"A sort of love letter to a vanished way of life, and a slice of English history at the same time, tracing as it does the lives of all the people who lived in Ashenden, a beautiful English country house, for over two hundred years."
—Penny Vincenzi, author of *Another Woman*

Praise for *Ashenden*

"The beauty of *Ashenden* lies in the interwoven tales that move us carefully through the years at irregular intervals, giving us intimate glimpses into not only the people who occupied the house but inside the heart of the very building itself."
—*Historical Novels Review*, Editor's Choice

"We are reminded of *Brideshead Revisited . . .* well observed."
—*The Times Literary Supplement*

"A mixture of short stories about the people who admired the grand house, found love and heartbreak inside its walls, and recovered in the green expanse that was part of the property. . . . Elizabeth Wilhide smoothly moves the story along while it remains in place at the same time. It's a very effective way to tell the story of the house and make it more than simply a structure of bricks, glass, and wood. It becomes a living part of the story and, in fact, the story itself. . . . A lovely story and a satisfying read."
—Bookreporter.com

"Rich and absorbing . . . personalities are sharpened by Wilhide's fine ear for dialogue and her wry sense of humor. The novel's real value lies in its detail, the patches of finely embroidered description, and in its subtle observation of behavior and tastes."
—*Financial Times*

Ashenden

—✕—

ELIZABETH WILHIDE

Simon & Schuster Paperbacks
New York   London   Toronto   Sydney   New Delhi

Simon & Schuster Paperbacks
A Division of Simon & Schuster, Inc.
1230 Avenue of the Americas
New York, NY 10020

Originally published in Great Britain by Penguin Group

Published by arrangement with Penguin Group Ltd.

First Simon & Schuster trade paperback edition November 2013

SIMON & SCHUSTER PAPERBACKS and colophon are registered trademarks of Simon & Schuster, Inc.

For information about special discounts for bulk purchases, please contact Simon & Schuster Special Sales at 1-866-506-1949 or business@simonandschuster.com.

The Simon & Schuster Speakers Bureau can bring authors to your live event. For more information or to book an event contact the Simon & Schuster Speakers Bureau at 1-866-248-3049 or visit our website at www.simonspeakers.com.

Designed by Jill Putorti

Manufactured in the United States of America

10 9 8 7 6 5 4 3 2 1

The Library of Congress Cataloging-in-Publication Data has cataloged the hardcover edition as follows:
    Wilhide, Elizabeth.
Ashenden / Elizabeth Wilhide.—1st Simon & Schuster ed.
    p. cm.
    1. Country homes—England—Fiction. I. Title.
PS3623.I5444A93 2013
813'.6—dc23   2012014720

ISBN 978-1-4516-8486-5
ISBN 978-1-4516-9789-6 (pbk)
ISBN 978-1-4516-8487-2 (ebook)

In memory of my mother

Contents

Ashenden

1

The Cuckoo's Egg: 2010

Winter has been hard on the house, the bitter cold eating into the honey-colored stonework, causing portions of the façade to crumble and flake away. Even in the external areas that are less exposed—under overhangs, for example—where the weeks of severe frost have been prevented from doing their worst, fresh staining has appeared in ugly blotches that bloom like malevolent flowers of decay.

Ashenden Park, built towards the end of the eighteenth century, and one of the finest late Palladian houses in the country according to those who make it their business to judge such things, was once surrounded by thousands of acres. Over the years the estate has shrunk to grounds of under a few hundred, which is nevertheless more than enough to provide an uninterrupted view from all sides.

Look around. It is as if the house were an island domain in a sea of green. In front, land slopes away, then rises to a gentle hill dotted with stands of trees and grazed by deer; behind, terraces descend more abruptly to the river, the modern world nowhere in evidence. The principal block, like the two smaller pavilions that flank it, is crowned with a pediment on the main elevation. Its centerpiece, and the focus of the symmetry of threes and fives and sevens, is a recessed columned loggia that soars from the first floor to the roof. At the lower story a continuous wall topped with a balustrade links the buildings together and makes elegant sense of it all. From a distance, as you come up the drive, for instance, the crisp lines of the architecture appear intact and it is possible to appreciate the clarity of the design more than two centuries since it sprang from a drawing into life, from a mind into being.

Look again. Up close the deterioration is brutal and alarming. Stone teeth missing under the roofline, rotten sills, the dull blank eyes of windows. Another winter as severe as this, the rot will find its way indoors and there will be serious trouble. Already the roof is leaking and the background heat that has been maintained in the principal rooms is barely enough to ward off the damp.

The house is much smaller than a palace, smaller too than many others of its type, yet much larger than most people today would recognize as a home. How many rooms? It depends on how you count them. About two dozen in the main block, give or take, not including hallways, landings, staircases, of which there are many. The side pavilions, once service quarters, are houses in themselves. Altogether it is a mansion, perhaps, but here is a trick of the architecture: a mansion that feels both generous and human-scaled. Were you to see it from above, from the flight path to Heathrow under which it lies, you might imagine yourself picking it up and placing it in the palm of your hand for safekeeping.

The house contains time. Its walls hold stories. Births and deaths, comings and goings, people and events passing through. Some of the occupants of the Park (and not all its occupants have been owners) have treated it well; others have been criminally careless. For now, however, it lies suspended in a kind of emptiness, as if it has fallen asleep or someone has put it under a spell. This silence won't last: can't last. Something will have to be done.

Charlie Minton, fifty-seven years old, twice married, father of one, woke up and for a moment didn't know where he was. It was a familiar feeling: over the years he'd woken up in boardinghouses, tents, three-, four-, and five-star hotels, shacks, on the backseats of cars and airport floors, in Beirut, Tokyo, New Orleans, Rio, and Pretoria, and had had the same momentary feeling of dislocation. It was part and parcel of the itinerant, unsettled life he had once chosen for himself and sometimes still hankered after. Now, he thought, this gray light could only be England, and as he came more fully into the day, something even worse occurred to him, which was that he was at Ashenden Park. More specifically, he was lying in bed in one of the spare rooms in the south pavilion, part of the house converted by his aunt and uncle over thirty years ago for their retirement.

He burrowed under the duvet, but any hopes that his mind would drift back to sleep and leave him in peace for another five minutes came to nothing. How could it, when every morning for the past two weeks the same dead weight had landed on him as soon as he had opened his eyes?

Over a fortnight ago, a February evening, he had been sitting at his worktable at home in the apartment on the Lower East Side he shared with his second wife, Rachel, correcting the proofs of a catalog to accompany a retrospective exhibition of his photographs. It was the kind of judgment that needed daylight, and he had moved away from the deceptive warmth of the Anglepoise to stare out of the window at snow flurries blown upwards and sideways in the sodium glare. He was thinking that he didn't much like the word "retrospective"—it reminded him how old he was—when the phone had rung. The dog, snoozing in her basket, raised her head.

It was Rachel's night at the Sita Center and she would be calling to say that she had yoga brain and should she pick up a takeout or was there something in the fridge. But as he reached for the handset, snug in its cradle like a papoose, he'd thought it was odd she was calling on the landline. Rachel always called him on his cell.

It hadn't been Rachel and it had only been when he'd picked up the phone that he'd noticed the red light was blinking.

Down under the duvet, clinging to his body heat on a cold, damp English morning, Charlie remembered his wife coming through the door of their apartment that February evening in New York, dumping her bag of yoga kit, snowflake stars melting on the little black ankle boots he'd given her for Christmas. Greeting the ecstatic dog, whose claws skittered across the waxed floorboards. Then taking a look at his face and asking what was the matter.

For a moment he had considered not saying anything at all. Pretending nothing had happened. Then he told her that his sister had just called with the news that Reggie was dead.

"Your aunt Reggie?"

He nodded.

"Oh, I'm so sorry, honey." She came across the room to give him a hug and he could smell sandalwood in her hair. "That's too bad."

At this point anyone else would have said that his aunt had been over ninety and had had a good, long life. But Rachel never said the obvious thing, which was one of the reasons he loved her.

"When did it happen?"

"Around noon their time. Ros was pretty upset. She's been trying to get hold of me all day." Ros was his sister.

"Didn't she try your cell?"

"Repeatedly. Bloody useless network."

Rachel rubbed his arm. "You planning on going over for the funeral?"

Before he could answer, he had to tell her the rest of it, knowing that would mean there was no further retreat from reality. "Reggie's left us the house. Me and Ros."

Rachel drew back. "That big old place?"

"Ashenden Park."

Ashenden Park. An image of its tawny stonework, its severe classical symmetries, formed itself in his mind. His uncle Hugo— his mother's brother—had bought the house just after the war and, together with his wife, Reggie, had saved it from what would have been almost certain destruction. The two of them had been devoted to one another and the house they had painstakingly restored but they had never had children of their own.

"I thought it was going to be donated to the country or something."

"To the National Trust." His breath constricted in his chest, and he felt the same sensation he'd had when he'd heard the news twenty minutes before: that of opening a door and stepping into space. Falling down, down, down, his feet scrabbling for a floor that wasn't there. "That's what we all thought."

"Is Ros sure?"

"She rang Reggie's solicitor this afternoon and he told her. We've inherited the house and whatever's left of the trust Hugo set up for her. I'll have to get over there straightaway."

Rachel's face registered internal adjustments, shifts of perspective. Yet, and this was another reason why he loved her, she did not rush to offer her opinion or second-guess his own. She held back. Only this late in life had he come to understand the paradox of true intimacy: that it depended on this type of respect.

He said, "Whatever happens, it's not going to be quick. I'll have to cancel my seminars at Parsons. Take a leave of absence."

"The exhibition?"

He shrugged. "Let's eat. We'll talk after."

Now, two weeks later, on this soggy gray morning at Ashenden Park, lying in the hollow of the mattress, the slightest movement accompanied by the creaking of the tarnished brass bedstead, the percussion of its springs, Charlie thought about what a good buy those little black ankle boots had been and how much he would like to see Rachel wearing them this very minute. He badly missed his wife.

In his first marriage, Charlie had experimented with similarity, shared interests, and things in common. He had since come to the conclusion that opposites worked better. People always imagined that opposites clashed, but in his experience similarities did, each vying for the same piece of ground. Opposites didn't have to mean conflict, wars of attrition, any more than they had to attract; sometimes, they made for smooth-running train tracks.

He and Rachel had met eight years ago at a Parsons fund-raiser: his seminars were beginning to be popular with the students and there was a rumor that he might be offered tenure; she was a graduate of the textile department, a "funky knitter" according to a colleague who'd noticed where Charlie's eyes were straying, and "the daughter of Jacob Gronert, one of our foremost benefactors," according to a glad-hander from faculty administration who had eventually introduced them. She hadn't looked like a knitter, more like the answer to hopes he hadn't entertained for years. A week later they first slept together; three months after that (which was two months after the attack on the Twin Towers), she had moved into the Lower East Side apartment he'd rented ever since the days when no cabs would go there. The following summer they were married.

For the first time ever Charlie discovered that it was possible to enjoy domestic life, to look forward to seeing someone else's toothbrush in the bathroom morning after morning. The same someone's toothbrush.

He bagged up a lot of his old stuff and threw it away. Together they bought new stuff. They sanded the stained floorboards and got a puppy. He was offered tenure, she exhibited her pieces here and there in SoHo galleries, then started up a blog called "Wool and Water" just as the craft revival was beginning to break, which led to a shop called Wool and Water in Tribeca, where she sold Peruvian hand-dyed yarn, skeins of fair-trade cashmere, and ran evening classes for the stitch-and-bitch brigade. Which led to a book, also called *Wool and Water,* with an explanatory subtitle for those unfamiliar with the *Alice in Wonderland* reference. (Even now some people came through the door of the shop expecting to buy bottles of Evian.) It was around this time that her parents, who hadn't approved of her marrying him, warmed up a little and her father suggested advancing her the capital to expand the shop into a chain. When Rachel turned her father down, Charlie couldn't have been prouder of her determination to own her own life.

A twenty-five-, thirty-five-, forty-five-year-old Charlie, riding along in the backseat of some clapped-out township taxi with his beaten-up Nikon F while the driver casually leaned an assault rifle out the window, or drinking in the bar of a scuzzy Macedonian hotel with stringers, indiscreet diplomats, and local mafia, or failing to show up on the second (and last) occasion when one of his photographs won a press award because he was sweating in a Mexican jail near the border, would not have recognized this fifty-seven-year-old Charlie, this home improver, wife lover, dog owner. But when he looked back on those exploits now, polished by many retellings, he recognized they were little more than approximations of the truth, which edited out the boredom, fear, and bad behavior that had led to them or been their direct consequence. They didn't even correspond to the occasions when he had taken his best photographs. Such was the benefit of hindsight and, however late in life, a good marriage.

Charlie poked his nose out from under the duvet and squinted at the digital clock. Nine forty-three. *Shit.* The surveyor was coming at ten thirty. He threw back the covers, got up, and reached for his boxer shorts. (He had never owned a dressing gown. Refused to own a dressing gown.) In the bathroom he pissed and then turned on the shower and stood under it, ready for punishment. As the water ran hot and cold, spurted and dribbled, he soaped his chest hair, which was graying, and regarded his penis, which had curled back into itself, the memory of Rachel in her little black ankle boots now subsiding.

Downstairs, Charlie could smell bacon cooking. His sister, Ros, would already have eaten her muesli and drunk her herbal tea: the bacon was for his benefit.

The kitchen was on the ground floor of the pavilion and occupied part of what had once been the old laundry. The floor was the original stone paving. The rest of it dated back to the 1970s conversion, which represented well over a lifetime in terms of domestic appliances and contemporary cabinetry. The microwave didn't work and two of the wooden drawer fronts fell off if you tugged them too hard.

When he went through the door, the smell of bacon cooking became the smell of bacon burning. He was aware of an atmosphere. His aunt's former carer, Elaine, was sitting at the kitchen table again, nursing a cup of tea and clutching a balled-up tissue, and Ros was being vicious with the grill pan.

This morning his sister's dark hair was springing up in wild tufts and she was dressed, like him, in T-shirt, sweater, and jeans. As far as appearances went, the family resemblance was strong; under the skin, they were chalk and cheese. She liked the country; he liked the city, any city so long as it wasn't in Britain (he made an exception for Glasgow). She was mildly religious and a disillusioned Labour voter since the war in Iraq; always an atheist, since 9/11 he had become a defender of the "war on terror." She had pleased their parents by following their father into medicine; he had perplexed them by "throwing away" his degree to risk his neck taking pictures in war zones and other regions of the world where the Foreign Office advised you not to go.

"Morning," he said, and got no answer. The lilies on the windowsill, floral overspill from the funeral, were well past their best, their sweet, slightly druggy scent fading. He seated himself at the end of the table, where he wouldn't have to look at Elaine's brimming red eyes, and reached across the table for the paper.

The election was expected at the beginning of May. A soldier had died in Helmand Province. He read those two items and the op-eds that related to them and skimmed the rest, barely glancing at the headlines. Page after page featured celebrity or popular news of one kind or another, retold in inverted quote marks to distinguish these reports from what had already been aired online or in the tabloids, along with bylined columns chatting as if there were all the time in the world to read about children losing clarinets on buses, dogs having operations, or (and these were by men) the inadequacies of men when faced with Hoover bags that needed changing. Lately he had noticed that the entire paper—news, op-eds, columns, features, and reviews—seemed to be written by the same three people.

Bloody England, thought Charlie. Bloody, bloody England. Every time he came back, the country had shrunk a little further into pettiness, the national conversation a low-level uninformed grumble that occasionally boiled over into a splutter of unfocused rage. He strongly held these views and hated himself for having them. (He also strongly held the view that the country encouraged self-hatred.)

A mug of tea and a bacon sandwich landed on the table in front of him.

"Thanks," he said to Ros. "You shouldn't have. I could have done that."

Ros said, "Helen called. Luke's coming on Saturday."

"Right." Helen was his ex-wife and Luke was his nineteen-year-old son.

"And David Barraclough called from the bank. He wants to know whether we've come to a decision. I said we hadn't. Then Fresher's called to confirm the survey. They'll be here in twenty minutes. And your friend Jules rang just now with the number you were asking about. I wrote it down. It's on the pad over there by the phone. What number were you asking about?"

"He knows someone at the National Trust."

She dropped the grill pan in the sink with a clatter, squeezed washing-up liquid into it, and ran the tap. There was a hissing sound, a warm smell of singed detergent.

"You're a one-woman app," said Charlie. He meant it as a compliment. His sister ignored him.

Elaine shoved back her chair, scraping its legs against the stone floor. She was wearing a bulky sweater patterned in gray lozenges, the same color as the roots of her dyed maroon hair. "Well, I'd better be getting along. Thanks for the tea."

"No problem." Ros turned away from the sink and gave her a brisk hug. "Now don't brood. Promise?"

Elaine nodded.

"I can give you something to help you sleep, if you want."

"I'll be all right."

"OK," said Ros. "Mind how you go."

"What on earth's the matter with that woman?" Charlie said, after the door closed behind her.

Ros was scrubbing away at the grill pan. He pitied the grill pan.

"I've told you a hundred times. She blames herself for Reggie's death. She thinks she failed in her duties."

Charlie considered this last statement, which he happened to agree with. As he understood it, despite the fact that there had been snow on the ground the day Reggie had died, she had insisted on going over to the house. Instead of talking her out of this plan, Elaine had escorted her from the south pavilion across the icy courtyard and left her (again at her insistence) to wander around the house on her own, upstairs and down, until Tony Knoll, the caretaker, had found her, looking "gray about the gills," and helped her onto her old marital bed, where she had passed away.

"I know what you're thinking," said Ros, drying the grill pan and banging it into the oven, "and it's not Elaine's fault. As I keep saying. After all, Reggie was over ninety. She had a good innings. It wasn't as if Elaine didn't try to dissuade her from going over there."

"Obviously she didn't try hard enough."

"She was her carer, not her jailer. Besides which, Reggie got bloody stubborn in her old age. Not that you'd know. The last time you saw her must have been a good fifteen years ago."

"Nonsense. I saw her when I came over after Mum died."

"No, you didn't. Reggie was ill with flu at the time."

"OK, OK, OK." Charlie put up his hands.

Ros took off her apron. There was nothing domestic whatsoever about the way his sister, the doctor, wore an apron. Down the hall from the kitchen the doorbell rang.

"That'll be the surveyor."

"You coming?"

She shook her head. "I have to be at the surgery in a while."

The GP clinic where Ros worked part-time was forty minutes' drive away in a small town on the other side of Reading, which was also where she lived with her husband, Geoff, and her daughter, Maisie, who was now in her first year at university. Yet while Ros continued to commute to the surgery for her shifts, every night since Reggie had died she had stayed at the Park. This struck Charlie as odd. Perhaps she didn't trust him not to flog off the silver;

perhaps she was avoiding her husband; perhaps she was suffering some sort of menopausal fugue. This last thought he registered as possibly sexist. It had been years since they had been under the same roof for any length of time and he was beginning to wonder whether he knew her as well as he thought he did.

"By the way," said Ros, "I've invited Marjorie Thurston for supper Friday evening."

"Who's Marjorie Thurston?"

"I introduced you to her at the wake. She knew Reggie well. She's active in the village historical society."

"I can hardly wait," said Charlie.

"Ask the surveyor about the roof," said Ros. "We need to know how bad it is."

The surveyor turned out to be two surveyors and an assistant, all wax-jacketed. What would be the collective term for surveyors? Charlie wondered. A doom? He led the three of them across the courtyard and out onto the drive. "I imagine you'll want to start with the main block," he said.

"Good a place as any," said the balding one, who had introduced himself as Neil Fielding.

There were two entrances to the house, not including the archways that led to the courtyards which separated it from the pavilions on either side. The formal entrance was reached by a flanking pair of enclosed staircases leading up to the loggia. Underneath the loggia was another door on the ground level, which Charlie unlocked. "After you," he said, switching off the alarm.

At this point, the second surveyor excused himself and said he was going to have a quick look at the stonework. He and Neil, the balding one, exchanged a professional glance.

Indoors the rest of them were greeted by a rank, sweetish odor. The pavilion where Reggie had lived out her last years smelled of old people and what they ate in unaired rooms: this was different. Charlie snapped on a few lights, one of which flickered and went out. Ahead stretched a long stone-flagged corridor, punctuated by niches and doorways.

"The house is on three floors," he said to Neil and the young assistant, whose spots, if joined up, would make a map of somewhere. "This ground level was mostly service areas originally, as were the pavilions. Over there are the internal staircases, a public stair and a smaller back stair. The old billiard room is at the far end. It's octagonal, like the two rooms above it. The principal rooms are on the first floor. The bedrooms are on the second."

"How long has this been shut up?"

"It's never been completely empty. Tony Knoll, the caretaker, looks after it."

"Heated?" The surveyor touched his fingers to the wall above a crumbling plinth and sniffed them.

"Background heat. A condition of the insurance. As is the caretaker. Shall I show you round?"

The surveyor shook his head. "No need. We have a copy of the plans." He nodded at the assistant. "Damp meter, Frank?"

Frank, the assistant, produced a small black metal box from his pocket. He handed it to Neil, who pressed it to the wall. The black needle on the display screen shot from left to right, from green to red.

Neil noted the finding. "Handy little gadget, this."

"I suppose it takes the guesswork out," said Charlie.

"Not a lot of guesswork in surveying, by and large."

Surveying was what his father would have called a proper job. "Well, I'll leave you to it," said Charlie, and went upstairs.

On the next floor he came out into the great void that rose up in the center of the house. Officially, it was known as the staircase hall, because it was a hall with yet another staircase in it, one made of stone and cantilevered from the wall, edged with a balustrade of wrought-iron filigree. Weak sunlight struggled down through the high clerestory windows. Something about its hesitant fragility made him think of his aunt. He was overcome by a sense of trespass and wondered whether his sister felt the same. Whether, in fact, the house felt the same.

The way the house had been designed meant that you never forgot the plan: it wasn't the sort of higgledy-piggledy place that invited you to get lost and charmed you once you had. Neither was it the sort of place where you were able to forget that it was the product of architectural thought. Standing in the middle of the staircase hall, facing forward, he knew exactly where every room was in relationship to each other. To his left, the formal dining room; immediately behind him, the octagon room; to his right, the drawing room. Ahead was the wide entrance hall, flanked on either side by the room his aunt had once used as her sitting room and the library where his uncle had pored over his auction catalogs. What little furniture remained was covered in white sheeting.

He crossed the entrance hall and poked his nose round the door of the library. To his surprise, his sister was sitting at his uncle Hugo's desk, on the phone.

"Oh, you startled me." Ros put a hand over her heart. "I'll call you back," she said, and rang off.

"Don't let me disturb you."

"It's no one important . . . I mean, nothing important. It was only Geoff."

"I thought you had to be at the surgery."

She checked her watch. "Soonish."

"Why don't go you home for a bit, Ros? I can look after myself, you know."

"I don't mind."

"Seriously."

"Perhaps I want to stay." Her expression, which had started off defiant, collapsed on itself, as if she had given too much away. "Here, look what I've found." She picked up a brittle, yellowing scroll and handed it to him.

"What is it?"

"The original deeds to the land. Hugo collected everything about the house he could lay his hands on." She gestured at a pile of buff folders on the desk. "These documents go back years. I'm glad I invited Marjorie to supper. This is a treasure trove for someone like her."

"Perhaps." He was not convinced. "Why are you doing all this?"

"I happen to think it's important to understand the history of this house before we make decisions about its future."

"It's not the house's future we should be worried about, it's our own." Charlie put the deeds back on the desk. "How's Geoff?"

"Geoff's fine."

"Coping OK?"

"He's busy. Rushed off his feet."

Geoff was an anesthetist. Could anesthetists be rushed off their feet? He hoped not. "Poor Geoff."

"Oh, you know, he loves it really."

Charlie pulled out a chair, brought it over to the opposite side of the desk, and sat down. He felt like one of his sister's patients. A patient with a symptom he didn't particularly want to disclose because he dreaded the diagnosis that would follow. "What does he think about you inheriting the house?"

"Is this your way of asking what I think?" said Ros, rearranging the files on the desk. "If so, I happen to think that it's far too early to come to a decision about what to do with it. We don't even know what the survey's going to reveal yet."

"No, but we do know more or less where we stand."

And that, they both knew, was on shaky ground. Preliminary discussions with the bank and his aunt's solicitor indicated that estate liabilities significantly exceeded available assets. The most recent heating bill alone was eye-watering. (He had never seen a four-figure heating bill before.) On top of that, death duties were going to be astronomical.

Although Hugo had left Reggie very well-off, she had survived him by many years, during which time the house had become much more expensive to run and keep in basic repair. Not wishing to touch the capital, she had apparently muddled through by selling things, which presumably accounted for a couple of missing paintings. Under normal circumstances, the investment portfolio Charlie and Ros had inherited on their aunt's death would have been almost enough to compensate for the shortfalls they now faced. But that, of course, had been before the credit crunch. "Double whammy," was how David Barraclough at the bank had put it. Which was a bit rich, considering.

"You have to agree," said Charlie, "it's not looking good."

"It's early days yet. There are lots of options we can explore," said Ros. "Lots. Renting out part of the house, converting part of it, selling off some of the land, doing a deal with the Trust. I've made a list."

She rummaged around on the desk and handed him a sheet of paper.

Charlie took it. She had indeed made a list. A list of many numbered points. She was methodical that way. He scanned it, conscious of her scrutiny. "You haven't asked me what I want to do."

"That's because I know what you want to do. You want to sell."

"Oh yes, here it is, option six. The last one."

"We don't want to be too hasty," said Ros.

Later, two o'clock in the afternoon his time, nine o'clock in the morning her time, Charlie Skyped his wife. He understood how tiny cameras in laptops thousands of miles apart allowed him and Rachel to watch each other's moving mouths as words came out of them, but it never ceased to amaze him. Scuppered him too. What technology offered, he had come to believe, was a ballooning of desire, not its satisfaction. Seeing his wife smile, brush her hair behind her ears, pull a face, what he wanted most of all was to climb through the screen and touch her, and this he could not do. Perhaps it might have been better, he thought, if he had had no option but to hold her in his mind while he wrote her a letter. He was old enough to remember when people did that.

Through trial and error, he had discovered that at Ashenden Park the wonders of technology worked only in the small room in the north pavilion that Tony the caretaker used as an office. That ruled out Skype sex and put a certain restraint on their video conversations. It also helped them to keep to their agreed limit of one

Skype a day. Skyping was free only in pecuniary terms. There was always the dull ache of separation to pay after you hung up the call.

"I miss you. I miss the *Times*," Charlie was saying. On the screen he could see the dog lying on the bed behind Rachel. The dog wasn't allowed on the bed. "I miss Paul Krugman."

Rachel laughed. "You can always read the *Times* online."

"It's not the same. I like the real thing. I like turning real pages."

A small delay. "You don't agree with Paul Krugman. Did the surveyor come?"

"Sometimes I agree with him." Another small delay. "Yes, they did. Surveyors in the plural. I should have realized with a place this size." He wanted to take a bath in her American accent. It was home to him. For some reason—possibly to do with public school—his British one had proved more indelible over the years than he had expected. Early on, that had proved useful. Waitresses tended to melt, for example. Not so much now, when most of the bad guys in Hollywood movies sounded the same as he did.

"We miss you too," said Rachel, stroking the dog.

That night back in February, after Ros had rung, he and Rachel had agreed that he should go over to England on the first available flight and she should follow once she had arranged for her assistant, Marisa, to mind the shop and persuaded someone, possibly also Marisa, to dog-sit. Weather had come between them. The snow flurries that were still falling as Charlie's plane took off the next day from Newark became a blizzard that closed the airport eight hours later. When he had landed at Heathrow, the two inches that were paralyzing the British transport system were the direct equivalent of the two feet that had temporarily put the East Coast out of action. Honey, I shrank the snow, he had thought, queuing for a taxi behind a woman wearing four-inch heels and complaining how slippery it was.

"Have you discussed things with Ros yet?" said Rachel on the screen.

"We talked a bit this morning. I think she's stalling for time. She's been digging around in the library, pulling out all the stuff my uncle collected about the house. Plus she's got this friend of Reggie's coming for supper Friday night. I'm guessing emotional blackmail is the general idea."

"You look tired," said Rachel.

"Do I?" said Charlie. He wasn't sleeping well without her. She looked tired too, tired and pinched. Sort of washed-out. He hoped that meant she wasn't sleeping well without *him.* "How's the shop?" The blizzard that had prevented Rachel from flying out to join him had marooned Marisa in Brooklyn for a day and made a significant dent in the takings of Wool and Water, which normally did its best business in the colder months.

"Not too bad. Picking up now, thank God. This woman came in today and bought three hundred dollars' worth of merino. Sort of a rust color. She's never knitted before, so I signed her up for some lessons."

"That's good."

Rachel moved her head and her face disappeared.

Back again. "Sweet, I gotta go."

They said their good-byes, hands to screens, and the call was over. He felt an immediate letdown that placed him squarely back in Tony's low-ceilinged office, with its dull view of the cobbled courtyard. March was daffodils in Wordsworth country on the wall calendar behind him, which advertised a local garage, and a furred kettle, a jar of instant coffee, and a couple of stained mugs huddled on a battered tray on the table.

As soon as Charlie came out into the courtyard, his laptop under his arm, Tony materialized from somewhere. He had a habit of doing that.

"Get through all right?"

"Yes, thanks."

"How long are that lot going to be here?"

"You mean the surveyors?" He shook his head. "I don't know."

Tony was bright as a squirrel in his anorak and Thinsulate hat. Despite the weather, he was wearing Lycra shorts on his lower half. He was ex-army and a keen long-distance cyclist. "I thought it best not tell them about the damp patch in the octagon room."

"There's no point hiding anything from them, Tony. We're *paying* them to find out what's wrong, for God's sake."

"Shall I tell them about the ghost, then?"

"What ghost?"

"Just joking. By the way, Claire wants to know if you're going to sell up to the Russkies."

Claire was Tony's invisible girlfriend, whom no one had ever met—"imaginary girlfriend, if you ask me," according to Ros—and who had an uncanny ability to ask the questions to which Tony wanted to know the answers.

"The Russians?"

"Seeing as they're the only ones with any bloody dosh."

"We haven't made up our minds what we're going to do yet."

"'Course, you could always try footballers, Claire says. More money than sense."

Up in the spare room in the south pavilion, Charlie placed his laptop on the rumpled bed, pulled out his cell, and dialed the number of the National Trust contact, the direct line of Trisha Greeling, assistant director of historic properties.

"I'm not at my desk at the moment," said Trisha Greeling, "but please leave a message after the tone and I'll get back to you as soon as I can." A tone. "Please speak after the beep," said a different singsong voice. "If you want to rerecord your message at any time, please press one or press hash to go back to the operator."

"For fuck's sake," said Charlie. After the beep he recorded a message. Then he picked up his Nikon digital SLR ("the Hulk," Rachel called it), banged out of the room, went down the stairs, and slammed the door behind him.

The flat gray light of early spring was fading as he crossed the drive, went down a shallow dip and up the long slope that led to a stand of trees silhouetted on the horizon. He walked fast. At the top of the hill, the ground fell away. There were still a couple of tongues of snow in sheltered areas.

Memory played a trick on him. This landscape, where he had grown up, ought to have reminded him of his childhood, yet here in the middle of Berkshire countryside he was back in the Falls Road, Belfast, for no good reason he could understand. Twenty-three years old, prowling around half-smashed and careless of his own skin to the point of madness. He'd stopped to light a fag in a doorway and in that instant two men had hared round a corner and lobbed a petrol bomb into a downstairs window of a terraced house. His hands had shaken as he'd fumbled for his camera. Click, click, click. And that would have been his first photograph to be published in a national newspaper, except the picture editor thought he had recognized one of the men as an off-duty UDR officer and spiked it. If he closed his eyes, he could still smell the grimy, coal-blackened street and see the fire roar out of the broken window. The ambulance had got there too late. No phone boxes in the street, or at least none in working order. Over the years, that knowledge had done little to erase the guilt of taking the picture first, then trying to find a phone box to ring for an ambulance afterwards.

Charlie held his camera up against the view and took a few shots, framing each with instinctive care. The grand old house with its eighteenth-century symmetries, the wooded acres that surrounded it, the brown river in the distance. All this was his—his and his sister's—if they wanted it. And who wouldn't want a sodding great chunk of English heritage? Who would not want the hand of history to clap them on the shoulder and say, Welcome to the club, old chap?

From the hill he stared at the house, the monstrous egg a cuckoo had laid in his life. He almost felt sorry for exposing its weaknesses and structural shortcomings to the wax-jacketed surveyors, for its being the subject of a list, for its being a weight on his mind. Yet when he tried to imagine bringing Rachel to live here, he failed. It wasn't the scale of the place or its market value, nothing like that. Her parents' house on Long Island was bigger, probably worth more, and oozed comfort and amenities, and that wasn't counting the Fifth Avenue apartment, the ski lodge at Vail, or the villa on Anguilla. Or the boat, which was larger than the walk-up on the Lower

East Side where he and Rachel lived. Instead, it was the fact that given all the effort Rachel had made to pull away from the gravity of her family orbit, the last thing he would want to do was to lock her into his. Nor could he imagine what the seepage of daily life in twenty-first-century England would do to them both. The drip, drip, drip of a small island at the fag end of its history and refusing to admit it. To live in this country now was to be perpetually standing in six inches of muddy water with a sodden mop, a brimming bucket, and a blocked drain.

Out of the corner of his eye he saw a deer standing on the fringe of a copse twenty, thirty feet away. Such a quiet, finely made, nervous thing. As he lifted his camera, it darted for cover.

On Friday night Marjorie Thurston came to supper. She was a tall, angular woman in her midseventies who had retired to Lower Ashenden after a career in the civil service and had since self-published an illustrated guide to its history, to which his aunt Reggie had apparently contributed a foreword. Charlie had known dons like her. The gray hair cut in a bob, the protuberant eyes with saddlebags underneath, the air of not suffering fools gladly or at all. He remembered a floundering tutorial he had once had—one of many, it had to be said—and the acerbic voice issuing from the armchair on the other side of the hissing gas fire: "You have *some* cerebral capacity, Charles. *Use it.*"

Ros had cooked a fish pie and set the kitchen table with good china and Reggie's silver candlesticks. Most of the meal passed in a halting question-and-answer-type conversation, during which Charlie learned rather more about the village historical society than he wanted to know. The weather was mentioned a few times, as an opening gambit and at points thereafter. Gardening, as a topic, failed to get off the ground, since only Marjorie knew anything about it.

"Marjorie?" said Ros. "May I help you to more?"

"Thank you, no." Marjorie folded her napkin beside her plate.

"At my age, one's appetite is not what it was. Would you mind awfully if I smoked?" This was a challenge or a statement in the form of a question.

"Not at all," said Charlie, getting up to fetch a saucer. "I'll join you."

"You've given up," said Ros.

"I still have one from time to time."

"That'll be news to Rachel."

"Oh," said Marjorie, raising her eyebrows. "Shall I go outside? I believe that's what people do these days."

"Of course not," said Ros. "It's far too cold. Stay right where you are and I'll fetch those estate papers I was talking about." She left the room, her trainers squeaking away down the hall.

"Have one of mine," said Marjorie, offering him the packet.

"Thanks." He lit up. "How long did you know Reggie?"

"About fifteen years or so. I met her quite soon after I retired to the village. Your aunt was a remarkable woman. She will be much missed." Marjorie, nudging ash into the saucer, asked if they planned to carry on their aunt's charity work.

Charity work? It would be charity work to take on the house full stop. "I don't know. Inheriting this place has come as a shock to us both, to be honest."

"Why should it have done?" said Marjorie. "Your uncle Hugo and your mother were brother and sister, as I understand it. Traditionally estates do tend to pass to the nearest relatives on the male side."

Charlie shrugged. "We didn't feel so connected to Hugo and Reggie when we were growing up. I mean, we saw them and all that. But they were glamorous and wealthy and we were a pretty ordinary family, really. My mum was what you might call a housewife. She was a nurse in the war, which is when she first met Dad, who was a doctor. We never expected to inherit the house. We always assumed it was going to the National Trust."

"You mean that's what you hoped."

"Personally I'd rather not have been saddled with it, if that's what you're saying."

"One can't always choose one's responsibilities in life."

Charlie's head was swimming from the fag. "Isn't that rather fatalistic?"

"Not at all." Marjorie rearranged the scarf at her neck, which was held in place by what could only be described as a woggle. "When you get to my age, it's always tempting to regard the past in too rosy a light. I do try to resist that. But it seems to me that you are in the fortunate position of being able to preserve something of true excellence. And so little of true excellence remains in this country. I should say it's a question of duty, if that isn't too old-fashioned a word."

It was past eleven and Marjorie had gone. The kitchen table, now cleared of dishes, was spread with eighteenth-century architectural plans, nineteenth-century housekeeping books, builders' estimates, old photographs, and letters that bore the faded, inky, spidery marks of quills and steel-nibbed pens.

"Was there something wrong with my fish pie?" said Ros. "There's so much left."

"It was fine."

Charlie poured himself another glass of wine. His sister's fish pie had tasted of cod-flavored wallpaper paste and he could feel sludge impacting his digestive tract, floury sediment silting his arteries. He ought really to get back to running.

Ros busied herself with the estate papers, collecting the yellowing, brittle pages together. "Marjorie was fascinated by the wartime stuff, I thought."

"She was."

"Did you see her face when I showed her those Victorian ledgers? Fifteen shillings to build an ornamental pond, it's unbelievable. Figures never lie."

"They don't," said Charlie, toying with his glass. "Look, Ros, I spoke to the surveyors today before they went."

"Any more wine left?"

"A bit."

She tipped the bottle over her glass. A dribble came out. "Go on. You spoke to the surveyors."

"They'll put it in their report, but they said that in their opinion the stonework's going to need a lot of work."

"Well, that's obvious. How much work?"

"About a million pounds' worth."

Her head went back as if he had slapped her.

"And that's not counting the roof." He paused. "There's something else. I finally got through to that National Trust contact Jules gave me."

"And?" she said.

"We had a chat, quite a longish one. It seems the Trust isn't taking on any more stately homes. Their portfolio is full."

"I see." As a child, Ros had always been the braver of the two of them. Not a crier, a whinger, or a wailer. Stoical with the scraped knee, the bump on the head, the wasp sting. Now he could see the effort she was making to control herself.

"Trisha Greeling, the woman I spoke to, didn't rule it out entirely. But she did refer me to their more recent acquisitions—a Manchester workhouse, a terrace of back-to-backs in Salford, and the house where John Lennon was born. Or maybe they haven't bought the Lennon place yet, I forget, but you understand what I'm saying."

"Cheap. Cheap to buy and cheap to run."

"A shift of priorities. All part of the heritage, as she reminded me." Charlie wished he hadn't had that cigarette, because now he wished he had another. And another. A pack. "She's going to think about it and we'll speak next week, perhaps meet, but frankly, it doesn't look hopeful. I'm sorry."

"No, you're not."

"You've got to see that the sums don't add up."

Ros placed her hands on the table and spread her fingers. "It's been less than three weeks, Charlie. We haven't even started to explore the possibilities. OK, so it looks like we'll probably have to rule out the

Trust. And it's going to cost more, a lot more, than we thought. But do you really want to sell this house and see it ripped apart?"

"It's Grade II listed. No one can rip it apart."

"A Grade II listing only protects the exterior. We sell this place to a pop star or whoever and the next thing you know there'll be a Jacuzzi in the octagon room. All the work that Hugo and Reggie did to restore this place will be smothered in crap."

Families had their fictions. Here was Ros, the healer, the restorer of health and life, and here he was, the voyeur, the bystander of loss and destruction. Truth was, they both bought into it.

"We have no choice."

"There's always a choice." Ros dropped her head in her hands, then raised it again. "What about your father-in-law?"

"What about him?"

"If we put together some sort of business plan, perhaps he might put up a bit of capital."

"Absolutely not!" Charlie pushed back his chair, stood up. He was furious. "It's taken Rachel years to work out how to live her own life. If you think I'm prepared to throw all that away by asking her father for money to fix up this place, you can think again."

Ros twisted round in her seat. "It would be a business opportunity, not a handout."

"No, it wouldn't be a business opportunity. It would be like cutting a hole in your pocket and seeing how much poured out on a daily basis. And before you get on to my father-in-law's generous donations to charity, let me tell you that he knows down to the last cent the difference between a good cause and a lost one."

"OK, some other investor, then."

"Yes, they're thick on the ground these days. Queuing up round the block to throw money down a pit, last time I looked."

"Oh, for God's sake, Charlie, stop being so negative. I know you don't want to live here and I'm not even suggesting that that would be necessary. But your son might want to one day. Have you considered that?"

He might have been more shocked at this blow beneath the belt had he not realized, to his shame, that he hadn't considered his son's views at all. Not once, not for a moment. He might as well not have had a son.

"Don't bring Luke into this."

"Why not? Maisie is part of this too. Hugo and Reggie must have trusted us to look after the house for future generations or they wouldn't have left it to us."

He ran the tap, poured himself a glass of water, drank half of it, set it down. "We don't know what their reasons were. That will was drawn up years ago, before Luke and Maisie were even born. Things were different then."

The kitchen clock ticked. It was nearly midnight.

Charlie drank the rest of the water. "OK," he said, "for the sake of argument, let's say Hugo and Reggie did trust us to look after the house. But looking after the house means making the right decision about its future. As things stand, we can either keep it or we can save it. We can't do both. If we try to hang on to it, we'll lose it sooner or later. The only way this house is going to survive in anything like its present form is if we sell it to somebody who has enough money to look after it properly."

"You don't know that."

"I'm being realistic."

"Is that what you call it?"

"For fuck's sake," said Charlie, gesturing to the piles of papers on the kitchen table, "look at all this stuff you've been digging up. All this stuff Hugo collected. What does it tell you? This house has never stood still. Not once. They put in an ornamental pond one minute, they change the wallpaper the next, they remodel the whole thing from top to bottom when they've got the cash. Then they try and flog it off when they're skint. So what if a footballer or an oligarch or some celebrity from reality TV buys it and puts a Jacuzzi in the octagon room? Or turns Reggie's old bedroom into a walk-in closet? Darcy would have installed a fucking plunge pool at Pemberley if he'd known a decent plumber."

Ros didn't laugh, but a ghost of a smile appeared on her face, enough to convince him that he was getting somewhere, that this dead weight might lift, or shift.

Then her phone went, buzzing and squirming on the kitchen counter.

"Geoff?" he said, handing it to her.

She looked at the screen. "Maisie. Term's only half over. She can't have run out of money yet." She punched a button. "Hi, sweetheart! What's up? No, don't worry, I haven't gone to bed. Oh, good, good, you got the package, I'm pleased. How about that dress? Did you buy it in the end?" Ros chattered on brightly, looking as if she had just been given a transfusion of freshly oxygenated blood.

Charlie squeezed his sister's shoulder and murmured, "Don't wash up. I'll do it in the morning."

She nodded and waved, her ear pressed hard to the phone.

Three a.m. UK time, ten p.m. New York time, Charlie crept down to Tony's office with his laptop. 19,081,487 people were on Skype. None of them was his wife. Beside her name was a little gray cloud with a white x in the middle of it. He tried her cell but it was switched off and he went straight through to voice mail. He left a message. Then he emailed her and texted her to tell her that he had emailed her.

Charlie missed his wife. He had a wife-shaped hole in his life. But that was only temporary. He could buy a plane ticket right now and that hole would be filled. What was beginning to dawn on him was that his sister had a child-shaped hole in hers, which was only going to become bigger as time went on. Somehow he had to persuade her that the Park wasn't the answer to an empty nest. It was a cuckoo's egg and given half the chance it would hatch and swallow them whole.

2

Stonework: 1775

You would never think much of the stone if you saw it lying in the ground. In its bed under the earth, it's yellow, almost soft to the touch. But bring it up to the air, let it dry so all the sap goes out of it, and it turns pale and dense and hard. Bath stone: it's a stone fit for palaces, fit for fashioning whole cities, fine cities made of terraced squares, crescents, and circuses.

At Combe Down, Farleigh Down, Box Hill, it's hot, backbreaking work. The quarrymen follow the stone in its bed, scraping, scraping away, freeing large blocks of it with their jadding irons. Underground in the loading bays the blocks are winched onto wagons that straining horses pull to the surface. When the stone is seasoned in the sun, masons square it and tramways deliver it to building sites or to quaysides where it will travel by water to whoever wants it and can pay for it. The farther it travels, the more it costs.

Late at night, the candle burning low, James Woods sat at a battered oak table in an upstairs room of an old manor house in the middle of a Berkshire estate. A sheaf of drawings was paperweighted by his right hand, and an accounts book was open in front of him. He turned the pages. Accounts rendered, accounts paid, accounts unpaid: foreman's wages, rubble by the hundredweight, sacks of lime, the hiring of sawyers, jobbing labor, draft horses. The figures weren't adding up. It worried him.

Woods was an architect. Drawings, figures, worry—they all related to his present commission, which was to replace the old manor with a substantial new house. Every job had its problems but this one had been more difficult than most. Not least because it had cost him many uncomfortable hours on the road, traveling down from his home in York, and many wasted days waiting for progress that never happened. So far, this site visit had been no exception.

The window was open and the soft southern air carried with it a hint of the nearby river. Around him floor timbers and roof joists ticked and creaked and groaned, as if the old house knew that its days were numbered. It was a miserable place, on the whole: ill-proportioned, dark, alive only with mice. Brick-built, whereas the house that would replace it would be constructed of stone. They made a beautiful brick in this part of the world, mellow and easy on the eye, but to his mind a pile of bricks amounted to a pile of bricks however tidily they were assembled. A pile of stone was a monument.

Woods, who understood stone, had been trained by a master mason. A broad, square Yorkshireman, with sharp gray eyes that were amused by the world but not fooled by it, Woods had made his living as an architect for almost thirty years. When he was young, others had tried to talk him into setting up a practice in London, but he knew there was money in the north and fewer competitors to go after it and had stayed where he was. The work had flowed like a stream. He had designed session houses and prisons, churches and follies, and a great number of large country houses, chiefly in his home county. Over the years he had gained a reputation for thoroughness and precision, which was deserved, and he rarely turned down a job, no matter how small or how troublesome.

Most of his patrons were concerned with appearances. They wanted to know what their buildings would look like, what their money would buy. Man or woman or collective body, they almost always wanted what their neighbors had, or their peers, or what was in fashion, and if you had designed the houses of their neighbors or their peers, or the local assembly rooms, a racecourse grandstand, a town hall, or a much-admired bridge, it was easier to persuade them to leave matters of style in your hands.

Drawings helped only up to a point. What people generally understood by architectural drawings were pretty pictures of façades, external elevations, and decorations for interior walls and ceilings. Producing these for comment and approval kept his apprentices busy for hours that could have been better spent on something else. No one outside the profession, to his knowledge, had ever seen a plan and understood how three dimensions sprang from two. Give a layman a plan and he would hold it upside down and ask where the front door was.

This commission had been different. There had been no argument about style or accommodation, no need to persuade or cajole. Drawings had been passed without a murmur. His recommendation as to where on the estate the new house should be sited, his proposals for landscaping had gone unchallenged.

Yet there had been trouble from the beginning. And in Woods's experience, trouble came in one chief form: money, or the lack of it.

There was a knock on the door and Joshua came in without waiting for an answer. Joshua Wainwright, nineteen years old, was the best and brightest of his apprentices. A devourer of treatises and pattern books, a natural draftsman, a quick learner. And, in the way of the young, a taker of liberties.

"What do you want, Joshua?"

"I thought you'd still be awake."

"So I am," said Woods. He closed the accounts book, rubbed his eyes. "Have you prepared the drawing for the foreman?"

"I have. But I doubt he'll look at it. He hasn't looked at the others."

"If he chooses not to, that's up to him. A drawing is an instruction, but it is also a record that an instruction has been given. That comes in useful more often than you might think."

"Yes, sir, so you've told me," said Joshua, shielding his candle from the open window. "I came to see if you wanted a bite of supper. Do you want me to fetch you something? The old woman's fast asleep in the chimney corner, but I know where she keeps the food and drink."

"That doesn't surprise me," said Woods. The boy ate like his legs were hollow. He shook his head. "No, I should go to bed. And so should you. There'll be plenty to do tomorrow when the stone arrives."

"They say," said Joshua, not leaving, "that More's up from London, staying with one of his friends. Not five miles away."

"Is that what the housekeeper told you?"

"No, the girl who brings the eggs in the morning. Daughter of one of the tenant farmers."

"A reliable source," said Woods drily.

"News is all over the neighborhood," said Joshua, still not leaving. "Tomorrow, when the stone comes, do you think he'll be here to see it?"

Woods rested his hand on the accounts book. It was Joshua's first trip south, the nearest he had come to the capital and what he must imagine to be the sophisticated taste and refinement of its inhabitants. Little did he know.

"I doubt it. He hasn't paid for it yet."

Sir Frederick More, who had commissioned Woods to design and build the house, was a fellow Yorkshireman. In all other respects they differed. Woods had made an honest living in the county where he had been born. More had made a fortune in Bengal by rising through the ranks of the East India Company and laying his hands on every material advantage, legitimate or otherwise, that fell his way. Several years after he returned to England, bought the Berkshire estate, and engaged Woods as his architect, shares in the East India Company collapsed and bled him of money, thousands of pounds lost in a single day. Hard on the heels of that calamity, a parliamentary inquiry found him guilty of corruption, fined him a vast sum, and stripped him of his seat in the House. The charge of corruption related to his dealings in the Dorset constituency he had bought his way into, but there was also the matter of the taxes he had unfairly levied in Bengal, for which he was investigated and publicly censured.

Woods had thought the job was dead, had written it off and filed the drawings. To his surprise—and to the surprise of many others—More, who had been Mr. More then, and a widower with small sons, had somehow survived the scandals, clawed back his position in society, and married a second wife, who was rich. He was now a baronet and a member for a different borough.

That was the way of the world and there was no cause for Woods to complain about it. If More had not married money and rebuilt his life on the proceeds, work on the house would never have resumed. Yet he could not say he had ever warmed to the man.

More had always been slow to pay. Since the inquiry, however, he treated every account presented for settlement as yet another outrageous fine unjustly imposed upon him. Funds dried to a trickle and for long periods work on the house stopped altogether.

Sometimes Woods found himself wondering whether his patron wanted to see the house built at all, whether his reluctance to pay arose out of a deeper ambivalence. Memories were short, it was true, but the house was now unlikely to serve its original purpose as a place where a political career might be made. A number of More's friends from the East India Company, who had also chosen to settle in this Berkshire valley on their return from the subcontinent, had not been so successful in restoring reputations tarnished by fraud. Their proximity, and the relative nearness of the estate to Westminster, might no longer be regarded as advantages.

Writing from York, before this last site visit, Woods had tried to make it as clear to his patron as he could. Once the stone was ordered, as soon as it arrived, there could be no going back. *Please advise me of your wishes. I beg to remain, as ever, your humble servant.* A polite form of words: he was neither especially humble nor anyone's servant.

Two things happened overnight. It rained and the Gypsies returned to the wood.

"That's all we need," said the foreman, nodding in the direction of the camp, or where it was said to be. "Gypsies. You'd think they'd have a care for their necks. Trespass is a hanging offense."

"It's no business of ours."

"When they thieve our tools or our horses, it will be. Besides which, they're bad luck."

"I'll speak to the steward. It's his job to deal with them." Woods was more concerned about the rain. Moving stone from the river-bank to the site was going to be difficult on soft ground. "Have you cast your eye over the drawing, Mr. Wilkes?"

The foreman, Wilkes, clearly hadn't. He spat. "I know my trade."

"Then you'll understand that the stone must lie in the building as it lay in the ground. That's the way to get the best out it." Bath stone was a freestone, which meant you could cut and square it in any direction. It wasn't like slate, which you split along its planes and which was strong only against the grain. Even so, Bath stone came from the living earth and had its preferences. "You'll need to pay close attention to the way the faces are marked."

"I hear you, sir. But first let's see them blocks arrive safe and sound."

Two days ago Woods had received word that the first of the shipments had reached Reading. "I hope we may depend on that."

It was the second week of May. Early-morning mist hung in the valley. Towards the east, pink promised the sun; on the low-lying ground hares bounded out of thinning, shifting veils of gray-white and vanished as if they had never been there.

Fields, woods, a waterway, a little straggle of a village huddled round pump and green, some way off a church and churchyard, all sheltered between gentle, rounded hills. This was ancient land, deeply settled, tilled, and husbanded through good times and bad, a country of yeomen and squires.

Ancient land, in a time of transition. The countryside was not as open as it once had been. In this age of exclusion—of money made else-where in cities and trade—ditches, hedges, fences, and walls enclosed fields and woods into parcels of ownership and put a price on every tree. The common land, where generations of villagers had grazed their livestock and scratched out a living, was fast disappearing, taking with it all the old ways. No one knew yet what the new ways would bring, but the poor, who found themselves poorer, had reason to dread them.

The sun rose and burned off the mist. Light caught the windows of the old manor house and reflected off broken, faceted panes, glanced up the leaning chimneys, and grazed the irregular roofline. On the upper story a casement squeaked open and a dust cloth shook out of it.

In front of the old manor, daylight laid bare the raw scars of trenches and earthworks that had been dug into the chalky soil, exposing flints and whitened animal bones. The foundations of the new house, which made its plan tangible and real, scored an intention of building into the ground.

Gazing at the trenches, Woods was aware that an intention could always be reversed, if not by human will, then by the lack of it. Left alone, the foundations would become waterlogged, the sides would erode and eventually fall in, and grass would grow over the top. The ground would stitch itself up. To build was a form of human folly that pitted itself against forces of nature bent on reclaiming their own. To imagine otherwise, to imagine that what you built might last, was akin to madness.

"I hear the Gypsies are back."

Woods turned. Joshua, unshaven, red-eyed, and slipshod, a gray blanket draped round his shoulders, was chafing his hands.

"So rumor has it."

The mist had lifted and the sky was clearing, but there was not a trace of the camp to be seen nor a sound to be heard, not a wisp of smoke, not a single child's cry, not a dog's bark to break the morning silence. The Romany were masters of stealth, a law unto themselves. By now their fires would be covered, and their shelters, formed of supple hazel twigs covered with skins, were fashioned to blend into the woods.

"Wilkes thinks they're bad luck."

"My mother thinks so too," said Joshua, yawning.

"Your mother is an excellent woman, but all females incline towards superstition. Bad luck is bad judgment."

Joshua's mother was a handsome widow from Thirsk. She had been left comfortably off and was no more inclined to take another husband than Woods was inclined to take any wife: their arrangement, conducted discreetly over the years, suited them both. A widow's company was one thing, and a fine thing in moderation, but he would never have taken on the lad had he not seen his promise for himself. None of this was spoken of.

Joshua shrugged. "Did Wilkes read the drawing?"

"No."

"I thought as much."

"Get yourself dressed. You're a sight," said Woods. The lad must have sat up drinking until the small hours, judging by the state of him. "You should have listened to me last night and gone to bed."

"I did," said Joshua, drawing the blanket around him. "So you needn't look at me like that. But then I had such a strange dream. It woke me and I couldn't get back to sleep again."

Woods was unsympathetic. "And Nurse didn't come to tuck up your covers."

"No," said Joshua, shivering. "Nurse didn't come. In my dream the stone was floating up the river. Piles and piles of it, stacked high."

"Then let's hope your dream was prophetic."

Joshua stared into the distance for a time. He was a good-looking lad, tall and dark, not yet grown into his rangy frame. Normally his intelligence was a flare of energy; this morning he was subdued. He shivered again. "Let's hope not. It was a terrible dream."

"It's the waiting," said Woods. "You'll get used to it. A good deal of this work is to do with waiting. It takes its toll on the nerves."

"My dream was not about waiting. It was about harm." Joshua shook his head, as if he might dislodge something in it, and went off to the manor.

Gypsies, dreams, a pattern of leaves in a teacup. Bad luck was nothing more than bad judgment, thought Woods, and bad judgment you could do something about.

*   *   *

They had made a kind of roadway of split logs from the site to the landing stage at the riverbank, skirting the steepest part of the slope. The roadway was Wilkes's notion and the rabble of men he had hired as jobbing labor had been sawing and splitting and tamping for days. When Woods walked the length of it later that morning, he could feel the timber teeter under his boots. The earth was sodden.

He called one of the men over. "See this?" He bounced on a split log and splashed his boots with mud. "This, all this"—he gestured up and down the roadway—"needs to be backfilled. It's not going to hold the weight with the ground so wet. Where's Wilkes?"

The man didn't know. Wilkes had his team of craftsmen, a tight-knit group, chiefly masons and joiners. These rough laborers were disaffected, unused to pulling in harness. Itinerants or villagers, largely unskilled, they were aged by hardship beyond their years.

"Tell the rest of them," said Woods. "Don't use the coarse rubble. The finer gravel is better. There's a pile of it up on the south side of the site, so you'll need to cart it down in barrowloads."

The man stared at him and nodded his assent, which under the circumstances meant next to nothing.

Woods gazed downriver in the direction of Reading. In his mind's eye he was pulling the stone closer and closer, willing it along. The worst, surely, was over. The journey down the Avon from Bath to Bristol, then into the open sea, skirting the treacherous west coast, along the Channel to the Thames estuary, was hazardous even in good weather, and the threats—piracy, rocks, the French—were many. Now a mere few miles of inland waterway remained.

Despite what he had said to Joshua about waiting, and the need to learn how to endure it, Woods was not a patient man on the whole. He may have been stubborn, meticulous, and precise—qualities which were in themselves forms of patience or of subduing the will to a greater end—but waiting upon events that were in the control of others was not in his nature. After watching the river for a while, during which time one lone heron lifted slowly up from the water, and coots and moorhens scuttled in the shirring, hissing reeds, he returned up the muddy slope.

On the way back, he saw Joshua, now dressed and shaved after a fashion, coming from the manor. As they passed each other, Joshua frowned, put up his hand, and moved his mouth as if to say something. Woods, the stone on his mind, gave him a brisk nod and went on with no further acknowledgment. The lad had to learn how to stand on his own two feet.

Later, during the long and unanticipated years of his old age, Woods would have time to regret his reluctance to show close affection. Joshua was near enough a son; he'd known the boy half his life and he had all the qualities anyone might wish for in their own flesh and blood. Warmth was due him and warmth Woods may have felt but rarely showed. Others might have put it down to a north-country reserve bred in the bone, a lid clamped down on sentiment, a suspicion of smooth and emollient words. But he knew the origins of this reluctance lay in something less excusable. On the few occasions when he allowed himself to think about it, he recognized it as a form of selfishness. He had lived a long time alone and on his own terms.

When on site, it was Woods's custom to eat sparingly during the day, and his afternoon meal was cheese and bread, washed down with half a jug of small beer. The cheese was good, the bread a little stale, the small beer so weak it would have been fit for the nursery. He pushed the plate and jug aside. Work, not food, was the remedy for waiting.

Woods could work anywhere. Upstairs, in the bedchamber, where he had been worrying over the accounts books the previous evening, or downstairs, here in the great hall, which was where the daily site business was conducted; if need be, he could work on the road in jolting carriages and stagecoaches (he had often found movement conducive to design thought). Now he sat at the midpoint of the long refectory table that bisected the great gloomy hall of the manor, an orderly chaos surrounding him, and reached for a scroll of drawings. The drawings were of a smaller, simpler commission, a design for a little classical pavilion or temple, a trifle to stand in the grounds of a house he had built fifteen years ago near York. When he unrolled them, his right hand knocked against a shard of pottery resting on the tabletop and sent it flying. He just managed to catch it before it fell and smashed on the floor.

The men were always bringing him such things, relics that they unearthed during the digging of the foundations, wanting to know what they were, or imagining that he might find some inspiration in them or use for them. Most of their findings were unremark-able: bits of broken tiles, old sections of beams, rusting metalware. This pottery shard was of a different order of discovery and he had brought it to the attention of Joshua, who had humored him by pre-tending an interest in it. The fragment was irregular and of varying thicknesses, a segment of an earthen vessel made of coiled, fired clay. Into its rough unglazed surface a hand had pressed a pattern of indentations with some sort of blunt-ended tool. His fingers traced the spiraling lines. The shard was ancient, he was certain of that; how old he did not know. In the regular pattern he recognized a tension that was familiar. Material knew how it wanted to be shaped—that was form. Material told you how to embellish it—that was decora-tion. Sometimes the marriage was perfect.

Woods laid the pottery fragment back on the table. At the same moment the door was pushed open and Joshua appeared with news on his face.

Despite himself, Woods felt anticipation tighten his chest. "The stone?"

Joshua nodded. "It's come."

Andrea Palladio's *Four Books of Architecture* and Sebastiano Ser-lio's *Seven Books of Architecture:* these two treatises were Woods's constant companions and his teachers. The rules and proportions set out in their pages formed the guidelines by which he built and the ideals to which he aspired. As he accompanied Joshua down the slope to the river, he thought that even the masters, Palladio and Serlio, would have been struck by what he saw in front of him. Here were the building blocks of the classical order; here, in raw form, were plinth, column, architrave, frieze, and cornice.

Sometimes when Woods looked out over the trenches and earthworks of the foundations, as he had done earlier that morning, he was surprised not to see the house already complete, it was such a fully formed thing in his mind. A thing, moreover, of inexpressible joy and delight. Of love. During his life he had known love twice (one of the women had died and the other had married someone else) and the sensation of building was the closest he had ever come to that enraptured state. Building was a voluptuous pleasure; taste it once and you wanted more. Now as he saw the stone waiting to become architecture, waiting to become what he held in his head, he was gripped by desire. It was nothing to do with ownership. This type of possession was entirely imaginative, and so the longing was infinitely renewable. Patrons, who inhabited your buildings once they were finished and sometimes spoiled them, were a small price to pay for it.

Men were swarming around and over the barge, making it fast to the landing stage, removing the canvas covers from the stone and hitching the blowing draft horses that had pulled the barge upriver. On the bank, two wagons were drawn up, fresh horses nodding in their leather head collars, and an arrangement of pulleys and winches was being assembled to hoist the cargo to land.

A small crowd was gathered on the riverbank. Among the villagers, dumbstruck for the most part, he spotted the local blacksmith, innkeeper, and parish priest. Even the girl who brought the eggs in the morning was there, a red kerchief crossed over her breast, and the old housekeeper had roused herself out of the chimney corner.

"Was I the last to be told?"

"Word gets around," said Joshua.

In the pale spring sunshine the uncovered blocks radiated their own glow, as if they were lit from within. England was a wet country; Bath stone was porous. You had to keep it dry on its travels and detail buildings to protect it from rain, which called for deep overhangs, among other things. This afternoon what the stone drank was light.

"I had no idea it was so fine," said Joshua, wonder in his voice.

"You get what you pay for," said Woods.

"Or what you haven't paid for. Is that how it works?"

"On occasion," said Woods.

He went to speak to Wilkes, who was directing the men, and asked him if the timber roadway had been made stable according to his instruction.

"Begging your pardon, sir," said Wilkes, raising his voice. "Do you take me for a fool? So far as your instruction goes, I'd already given the self-same one." The sharp words threatened an open quarrel.

In the bright glitter of the foreman's eyes Woods recognized the hunger he felt himself. An architect was only as good as his crafts-men and the craftsmen were only as good as their foreman. Wilkes was skilled and experienced, and well paid on both accounts.

"Then I shall leave you to it."

"I thank you for that, sir." Wilkes signaled to the men.

The horses pulled forward and the rope tightened over the creaking winch. The first block, nestled within its cradle, was lifted off the barge and over the riverbank, its great weight a pendulum of doom.

The stone swung in the sky, to and fro, back and forth, long enough for everyone to wonder what it would do to a skull. Gasps came from the crowd, some of whom ducked. Others put their hands on their heads. A few scrabbled up the slope and out of the way.

Then slowly, slowly the horses were made to reverse, the rope slackened, and the descending block was grappled onto the back of a wagon. Cheers of relief greeted its landing.

More gasps, more cheers as the second block came ashore. By the fifth, the crowd was bored of the spectacle and fell silent. By the sixth, they began to disperse. Only a few remained to see the wagon laden with stone begin its progress up the roadway to the site, and none, bar the workmen, were there to see it arrive.

So it went all afternoon. The first barge was unloaded, pulled away from the landing stage, and moored downstream, and the sec-ond barge had arrived when the light began to go.

They covered the piles of stone for the night. One by one, the workmen drifted back to their billets in the outbuildings of the manor.

"Will you dine with us, Mr. Wilkes?" said Woods.

The housekeeper had made pigeon pie. More pie than pigeon, truth be told. Over the meal, they talked about the day's work. Above the flames flickering in the hearth the ceiling was lost in darkness.

Joshua, chasing the last morsel around in the dish, remembered Woods saying, *Better make an enemy of your patron than your fore-man.* As good as his word, he was mending bridges, discussing with Wilkes the arrangement of the stone on the site, what covers, what pallets would be required, although he needed advice on none of these questions.

"I thought your roadway served us well," said Woods.

Wilkes swallowed and rubbed his mouth on his grubby sleeve. "A dry night or two and it will set hard."

Joshua's eyelids drooped, then jerked open again. The day had been long and he wanted his bed. He rose from the table. "Well, I'll make one less." Wilkes had got onto the Gypsies again, like a ter-rier worrying a bone. Woods waved his hand in an absent gesture. Joshua took a candle, stumbled up the stairs that pitched under his feet, and went along the gallery with its squeaking floorboards. In his bedchamber, where cool spring air dampened the worn linen sheets, he fell asleep almost immediately and dreamed of nothing.

They were lucky with the weather. Day after day was dry. The road-way compacted under the weight of the wagons that trundled up it and the stone accumulated in neat, square, honey-colored piles. Woods had intended to start building as soon as the first blocks were unloaded, an intention that was fueled by a desire not to waste the opportunity offered by the dry weather. Yet, despite what he had said to Joshua about the unlikelihood of More showing his face when there was an account to settle, the knowledge that his patron remained in the neighborhood held him back. He made inquiries, established where More was staying, and wrote to inform him that the delivery of the stone was proceeding. In return, he received a brief reply that said neither one thing nor another.

Woods had often observed that the laying of the foundation stone wedded patron to house, even if the stone had to be removed and reset in a proper fashion afterwards. While there was still a chance that such a ceremony might flatter More into releasing the funds that would spur progress, he was willing to delay. Now the last barge was half unloaded and the men were looking at him with question marks on their faces. One more day, he told himself, and then he would wait no longer.

He had set Joshua the task of recording the old manor before they pulled it down, and this morning he could see the lad sitting some way off, dutifully working on a drawing of the north elevation. In his own mind the site was already cleared and the new stable block built on top of it. In his own mind carriages were pulling up and people were alighting from them.

There wasn't a single right angle in the old manor, thought Joshua, rubbing a stale crust over his charcoal marks to correct what he had drawn. Not a one. Everything leaned. Squinting against the light, he saw Woods surveying the stone piled up alongside the trenches dug for the foundations and even from a distance he could sense his impatience. He quickly sketched in the architect to give a human scale to the drawing and then scrubbed this out too. The sketch was very lifelike and therefore somewhat disrespectful.

During the five years that Joshua had been apprenticed to Woods, he had learned that staircases must have odd-numbered treads, which types of timber, brick, and stone were suitable for construction, how to mark out foundations in straight lines, how to burn the ends of piles and drive them down into the earth, how to joint dressed stone with thin mortar so the wall was a smooth skin, the properties of lime and sand, the importance of model making, and many fine points of architectural drawing. He had studied the masters: Vitruvius, Alberti, Palladio, Serlio. He had been taught to read a site like a book: to identify the direction of the wind and the aspect that would bring light into a building, to investigate ground conditions. Standing unremarked on the sidelines, he had seen for himself how a combination of mute resistance and cunning could deliver an architectural vision intact and uncompromised, despite the best efforts of patrons, with all their absurd vanities and contradictory demands, to thwart it.

For most of his apprenticeship what Joshua had wanted was to emulate his master, to conceive designs that would meet with his approval, and eventually to achieve a reputation as solid and distinguished as his. In recent months, however, ideas of his own had boiled up in his head and filled his sketchbook, and he was shocked to find that, despite what he had absorbed so eagerly from Woods and the books in his library, what he had drawn was very different. So different that the drawings almost seemed like a kind of heresy.

In the pages of his sketchbook sprouted soft, fluid buildings, buildings that were more expressive of feeling than reason, less mathematical and austere. Fantastical, freakish buildings that could never be built, their plasticity unattainable in any kind of known material. Woods, he knew, would see the designs as aberrations, the products of disordered thought, which was why he kept them hidden.

Joshua looked up from his drawing of the north elevation and saw that Woods was gone. He put down the board on which he had pinned the paper, covered it, and set off in the direction of the woods.

He liked the woods. He liked their quickening smell in these mild spring days, the life stirring, the trees budding, the crack of twigs under his boots. He walked a while, swishing his feet through the dry leaf litter, until he came to the clearing, a little vaulted space where he had seen the Romany girl.

The day he had seen her, she had been cutting mushrooms with a small knife and gathering them into her apron. When he blundered through the undergrowth and surprised her, she dropped the corners of her apron, scattering the mushrooms on the ground. She stood stock-still, their eyes had met, and he had wondered if she would use the knife on him. Then she had run away deeper into the woods, her dirty bare feet making next to no sound.

Joshua hadn't seen her since, although not for want of trying. He sat down on a tree root, pulled his sketchbook out of his pocket, and turned to the page where he had drawn her. The snap of her dark eyes, her black hair streaming behind her when she had fled. An impression of color, and an abiding sense of connection, which kept drawing him back to this place. He had never come across anyone like her.

A noise startled him. For a moment he thought the Romany girl had returned, but when he looked up, he saw that the steward, Hastings, had come into the clearing. Hastings was not much older than he was; he had a swaggering walk and a mean mouth. As always, he was accompanied by his dog, which ran over panting, poking its wet nose in everywhere.

Joshua fended off the dog and hastily closed the sketchbook. "Good day, Mr. Hastings."

"Don't let me disturb you," said the steward.

Hastings had made several attempts to run the Gypsies off the land and none so far had succeeded. Somehow the Romany always got wind of the plans and moved their camp each time. A good portion of the estate, which covered thousands of acres, was wooded, and finding a handful of people who were expert at the art of concealment was a poor game of cat and mouse.

The locals were easy to intimidate. Arrest a trapper, a herder, a woodcutter. Change the language. Call the trapper a poacher, the herder a trespasser, the woodcutter a thief and hang them or send them to prison. That taught the villagers they were no longer free to snare hares for their pots, graze their sheep on the uplands, or fuel their fires. The Romany were different. What did they care for surveyors with telescopes and chains? Title deeds, fences, and walls meant nothing to them. Land was land. They roamed and lived lightly on it. They took what they needed and moved on, covering their traces, melting away.

"Must be hard work, drawing trees," said Hastings, his mouth twisting up to one side.

Joshua kept his hand clamped on the cover of the book and eyed the man warily. "Drawing is work. It takes practice."

Hastings said, "I know a man who can tell when an oak is ripe for the felling by the taste of the acorn. I call that proper skill."

"I have heard of such." Joshua made to shove the sketchbook in his pocket.

Hastings was too quick for him, snatched it out of his hand, and flicked through the pages. Laughed. "Is this what you call work?" he said.

The sketch he held up was of a round building, raised on columns, with a spiraling stair in front. "It's what I call thinking." Joshua's heart was hammering. Don't turn any more pages, he thought.

Hastings turned more pages. "And this?" he said, holding up a sketch of a tower. "Don't tell me. It's more of your thinking. You ask me, I'd say it was the work of a madman."

"I don't ask you, Mr. Hastings. You do your job and I do mine," said Joshua. "Call off your dog."

"Bess!" Hastings called the dog, which was chasing round in excited circles, nipping at Joshua's heels. "Catch," he said to Joshua, and threw the book at him. It fell on the ground, open to the page where he had drawn the Romany girl.

There was a silence as they both stared at the drawing. Joshua got up from his perch on the tree root, his breath shallow and fast. As he recovered the sketchbook, he felt the steward's eyes shift to him and heard his thoughts.

"Where did you see her?" said Hastings in a quiet voice.

"Her?" said Joshua.

"The girl in your book."

"I made her up. I imagined her. Just as I imagined the buildings."

"Oh yes? Then you've made up the very likeness of a thieving Gypsy." Hastings narrowed his eyes. "You'll want to tell me when and where you see her next. That's something I'd like to know."

"I'll be sure to tell when she next visits my thoughts," said Joshua, with greater defiance than he felt. The man was not fooled.

"What's all that writing? Under the drawing."

"It's a poem," lied Joshua. "Do you want me to read it to you?"

"I want you tell me when you next see that girl," said the steward. "Or any other of her filthy tribe." He rubbed a finger inside his neckcloth. "I don't rightly understand your notion of work, but making things hard for those that break the law is what I do for a living." He called the dog to heel and went off.

When he had gone, Joshua opened the sketchbook to the page where he had drawn the Romany girl. Underneath, in the neat lettering that Woods had taught him, was a description of their encounter, the date, the place, the gathering of the mushrooms, the knife. He let out a long sigh and thanked his stars that Hastings could not read.

As he put the book in his pocket, rain began to patter on the ground. In a matter of minutes, the patter became a drumming, a hissing, a roaring. There was a flash of lightning, followed by a low rumbling roll of thunder.

Joshua came out of the woods into a downpour. It was as if the sky had burst and all the preceding dry days had saved themselves up for this flood. Rain was pelting down, drenching him to the skin, running off the dry ground in muddy rivulets. There was a kind of exultation to it. He pulled up his coat collar and ran. When he reached the spot where he had been sitting earlier and sketching the old manor, he found the drawing sodden and ruined.

He looked around, expecting to see men laughing and rushing for cover from all directions. Instead, over the insistent sound of the rain, he heard shouts and sharp cries of panic come up from the riverbank. It was his dream, he thought, his terrible dream, as he slid down the slope to meet it.

The storm took them by surprise. One minute they were joking, negotiating the by-now familiar routine of loading the stone onto a wagon and nursing it up the hill, the next it was chaos. Rain, hail, lightning, thunder.

The force of the deluge loosened the timbers of the roadway, and a wagon laden with stone veered sideways and threatened to discharge its cargo into the river. At the sound of the thunderclap, one of the horses hitched to the wagon slid off into the mud and the other reared, its eyes wild and rolling back in its head. Yoked together, they skittered and thrashed in opposite directions as the men ran about, unsure where to push or to pull. All the while, rain sluiced down the hill.

Woods could hear the foreman shouting. Then, looking up the slope through the teeming rain, he saw Joshua sliding down it.

"Get back! It's going over!" yelled Wilkes, waving his arms. "Get back!"

Afterwards, Woods was never sure of the order of events, although he tried to reconstruct it in his mind many times. He had been standing by the wagon, that much he remembered, and he remembered, too, the sight of the stone tipping off the top, the certainty that it would be lost in the river. The rest was as blank as a sheet of paper.

When he came back to himself, he was lying on his side on some sort of litter, which was jolting over the ground. He saw a man's hand, black hairs on his knuckles, gripping the side. The next time he opened his eyes, he was in bed. Wilkes was there and a few other faces he recognized but could not put names to. His head was lifted and brandy was spooned into his mouth.

On what he would later learn was the third day, he asked for Joshua. Wilkes—he thought it was Wilkes—rose from his seat near the window.

The doctor had been, bled and cupped him. But it was the housekeeper's tea brewed from bitter herbs that had cleared his raging, aching head. This morning he had a sharpened sense of himself, of his limbs working, of being a whole person. "Joshua?" he said.

Wilkes sat himself on the bed. Rubbed his nose, then his eyes. "Friend," he said, absently patting and smoothing the counterpane. "The boy is dead."

Joshua was dead, and Joshua had saved him. Had seen the wagon going over, the stone beginning to topple, and pushed him out of the way with so much force that he had been knocked unconscious. The stone had fallen and crushed Joshua instead.

"I want to see him," said Woods, raising himself up against the bolsters, fighting the bedclothes.

Wilkes shook his head.

"I want to see him, do you hear?"

"We buried him this morning."

Woods remained on site for another few months. The stone rose in its courses and the house took the shape he had imagined, growing up from the ground story by story, but the delight had gone out of the building for him. At the close of each day, he often found himself in the churchyard, where the lad's unmarked grave was a hillock of earth. They had given him Joshua's sketchbook, which they had found in his pocket. At first he had thought he might send it on to the boy's mother, the widow, along with the letter that it had taken him five days to compose, but some of the sketches were bloodstained and he thought it better not to. Truth be told, he wanted to keep it.

He didn't understand the designs Joshua had drawn—unbuild-able, fictional things—but he recognized the independence of thought and marveled at it. Woods knew he was a competent fol-lower of patterns, of rules; he was not, and would never be, an origi-nal. If the boy had lived, eventually the teacher would have become the taught. That was clear to him.

The steward, Hastings, came to see him one day, wanting to see the drawing of the Gypsy girl, wanting to know what was written underneath it. Woods told him he had burned the book.

In their own good time, the Gypsies left the woods and went elsewhere. In his own good time, More came in his carriage to in-spect progress. He was on his way back to London and talked at length of the trouble in the American colonies, and promised to pay for the stone, although it took another six months to get the ac-count settled, by which time the trouble in the American colonies had become a war.

Bath stone killed Joshua. It wouldn't do for his grave. Back in Yorkshire, Woods commissioned a granite slab and paid for its inscription and transport.

The widow refused to see him. He did not blame her. The office was busy with several new commissions, one of which was a house in Beverley for a wealthy Catholic family. In Berkshire, Wilkes wrote to him, the roof was on. On Woods's drawing table lay the pottery fragment the men had unearthed during the digging of the foundations.

When he had shown the shard to Joshua, the lad had asked what type of tool might have been used to make the indentations—the blunt end of a stick, a piece of bone? It was then that it had occurred to Woods that in profile the dents looked very much like the cross-section of the reeds that grew down by the river. They had tested this out, making impressions on a smooth patch of damp soil, and the results staring up at them from the ground had slipped the hand of the present into the past.

3

A Book of Ceilings: 1796

In twenty years the stone has mellowed and the house has lost its raw, stark newness. Now it sits naturally in a landscape that has taken much art, much time, and much expense to achieve. Contoured into flattering vistas, planted with clumps of trees and grazed by deer, the park is enclosed by high walls and defended by two stone gatehouses, in case anyone is in any doubt about ownership and entitlement.

From the outside, you might think the house has always been here. Yet inside, it isn't finished. Only a few of the principal rooms, designed for entertaining and society, are completely furnished and decorated. The structure may be sound and weathertight, but what is missing are the people to inhabit it.

At the age of seventy-six, James Woods was traveling south again, this time in the company of his nieces, Hannah and Maria. Their destination was Fawley Court in Buckinghamshire, where he had been asked to design a pair of lodges. The commission had come when Woods was midway through a survey of York Minster he was conducting on behalf of the diocese. He was busy and could have refused the work. Always careful with money, he lacked for nothing and had nothing to prove, but he hadn't turned down a job in half a century and was not about to do so now.

It had been Hannah's idea that she and her sister should accompany him. Maria, she said, needed a change. It would do Maria good. Neither of his nieces had ever left Yorkshire, and Hannah's notion of adventure was a visit to Harrogate. It was so unlike her to put forward such a proposal that he had agreed, thinking that there must be a reason behind it, but not wishing to ask what it was.

It had been Maria's idea that they visit Ashenden Park, as it lay on their way to Fawley, which was a few miles away down the Thames. She had heard so much about it and she had always wanted to see it. To this, he had also agreed, with a heavier heart. After Joshua had died, he had returned to Ashenden only once and that had been twelve years ago. The memory was less painful now, but he would have preferred not to revisit it.

The journey south had taken them through so many clamorous towns and staging posts, so many dead wastes and empty fields, that the creaking, jolting carriage had become a kind of refuge, a welcome familiarity among the confusing changes of scene. Something to shield them, too, from the unrest and distress of the country, the blank hungry faces at every turnpike, the deserving and undeserving poor trudging back to cots with a few crooked branches lashed to their backs or howling drunk in the lanes. This afternoon, after such a long time on the road, it was strange to think that they were approaching the first of their destinations, places that had come to seem beyond reach.

As they rattled through the gates of Ashenden Park, Maria leaned out of the open window, her thin face turned into the sun. Her watercolors, which had slid out of her portfolio, littered the floor, and there was a crumpled shawl beside her. Her sister, seated opposite, was reading a letter from her son.

"Look at this landscape, Hannah. Look at the green. Have you ever seen anything greener? If I were to paint it, it would have to be on white paper. Not like home, where you'd want a duller ground. Pale gray perhaps."

Hannah raised her eyes for a moment. "What difference would it make? The colors go on top."

"Precisely." Maria drew in her head and fell back against the buttoned seat. Before they had left Yorkshire, she had cut her hair short, and dark wisps of curls escaped from under her cap. "What do you say, Uncle James?"

"We are on chalk here. I am inclined to agree with you. In my experience, you have to respect what lies underneath."

His nieces were kind and affectionate women. Hannah believed he did too much. The word "retirement" was often on her lips. She pointed out quiet villages where it would be pleasant to spend one's later years and thought of quiet occupations, such as fishing, it would be pleasant for him to take up. Maria sometimes asked questions to which he did not have the answers. Aside from that, they were good companions, and had not complained once since they had set out days ago.

When they came up the drive and the house appeared, they fell silent. Then Maria said it was beautiful, Hannah said she had no idea it was so large, and Maria replied it was not large, it was exactly the right size. The driver had already jumped down, turned out an ostler from the stable block, and was setting the steps under the door.

"Give you a hand, sir."

"I can get down well enough," he said. "Help the ladies."

He found that he needed a little time and walked along the frontage towards the north pavilion, which housed the kitchen. In his head he counted his paces, measuring out the yards, the way he had done before the land had been surveyed, when the old manor had still been standing.

The girls—he had to remind himself they were grown women, and in Hannah's case with a family of her own—were waiting for him, sharing a parasol. No one would ever take them for sisters. Hannah was fair, placid, and getting a little stout. Maria, small and dark, was quick and sensitive. She had never married.

"This wonderful color," she said, as he joined them, "what is it?"

"Bath stone." He touched his hand to the wall and ran his fingertips along it. "It's warm. It holds the light. You used to get a similar quality from the quarry at Headington. Headington stone built Oxford, but the best of the quarry has been worked out long since. This was more costly." He frowned at the memory. "We had to bring it up the river by barge."

They went through the central archway at the lower level. Woods rang the bell. He was glad that he had taken the precaution of arranging the visit to coincide with a time when his former patron, More, would be away.

After a time, the door was answered by the housekeeper, a capable-looking young woman with dark eyes and a receding chin. A small boy with the same dark eyes and receding chin was hiding in her skirts.

"You will be Mr. Woods." The housekeeper smiled. "And these ladies must be your nieces. Welcome to Ashenden. I must say, you couldn't have picked a better day for your visit. Isn't it grand to see the sun?"

"Mrs. Hastings, I should like to show my nieces the loggia first. Would it be possible to admit us above?" He explained to Maria, "You'll have a better impression of how the apartments are arranged if we go in by the principal entrance."

The housekeeper, shooing the boy away, said that it was just what she would have advised herself. "Have you been here before?" she asked Maria. "No? Well, a pleasure awaits you. I shall go and unbolt the doors."

Woods led the way back through the vestibule to a pair of stone staircases rising to either side.

"Which one do we go up?" said Hannah.

"Does it matter?" said Maria.

They went up the left-hand side and soon Maria was well in front. The stairs were enclosed, narrow, and plain. They could have been climbing up a curved tunnel or a shaft cut from solid rock.

Woods was thinking about arrival. What he had never attempted to explain to his patrons, and what he could barely describe to himself, was his conviction that a house conveyed richness through experience. Any fool could dream up a grand front, sit it on a hill, or move earth around until it appeared to command its surroundings. That was all very well if you were in the business of selling engravings. To make a house come to life was a different matter altogether. Arrival was the beginning of that process. Arrival began the moment you first saw a house and ended when you crossed the threshold and entered the first apartments. It was a question of sequence.

Up ahead he heard Maria exclaim. He turned to Hannah, who was perspiring and a little out of breath.

"She has been looking forward to this visit so much," she said.

He nodded. Sometimes he worried that he made his preference for Maria's company too obvious.

On the way up the stairs, Maria had the kind of anticipation she felt turning the pages of a book, without knowing exactly what she was expecting to happen next. As soon as she came out onto the loggia, it was as if someone had given her a pair of wings. The roof soared two full stories overhead on Ionic columns, the warm stone glowed in the late spring sunlight, and the landscape fell away in front of her, rising in the distance to a gentle hill.

Footsteps and the swish of skirts announced the arrival of the others.

"Are you trying to fly?" said Hannah, with a laugh.

Maria dropped her arms to her sides and spun round. Her eyes were brilliant. "It is wonderful. Do you not think so?"

"It is very fine."

Maria lived in a world of sensation, where other people's feelings streamed through the pores of her skin and mingled with her own, which then streamed back in the other direction. At that moment, she was aware that her sister, who was all goodness and patience, was worried that she would pay for her excitement later and that her uncle, who had gone over to the balustrade to look at the view, was struggling not to show how much it moved him to see the house again, and that the housekeeper, standing on the other side of the door in the shadows, was waiting. She was aware of the heartbeats of every deer in the park and every breath of air rustling the leaves of the limes, chestnuts, and beeches that grew there.

"It took seven years to move the earth for that hill," said her uncle, clearing his throat. "When I was last here, none of the planting had been done."

They went indoors. There Maria had a new feeling, which overpowered her to the extent that she barely heard the housekeeper telling them where they could go and where they could not. She saw now that what she had experienced on the loggia was only a preparation.

She stood in the center of the hall and the whole house made itself known to her. If she stretched out her fingertips, she felt she could touch every part of it. To left and right, rooms aligned with each other behind closed paneled doors. Directly ahead, through a series of unfolding spaces, she could see a window all the way across on the opposite side. Held within the poised symmetries, she felt tears come to her eyes.

Hannah asked a question about the doors and was told they were Spanish mahogany. Then the housekeeper said to ring the handbell next door if they needed her. Her uncle made slight, unnecessary adjustments to his clothing, took out his pocketbook, and handed over a number of coins.

"Thank you, sir. Most kind and generous of you."

"Not at all." Her uncle said, "Many years ago, there was a Hastings who was steward here."

"Yes, sir," said Mrs. Hastings. "He is still the steward here and he is my husband." She pocketed the coins and bobbed her head.

After Mrs. Hastings had gone, they stopped being a party of visitors and became three separate people. Her uncle weighed the room in his eyes, ran his fingers across the ribbed contours of a pilaster, and gave a bronze Indian deity writhing on a console table his full disapproval. Hannah strolled across the floor.

"Happy, Muzz?" she said, slipping an arm through hers.

"This house is perfect."

Hannah gazed up at the ceiling. "The decorations are pretty."

Maria fought an impulse to point out to her sister the difference between decoration and architecture. Fingers of light beckoned through the window on the opposite side of the house, an open invitation. The enfilade tugged at her. So did her better nature.

"What did Henry say in his letter? You must tell me all his news."

"Later," said her sister, releasing her with a pat. "Go and explore. Don't worry about me. I shall dawdle along in my usual fashion."

Afterwards, Maria would remember the afternoon as a series of shining fragments overlaid on a mental map. She had studied copies of the plans and thought she understood them. The musical succession of volumes took her by surprise. You could, she discovered, breathe light, just as you could breathe air.

She went through the open door in front of her, where the housekeeper had gone, and found herself in another soaring space. At the heart of the house a great staircase rose up and up, its shallow stone flights cantilevered from the wall, the balustrade wrought-iron filigree. Light slanted down from a ribbon of clerestory windows and there were glimpses of vaults and galleries above. Here was the lunar partner of the robust sun-warmed loggia, all coolness, smoothness, and delicate plasterwork wreaths.

Hannah drifted out of the hall and went over to admire a flower arrangement at the base of the staircase. Maria had been meaning to go onwards, towards the beckoning window she had seen when she first crossed the threshold, but a glimpse of a room to the left presented her with the opportunity to delay the pleasure.

She left Hannah behind and came into what was the formal dining room. A screen of columns separated a sideboard from a long, bare mahogany table, creating another little loggia, an open antechamber where liveried footmen would stand. Overhead, the ceiling was complicated geometry, lunettes and medallions painted in grisaille.

Soon after her mother had died, when it was becoming clear she was going to have to live with Hannah, who was then newly married, she had spent a fortnight staying with her uncle while the family home was let and its contents dispersed. He was working on the design of another great house then; he was always working and often sketched his way through dinner. She could not remember him talking much about her mother, although her absence had filled every silence that had fallen between them. Instead he had talked about architecture and shown her books. *A Book of Ceilings* was one of them. Her uncle took most of his ceiling designs from its hand-tinted plates, and she recognized the cherubs peeking through acanthus fronds in the central medallion from one of them. It was like meeting an old friend.

Aside from the table and sideboard, the room was empty, awaiting entertainment. There was a dead butterfly in the grate of the fireplace and a fly buzzing against the window at the far end, trying to find its way out. She stood at the window for a while, looking out over the gardens at the rear of the house, which sloped down to the river. That soft green, which asked to be painted onto white paper, was so different from the green she knew.

From the beginning Hannah had done everything to make her welcome. Sometimes Maria thought it would have been easier if her sister had openly resented her or had acknowledged that she would rather have had her early married life to herself. They had set aside two rooms at the back of the second floor for Maria's use, a bedroom and a small adjoining parlor that faced west into the setting sun, where she had put her mother's desk and a bookcase. Mr. Milford, Hannah's husband, whom she found difficult to call Robert, had stood in the doorway, thrusting his hands in and out of his pockets, and explained that they had wanted her to have somewhere private to ask friends to tea and work at her drawings. "We want you to consider this your home," he had said. In those first months, a succession of men with damp palms, sudden laughs, and droning conversation had appeared downstairs at the dinner table, produced from some inexhaustible supply of widowers and bachelors in the North Riding. Perhaps it was hard-hearted and ungrateful of her, but she could not bring herself to marry one of them. Then the children began to arrive, bringing noise and small calamities, and no more single men were invited to dinner. Instead settled couples came; Maria ate more often in her room and slowly became an aunt, which she had never imagined as the principal role of her life.

Tomorrow they would be at Fawley and then they would be halfway through their journey. She had been looking forward to this week so much and for so long, her expectations had altered the way time worked and made it slip away too fast. It was the opposite for Hannah, she thought, the minutes dragging the farther they traveled away from home and her family.

The fly flew in straight lines, turned at sharp angles, hit the glass repeatedly. She reached up and pulled down the sash, but it could not seem to find its way out.

At that moment Woods was in a warm, south-facing room with a white marble chimneypiece and a pale pink-and-green ceiling (Richardson, *A Book of Ceilings,* Plate IV). You never knew how people would use a house. From its furnishings, the room was clearly where the family chose to live and eat when they did not have visitors, which is what he had intended, although he would have preferred that they had surrounded themselves with fewer belongings. Not for the first time, he wondered why people paid for architecture and then did their best to obscure it. A housemaid, who was dusting a collection of porcelain set out on a japanned commode, blushed, curtsied, and withdrew.

"There you are, Uncle." Hannah poked her head round the doorway. "Well, this is comfortable, I must say."

"Where is Maria?"

"I thought she was with you." She came into the room and stood examining a Dutch still-life painting, her hands folded in front of her. "Very lifelike. You could eat those pears, couldn't you? But I don't care for that fly."

"The fly represents death and decay. It is supposed to be a reminder of our mortality."

Hannah put her head to one side. "Still, I think it would be a prettier picture without it." She moved away down the room, her skirts murmuring behind her. What caught her attention next were half a dozen ivory elephants, descending in size, penned in a glass-fronted cabinet. She looked at them for a long time. "Do you re-member when Henry was little," she said, "and we took him to see the giraffe?"

"I do."

They had brought the beast up from London and taken it through the Shambles. The crowd had been terrified, but not as ter-rified as the giraffe, which had shivered and trembled on its long spindly legs, its great eyes pools of dumb sorrow, silver mucus trail-ing from its nostrils. It had died on the return journey.

"Afterwards Maria painted one of the nursery walls with all the animals going into the Ark, two by two. Henry called the giraffes Mr. Henry and Mrs. Henry. When the children were older, she asked them if they would like something else instead, but they re-fused to let her paint over it." She smiled and shook her head. "It has become quite shabby and faded. Robert wants to put up an Indian paper now the boys are all at school and buy a pianoforte. He thinks we should have musical evenings. Apparently everyone has musical evenings. The trouble is, we're not musical."

Hannah's laughter, rich and full-throated, always came as a sur-prise. Her husband, who was a man of few words and too many, de-pending on whether or not what was being discussed touched upon his line of business, had always struck Woods as a person who took the virtue of common sense to an extreme, even for a Yorkshire-man. Yet he remembered once seeing the pair of them, sitting on the sidelines at some family occasion, overcome by a private joke, wiping their eyes, and had understood that what he was seeing was a good marriage.

Hannah went to look out of the window, commented on the gar-dens, and asked if he thought anyone would mind if she sat down for a while.

"I don't see why they should."

She considered the options, then placed herself at the end of a settee upholstered in damask, crossed her ankles, and closed her eyes for a moment. A little while later, when he left, she had taken out her son's letter and was reading it again.

Maria opened a door at the rear of the dining room and found herself surprised by the end of the enfilade. The architecture had played a trick and delivered her, via half a circuit, into this octagonal space.

She was shocked by what she saw. The faceted room, four times the size of her own, was raw, undecorated and unfurnished. The beckoning window she had seen from the hall had no hangings and the glazing bars were rough to the touch. It was as if a piece of music had come to an end, trailed into nothing, and she had been cheated out of a round, harmonious chord. They had money, these people. Why hadn't they finished their house? Her mind flooded with sympathy for her uncle. It was hard enough to design a house, to conceive every last detail in your head, and then hand it over for other people to live in. To visit, years later, be told where you could and could not go, and find it still incomplete was the worst insult she could imagine.

Her foot disturbed a heap of tools concealed under a canvas, and a nail rolled across the floor. When she bent to pick it up, she felt the familiar pain again and held on to a windowsill until it passed, cold sweat mushrooming on her lip and forehead. She was glad she had cut her hair and lost its dragging weight. It made the nausea that came after the spasms more bearable.

These past months, suffering had crept up on her. It had started as a rumor of discomfort, explained away in the many different ways you explained such things to others and yourself. Then had come a time when it asked her to pay more attention to it. Now she was surprised when she turned a corner and it was not there. She tested the point of the nail, pressing it into the center of her palm.

What put the idea into her head of gouging her initials into the bare plaster she did not know. All she knew was that once it was there, it was irresistible. Perhaps it was the same impulse that made schoolboys plunge the tips of their penknives into desktops, or lovers score hearts into trees.

M. G. Maria Gilmour. She scraped away with the nail, a dizzy rush in her head. Scratch, scratch, scratch. Plaster trickled down the wall. She dug deeper and deeper, her breath quick and shallow. For some reason, it was important to do it properly, to fashion the characters with proper tails and feet as if they were printed or chiseled in stone. It was important to make them as well as she could.

The moment she finished, she was appalled. The dizziness went, the rush in her head, and in its place came cold horror. She felt as if she had murdered something, smashed a poor creature's skull with a rock. The letters were under the sill where you would have to bend down to see them, but they might as well have been ten feet tall and picked out in gold. What she had done was brazen, irreversible, and there was nothing, nothing at all, she could do about it.

She put the nail in her pocket, went into the staircase hall, and stood shaking in the white light that was pouring down from the clerestory like some sort of divine admonition. What had possessed her? She fancied she could feel the nail burning through to her skin like a brand.

Her uncle came out of a doorway to her right. "Your sister was looking for you." He nodded the way he had come, then stopped. "Is anything the matter?"

"No, nothing. I am a little overwhelmed, that is all."

He grunted and gave her elbow a squeeze. "Truth be told, so am I. It has been many years."

"Uncle?" He was, she saw with dismay, making his way to the octagon room.

"What is it, my dear?"

She ought at least to warn him. "The room is not finished. It is quite bare."

"Does that distress you?"

She nodded.

"Better bare than done badly."

The entire time her uncle spent in the octagon room, her heart was in her mouth. She moved away from his sight line, dreading the moment when he discovered the damage she had done. A little while later, Hannah appeared, yawning, and told her what Henry had said in his letter, at length.

"Vats of burning oil is what he has in mind."

"Burning oil?" said Maria, hearing only the drumbeat of her fear.

"His plan to defeat the French," said her sister. "Robert says he reads too many books and his imagination runs away with him."

Then her uncle came back into the central hall, smiling. It was agreed they should look at the gardens while it was still light, and Maria felt a wash of relief so sudden it brought tears again to her eyes.

Hannah came down the stairs of the inn, her way lit by the candle that danced shadows on the walls. It was not the worst place they had stayed; it was not the best. The beds were clean, she could say that much, but their room was at the back, overlooking the stable yard, and it was noisy.

She found a serving girl in the passage and told her what she wanted. "Right away."

"Yes, ma'am. Please to wait in the parlor. I won't be long."

It was late and the fire was burning low. Hannah sat herself on one of the high-backed settles and let out a sigh. Her feet hurt and she slipped off her shoes. The candle made a puddle of light on the table in front of her. The parlor smelled of stale ale, tobacco, and pies.

"Hannah." His voice came out of the darkness.

"Uncle? Is that you? I thought you had gone to bed."

"Not yet." He cleared his throat. "You sound tired."

"I am a little weary."

"And Maria?"

"She has had a wonderful day."

"I am pleased." A pause. "She isn't well, is she?"

"She will be right as rain in the morning."

"I'm not blind."

Hannah stared at the candle. She wondered whether Maria would have had a better life if her uncle had offered her a home after their mother died. It was what she had wanted, but nothing had been said during her stay with him and she was not the sort of person to ask. Maria never asked for anything.

"I think she was surprised that the house was not finished."

"They have run out of money. The estate is heavily mortgaged, so I hear."

"Oh," said Hannah.

"The son is a gambler. They say he has debts all over Europe."

"What a pity."

"The house will survive. It's strong. It has good bones."

The serving girl came into the parlor with the jug and asked if she should take it up.

"No," said Hannah, relieving her of it. "Thank you for your trouble."

"Hannah?" said her uncle. "Is Maria . . . ?"

"Maria wanted to come. It's all she's talked about for weeks."

"You said it would do her good. What's wrong with her?"

"Dr. Thirwell doesn't know."

"Perhaps she should consult another physician."

"He's the best in York."

"We're near enough London. I could make inquiries. We could delay our return long enough for her to see someone else."

In the dark, the conversation was naked and unguarded.

"I have already suggested that. She forbids it."

Hannah took up the candle and saw that her uncle was sitting in front of tiny sketches. For once he looked his age. He raised his eyes and the whites caught in the light.

"She carved her initials under one of the windows in the octagon room. M. G."

"M. G. could be anyone."

"Fresh plaster dust on the floor."

Hannah pressed her lips together and nodded. "I'm glad."

Upstairs, she found Maria crying into a pillow so no one could hear. "Hush, Muzz. I'm going to give you a little stronger dose tonight."

Her sister lifted her head. Strands of hair were stuck to her face. "Don't. I shall be fit for nothing tomorrow."

"You need it. Perhaps it was a mistake to stay so long in the gardens. But they were pretty, weren't they?" She measured out the drops. "Drink it up."

Maria struggled to raise herself against the bolster and took the cup. "I have been thinking about that boy we saw in Leicester. Was it Leicester, or somewhere else? I cannot recall."

"Which boy, my love?"

"He had curly hair, and a little sister, and they were so destitute, so ragged."

"I remember. You gave him money. Yes, it was Leicester, I believe."

"Will it have helped, do you think?"

"It is good to be charitable."

"That is not what I'm asking."

"I don't know. We do what we can, that's all we can do. Come on, my love, drink it up."

"Poor Hannah. You haven't had a decent night's sleep since we came away." Maria lifted the cup to her lips, swallowed, and made a face. "I am such a nuisance to you, such a burden."

"Hush. Don't talk nonsense. All gone? Good lass." Hannah took the cup. "Uncle was in the parlor just now."

"Was he?"

"He'd been drawing. The Fawley lodges, I expect. Turn over and I'll rub your back." Through the nightdress, her sister's skin was hot and her shoulder blades sharp, her spine distinct bumps you could count. How many times had she done the same for her children, she thought, her fingers circling and soothing? When she felt the drug begin to work, she took her hands away. "Let me tuck you up."

Maria's eyes were dimming. She murmured something indistinct.

"What did you say?"

Hannah bent down to hear the words breathed into the pillow, but she did not catch them and they vanished into the air.

*   *   *

The next morning Woods rose early and left the inn just as day was beginning to break. The church was a little set apart from the village, down by the river. He let himself in by the lych-gate.

It did not take him long to find Joshua's grave, with its great impervious slab. Granite, Woods thought, had been a mistake. All around the churchyard, gray headstones slanted out of the ground like so many loose teeth. Time was eating into the names and lichen was blurring the dates, settling the dead into the earth and into the past, which is where the dead must live. By contrast, Joshua's marker might have been put up yesterday. He bent and ran his fingers over the chiseled inscription as gently as one might brush a child's cheek.

Hannah slept late and when she woke, Maria was up and already dressed, sitting at the small table by the window, working on a watercolor, silhouetted against the light.

Hannah rubbed her eyes, slipped her legs out from under the covers, and reached for a robe to pull over her nightdress.

"What are you painting?"

"Come and see. I daren't hold it up, it's still wet."

It was a fluid, tremulous sketch, green and alive.

"Do you like it?"

"I do," said Hannah. "The gardens were so pretty, weren't they?"

Years later, somewhat faded, the picture was still hanging on the landing of Hannah's house in York, where she passed it every day and no longer saw it.

4

The Portrait: 1837

Appearances are deceptive. In the heat of midsummer you might be fooled into thinking that the house faces the future squarely and untroubled. Where sunshine splashes on the stonework and the stonework drinks it up, everything appears permanent, orderly, and solid. Never mind the shut rooms, the curls of peeling wallpaper, the slates missing on the roofs of the pavilions, the broken turret clock of the stable block. Never mind what's faded and old or what has never been completed for want of care and funds. Moths in the carpets, worm in the wood, silverfish in the books: these temporary intrusions can be tolerated, might one day be defeated and banished. This is what the light promises to make good. And with the light, soft fingers of air playing about the symmetries like music, sudden laughter behind closed doors, or footfalls on the staircase that twines up in the center of the house under the high clerestory windows.

Over the chemise went the corset. "Tighter," she said, holding her breath as the maid tugged the laces and the boned gores thrust up her breasts and gouged her armpits. Over the corset went the starched linen petticoat. Over the petticoat and corset went the sprigged cotton skirts and the sprigged cotton bodice with its wide stiffened sleeves. Her hair loose over her shoulders, she lowered herself to the chair in front of her toilet table and waved away the lace cape. The day promised to be hot.

The third week of June, the King was dying and the country had said its prayers. Five days earlier Georgiana More had come down to Ashenden for the summer, accompanied by her maid Benson, her four children, the French governess, a nursemaid, two footmen, and a dog. She had written ahead to advise the housekeeper to make the house ready, or as ready as somewhere that had never been finished and was now falling down could be. The country seat of the Mores, crumbling, derelict, unkempt. To Georgiana, if to no one else, beloved. Ashenden Park had taken possession of her when she had first seen it shrouded in dust sheets early in her marriage, the last of the tenants gone, and unlike a husband or a lover, it had never let her go. Some houses you lived in; others lived in you. Over the years she could have done more to improve it if there had been proper money to spend. Yet she was pleased with what she had accomplished through cutting and contriving. The vivid Indian paper in the octagon room, got entirely by wheedling and which she still had not paid for, was a case in point.

"You have made a palace on a shoestring," had been Delgado's verdict. Delgado, her former lover, a penniless young scribbler with dark, oiled ringlets, an exotic parentage, and an ambition to avoid bankruptcy long enough to get into politics, knew better than most how to manage on very little. Disastrous speculations in South American mining shares had brought him to the brink of ruin, and apparently whole days passed when he dared not go out for fear of being nabbed by his creditors. She did not doubt the story; in fact she had lent him money on the strength of it.

She had adored Delgado, his fine slender hands and compellingly ugly face, and counted their three years together as the happiest of her life. Even now, after she had extricated herself from the affair by the simple expedient of taking someone else into her bed, he often wandered uninvited into her mind. Her desertion had made him miserable, so she had heard; he would get over it. Soon enough he would find someone else, a rich widow perhaps. Delgado liked older women. She thought she had probably cured him of his preference for those who were married.

The little dog, Blanche, was worrying a slipper, tumbling over it, shaking it, growling, and generally revealing a base terrier ancestry.

"Do I turn her out, my lady?" Benson asked the looking glass.

"No, let her stay. She's trying her best to amuse us. Aren't you, *ma petite chérie*?"

She reached down, the dog nipped her, and she swatted her on her white whiskery nose. Immediately she regretted it, for to love a dog means to anticipate loss and the suffering that comes with it. The short lives of dogs couple love with death.

A hundred strokes of the hairbrush. The bone comb scoring the parting, the maid's fingers deft with pins, looping up the glossy brown coils so that they kissed her cheeks. Georgiana turned her head to one side and the other.

"My lady is so beautiful," said Benson, admiring her handiwork.

By candlelight, possibly. Daylight had no respect for her now. By daylight she was becoming *une rose fatiguée*. At sixteen, she had been unable to imagine thirty. At twenty, thirty-five. She was thirty-seven.

"If I may suggest?" The maid touched a dark bloom on her neck beneath her earlobe. "A touch of powder here."

The mirror held their amusement. "Oh! I hadn't noticed. Yes, we had better cover that up."

"It wasn't near so dark yesterday." Benson puffed powder over the love bite. "Will that be all, my lady?"

Georgiana stared through the window of her dressing room over the bright park. Sometimes she worried about the blankness of her mind. "What time is it?"

"Near noon."

"Where are the children?"

"The boys have gone down to the river with James. Miss Clara wanted to go with them but Mademoiselle wouldn't let her."

"Poor Clara. We females deserve better in life, don't you think?"

Benson said that she was happy with her situation.

Georgiana envied her. "Any news of the King?"

"No, my lady."

No news meant no mourning; more to the point, no summons from her husband ordering her back to town.

"Then I shall want the oyster silk later. I am expecting company." Their eyes met again in the looking glass, complicit.

The letter had arrived, the one she had been waiting for. How quickly you recognized handwriting, she thought, the pen strokes that formed her name sending a spark leaping inside her. Along with the spark, a shiver of risk, born out of the suspicion that this time she might be going too far. The note—it was no more than a line—said he would be arriving on Wednesday. Wednesday was today.

When Benson had gone downstairs, removing the dregs of her breakfast chocolate, Georgiana unlocked the traveling writing desk that stood on her toilet table and opened it. The desk had been a gift from her father on her eighteenth birthday, and the Langville crest was inlaid on top. Inside, tied up with black ribbon, were all the letters Delgado had ever written her. She drew out the packet. So many words. The endearments, the poetic raptures, she had by heart, but there were other passages she did not understand even now, references to books she had never read, quotations in languages she did not know, the playful wit of a mind that needed another to spar with it. At the beginning, it had not mattered that he was much cleverer than she was. He had been her dearest heart, her petted boy, starved of the loving attention it was in her nature to bestow. Towards the end they both knew must come, he had started to make her feel stupid. What was worse, he had started to enjoy it.

Folded into a visiting card was a black curl whose smell of pomade was faint and fading. She sniffed it and stared at it for a while, remembering the occasion when she had snipped it off with her silver embroidery scissors, then she put everything back in the desk, locked it, and returned it to her bedroom. The note signed "D. M.", which had arrived that morning, she left in plain view. No one could make anything of it, after all.

Wednesday was today and today was half over. Georgiana left her apartments and made her way across the hall to the loggia, the dog scampering ahead barking at nothing. Then she stepped into the light. It was a bright cloudless day, the sky a big blue bowl. In front of her was the familiar view, the land sloping away beyond the stables and then ascending in a gentle rise. "Queen of all she surveys," she could hear Delgado saying. The sun was almost directly overhead, shrinking the shadows cast by the stands of trees to small dark islands on the undulating green turf. A bubble of pleasure rose inside her. Here she was always herself. Her husband did not share her love of Ashenden; he preferred town, or abroad. Long ago, she had accustomed herself to the fact that her marriage was an odd sort of reel where partners seldom met and never by choice. It had not taken her long to learn that this was preferable to the alternative. One should not be frightened of one's husband, yet it was surprising how many women were, and how many bore the marks of brutality and scars on their hearts. Those love tokens could not be covered with powder. In a corner of the loggia Blanche squatted and piddled on the stone floor, the wet trickling away down the stairs.

A cough. "My lady?"

She turned. "Mrs. Trimble. What a beautiful morning."

"Yes, it has been. If it keeps fair this afternoon, they will be certain to get the hay in." The housekeeper was a dry, spare person of extreme competence who had never got the hang of subordination. For that, Georgiana envied her too. "Benson informs me you are expecting company. Have you instructions for Cook?"

"A light meal, I think, in this weather."

"I'm told the strawberries are ripening."

"Strawberries, yes. And I should like champagne. Do please ensure that it's chilled. There's nothing worse than warm fizz."

If she was expecting a murmur of agreement, none came.

"Numbers?"

"There will be two of us. We shall dine in the drawing room."

"As my lady wishes." The housekeeper made a gesture that was neither a curtsy nor a bow but somewhere in between.

"Mrs. Trimble?"

"What is it, my lady?"

"Tell Mademoiselle she is to take Clara down to the river. It is too fine a day for her to be indoors. If someone will find her a net, she can play at fishing along with her brothers."

Georgiana delighted in her children and kept them closer than most mothers of her acquaintance. The summer would do them good, the older boys in particular, who were now at school and who needed to run a little wild in the holidays. She was a great believer in the free spirit, she had told Delgado. Ah, a devotee of Rousseau, he had said, but that had been another occasion when she had not known what he was talking about.

"Two to dine. Champagne and strawberries," said Mrs. Trimble, coming briskly into the servants' hall. "Otherwise, Cook, my lady leaves it up to you."

"Makes it simple."

The servants' hall, on the lower story, had a subterranean quality and was poorly lit. It never warmed up, not even in the height of summer. The table where they ate their meals was strewn with copper jelly molds drying on linen glass cloths.

"Jane," said Mrs. Trimble, addressing a housemaid, "take a mop to the loggia."

"The lodger, ma'am?"

"The *porch*. The dog's made a mess on the stairs again. Then see to it that the blue bedroom is aired and made up for my lady's guest."

"Yes, ma'am."

"Does something amuse you, Thomas?"

Thomas, a local boy whose real name was Jed Jenks, had had his eyes opened by a few seasons of London life and now wore his hair in a fashion that gave the village something to talk about.

"Begging your pardon, ma'am, but why bother? We all know that bed won't be slept in."

"Begging *your* pardon, sir, but there are standards to uphold. No visitor to this house will ever lack proper accommodation. Keep your comments to yourself in future."

While it might have been Mrs. Trimble's custom to volunteer information to her superiors which was not required and had not been requested, about haymaking, for example, that did not mean she tolerated it in her staff.

"She's got a love bite on her neck the size of a plum." He winked at Jane, who let out a shriek of laughter.

"That's enough!" Those two wanted watching.

Chilled champagne meant ice. Mrs. Trimble pinched the bridge of her nose, a gesture that was much imitated behind her back by some of the younger servants. How was she going to lay her hands on ice? The drains of the icehouse had been blocked for six months and she doubted what was down there amounted to more than slush.

"Where is Mr. Hastings?"

"He was out in the courtyard earlier," said Thomas.

"Thank you, Thomas. Glad to hear you are useful for something."

"No trouble, I'm sure."

Mrs. Trimble went out into the courtyard that separated the main house from the north pavilion. "Mr. Hastings?" The second time she called, he came into view, accompanied by the lurcher, Jess.

The steward was a slouch-backed man, with long furrows in his cheeks and a receding chin. He'd had been at Ashenden since he was a boy, in the days of the 1st Baronet, when the house was new and his parents were in service here, his mother housekeeper and his father steward before him. He gave everyone to understand that times had been much better then. All indications were he had been disappointed in life, which was true, and the lack of a Mrs. Hastings was one of those disappointments. Not for want of trying, she had gathered. A fortnight after she had arrived at the house, he had asked her to marry him, a proposal made with all the bluntness of a horse trader or a farmer at a corn exchange. Naturally she had refused; the man was singularly unappealing. Besides which, unlike most housekeepers, whose "Mrs." was a courtesy title, hers reflected a legal status. Mr. Hastings was not to know, nor did she enlighten him.

"What is it, Mrs. Trimble?" Hastings stood in the cobbled yard, feet apart, as if he were braced on the rolling deck of a ship. Beside him, the lurcher flopped over, panting in the heat.

"My lady wants *chilled* champagne."

"Does she?"

"She is expecting company."

"That will be the writer, no doubt."

"I have no idea whom she's expecting. I need ice. What do you suggest?"

Hastings rubbed his face. "If it's ice that's wanted, I suggest they find the money to repair the icehouse, ma'am."

"Failing that?"

He tugged at the hat he wore summer and winter, lowering it over his eyes. "Failing that, we send someone over to Whiteleys and fetch some."

"There's an icehouse at Whiteleys?"

"There is."

"I didn't know."

"No reason why you should."

This statement was designed to impress upon Mrs. Trimble the fact that she was a relative newcomer to the estate and surrounding area and that Mr. Hastings was the old hand who could be relied upon for local knowledge. As such it was successful and put the housekeeper into a bad mood for the remainder of the afternoon, during which time Jane the housemaid bore the brunt of it and was in consequence sharp with the bootboy. Much later, the bootboy punched his thin pillow, said to himself how unfair it all was, and fell asleep dreaming of running away and joining the navy.

In the early afternoon Georgiana drifted down to the riverbank, forgetting the children would be there. The grounds at Ashenden had been laid out with a precision that was now blurred by neglect.

She knew nothing of gardening and descended the terraces with an abstract impression of abundance that failed to distinguish weeds from desirable plants, passing through clumps of little white flowers, big white flowers, and the scarlet stains of poppies, the murmuring hum of bees, a wayward creamy rambling rose with a deep musk scent, greenery drooping in the heat, and an infestation of something thorny that snagged her skirts.

The dog yapped. The cries of the children came up to greet her. They were all in the river, except Clara.

Georgiana's two older boys, Frederick and Edward, were fighting again and it was clear that Edward, as usual, was coming off worse, spluttering and throwing feeble punches while his brother tried to hold his head under the brown, churning water. "Drown and see if I care!" Frederick was saying. "Damn little fool. Weakling!" For a moment Georgiana thought about turning around and going back to the house. Too late: Clara had seen her.

Clara got up and ran across to her, her dress streaked with grass stains, and asked her to please, please stop Freddie being so awful.

"Go back under the parasol, my love. You are becoming quite pink."

The youngest, George, who had been paddling in the shallows, scrambled onto the bank, seeking the safety of dry land. By now, Mademoiselle had got to her feet and was calling and waving her arms in a helpless and agitated manner, while the footman stood around with his mouth open and did nothing.

"James!"

"My lady?"

"What are you thinking? Stop them at once!"

"My lady."

The footman took off his shoes and stockings and waded into the water. After a tussle and a struggle, Frederick was persuaded to release his brother, who slithered onto the bank near Georgiana's feet, where he lay panting for a while.

"Don't snivel, Edward," she said. "Be a man."

Frederick strode out of the river and picked up his fishing rod.

She called him and he ignored her. He cast his line, reeled it in, and whipped the rod out over the river again with a closed, self-satisfied expression on his face that reminded her of her husband. Her eldest son, who would be the 4th Baronet one day, had her lustrous hair ("nut-brown hair," Delgado had written in one of his letters) and had always been robust, unlike little George, the youngest, whom they had to keep an eye on. From time to time, and this was one of them, she worried that in other respects Frederick took after his father, who had inherited the title, the London house in Carlton Terrace, and Ashenden at the age of five, among other things bred into his nature, including his own father's disastrous taste for gambling and a streak of cruelty she believed came from his Teutonic mother. Georgiana was of French descent herself and distrusted Germans.

"May I fish now, Mama?" The fight over, Clara was back. "Might I, do you think?"

"What is that dirty thing?"

"It's a net. Cook gave it me to catch tiddlers."

Forgetting that girls ought to be allowed to play at fishing on fine days along with their brothers, Georgiana pulled a rose leaf out of her daughter's curls and told her she was pink and should go back under the parasol.

"Mama," said Edward, his face smeared with river mud. "Freddie called me a *damn fool* and a *weakling*."

"Be a man, Edward. Don't snivel. And don't curse."

"I'm not cursing, Mama, I'm saying what Freddie said. Freddie was cursing."

George sat shivering on the grass in his damp things.

"Wrap him up, Mademoiselle," said Georgiana. "I don't want him catching a chill."

"Yes, my lady."

"You must learn to control the children better. That was quite out of hand."

Then, to a chorus of "Might I fish, Mama?" and "I'm not cursing, Mama, I'm saying what Freddie said. Freddie was cursing," and teeth chattering from little George, Georgiana pleaded a headache and went back to the house. Fixed in her mind was a picture of Frederick, casting his line and reeling it in, the king of all he surveyed.

Midafternoon Mrs. Trimble was making calculations, the sort they didn't teach you in the schoolroom. Whiteleys was three miles away. My lady's visitor was arriving at some unspecified time before dinner. The champagne had to be chilled before then. Ice melted in the sun. It was a warm afternoon. How late could she leave it before she sent one of the footmen to fetch the ice from Whiteleys in the cart, ice that would begin to melt as soon as it came out of the icehouse, even if the wooden icebox with its inner metal skin was well packed with straw? She would have liked to ask Mr. Hastings his opinion, but Mr. Hastings was out with the haymakers and in any case she would rather have died than have handed him an advantage on a plate.

The housekeeper's room faced south across the courtyard in the direction of the main house, which shaded it. To its plain furnishings and severe walls she had added a few things of her own, a number of books and ecclesiastical prints that had belonged to her father, who had been a curate in Kent, a length of tatted lace worked by her mother, which hung limp over the bureau, and a faded miniature of a man to whom she had once been briefly married, until he had gone off his head and they had locked him up. These things had been with her at Priestlands, at Gritchling Manor, and at Fordingstone Hall, occupying much the same places in rooms that were much the same. She barely saw them anymore and did not see them now.

What she saw was a vista of problems and difficulties. Blocked drains in the icehouse was only the half of it. It rained into the maids' rooms above the laundry in the south pavilion and most of the panes in the glasshouses were cracked or broken. Pictures had disappeared upstairs, leaving behind sad tidemarks on the walls, and the furniture was thinning. The most recent departures, both from the little drawing room, were a japanned commode and the "fly painting," so called because every new housemaid swished her duster at the fruit thinking the fly was real. Ashenden was a grand house, a beautiful house, but no one could say that it was in the best repair. In certain lights—a low winter sun could be particularly unkind—you might say it was desolate, particularly in rooms where the plastering had not been completed. Any day now the household would need mourning, black crêpe bands, edgings, and trimmings, and how that would be managed, failing the discovery of some funerary goods stashed in a cupboard that hadn't been opened in half a century, she did not know. The account book, lying in front of her, told her that they couldn't rely on credit from the haberdashers of any town in the immediate vicinity. Dye, she thought, making a mental note.

Her previous employer, Mr. Wilmott, had told her what to expect when she had given notice. "Why do you want to go and work for the Mores? He is a brute and her behavior is a scandal. They have no money. It has all been gambled away. You will not like it there."

Mrs. Trimble had no answer for him. She could not explain the restlessness that drove her from one position to another any more than she could explain it to herself. It was simply that work steadied her for a while, then her husband's face reappeared at night more and more often, which was when she knew it was time to move on.

Mr. Wilmott had an excellent memory for someone his age and spent the next half hour recounting the declining fortunes of the owners of Ashenden, down to the last card played and lost, while she stood with her hands folded in front of her. "You give excellent service, Mrs. Trimble," he had said, clutching the edge of the rug that lay over the bony peaks of his knees. "And I shall of course give you a good character. However, I believe you are making a grave mistake. The house was only half finished to start with and now it is falling down round their ears. You will not like it there at all."

Her previous employer had been wrong in one important respect. She had gone to Ashenden with no particular expectations beyond a change of scene. What she had not bargained for was finding a place where she felt she belonged the instant she arrived. Charlotte Trimble rested her hands on her writing table. Ashenden was precarious. But it was alive and she needed its emergencies and its precariousness as much as it needed her. They kept everything else at bay.

Her room was next to the scullery and kitchen on the ground floor of the north pavilion. She pinched her nose, got up from her seat, and went out to give orders. Whomever my lady was expecting, it was not her husband. That called for an element of management, but also a degree of thanks.

"Rose," she said to the nursery maid. "Is the children's tea ready?"

"Taking it up now, ma'am," said Rose, fetching a tray.

"James?"

"Here, ma'am." James was a simple soul who had never mastered the footman's art of melting from view whenever a job needed doing. Thomas, younger and not long in service, had been a much faster learner and might at present be anywhere.

"Take the trap and fetch some ice from Whiteleys, as much as they can spare. The bigger the blocks the better. Chippings won't do in this heat. Promise them whatever they want in return that we can reasonably give. You know where the icebox is."

"Ma'am."

"Plenty of straw."

"Ma'am."

"Off you go."

James headed towards the archway that led to the stables.

"James?"

"Ma'am?"

"Any news of the King?"

"No, ma'am. I expect we'll hear the bells."

In the steamy kitchen Cook was getting on with her preparations and waved at her with floury hands. Little Benson appeared and asked if she might have a drop of hot water for my lady's bath.

"Be my guest," said Cook, her cap soaked with sweat.

"Thomas should carry up the cans for you," said Mrs. Trimble. "He hasn't done a hand's turn all day so far as I can tell."

Benson said no matter, she could manage herself. She poured out hot water from the big kettle on its trivet over the fire, wiped the damp hair off her forehead, and went into the yard to fill the can from the pump.

"Plucky wee mite," said Cook, kneading dough with her knuckles. "You'd never think she had the strength to look at her."

"Her head's full of nonsense," said Mrs. Trimble, knowing full well who had put it there. "Have you all that you need, Cook?"

"Bless you, ma'am, all I need now is some notion when they will be sitting down to eat. You give us a nod when the company arrives, if you will. It don't do to cut the 'sparagus too soon, the flavor goes out of that quick."

Mrs. Trimble came out of the kitchen into the glare of the court-yard. In a house such as Ashenden, there were always a hundred things that could be done at any moment, especially when the family had just arrived. Despite the maids and footmen who had come down from London, they were understaffed by any standards. There was no butler, so Hastings would put on his rusty black frock coat this evening and pour the champagne. Rose, the nursery maid, would help out later in the kitchen. Most of the care of the children fell to Mademoiselle in any case, who pretended her birthplace was Toulouse when it was really Tunbridge Wells. As for Thomas, Mrs. Trimble briefly considered hunting him out and setting him some arduous and unpleasant task, and then decided she would see to the flowers first.

Georgiana lay in the bath in her dressing room while the maid combed and plucked her way through her hair. Over the tub's curled copper rim she could see across the bright park.

"Have you found any more?"

"No, my lady, not a one."

"Are you certain?"

"No more gray hairs, my lady. Just the five, I swear to God."

Five gray hairs. For pity's sake. She trailed her fingers in the water and closed her eyes.

It had been another summer evening, a year ago, when she had introduced Delgado to the Lord Chancellor. Delgado had been as nervous as a cat; he'd changed his waistcoat three times, then settled on the most unsuitable. Before the great man had arrived, she had soothed and reassured him, all the while knowing that if the evening was as successful as she hoped, she was writing herself out of his future.

The evening had been a triumph. Delgado had charmed and impressed—my God, the man had a silver tongue—and by the time the carriages had rolled away down the drive, he had secured the patronage of one of the most powerful politicians in the country. He had not been able to disguise how delighted he was, which she had taken as a form of gratitude, none other being on offer. Looking back, those were their last happy days. Afterwards the whispers began and there were hints of a *ménage à trois*, which was ridiculous—everyone knew she had no appetite for men as old as the Lord Chancellor. Then Delgado had started to distance himself, to talk over her head, and soon after she had ended it.

Her husband had never seen Delgado as a threat; most of the time he had been abroad and not seen him at all. Otherwise, he had been amused by him, as most people were. Perhaps he felt the kinship of risk: betting on the tables and betting on mining shares were not a world apart. Two years ago she and Delgado, her husband, and Mrs. Gibson, one of Delgado's former mistresses, had made a foursome at the seaside, which she supposed was a *ménage à quatre*. She remembered standing on the front, the tide out, thinking she ought to be happier about the arrangement than she was, while high-stepping birds plunged their thin tapered bills into the sand's slick curls.

She opened her eyes. "Where are the children?"

"They're having their tea. I saw Rose taking up the tray earlier."

A sucking, sloshing noise and Georgiana stood in the tub. "Tell Mademoiselle to bring them down before bedtime." Other mothers might have washed their hands of their duties for the day, but she was not like other mothers. She always made a point of saying good night to her children.

Benson stood on tiptoes to hold out the bath sheet, turning her head away.

"Benson."

"Yes, my lady."

"It could have been a little warmer."

"Begging your pardon, my lady."

"Never mind. You may leave me now. I should like to rest for a while."

Benson dried her and wrapped her in her robe. "Yes, my lady."

Georgiana went into her bedroom, leaving damp footprints on the floor, and closed the door. Then she unlocked her traveling writing desk and took out Delgado's letters.

Rose carried the tray down to the kitchen.

"Didn't they like my lovely food?" said Cook, sifting through the remains. "Shame to see this go to waste." She scooped out a coddled egg with a dirty teaspoon, heaped it on a crust, and popped it in her mouth.

Rose said, "Oh no, Miss Clara and Master Georgie are greedy little pigs, they are."

"So it was other two turning up their noses, was it?"

"They wasn't there." Rose's face was as round as a moon.

"Off wandering, I expect," said Cook, "the rascals," and thought no more of it until Mademoiselle came below stairs an hour later, wringing her hands, saying she could not find the boys anywhere, and Thomas appeared, for the first time that afternoon, with news.

"Are you sure?" said Cook.

"I got eyes in my head. That fowling piece was there this morning and it ain't there now."

"Oh, my Lord," said Mademoiselle, her vowels going English, her face going white. When she told them what had happened in the river, Rose threw her apron over her head and began to wail.

"You'd best find Mrs. Trimble," said Cook.

Mrs. Trimble was in the hall, sucking her thumb where a rose thorn had pricked it, when Thomas came to tell her that Frederick and Edward were missing, and so was a gun from the gun room.

"What on earth were you doing in the gun room?"

Thomas opened his mouth.

"And why was the gun room unlocked?"

"Mr. Hastings—" began Thomas.

"Never mind your excuses." She would get to the bottom of *that* later. "Who saw the boys last?"

Edward had been gone for a couple of hours. Frederick had not been seen since early afternoon when Mademoiselle had brought the younger children back to the house.

"They was fighting earlier," said Thomas. "In the river. Frederick almost drowned Edward, by all accounts."

Mrs. Trimble caught her breath. It might be nothing, but on the other hand it might not, and it was her duty to imagine the worst in order to prevent it from happening. The brothers hated each other, and a gun in the hands of either of them didn't bear thinking about. A little bird beat its wings against her rib cage. Heaven help her, but for such moments she lived.

"Search the outbuildings and when you've done with that, search the grounds. Get the bootboy to help you. Don't forget the privies, the stables, and the wood store, and hurry up about it. Not a word to Benson or my lady."

"Yes, ma'am."

Down in the servants' hall it was female pandemonium. Mrs. Trimble dispatched Mademoiselle to look in the attics and Rose to the laundry, the dairy, and the maids' quarters above. She sent Cook back to her preparations and toured the north pavilion herself.

Some still, quiet part of herself observed, from a distance, as she went through cupboards and stowing places and checked the rooms upstairs where the mice gnawed behind the skirtings and distemper fell like snow. She had felt this detachment before, exploited it, and over the years it had earned her a reputation for being dependable in a crisis.

In truth, there had only ever been one crisis in Mrs. Trimble's life; all others were pale imitations of it. That crisis had occurred three years into her marriage, when her husband went mad. Richard Trimble, a curate like her father, had never been the most robust of souls; she had known that when she married him, but she believed him to be a good, kind man, who needed the settled life she could provide, just as she needed to leave her family home and run her own household. At first his mental disturbance had taken the innocuous form of an excess of ordinary activity: an excess of reading, an excess of walking, an excess of words, followed by an excess of sleeping and an excess of silent brooding. Then he had taken leave of his senses altogether and she had recognized neither her husband nor a fellow human creature in the violence of his mind and his actions.

When they finally came for him, on a crisp October morning, it had taken three men to subdue him and bind him with leather straps. He'd been raving for days upstairs, unslept, crashing into the furniture, howling at the moon. The village children had taken to throwing stones at their door. The men had bound him and dragged him out, gagging him with another strap between his teeth, and she had watched at the parlor window, dry-mouthed, her bruises blackening, as if she were standing outside of herself. Then they had forced him into the back of a dark shuttered chaise and driven him away.

Up in the male servants' quarters at Ashenden Park, searching for the missing boys, Mrs. Trimble was observing herself again with the same sense of detachment. There was a heavy odor of feet and unwashed bodies and she was trying to open a window, straining at the stuck sash, when she heard someone arrive below. Her first thought was that James had returned with the ice; then she looked down and saw a chaise draw up in front of the stable block.

Chipped paintwork spelled out a Reading address in garish letters and the horses were ill-matched and blowing. Hired, she thought. The driver took his time setting out the steps, as if the fare didn't cover the service or the passenger didn't merit it. Then he opened the door and a man stepped out into the early-evening sun.

He was of average height and build, perhaps thirty, no more, with a contained way of moving that spoke of uncertainty rather than anything studied or cultivated. Even from a story above, it was clear the impression the house was making on him. He stood and took it in, like you would absorb a blow, then looked up.

My word, there was a face.

For a moment, she could have sworn he met her eyes. The next he was reaching into the chaise and drawing out a large black portfolio fastened with ribbon.

The hired chaise and the package suggested a delivery. The face told a different story. All of which placed the visitor somewhere between tradesman's entrance and front door. Somewhere uncomfortable. My lady's guest, thought Mrs. Trimble. Here was a collision of emergencies. The bird beat harder under her rib cage as she left the window and hurried downstairs.

Mrs. Trimble greeted the visitor at the door on the lower story and ushered him up the side stairs. He had given his name, which she did not catch, said he had come from town to see her ladyship, and kept hold of his portfolio. She noticed that his fingernails were edged in dirt, that his coat was not of the best quality, and that whoever had shaved him had done a poor job of it. Halfway up, she turned, caught his bold black eye, and blushed, which annoyed her.

The housekeeper sometimes wondered what her clergyman father, or Mr. Trimble himself, would have made of the immorality of the household where she earned her living. She couldn't say that Mr. Wilmott hadn't warned her. When the writer, Mr. Delgado, had made the first of his many visits, she had thought long and hard about handing in her notice. Over the years, she had fallen out of the habit of praying, but it seemed a conscience was not so easily discarded. That was before she had met the 3rd Baronet and discovered that a spoiled, foolish woman who broke her marriage vows could still arouse her sympathies.

The writer, no gentleman to look at, had proved to have a certain sensibility or delicacy of manners. Whatever happened at night, before dawn he was always back in the room that had been made up for him. Never any trouble with housemaids being surprised drawing curtains or laying fires. This visitor, however, was a different matter altogether. She was at a loss what to do with him. The blue bedroom no longer seemed appropriate. Wherever he laid his head, she decided she would excuse Jane from her duties tomorrow morning.

When they came up the stairs into the central hall with its soaring staircase, she noticed the same uncertainty come over him that she had seen from the window. Worried about putting a foot wrong. Worried about being seen to worry about putting a foot wrong. Then he asked if there was somewhere he could leave his portfolio, saying that he'd "like to keep it a surprise for now," and drawn into that small conspiracy against her will, she suggested the library.

Something about that suggestion shifted the balance between them. In the library he stood for a moment, then set the portfolio on a stand, stroking the black cover with the flat of his hand. Mrs. Trimble recognized ownership and ambition when she saw them and asked him to wait outside. After she had spoken to Benson over the yapping dog, her mind on the missing boys, and gone down the stairs, she realized that she had forgotten to ask the visitor whether there was news of the King.

When the housekeeper left, David Maurice went over to a window and stood looking out across the park. He was sensitive to light and the light was exceptional, a prize in itself. It sank into his eyes and from there into his bones. The chaise that had brought him from the staging post on the Bath Road had gone, along with its surly driver. The land fell away in front of him and rose up to a gentle hill dotted with stands of trees, grazed by deer.

It was not entirely what he had expected. From time to time Georgiana hinted they were short of money. Easy enough to imagine creditors petitioning at the doors of a town house: you saw it all the time. Here it was a different story. Ashenden was substantial, solid and real. He hoped that meant he would be paid. The journey from London had been an extravagance, if uncomfortable.

The rich had their own ideas about poverty in any case. David Maurice knew what it was like to have nothing. It was turnip tops and ragged breeches; it was the sour stink of poteen and mildewed sod. It was bare-arsed children scrapping in the mud and his empty-handed father, staring into the fire until it went out. Once he had seen a woman eat a rat. Worse than that was the shrinking view, until all you could see ahead for yourself was more of the same. His father had wanted him to be a bricklayer like himself—"ye'll need a trade"—as if that guaranteed someone would pay you a living wage, despite all evidence to the contrary. Still, they hadn't always been poor and perhaps it was the better times his father had been thinking about or hoping for.

The lithograph had changed his fortunes. That was the story he told and it was almost as much of a fiction as the name he went by these days. The fact was by that time his fortunes had already changed, along with the rest of the family's. When his father found regular employment at the new yard, there had been schooling of a kind for him and afterwards a placement at a bank, banking having replaced bricklaying in his father's ambitions for his eldest son. Two dull years, and then the famous author had visited Cork.

The Scotsman had been mobbed. They were waving copies of his books under his nose and shouting passages from them. David Maurice (or McNorris as he was then) had leaned out of the first-floor window on Lee Street to sketch him. "You've caught him to the life," said O'Keefe, passing. Later, he'd worked the sketch up to a portrait. His pencil always did what he told it to. Then he took it to the print shop and the print sold well enough for him to leave the bank and enroll at the art school.

David Maurice came away from the window and walked back into the library through streams of dust suspended in the slanting light. He was trespassing, he knew, but then his whole life was a trespass. The black portfolio, tied with black ribbon, was propped on the stand, which stood in front of a mahogany desk topped by an acreage of green tooled leather. On the walls were faces. He knew enough about these houses now to understand that this was one of the places they kept them, these frowning forefathers, in here along with the books and ledgers bound in calfskin. Or strung along some corridor or stairway. Above the fireplace was a red-cheeked man, three-quarter view, hiding his chin in his white neckcloth. You could see he was proud and acquisitive. Whether there was anything else to his interior life, the artist had not recorded it.

You painted what they paid you to paint. You drew what they wanted you to draw. Prints of famous people sold well. Those were the most important lessons he had learned as a working artist, along with the fact that exhibiting at the Royal Academy was the best way to attract patrons. He had not made enough money yet to be offended by the fact that some people called him a "society painter" and meant it as an insult.

Last winter he had drawn Delgado, lazing in one of his familiar poses, in the rooms they used to share. When he'd turned it up the other day among his papers, he could remember exactly what they had been talking about (politics), what the weather had been like (misty with a drizzling rain), and the smell of the Bengal cheroot his friend had been smoking. The sketch had been done off the cuff and he doubted Delgado even knew he had committed his likeness to paper, otherwise he would have somehow managed to get his hands on it. Delgado was one of the most charming and persuasive men he had ever met, but also probably the vainest. They no longer shared rooms and when they met it was at a distance, the betrayal between them. It had been Delgado who had recommended him to the Mores. Sometimes he wondered who had betrayed whom.

He was aware she had come into the room when he caught her

musk-rose scent, and all at once he could feel the heat prickling along his skin and up his neck into his hairline. He turned and their eyes met.

"They told me you'd arrived."

"Lady More. Georgiana." Some apology seemed necessary. "Forgive me for intruding. I was told to wait in the hall."

"Never mind." She made a remark about how warm it was, fanning herself, which wafted more of the intoxicant in his direction. "Perhaps you might care to refresh yourself with a swim after your journey. We shan't dine for a while." Her lips tucked themselves up at the corners of her mouth. "Or perhaps you can't swim."

As a boy he had once swum from Blackrock Castle to Little Island, quite some distance in tidal water. He did not think she would be interested in the exploit. "I shouldn't want to squander a minute of your company."

She stopped in front of the stand and stretched out a hand to touch the black cover of the portfolio with her fingertips. "Is that what I think it is?"

He nodded and realized he had undermined his own strategy.

"May I see it?"

"Later."

"Are you teasing me?"

Was he teasing her? He did not know. All he knew was that he wanted to delay the moment.

"Very well, Mr. McBrush," she said. "Later. After dinner."

Mr. McBrush, Mr. O'Daub, or Painter was what she called him. She had seen through the pretense of the assumed "Maurice" straightaway, or it was possible that Delgado had talked about him and his lowly origins. He was careful with his voice and his vocabulary, but sometimes when he was with her, he could hear the vowels change in his mouth. Slips of the tongue.

Her eyes strayed to the portrait of the red-cheeked man over the fireplace. "What do you think of that picture, Painter?"

"Competent," he said.

"Not up to your standard?"

"Perhaps it is a good likeness. I wouldn't know."

"Tell me what you see."

"A hard man." The vowels slid around.

She laughed, showing her biteable white throat. "Then it must be a good likeness. That's my husband's grandfather. He made a fortune in India. When he came home, they fined him for corruption, which was no more than he deserved. Then he married well for a second time and set about building Ashenden on the proceeds. As it turned out, he couldn't afford to complete it. His son's debts saw to that. And my husband has taken up where his father left off. What the pair of them have lost on the tables would have built a palace ten times over. Did I tell you my husband tried to sell the estate?"

"No."

"It was several years ago." She went on to say that an awful common man called Anderson or Ferguson, she couldn't remember, who had made a good deal of money in buttons, or something like that, had set his heart on it. "He used to drive past in his carriage and look in the windows, as if he might snap his fingers and it would be his."

He knew, whether she knew it or not, that she was talking about the haberdasher James Henderson, whose fortune was feeding a growing reputation as an art collector, but who had not yet collected any of his own pictures.

"Why didn't he buy it if he wanted it so badly?"

"I expect he couldn't afford what my husband was asking for it. I can't say I was displeased."

Ever since she had entered the room, he had been hoping for an acknowledgment of their intimacy, a gesture of affection no matter how small, and he was beginning to wonder if she had cooled towards him, if the affair was over. Rank, as much as patronage, gave her the upper hand in all their dealings with one another. Perhaps it would be better, despite his present disappointment and ill ease (not to mention the expense of the journey), that it should end after all.

She must have read something of this in his expression. Moving close, and with a boldness that made his heart race, she reached up to grasp the stuff of his coat and kissed him full and deep on the mouth. "Mr. O'Daub . . . oh, how I've missed you."

Rose ran into the kitchen, strands of hair stuck to her cheeks, and said James was coming and he had one of the boys with him.

"Which one?" said Mrs. Trimble.

Rose was out of breath and couldn't say.

The trap was pulling up in front of the stable block when Mrs. Trimble came through the courtyard at a trot. Frederick jumped off the back.

She seized him by the arm. "Where is your brother?"

The boy was carrying a dead water rat by the tail. The brown fur was matted with black blood, buzzing with flies.

"I said, where's your brother?"

He nodded back at the trap.

Relief lit the touch paper of her anger. "Get yourself indoors, Frederick. Straightaway. And put that dirty thing down!"

"*Master* Frederick. I thank you to address me correctly."

He strode off into the courtyard, his eyes hard like marbles. Like father, like son. Seeing him go, swinging the rat by the tail, she itched to run after him and beat the living daylights out of him.

Thomas, always eager for a drama, appeared to see what all the fuss was about, and she told him to help the stable lad take the icebox into the yard. "No need to shout, ma'am," he said, waggling a finger in his ear. "I hear you plain enough."

Edward got down from the trap, yawning and rubbing his eyes.

"Thank the Lord," said Rose.

"I think he's had too much sun," said James, who clambered down afterwards. "He's been asleep most of the way back." He was carrying the fowling piece, broken at the breech, in the crook of his elbow.

"Take the boy to bed, Rose," said Mrs. Trimble.

Edward said that he was hungry.

"Supper first, then bed."

"What if my lady wants to see the children?" said Rose.

"Her visitor has arrived. I doubt she'll ask for them."

Rose led the boy back to the house. Mrs. Trimble watched them go, then turned to the footman. "What on earth possessed you to take them out like that without telling anyone? You've given us all a fright."

James shrugged. Putting thoughts into words—or having them in the first place, she suspected—was not his strong point, and it was a while before she got the story out of him and reassembled into an order that made sense. The gist was he'd thought it would be a nice treat. For Edward, that is. When he'd found the boy lurking about the stables with a long face and had said how about they go fetch the ice together, remembering the thrashing his brother had given him in the river (had she heard about that business?) and thinking somehow it would make it up to him, the boy had jumped at the chance. You had your tea? he had asked, and Edward had said yes, he had had his tea, thank you. Then go and tell them where you'll be, he had said, and the boy had gone off to tell them and how was he to know that he hadn't? They'd come across Frederick on the way back from Whiteleys. He'd been in one of the fields with the haymakers, with the rat and the gun, and he'd managed to get the gun off him and persuade him to come home. It had taken some doing. The haymakers had the jugs out by then.

"You know what it's like . . . thirsty work."

"What are you saying, James?"

He scuffed his toe on the ground and pulled his ear. "I wouldn't be surprised if the lad's had a few." The ear received more of his attention. "To hear him talk, you'd think he'd shot a buck."

Those were the most disrespectful words that she had ever heard him utter about one of the family, and as soon as they were out of his mouth, he blushed to the roots of his hair.

It was then that the passing bell began to toll, slow and deep, marking each year of a life. As the sound came across the hushed fields, they counted in silence.

"God rest His Majesty's soul," said Mrs. Trimble at the end.

"Amen," said James.

Mrs. Trimble glanced up at the turret clock, which was broken and could not tell her the time. They were in a backwater here; the news was probably hours old. The end of an era. What would happen to the country now with a girl on the throne, the Lord only knew.

"It is a beautiful house."

"The moths like it," she said. "And so do the beetles and the silverfish. They adore the carpets and the furniture and the books. Positively dote on them."

They were eating in a pink-and-green room, and what they were eating was also pink and green. Asparagus, that was green, and very green it tasted too. And something trembling in aspic, which for some reason made him think of a baby's bottom. He was not sure how to deal with it. It wasn't a chop, put it like that.

The butler in his worn frock coat hovered in the shadows. From time to time he came forward to pour the champagne and the furrows on his face would sharpen into charcoal lines. A bitter man, thought David Maurice. He'd seen the same type in the murk of Cork alehouses, men with grievances they nursed to themselves along with their grog. Not a drinker, this one, he thought, rather a person pickling in his own sour juices.

Georgiana sipped from her glass, made a face, and said that she had asked for the wine to be iced, not frozen. "It is so cold, it sets my teeth on edge."

"I beg your pardon, my lady."

David Maurice glanced up from his cracked gold-rimmed plate, but the man's face was a professional mask. He had never become accustomed to the way they were with their servants—ignoring them one minute as if they were blind, deaf, and dumb, and carved from stone, taking them to task the next, like little children who wanted the world and saw no reason why they shouldn't have it this instant. What made him uneasy was the fact he never knew which side he was supposed to be on. He smiled at the butler, smiled at Georgiana, who was feeding the dog from her plate, then squirmed in his seat. He noticed how her plump rounded arms tapered to narrow wrists that you could encircle with one finger and thumb.

Fish was next, with a remote taste of mud, and more champagne, which washed the taste away. There was a small, fine bone lodged in his teeth and he didn't know what to do with it. In London, dining with his friends, talking about books and plays and paintings, it was not the sort of thing that concerned him.

The food came in unpredictable relays and was served by a pair of footmen, one knowing and leering, whose gaze he avoided, and the other raw-boned and simple, who appeared to have hurled his clothing on his back and his wig on his head, because nothing was straight. As they handed round the dishes, by turns ingratiating and inept, it occurred to him that footmen were ordinary fellows who assumed the part when they put on their livery, just as he was an ordinary fellow who had altered his accent and origins to present himself as an artist. The idea was disturbing. By the end of the meat course he was more than a little drunk and the truth was he couldn't have said what they ate after that. He was conscious only of the light fading as the long day wore itself out like an overexcited child.

Georgiana got up from her chair with a harsh rustle of silk and told the butler that they would have another bottle of his "frozen champagne" in the library. David Maurice rose to follow her, hearing a faint shrilling that might or might not have been coming from inside his own head. Drink had blurred him. All the talk at dinner had been of Delgado, what he was doing, who he was seeing, and whether or not he would win his seat, none of which he knew the answers to. Delgado would have to marry, she had said. Someone in his position, with his ambitions, had to marry money. "I wonder who will be fool enough." Then she had laughed. In a moment of sobering clarity, as they walked through the echoing spaces of the house, feeling the blood heat of her creamy arm through the cheap cloth of his coat, he realized that she was still in love with his former friend (he supposed Delgado had been his friend) and that it was the type of love that you never got over. "Well, so much for all that," she said, leaning into him. "Let's make the most of the evening while we can. Now the King is dead, no doubt my husband will summon me to court tomorrow. A parade of respectability suits his purposes on occasion."

The library walls, between glazed shelves of dull brown books, were the same green as the awning that shaded the bank on Lee Street in summer. Georgiana complained how stuffy it was, crossed the room, and opened a window, which struck him with amazement, as he had never seen her perform even so simple a task when there was a bell to summon someone else to do it. The night air came in, sweet with the fragrance of white flowers and mown hay. Even now, it was not quite dark: candlelight and twilight took it in turns to trade places with each other so that it was hard to say whether it was brighter or dimmer indoors or out.

"Show me," she said, her eyes straying to the portfolio. "I want to see what you have made of me."

"I have made of you what you are."

"And what is that?"

"Magnificent."

"You have all the blarney of your countrymen," she said, but he saw the comment had pleased her.

As his fingers fumbled with the strings, he thought how the rich, even the poorest rich, could stretch time. At home they had risen with the sun and gone to bed when it set. It had been more or less the same after his father's luck had famously changed: he couldn't remember an evening when a candle had burned more than an hour after dark. Here on the shortest night of the year the sconces were lit, picking out the gilt letters on the spines of books he doubted anyone had read. Georgiana, he knew, had struggled to turn more than a few pages of Delgado's novels, including the most recent one that had immortalized their affair, mystified as to why it contained so much politics.

"Show me," she said, leaning over him, her breath sour-sweet with champagne and strawberries.

"Close your eyes."

Her eyelids trembled.

"Close them."

He had so little power over her, or over anyone, that when she shut her eyes, he was tempted to keep her standing there, the prisoner of her own curiosity and anticipation. Then he reminded himself he had a living to make, opened the portfolio, removed the plain sheet of paper that covered the watercolor, and told her she could look.

She didn't say a word. Not at first, and not for some long moments afterwards.

David Maurice had won the commission for the family portrait on the strength of his friend's introduction. Sir Frederick had sat for him briefly, long enough for him to get the measure of the man, which was to say long enough for him to see the way the man wanted posterity to view him. He found him to be one of those bluff, loud, unthinking fair-haired types, unconscious of their own cruelty, an impression that fitted with what he had already learned. The children, who could not be expected to sit, he had sketched in the nursery at Carlton Terrace on a number of rainy afternoons. He had to admit that some of those sketches were more realistic than what he had subsequently painted. As a matter of course, you shortened noses, pinned back ears, and added healthy robustness to spindly limbs. He had never known a mother or father who wished to see the warts on their children's faces.

Georgiana was a different matter. He'd had no need to gloss her beauty and she had made herself available for many sittings in which he could record it, savor it, and in due course pay it the physical tribute her veiled eyes and parted lips had invited. A few of the women he had painted before had responded in the same way— it was all that looking, he supposed, easily confused with admiration—but those encounters had been brief and had ended in shame on both sides and for different reasons. Often he wondered how this would end, but not when he was with her. She had a knack or an instinct for making the present infinite, and it was only when he was apart from her that he considered the danger to both of them, a danger of which she seemed entirely oblivious. Or perhaps it was simply that she liked courting risk.

The *mise en scène* of the portrait was the Middle Ages. Historical settings generally met with approval, so he'd found. The boys in hose, Clara in a trailing gown that might have come from any period, dogs in the foreground, one of which was Blanche. Sir Frederick, with his high forehead and drooping mustache, he had portrayed emerging from the darkness at the top of a stone stair wearing a suit of armor, the noble protector of his family. The armor was a gift, for it enabled him to improve the man's physique. Halfway down the picture, where the diagonal composition reversed on itself, was Georgiana, the wide wings of an ermine-trimmed velvet cloak framing the creamy whiteness of her breasts. She could have walked out of the picture into the court of St. James's and set a fashion. That was the entire point of the romance, as he understood it. It had not escaped his attention that this evening she was dressed in the same gown she had worn for the sittings and which he had painted.

Into what was becoming a long silence, he said, "I should like to exhibit the portrait at the Academy. With your permission, naturally."

There was no response. He was beginning to worry when she turned to him, her eyes lit with laughter.

"You've given my husband such a big lance!"

"It is a mighty pole."

"It's an *enormous* pole. And it's pointing at my head. As if he were about to knock it off."

"There is a reason for that."

"Oh? Do tell me."

"It is to do with the composition. If you follow the line of the lance downwards—see here—and the upwards line of the stave Master George has over his shoulder—see there—they meet at the center of the picture." He smiled, in what he hoped was not too false or patronizing a manner. "Which is, of course, you."

Well, the pole was something else. It had grown as he had painted it until it had assumed its monstrous proportions. What that lance said, what he intended it to say, was that the sitter had nothing to fear from the painter, but somehow he had managed, he saw now, to convey the reverse. He might as well have written "cuckold" on the shaft of the thing.

"I did not mean it to be so big."

She laughed. "Don't worry. He should be flattered."

They drank a little, toasting the portrait. They drank a little more, toasting themselves. By then, they were in her bedroom, with its blood-red walls, and she was lying back on a divan, the silk folds of her dress silver in the candlelight, her breath rising and falling. In another woman, the pose would have been submission; with her it was capture.

"What are you thinking?" she said, holding his gaze.

He had never wanted her so badly. "I am thinking that this is how I should like to paint you."

"Undo me," she said.

David Maurice woke, his throat dry and his head thudding. The shortest night of the year and already the sky was thinning and graying into light. Beside him, Georgiana was abandoned in sleep, her bare limbs tumbled about in the summer bedclothes. He kissed her shoulder and she murmured and turned her head away into the pillow. Among the clothing strewn on the floor, the silvery silk, the underthings, were scraps of paper, and it came back to him in a little rush of memory that after their lovemaking he had drawn her. He reached over the side of the bed and picked up the pages. The sketches were quick and vivid, but he thought that his pencil did a better job when it was sober. On the back of one of the sketches he started to draw her again, voluptuous and lost in sleep, the little death.

It was then that he heard noises, although afterwards he was to wonder whether the noises had come first, whether they were what had woken him. At first the sound was indistinct and far off, some minor commotion, and he imagined that the household must be stirring, the maids already up and going about their work. Then it came closer and he recognized a voice. It was More's.

More turned the handle and flung back the door. It was just as he had suspected. The grubby little Irish portrait painter in bed with his wife. The forked thing, the homunculus.

Fury seized him by the throat. "You!" The dirty tinker. He grabbed him, hurled him to the floor. Kicked him and kicked him again. "You! I'll break every bone in your body, so help me God!"

"No!" said his wife, her eyes wide, her hair loose and tangled over her bare shoulders. "No!"

"Madam," said More, lifting his hand to strike her, "how dare you shame me in this way!"

"I'll come to court with you," she was pleading. "I'll do whatever you want."

He hit her in the mouth.

Rose came to wake Mrs. Trimble when she heard the roaring and the screaming. By the time the housekeeper threw a shawl over her nightgown and went upstairs, it was over. They were all up by then.

Mrs. Trimble was known to be dependable in a crisis. She told Jane to sweep up the debris, sent Benson to her shrieking mistress, and dispatched Rose back to the nursery to calm the children.

She was heading for the pantry to fetch brandy when she found the visitor slumped halfway down the side stairs. One eye was swollen shut, his lip was split like a black fruit, and there was not a stitch on his back. In the kitchen she washed his cuts and helped him dress in the clothes she made James bring for her.

"I shall have you driven into the village. You must get yourself away as soon as you can."

"I must save her." His words were thick and his head was lolling.

"No one can save her now." She took that lolling head in her hands. "Do you hear me? Get yourself away while you can."

It was after he had gone that she discovered the dog dead on the loggia, its neck broken, its lively dark eyes dulled and glazed. Heaven help her, but she wept over that poor creature, who would never yap or make work for a housemaid again. She was wrapping Blanche in an old sheet, her tears dripping wet circles onto the worn linen, when More found her and dismissed her. She was to go directly, without a character, without pay.

5

Butterflies: 1844

The house slips through the fingers of the family who commissioned it, slips right away from them forever. Neglected for decades, on the brink of ruin and irreversible decline, it's sold and, in the nick of time, saved.

Six years of industry and expense pour into the house. What's unfinished is at last completed, what's broken is mended, down to the last cracked glasshouse pane. The old makes way for the new: paint, paper, furnishings, cloth, carpet. No detail is left untouched or unconsidered. No corners are cut. Only the finest will do.

Everything is put in working order. Drains, cesspools, and ice well are all rebuilt; the roof is comprehensively repaired. Progress arrives. There's running hot water, bells to summon staff in all the rooms, the conveniences of a new age. New gardens, new lodges, new gates, new cottages adorn the estate.

The house is full to the brim with life and activity. A large family, dozens of servants to look after them, animates its well-furnished rooms. A stream of visitors comes to admire and appreciate the richness of its appointments, the rare treasures hanging on its walls. For the first time in its history, the house serves the purpose for which it was built. After all these years, nothing's lacking, nothing at all.

On a wet morning in late spring the three youngest Hendersons were playing, with some seriousness, their usual game. It was a game perhaps more suited to the outdoors but, like the best inventions, it was capable of adaptation: if rain meant that furniture was forced to take the place of shrubbery, which itself stood for jungle, or staircases replaced trees as ships' rigging, the children's powers of invention were equal to the substitutions.

The game was "brigands." When numbers allowed (visiting cousins, for example, or other children they were expected to play with), there were fierce sea battles; there might also be a mutiny that ended in walking the plank. Treasure was hunted with the aid of maps erratically spotted with sealing wax and aged by candle smoke. Today the boys were "stalking."

To the uninitiated (and occasionally to participants), this variant of the game bore a resemblance to hide-and-seek. Yet there was a difference. To "stalk" you had to steal into a place—a room, a garden, a terrace—where unsuspecting others were gathered and inch around it undetected: not a single hiding place, then, but a succession of them, with the possibility of discovery at any moment. It was at times so exciting that you might almost stop breathing.

As a large family, the Hendersons naturally fell into ranks. Top rank, and so lofty as to be almost indistinguishable from parents, were the three eldest: Philip, who had recently returned from three years in America and was a complete stranger to John, the youngest, who didn't remember him at all; Rowena, who was almost a second mother; and Albert, of whom they were a little wary, as he meant them to be. Middle rank were Caroline, who wouldn't play with them anymore and cared only for what mirrors told her, and Wilfred, who was Wilfred. Reginald, Cedric, and John occupied the lowest rank, which gave them the freedom of outlaws.

"He is quite close," whispered Reginald underneath the sofa. "He is within our sights. Muskets at the ready, men." From his tunic belt he withdrew the musket he had earlier taken from the kindling basket.

"My muskirt is ready," John said in his ordinary voice.

"Shh."

"I have only my cutlass," said Cedric. "But it is a trusty blade, sharpened fresh this morning." His bandanna was slipping and he righted it as best he could.

They had slithered across the threshold of the little drawing room and were now peering through the fringing of the sofa's upholstery at the legs of the room's occupants. It was a low sofa and a tight fit, although very clean underneath.

"My muskirt is ready for blood," said John.

"Shh."

"Take your hand away. I *don't* like it."

"*Shh.*"

The feet of a maid passed by. A tray was set down. The feet padded off, muffled by carpet.

The house contained a great deal of furniture; there were many useful hiding places. On a signal from Reginald, the boys swarmed on their stomachs out from under the sofa, across a foot of Barbary Sea and behind a round table draped with a tapestry cloth that fell to the ground.

There was a tinkle of china and a murmur of voices in the room. "He raises the white flag," said Reginald. "He knows himself surrounded."

Cedric agreed that *he* was done for.

"My muskirt is ready," said John, and they both clapped their hands over his mouth.

Across a hazardous strait they reached the lee of a fauteuil. Then a bold crouching dash across the foaming, churning waters and they sheltered behind its twin. They were quite near their quarry now and were experiencing that giddiness which felt, thought Cedric, like thousands of butterflies emerging from their cocoons in your stomach, their dry feathery wings tickling up your insides. (Cedric was a natural historian when he wasn't a brigand.)

It was John, predictably, who allowed a few butterflies to escape.

"If you can't keep quiet, you must go below to your bunk," said Reginald in a hiss. "I say this to you as your captain."

"Aye, aye, sir," said John, and a few more butterflies floated free.

In the little drawing room, the Hendersons, new owners of Ashenden Park and agents of its restoration, were taking a late breakfast.

The lateness of the meal was not indolence. It was design, a scheduled point of contact in their busy days. Both had been up for hours.

Rain smacked against the windows. Such a cozy sound, thought Mrs. Henderson, applying herself to the egg in her eggcup.

Ada Henderson had a broad fair face and a figure to go with it. Only the set of her mouth and something sharp about her gaze hinted at the practical nature that had brought eight children into the world without losing a grip on one, and had supported her husband, James, in his commercial endeavors without his ever becoming unduly aware of the extent to which he relied upon her.

"I have had a letter from Mrs. Butterworth."

"Have you?" said Mr. Henderson, lifting a napkin to his mouth. He was a square-built fellow with cropped gray hair that did what it pleased on the crown of his head, which was mostly spring up in various directions.

A little scuffle and skirmish in the room, and their eyes flicked away to note the stockinged legs of their youngest, John, poking out from behind a table draped with a tapestry cloth, then met again, amusement tightening the corners of their mouths. *That game again* was unspoken.

"And what has Mrs. Butterworth to say?" Mr. Henderson raised his voice.

"Mrs. Butterworth," said Mrs. Henderson, also raising her voice to the required level of performance for their play-acting audience, "has most kindly accepted my invitation to spend a few days with us in a week's time." She referred to the letter that lay by her plate. "She will bring Florence and Bertram, although Mr. Butterworth respectfully declines on account of business." The Butterworths had been their neighbors in Clapham before the Henderson fortune had been made and the family had moved to Harley Street.

"I see." James Henderson forgot about the children under the sofas and behind the tables and laid his napkin, the white flag, beside his place rather too deliberately. "I was not aware you had invited the Butterworths to stay."

"Oh, I have been meaning to invite them for some time. But now that we are truly settled and straight . . ." She was thinking of the interminable repairs, the plastering, paperhanging, the suites of furniture ordered and upholstered, the arrangement of pictures.

"This is a mistake."

"The Butterworths are our oldest friends."

"A mistake," said her husband.

"We are not the sort of people, I should hope, who forget old friends. It has been ages—years!—since we were all together, and there is a limit," she said, "how far friendship can be maintained by correspondence alone."

"Have you thought this out, my dear?"

"There is nothing to think out. How could there be?" It occurred to her that they were quarreling. Many quarrels began "my dear."

"Have you thought about the expense?"

"James!" She gestured at the room with all its new furnishings, and by extension the sweep of her arm took in the whole house and all its improvements and embellishments. "Surely we have no need to worry about that. After all we have spent on this place." Her husband was a close man, some called him a very near man indeed, but she doubted that even he would tot up the cost of having dear friends visit for a few days.

"Not to us. To *them*."

"But as our *guests* they need spend nothing."

James Henderson regarded his fingers, which were short and stubby. "I am speaking of the expense of whatever they will have bought for the occasion. Which they will have bought for the sake of appearances."

"For heaven's sake, James, you are being quite foolish now. Old friends don't stand on ceremony. And they aren't extravagant people, as you know. When Beatrice came last to Harley Street, I distinctly recognized her brown merino from Clapham."

There was the incongruity of giggling and shushing from behind a fauteuil.

"Harley Street is not Ashenden. And an afternoon call is not a visit to a country house lasting days or more."

She refused to see the distinction. "And Harley Street is not Clapham. What of it?"

"There is too great a difference between us now. They will be uncomfortable and you will be uncomfortable." And you will regret how they will make you feel, he thought to himself.

"You are saying *you* will be uncomfortable."

"I shall not be uncomfortable. I am never uncomfortable."

This was not true, but she let it go by. "Then you can have no objection."

"It is a mistake. But I shall not forbid it."

"I should hope not!" she said, with some warmth. She shook her head. "Are these the consequences of wealth? That we should cast off old friends?" She was not prepared to entertain that of herself: she was ever the haberdasher's daughter and haberdasher's wife. So she firmly believed, failing to recognize the desire anyone might have to display their fine furnishings, especially to old friends.

Her husband let her have this last word, for there was always the possibility that she might be right. However, he consoled himself with the notion that the possibility was remote. The day lay ahead and he had plans for it.

"Come out, come out, you little heathens!" He reached down and caught hold of John, then Cedric, then Reginald, all wriggling and squealing, for this, too, was part of the game.

"We are taking you prisoner," said Reginald, who would not let go of his role, or his father.

"What have you here?"

"A bit of kindling."

"A butter knife," said Cedric.

John, who was not to be ignored, said that he also had a muskirt.

"You must put them back," said their father in his most terrible voice. "Or your mother will have something to say. As she does about most things."

A clatter from the breakfast table answered the rain beating on the windows. One was fortunate to have such a sporting father, thought Reginald, and it was a thought to which he would cling all his life, along with all the happy memories of the house and their childhood in it.

On Sunday a small crowd had gathered by the lych-gate, rather more than usually attended matins. Most were villagers, but there was a fair sprinkling of local gentry.

Philip, the eldest son, peering out of the carriage window, knew the crowd was there to see him. The footmen dismounted from the rear and opened the doors. He made no move to get out.

Instead, his sister Rowena got down first, one hand on her bonnet and the other clutching her basket, followed by his younger sister, Caroline, in her new frock, then his brother Albert, who had grown a fine shading of dark hair on his upper lip in his absence. Afterwards Wilfred, lost in his own world, and finally their father, James Henderson, who rarely went to church but who was making what Philip imagined was a public statement about the return of his eldest son from America. "Come along, Philip," he said, with a look on his face that equated religious worship with a branch of commerce.

Philip came out of the carriage into a spitting rain that any moment threatened to turn into a downpour. There were so many people who wanted to greet him and he barely knew any of them. You would think he had been gone thirty years, not three. The men wanted to pump his hand or clap him on the back, and the ladies wanted to ask if he had seen many bears, if it had been very cold or hot or savage or heathen, or if he had met George Washington. At first he explained that George Washington had been dead nearly fifty years, that New York and Boston, where he had spent most of his time, were God-fearing places on the whole, if a little rough and unfinished round the edges, and the weather wasn't so bad once you knew how to dress for it, although he had never experienced such dreadful mud. After a time, he said, "Very well, thank you," and "How do you do?" because no one seemed at all interested in his answers, only in their own questions.

They went into their pew, Rowena, Caroline, Albert, Wilfred, himself, and his father. John, whom he hardly knew and who had woken with a cough, was at home with his mother, along with Cedric and Reginald, who were too young for sermons. The family story, and they were a family who were bound to each other by stories, was that before their parents were married, they had discovered a mutual fondness for the works of Sir Walter Scott, particularly *Ivanhoe,* and that in due course they had named their children after its characters. Philip had never seen his father read any book that did not have columns of figures in it, but he supposed the story must have been true, so far as any family stories were true, because he had read the book himself and found them all there, except Caroline, whose name commemorated his father's first commercial success. (Aside from Rowena, the only other significant female in *Ivanhoe* was Rebecca, which would not have been suitable.) It was just as well, he thought, breathing in the chill prayer-book air, the greenish smell of damp, and the dust that puffed up from the needlepoint hassocks, that so many of them had turned out to be boys. That wry observation would not have occurred to him before he had gone away.

The *Ivanhoe* story was retold every time someone commented on what a pretty and unusual name Rowena was, which was roughly every time one of the family made a new acquaintance. Their chief narrative, however, which needed no retelling because they lived it every day, was the story of his father's rise from humble beginnings to immense wealth. Ever since Philip had stepped onto the gangplank in New York harbor to begin his journey home, the business, Ashenden, the house in Harley Street, and the art collection had been weighing heavily on his shoulders. (His father's radical views meant there would probably never be a title, which was one less burden to inherit.)

They stood to sing a hymn, the stone flags rose and fell like the ship's deck, and when Philip reached out to steady himself against the rolling of his sea legs, his hands met nothing. They were at the front. His father's wealth would have entitled them to a box pew, such as the one the squire's family had occupied for the three centuries that Whiteleys had been standing, but his father preferred to be seen as one of the people. Philip dropped his eyes to avoid the importuning stares of the congregation and told himself he would speak to his father tomorrow. It was the same promise he had made to himself the day before, and the week before that when he had landed at Liverpool.

The vicar climbed into the pulpit to deliver the sermon. Reverend Cummings was young, a new incumbent with red pimpled cheeks, and looked like he would be very unhappy if anyone handed him a baby to christen. Philip sat, folded his hands, and prepared himself to listen. Immediately his mind drifted.

Somewhere around Newfoundland the ship had run into fog. The captain explained that it was a common occurrence. For two days they had sailed through a white blur and only the slap of the waves against the side told him they were at sea, not suspended in nothingness between one world and the next. During the remainder of the voyage, which was uneventful, Philip had spent long hours at the rail staring at the water, one minute smooth and marbled so that it looked almost solid, the next dissolved into a spray that made his coat stiff with salt in the morning. On the way out he had been too busy being sick to look at anything except the lurching walls of his cabin. Now he discovered that you could watch water the way you watched flames in a hearth or clouds in the sky and the result was the same. There was something about it that stilled the mind. The day a thin dark line appeared on the horizon and all the other passengers came out to see it, he was sorry.

He did not want to be home. This morning when he had woken up in the unfamiliar bed in the unfamiliar room, he had thought he was back at the lake with Prentice and his friend DeWitt. It might have been the way light was swimming on the ceiling or it might have been the aftermath of dreams, which he never remembered but which often colored his moods well into the day. Now, sitting in the front pew with his family, or kneeling and murmuring "amen," he could smell the sharp tang of the pines that grew by the lake edge and feel the rasp of granite under his fingers as he lowered himself down into the tipping canoe. The first summer, DeWitt taught him how to paddle as the natives did, and he could still recall the way the blade struck the mud of the lake bed on his first attempt and the vegetable odors that came bubbling up. One winter the three of them had skated through a thin crust of snow past the swaddled men fishing over holes cut in the ridged ice and it had seemed miraculous to him that weather, which he knew as an inconvenience, could be such an elating force.

"Are you all right?" mouthed Rowena, from the far end of the pew.

He nodded. The three years he had been away had not been kind to his sister. At sixteen, there had been the faint promise of prettiness; at nineteen it was gone and did not look likely to return. The letters he had received from her had not prepared him for that, nor for the distance that had inserted itself between them. The few days he had been home he had never seen her without a basket, packed with charity of one form or another. There was one at her feet now, full of books she was delivering after church to a woman who had once been housekeeper at the Park. Buried somewhere at the bottom of it, he felt sure, was her sense of humor.

The service was over. His sister was standing in the porch talking to the vicar about the sermon. "This is my eldest brother, Philip," said Rowena. He shook the vicar's hand and was reminded of a mollusk.

"The world traveler," said the vicar.

"He's home now," said Rowena. "Home for good, aren't you, Philip?"

Philip said yes, he was home now. Then Rowena went off with her basket, and there were more people his father insisted on introducing him to, while Caroline and Wilfred linked arms and whispered, and Albert, with his shadowed upper lip, stood off to one side with his hands in his pockets, kicking a stone to and fro.

On the way back it began to rain. "Rowena will get wet," said Caroline, for whom the promise of prettiness was a certainty. The statement carried a hint of satisfaction with it.

"Rowena has an umbrella," said their father.

Everyone agreed it had been a cold spring. All along the lanes the may was out, but the white flowers might as well have been snow. Philip tilted his head against the misted glass and wondered where all the colors had gone.

Rowena had not returned by luncheon. No one, apart from Philip, seemed to be troubled by this. His mother was occupied with John and his cough upstairs in the nursery, where the younger children had already eaten. The only guest at the table was a Dr. Burgess, apparently a frequent visitor, who had a bulging forehead and no neck, and who had arrived in a gig direct from the bedside of one of his patients soon after the Hendersons had returned from church. Before they sat down to eat, his father told him that Burgess was "sound." That approval, as far as Philip could tell, was based on the doctor's willingness to listen to his father's opinions without voicing any contradictory ones of his own, bobbing in the wake of the great ship like some sort of highly respectful dinghy.

A week ago, when Philip had got down from the Liverpool coach and gone to meet his father at his London offices, he had been shocked at how short, stocky, and ordinary he seemed. Half an hour later, over chops in a chophouse, that fleeting impression vanished and the height, presence, vigor, and sense of purpose he had always associated with his father, and that had loomed over him while he had been away, returned with full force. When they said good-bye, his handshake had a point to make.

A self-made man was a man with a story to tell. The story Philip knew was that his father, James Henderson, a drayman's son from Somerset, had gone to work at a haberdasher's warehouse in the

City, married the owner's daughter, and become a partner. A few years later, watching a state procession among crowds lining the Strand, he had observed that Queen Caroline looked very poorly, bought up all the black stuff on the market, and made his first fortune when the country went into mourning soon after. There was a subsequent business triumph over imported silk, when he had outsmarted the excise men along with his competitors, and later a grand tour of the Continent with their mother, which pleasantly combined the unearthing of trade secrets with cultural education. Now the self-made man sat in the House, dined with reformers and radicals, collected paintings and estates, and expected his eldest son to follow suit.

A gong sounded. "Luncheon." His father consulted his pocket watch. "Come along, Philip." Dr. Burgess put down his glass of Madeira and wiped his upper lip.

Luncheon was managed with the competence and attention to detail that characterized all the family's affairs. It was punctual, it was neat, the linen snowy, the glassware glinting, and the silverware bright. At the head of the long table sat the head of the family, with Philip and Albert on his left facing Dr. Burgess on his right. Receiving instructions with the circumspection of an envoy, a footman in a powdered wig and blue coat with brass buttons cleared away Rowena's place, muffling the cutlery against the crockery with his spotless gloves.

"Miss Henderson will not be joining us today?" said the doctor.

"It appears not."

Over deviled kidneys, veal cutlets, and a fruit compote, his father talked about the bank failure in the United States that had been the reason why his eldest son had spent three years in New York and Boston, looking after the Henderson investments under the direction of his American associate, Mr. Ryder. "We've seen the worst, thank God," he said. "I'm happy to say we're back on a level footing. Now Philip is home, with his experience in the money markets, I expect him to be a valuable asset to our new bank in Moorgate."

The doctor bulged his forehead at Philip. "Tell me, what general impression did you form of our cousins across the Atlantic?"

It was a version of the questions Philip had been asked in the churchyard. The answer was that he had formed no general impression, only many specific ones. The hallway of the Boston boarding-house where he had lodged with Prentice had a particular smell, for example, a blend of rush matting, boiled bacon, and polished paneling, which he could summon up without any trouble. The same was true of the clamor of lower Manhattan, where Irish squatters huddled in shanties made of scavenged planks, pigs rooting in the mud alongside, or the sight of the dilapidated wooden villas that clung to the cliffs of the East Sound, soon to be swept under the advancing street grid that was schematizing the island and obliterating its rocks and ditches and shrubbery. Most of all he remembered what it felt like to be living in a country that was in a hurry to make itself. He frowned, looked round, and saw that the doctor was waiting for his reply.

"I cannot say, to be honest. Some Americans are much the same as us. Others aren't."

"From what I understand, they lack all social graces."

"I found them friendly."

At this moment, Philip was thinking of the frankness of some American girls, his landlady's daughter in particular, whom he had been very careful not to mention in any of his letters home. It had been difficult to restrain himself, since she had taught him things and changed him in ways he would never have imagined three years ago, and he would have liked to have communicated that to someone.

"Friendly?" The doctor laughed. "That is not surprising. If there is one thing Americans respect, it's money."

His father mopped his mouth. "Everyone respects money, Burgess. Philip acquitted himself very well. I had excellent reports of him."

Praise was a form of expectation, thought Philip.

By the time the dessert was on the table, his father had moved off the subject of banking and, via a short detour into the arts and some of his recent acquisitions, had arrived at the great topic of the day, the opportunities provided by the speed of modern transportation.

"You bought this house at precisely the right moment," said the doctor. "The railway changes everything."

"The truth is I wanted to buy it much earlier. When I first saw it, I knew there could be no finer setting for my collection. That was soon after I entered Parliament."

"You waited eight years!" said the doctor, doing the mental arithmetic. "My word, there's patience."

"Prudence," said his father. "More was asking too much for it and he knew it. After that unfortunate business I was able to get it for a reasonable price, considering that it included the timber, which was not in the original offer."

"You drive a keen bargain," said the doctor.

"There's no other kind." His father surveyed the dining room decorations, which were too subdued for his taste: "It might as well rain indoors" was his estimation of them. He had plans for the dining room. "Yet I cannot deny that the arrival of the railway has been a great advantage. I don't see why anyone will ever need a town house in future."

The doctor said that thanks to Brunel and fifty miles an hour, one might have houses anywhere.

"Which unfortunate business?" said Albert.

Philip glanced at his brother, whose face was a blank. Albert's face was always a blank when he was stirring things up. He knew full well what had happened to the Mores; they both did. The divorce had been all over the papers. The woman had been ruined; her lover, who had recently been elected to the Royal Academy, had not.

"Which unfortunate business?" Albert repeated.

Their father rose from his seat. Luncheon was over. "An old story, which need not concern you." He nodded at the doctor and asked him if he would be so good as to listen to his youngest child's chest, as it would very much ease the mind of Mrs. Henderson.

Philip followed his father and the doctor into the staircase hall, where the white light poured down from the clerestory onto the new green-and-gold carpet. From somewhere above he could hear young voices and little feet running to and fro. He saw Cedric, or was it Reginald, peeping through the balusters up in the gallery. (It was definitely Reginald, he decided.)

The cottage was down by the railway. It was not one of the new brick ones that were springing up from footings to flashings in what seemed like five minutes, but an old place with flint walls that squinted under its thatch a little way out of the village. Before the line had gashed through the countryside, there had been an orchard at the back. Now all that was left of it was a pair of gnarled apple trees on which the soot settled. When the roaring trains passed, which was more and more often, the teacups and plates on the dresser rattled against each other and chipped themselves.

In front of the cottage was a small garden that struggled against the odds to be cheerful and productive. Every time Rowena saw it, she was reminded of an uncomplaining invalid who, despite all evidence to the contrary, always insisted that she was "much better today, thank you for asking."

It was raining harder when she came through the narrow gate and hurried the short distance down the cinder path. The porch was as inadequate a shelter as her umbrella, little more than a covered step, and by the time Mrs. Trimble opened the door and ushered her over the threshold, she was rather damp.

Straightaway she could tell something was the matter. "I hope you are quite well, Mrs. Trimble?"

"Very well, thank you, Miss Henderson." The reply was too bright and so were the eyes. "What miserable weather! Come and warm yourself by the fire while I make some tea. You must not catch a chill."

The cottage was dark and small. Conscious that her Sunday skirts took up half the space in the parlor, Rowena stood in front of the smoky hearth, to one side of an armchair where a cat was sleeping, while Daniel in the lions' den stared down from the wall above. To either side of the chimneybreast were framed prints of churches blotted with brown spots. A length of tatted lace was draped over a small bureau in one of the alcoves. On it was a miniature of a young man in an oval frame. In the other alcove was a spare chair with a sagging seat. This was all familiar to her.

Mrs. Trimble came back with the tea tray, which she placed on a small round table two steps away in front of the window, insisted that Rowena take the armchair, shooing the cat off it first, and brought up the spare chair for herself. Before she sat down, she took up a letter that had been lying folded on the mantelshelf and put it away in the little bureau.

"It is a pity you were not at church this morning. I could have introduced you to my brother Philip," said Rowena. "He is quite a man now."

A roar shuddered the walls, danced the teacups in their saucers, and offended the cat, which shot out of the room. Mrs. Trimble consulted the clock on the mantelshelf. "The London train," she said, when it was possible to speak. "You were talking about your brother."

"Yes, I would love you to meet him. Perhaps I might bring him to call one day soon."

Mrs. Trimble smiled, but the smile did not go far. While they drank the tea and ate thin slices of bread and butter, Rowena wondered whether or not this was the right occasion to put forward her proposal. She reached down to stroke the cat, which had made a cautious, dignified return, but Puss was not in the mood for stroking.

After Philip left and there was no one with whom to share her thoughts, she had decided to make herself useful, with the idea that it might give her something to write about in her letters to him. So while pictures were hung and rehung in the new house, furnishings were delivered and sent back, and accounts rendered were queried to the last penny, she had gone into the village with one of the maids, bearing offerings of food and clothing. These were met with silence and stares and peeping round the shutters. "Give it time, miss," said the maid on the way home. "They don't know you from Adam." A few months later, the Godwin boy broke his arm in two places falling off the back of a stationary milk cart and she managed to persuade her father to send the doctor to treat him. Afterwards the blacksmith took a pair of boots for his youngest—"Thank you, miss, he'll grow into them soon enough"—and an elderly woman accepted a cabbage. None of this provided her with much to write about.

The day she met Mrs. Trimble, soon after the family had finally moved into the house, was the day the first express came through the village. She had taken Caroline down to see it. As the locomotive and the carriages sped past in a blur of Brunswick green, chocolate, and cream, everyone was waving their handkerchiefs from the top of the cutting and pretending to fall backwards and having to be revived, the women with embraces and the men, who were happy to oblige, with beer. Meanwhile the children were making as much noise as the train but going nowhere near as fast, which did not stop them from trying. The Godwin boy tumbled down the bank to horrified cries and narrowly escaped being showered by white-hot cinders.

Then it was gone. Plumes of gray steam hung in the air. All along the track the cinders glowed red and turned to ash.

"I suppose this is progress."

Rowena turned to see a spare, middle-aged woman in dark, plain clothing, her shawl fastened by a dull metal brooch in the shape of a leaf. "Good heavens, wasn't it fast?" Rowena pressed her hand to her throat, where her pulse was beating rapidly. "Everything must go by in a dream. I don't see how you would ever know where you were."

"Don't be ridiculous. Of course you would," said Caroline. "That is what the station signs are for."

The woman laughed, they introduced themselves, and Rowena discovered that Mrs. Trimble used to be housekeeper at the Park for the family who had lived there before them.

"Then you must know Hastings, our steward," she said. "Father says he's been at Ashenden ever since he was born."

"Yes, I am well acquainted with Mr. Hastings."

"He's very disagreeable," said Caroline.

"Caroline!" said Rowena.

"I am also well acquainted with Mr. Hastings's disagreeableness."

Rowena did not know what to make of the comment and chose to ignore it.

"What are they doing?" said Caroline, craning her neck to stare at the couples on the bank. "Is it a game? A country dance of some sort?"

"You had better take your sister home," said Mrs. Trimble, with a private nod, "before it gets worse."

Rowena moved round to block her sister's view. "It was a pleasure to meet you, Mrs. Trimble," she said, putting out her hand. "You are more than welcome to visit us at any time. My father has made a great many improvements, which might interest you as someone who knows the house."

Mrs. Trimble shook her hand and declined the offer.

"In that case perhaps I might call on you some day."

"I am not difficult to find."

Back in the parlor Mrs. Trimble watched Rowena coax the cat. The girl was not so dislikable once you got to know her. She meant well, and she was too young to appreciate that meaning well and knowing best often looked like the same thing to the object of one's charity. Mrs. Trimble suspected she was lonely and underoccupied, as one could be even in the midst of a large family.

Soon Rowena would unpack the books from her basket, Mrs. Trimble would thank her, and after the visit was over, she would add them to the pile upstairs, where they would remain untouched and unread. It wasn't the girl's fault that she couldn't bear to hear about Ashenden—the staircase hall carpeted, for pity's sake!—or that in casting around for other things to talk about during her visits, she had inadvertently given the impression that she spent most of her time with her nose in a book.

Volumes of sermons and histories of Berkshire were not going to feed her or keep her warm, any more than they were going to entertain her. The hens had stopped laying because of the trains, the soot-caked vegetables were inedible, and she was down to measuring out the coal in teaspoons. But she would rather have starved than ask for help. The letter in the bureau informed her that her savings, including the small bequest her former employer Mr. Wilmott had left her in his will, were almost exhausted. She would be penniless in a matter of months. Then it would be Reading workhouse, and no prospect that she could imagine was worse than that.

Another train roared past, as if on cue. Mrs. Trimble, a dull weight on her heart, poured out what was left in the pot. She would keep the leaves to brew again later, as they had already been brewed once before, in the full knowledge that economies were only economies until there was nothing left.

Rowena took the cup and spilled tea into her saucer. Generally the girl was composed to the point of blandness. Today she appeared to be engaged in an internal struggle, which made her fidgety and pink. She opened her mouth a couple of times, each time checking herself. Finally, she said, "I think—well, first let me show you what I have brought." Then she delved into her basket.

What she produced was a battered assortment of children's books with faded bindings and loose pages. Spelling primers. An atlas. La Fontaine's *Fables*. A collection of Bible stories.

"These are from the nursery," said Rowena.

"So I see."

"I should very much like your opinion about an idea that I have had. It is simply that for some time I have been thinking—and I am certain that I am not alone in thinking this by any means—" She swallowed and smoothed her skirts. "I should like to open a school in the village."

Reading and writing for the boys, reading for the girls, perhaps writing, too, for the more able ones. Basic sums, so that they could manage their own household accounts in future. The sorts of skills that would fit them for lives of service or other forms of suitable employment. After the hesitancy, Rowena was now in full flow. She had heard that the Butlers had lost their paddock because they had been persuaded to mark their crosses on a document they could not read. The blacksmith knew what to charge for replacing a shoe, but she had observed that he could not multiply that by four and come up with the same answer twice.

"I do not propose the children should be educated above their station, but it would be a great shame and a pity if they grew up to be as ignorant as their parents. Do you not agree?"

Mrs. Trimble had sometimes been asked to read a letter for a villager or estate worker (although not the unfortunate Butlers) and had on rarer occasions been asked to write one. For such services she had received small offerings in kind.

"There is a day school in the next village."

"That costs money."

"And your school would be free?"

"Of course. Although naturally the teacher would be paid."

"Subscriptions?"

"No." Rowena lowered her voice. "Money is not a particular concern. To be frank, I have a little allowance of my own and I am confident more might be raised if need be."

The girl had thought about premises too. There was an outbuilding at the vicarage which was unused and could be made serviceable with whitewash and perhaps a small stove. She had spoken to Reverend Cummings about it.

"The great advantage is that it has its own entrance by the lane, so it is somewhat set apart." She clasped her hands in her lap. Fervor had made her almost pretty. "There it is. What do you think? I should value your opinion."

Mrs. Trimble collected the cups and saucers and put them back on the tray, making more noise than was necessary. She wanted the girl to go. It was hard to hear about someone else's plans when you were staring at the dead end of your own future.

"I wish you well with your enterprise, Miss Henderson. You are obviously your father's daughter."

"That would be news to him."

Mrs. Trimble did not know what to make of the comment and chose to ignore it. A coal shivered in the hearth. The cat leapt onto the windowsill, washed his paw, and pretended he had no interest in the milk jug.

"There is one other thing," Rowena said, the workings of her mind playing across her face. "I should like you to run the school."

There were times when you lost your footing in the world, when the ground turned into air and you couldn't tell whether you were falling or flying. Mrs. Trimble stared at the crack in the lid of the teapot. A tremendous silence was coming from somewhere and it was as loud as a train.

Rowena must have heard it too, because she rushed to fill it. "You don't have to give me your answer now. But I do ask you to consider it. I cannot think of anyone better suited. Someone who loves books as much as you do would be an excellent teacher. Besides which, the villagers know you and I am sure that they would be happy to entrust their children to your care."

Mrs. Trimble thought of the unread books upstairs and the way the locals kept her at arm's length. It was almost laughable how people misread and misled each other.

"I am sorry. I don't think I'm the one you want. I was a housekeeper, not a governess. I have never taught anyone."

Rowena smiled. "And I have never opened a school. Come," she said, touching Mrs. Trimble on the arm, "we shall be babes in the wood together. In any case, you do yourself a disservice. Housekeepers manage and calculate and instruct, do they not? I cannot see how teaching children their ABCs and two plus twos would be beyond someone of your capabilities." She got up from her seat and shook out her skirts. "I understand you might be reluctant to give up your pleasant, quiet life. All I ask is that you think about it."

Mrs. Trimble followed her to the door, wondering which part of her life was pleasant and which part was quiet.

"Oh, good, it has stopped raining," said Rowena. "More to the point, by the time I'm back, I shall have missed Sunday luncheon."

"Is that a cause for celebration?"

"Yes. It is." She turned on the doorstep. "Please consider it."

For Philip, a dull week ensued. Tomorrow succeeded today, his father took the train to town, and all he had been meaning to say remained unsaid. The ground steadied and the faint rocking he felt when he was lying in bed disappeared for good. On dry land at last, he was homesick for a place that was not his home. What he had liked about America, he realized, was that so much of it was unmapped. Life there—thinking of the landlady's daughter again— had a pleasing quality of not being foretold.

Rowena went to the village again on Monday morning, and in the afternoon his brother Albert challenged him to a rowing race, which Albert won by two lengths. On Tuesday afternoon, Albert challenged him to another rowing race, which ended in a disputed draw. Tuesday evening Wilfred said hello in passing and Caroline asked him many questions about what Americans wore. At his mother's suggestion, on Wednesday he spent some time in the nursery with the younger boys. John clambered over his knees and slid down his legs. Reginald stood on his hands, twice, toppling a Noah's Ark and scattering the animals all over the floor. (Takes after Albert, Philip thought.) Cedric shyly showed him his collection of moths and butterflies, along with an unhatched blackbird's egg, pale greeny blue speckled with brown. On Thursday the egg exploded. Then on Friday afternoon the Butterworths arrived and life took a new turn for Philip.

Ada Henderson had given instructions that her visitors were not to be admitted downstairs but to be directed to the principal entrance off the loggia, and it was with a flurry of servants that they were received there.

"Beatrice!" she said, crossing the entrance hall to greet her friend, who was, she could not help but notice, wearing an altogether more costly and ruffled gown than her brown merino. Beside her was a slender young woman (seventeen, she calculated), with long-lashed brown eyes and a beautiful mouth. "And this, my goodness, must be Florence!" She remembered herself in time to mention the unprepossessing child, all elbows and teeth, holding tight to his mother: "And, of course, young Bertram!"

"My dear Mrs. Henderson. Ada!" said Mrs. Butterworth, releasing Bertram to clasp her friend's outstretched hands.

"It has been too long."

"Oh, it has. Indeed it has."

"How do you do, Mrs. Henderson," said Florence, in a voice to match the mouth.

"How do you do," said Bertram.

"Florence is quite the young lady," said Ada, linking arms with Beatrice and guiding her across the expanse of the hall. "I should never have recognized her. Such a beauty."

But Beatrice Butterworth, staring round at furnishings and paintings and wall decorations, was lost for words. Ada, seeing her friend's eyes linger on the heavy folds of the damask hangings, found herself saying, "The crimson drapery is from our own manufactory. The gold gimp, of course, was imported."

"Those valances," said Beatrice, her hand at her throat.

Ada said, "I was not entirely convinced about the green satin, but it is a handsome color, don't you think?" She maneuvered her friend through the huddled groupings of furniture and past an easel, taking pride of place, on which a painting was propped.

Florence asked about the painting.

Her mother found her voice. "I believe it is Mr. Henderson's Titian," she said, turning to Ada for corroboration.

"What an excellent memory you have," said Ada.

"One could hardly forget." She smiled and her hand fled again to her throat as they passed through to the staircase hall and embarked across the swath of its new carpeting. "My word!"

"Wilton," said Ada, and immediately regretted the comment. It sounded like boasting and she deplored boasting. To cover up for the lapse, she began talking about "arrangements"—which servants would attend upon them, which rooms they would take. But her friend was not listening. Instead her eyes were flitting here and there, up to the clerestory windows and down again.

"I had imagined," Beatrice said at last, "the house quite differently. It is clearly *very* well appointed."

"Let us get you settled and then we shall take tea," said Ada, entirely gratified by her friend's reaction. "After your journey, you will be in need of refreshment."

They took tea in the drawing room. Here Ada experienced afresh the great shock of Florence's beauty when the girl came through the door, all grace and self-possession. Her younger daughter, Caroline, began twiddling with her ribbons in a sulky and pettish way. Her elder daughter, Rowena, however, who had been prevailed upon to greet the visitors, appeared indifferent.

"Philip and Albert may join us later," said Ada. "But I am not entirely sure where they are or what they are doing."

"Albert has gone riding," said Rowena.

Beatrice said, "I can't believe Albert is already sixteen!"

"You would not think it," said Rowena.

"In any case you will meet them both before long," said Ada. She added that Mr. Henderson, who had business in town, would arrive the next day.

Ada poured and a maid handed round the porcelain cups and saucers, the silver sugar basin, with its monogrammed tongs, and the silver milk jug, with its gilt interior.

"I fear Bertram may have been a little apprehensive about his introduction to the younger boys," said Beatrice, taking her cup with a murmur of thanks. Bertram had been left, white-faced, in the nursery.

"That is natural," said Ada. "I daresay he scarcely remembers them. Or John, of course, at all."

"He remembers Reginald very well," said Beatrice.

The conversation began to pick up a little. Beatrice asked after the particular decorations and furnishings of the room in which they were sitting. Ada enumerated them, keeping a watchful inner eye on boastfulness. The Greek gods painted on the ceiling she omitted for that reason; also she did not know their names. Then Beatrice, having no other coin to offer, responded by enumerating her daughter Florence's accomplishments, which were many. No watchful eye there, thought Ada, as Beatrice described singing in the Italian language, painting in watercolor, and a prose composition that had been praised by the vicar of St. Barnabas as revealing a "maturity beyond her years." At the mention of Florence's fine needlework, Ada could not help but wonder why Providence, who had distributed its favors so unevenly between her elder and younger daughter, giving Rowena sense and plainness, and Caroline an empty-headed prettiness, should have awarded this Florence a surfeit of everything.

The arrival of Philip, hesitating, stooping in the doorway, was at first a relief. Here was her eldest, the heir, who was not at all bad-looking and was exceedingly well traveled for one barely twenty-two. A credit to any mother. Then she noticed him noticing Florence with an almost physical jolt and the tide of blush that rose over the top of his high collar to wash over his cheeks. "I'm afraid you're too late, Philip," she said. "We have drunk all the tea and eaten all the cake."

Rowena, catching Philip's eye, rang for the maid and instructed her to bring her brother a cup. She patted the seat alongside and he crossed the room, scarlet to the tips of his ears, and folded his long frame into it.

There followed a general discussion about Philip and his three years in America, as if he had not been in the room. He might not have been, for he did not contribute to it. It was only when Florence asked him, with a slight tilt of her head that made the one long dark-brown ringlet curl against her cheek, what he was presently engaged upon that he opened his mouth. "I have been working on some figures," he said, with a fresh blush that overlaid the previous one.

At this point conversation died.

Nor did it revive when various squirmings and shushings came from below the furniture. Catching sight of Bertram's thin leg and new buckled shoe peeking out from underneath a tapestry table-cloth, Beatrice was surprised at this boisterous, somewhat trans-gressive side of her son's nature that she had never before suspected he possessed.

"You aren't attending, Philip," said his father.

It was Monday morning, two days after the arrival of the But-terworths, and they were sitting in the small estate office beyond the library. No decorative schemes had been devised for it and no new furniture had been ordered. Nothing hung on the walls except a map of the local area showing the new railway line.

"Sorry, sir," said Philip, shaking himself out of a dream in which he and Florence Butterworth were exchanging a long, hungry kiss . . .

"Are our visitors distracting you?"

"Not at all."

"Good," said his father, running a pencil down the columns of figures in the ledger open on the table in front of him.

By any rough estimation, the Henderson fortune was into the millions, yet every week income was measured against expenditure, down to shillings and pence. What was at issue at present was how much time his father's architect, Mr. Bartholomew, was claiming to be spending on the improvements to Ashenden, set against observ-able results.

"He's spread himself too thin," said his father, throwing down the pencil. "There has been no progress on the stables whatsoever." The old stable block was derelict and would have to be demolished, which would improve the view from the portico, but the new sta-bles hadn't been built yet, which was holding things up. "I won't be cheated because he's too busy elsewhere with other clients."

Bartholomew and his father had known each other for many

years, during which time they had woven a fine mesh of mutual clients, interests, and business partners. It was a fabric as strong as any marriage, or so one supposed.

Ashenden had been in a terrible state when his father bought it. The roofs on the side pavilions were missing half their slates and were about to cave in. Indoors was bleak and the park was a heath. Only Bartholomew had understood what his father had seen. No one else had.

"If you ask me, I think he's done the impossible," said Philip.

"I don't ask you, Philip," said his father. "The man is shortchanging me. It's as simple as that."

"What have you paid him?"

"Two thousand, and he won't get a penny more. It's a five percent commission and he's given me a three percent return."

Philip knew this mood. His father had gone to court for much less. He glanced at the map on the wall. It was plain that the railway, not the stable block, was at the bottom of it all: specifically, Bartholomew's failure to persuade the Great Western to reroute the line away from the eastern boundary of the estate. Trains might be convenient for the transportation of people and paintings and furnishings, but they were not what you wanted to see or hear when you had paid a great deal of money for a derelict house. A screen of firs and forest trees was the remedy Bartholomew proposed; "a blot on the landscape to disguise another" had been his father's response, for which Philip had some sympathy.

At an ocean's distance, in America, he had understood that the contradictions in his father's nature were the price a self-made man in an old country paid for success. It was the reason why an advocate of the railway did not want a railway line near his house and why a campaigner for the abolition of slavery underpaid those he employed and accused them of cheating. Much as he loved his father, that did not make the contradictions easier to bear at close quarters.

"I have written to ask Bartholomew for his final accounts," said his father. "A great, great shame."

It was indeed a pity. The architect was a small fretful man who worried about his reputation to the detriment of his income and who had put his blood into the house. Philip remembered him darting in and darting out, spinning jobs like plates in the air. It was hard to say what would hurt him more, the loss of his fees or the withdrawal of what he must assume to be friendship.

"Whether or not it comes to court," said his father, "I should like you to handle it."

No! This came out as a nod.

"I've prepared the figures. All you need to know is written down here." His father pushed a few sheets of paper across the desk.

Philip got up to go.

"Pretty girls are ten a penny," said his father. "As you must be aware by now."

"Sir?"

"I trust you take my meaning."

Later Beatrice Butterworth would wonder how she got through the week. For there was so much to be got through and admired: dismaying numbers of meals with many courses and dishes, rooms and yet more rooms, walks through shrubbery and along the river, bright regiments of planting on the terraces, and, of course, children. There was such a great deal of everything, and admiration, she found, was exhausting. For Florence, who had become such an object of fascination, the visit must also have been tiring, albeit for a different reason. Only Bertram was in some new element.

As the days wore on, Beatrice found herself thinking more and more fondly about her own dear home, which was of a similar age to Ashenden and shared (on a very modest, terraced scale) its proportional sympathies. In her mind, its quaint deficiencies that were such a trial to housekeeping receded, and she longed for its quiet and unfashionable rooms, where several clear strides might be taken between furniture.

"One can have too much ebony, don't you think?" she said to her daughter on the last evening, as they were preparing themselves to go downstairs. "Such an oppressive wood. To say nothing of all the gilt."

"I am not clear whether you are objecting to the darkness or the brightness, Mama," said Florence. "Are you going to be much longer? They will be expecting us in the octagon room."

Her mother settled her locket round her throat on its black velvet ribbon and crooked her head. "I've been meaning to ask. What do you make of Philip?"

Florence replied that she thought he was very polite.

"Yes, he has been most attentive. To you, above all."

"And of course he is quite tall," said Florence.

"Long of limb," said her mother. "But polite, as you say, and well spoken."

"When he speaks," said Florence.

"A quiet, steady disposition."

"Quiet, certainly."

"Hidden depths," said her mother. "Your father was the same at Philip's age."

Florence colored with irritation. Philip had unsettled her in a way she could not put into words. "But clearly his chief distinguishing characteristic is that he is, or will be one day, very rich."

Her mother gave her a long look. "We should go downstairs," she said. "We are already a little late."

The octagon room was where the Henderson collection of English pictures was displayed, or where it was stifled, depending on how you looked at it. Florence came through the door with her mother and thought she could hear the Constable gasping for breath.

It was an overwhelmingly purple room, padded, trimmed, and tasseled to within an inch of its life. Beside the high altar of the hearth, with its steel-and-ormolu grate, Philip leaned against the carved marble chimneypiece. Across an expanse of Turkey carpet, beyond the tableau of the rest of the family gathered there, she saw him register her appearance with a sharpening of attention that seemed to indicate that he knew something about her that she didn't know herself. She was used to attention, but the quality of Philip's attention gave her a fluttered sensation that she was quite unprepared for. It was as if he had some sort of odd power over her that he might at any moment exercise.

"I very much enjoyed the archery this afternoon," she said, as he threaded his way through the furniture to her side. She could hear herself throwing out the bright words to put a little distance between them. Everyone was looking at them. Even Wilfred, sitting reading on the ottoman, was observing them over the top of his book.

"You've a real knack. A crack shot," he said. "That bull's-eye!"

"I was standing quite close."

Philip had butterflies in his stomach and elsewhere. "Not so close as all that," he said.

"Albert scored three bull's-eyes and he was standing much farther back."

"Oh, *Albert*," he said, longing to reach his hands about her narrow waist, to run his fingers through her curls—"spaniel's ears" Caroline disdainfully called them—and as if reading his intention, she moved away.

"Tell me about this painting," she said, peering at a still life of pears in a pewter dish surrounded by a dark broad frame. "It doesn't look English to me."

"No, it's Dutch. It shouldn't really be here. At least"—and here he paused, worrying that what he felt about her was written all over his face—"it should and it shouldn't. We keep the Dutch masters at Harley Street."

"I like the fly."

Philip, who liked the fly too, admired her for admiring it (although there was almost nothing he did not admire her for). He explained that the picture had formed part of a collection that his father had bought a few months ago, with the idea that he would keep whatever appealed to him and dispose of the rest. "This was one of the ones he was going to sell until he discovered that it used to hang here in the house when the Mores were the owners."

"Why was he going to sell it?"

"It isn't of the first rank," said Philip. "My father has very good taste." He could have added that his father liked to win and found many ways to do it.

"My brother is going to be very sorry to leave tomorrow," said Florence. "In fact, he has announced that he has no intention of doing so." She laughed into what was becoming a dangerous pause. "Bertram is revealing quite a new side to Mama. Quite an *adventurous* side."

"He has fallen in well with the little scamps, hasn't he?" And here Philip had a warm and curiously complicit feeling that they were parents discussing their own offspring.

A footman bearing a small silver tray with chased scalloped edges, on which stemmed crystal glasses of pale wine were arranged at geometric intervals, interceded. They each took a glass, Florence raising hers quickly to her lips to avoid the embarrassment of a toast.

"A toast," said Philip, leaning across to chink and spilling a little of his in the process. "I very much hope you have enjoyed your visit as much as your brother."

"I have," said Florence, and to an extent this was true. She had enjoyed the walks, the inspection of the glasshouses, the card games when it was raining, the smooth running of a household that delivered many delicious meals at appointed hours with no crying in the kitchen or fuss at the tradesman's entrance over bills. She had liked to see the younger children making their own world in this house, which for all its ebony, gilt, and purple plush was at ease with itself. She was even rather proud of her bull's-eye. To Philip she said none of this. Instead, she thought it might be really rather a relief to go home.

At the end of the evening, Ada Henderson sat in front of her looking glass and removed her garnet earrings and necklace, handing them to the maid to lay in the velvet-lined tray beside her diamonds. Not once during the Butterworths' visit had she worn the diamonds—what a pity tact was second nature to her!—and she now regretted this. A soft tap at the door, her husband entered, and she sent the maid away. He came across to where she was sitting and began to unhook her bodice as she took the pins out of her hair and brushed it out.

"Thank heavens that's over," she said, breathing more freely.

"I did warn you."

"And you were right." Ada thought how fortunate she was to have married a man of such sound judgment: it made for a well-regulated life. "It's very sad. Beatrice and I have grown quite, quite apart. The easy way between us has gone. What's worse, she has a new sly way of asking what things cost." She turned to pat his hand. "As if *you* would ever pay too much for anything!"

"As if I would," said her husband, returning the pat.

"And that wretched girl set her cap at Philip." She wriggled out of her sleeves and fumbled about her waist to undo the strings of her skirt.

"Hop up," said her husband. "It's got into a knot."

"What a siren that girl is!" said Ada. "I knew it the minute I set eyes on her. A fortune hunter of the first degree."

"I think that it is rather the other way round, my dear."

Ada said, noting the "my dear," "What do you mean?"

"I mean that it is evidently Philip who is smitten."

"Philip is far too sensible."

"Philip is a young man and Florence is a very pretty girl."

"I hope you are not suggesting—" said Ada.

"A very pretty girl and a most unsuitable one," said her husband. "Philip can do much better."

"Then we are agreed," said his wife, who, after much tussling, was down to her chemise, every ounce of flesh rejoicing. "Will you stay?"

"If you don't mind." Her husband, who had already removed his frock coat, was struggling with his neckcloth.

"Let me," said Ada, reaching to help him.

Separate bedrooms, which they had not been able to afford in their early married life, made for conjugal happiness, or so she believed. There was something very agreeable about having a choice.

After the Butterworths left the following day, Philip found himself in the staircase hall utterly at a loss, unsure whether to go upstairs or down or to stay where he was.

"There you are," said Rowena, untying her bonnet, as if he had been missing, not her. She had been out early this morning and missed the departure. "Come upstairs," she said, studying his face. "We'll go to my sitting room."

His sister's small sitting room looked over the river. The wallpaper was floral and he recognized some of the furniture from Harley Street, along with a brown-and-white pottery cow that was a childhood favorite of hers. There was a hole in the back where you poured in the milk and a hole in the mouth where the milk came out. The tail looped to make a handle. He remembered the tears at Clapham when their nurse forbade his sister from taking it to bed with her.

Shrugging off her paisley shawl, Rowena sat down and propped her feet on the fender. It was raining again and her shoes were wet through. "I've hardly seen you since you came back, what with the visitors."

"Well," said Philip, "you do make yourself scarce." Wherever did she go? he wondered.

"I can't be doing with all this sitting about, all this chitchat."

"You've become quite an oddity, Ro."

The old nickname brought a smile. "Haven't I? The fate of unmarried persons."

"You're only nineteen."

"I shan't marry, ever."

She leaned forward and began to ask him all sorts of questions about America, none of which concerned clothing.

"No, you tell me your news first. What have you have been doing with yourself while I've been away?" At his suggestion, the hunger on her face almost shamed him.

"Oh, I haven't been idle." Then out came a story about a little school she was planning for the village, all the ins and outs and whys and wherefores of it. How she hoped that Mrs. Trimble, the former housekeeper of Ashenden, would agree to be the schoolmistress; how an outbuilding at the vicarage could serve as premises. "What do you think?"

Philip said that he thought that the school was a good idea but perhaps she might think of someone better qualified to run it.

"Mrs. Trimble is the daughter of a clergyman. She strikes me as a very capable person and she is a great reader."

"All the same, a housekeeper isn't a schoolmistress."

"Anyone can teach. You taught me my sums and I taught Wilfred to read."

And Wilfred had never left off reading. Even when he wasn't reading, he looked like he was reading.

"It's not Eton or Harrow I'm founding," said Rowena. "At any rate, you will see when you meet the woman. From what I hear, More treated her badly and she hasn't been able to get a position since. Not that she's told me anything about it. She is too proud for that."

"Is this about providing a school for poor children or finding employment for a housekeeper fallen on hard times?"

Two spots of red appeared in the exact centers of her cheeks. "It's about righting wrongs. I thought you would understand."

"Of course I do, Ro. I think it is a splendid idea." He nodded and got up from his seat.

"Must you go?"

"I have some figures to look at. We'll talk about my travels another time, I promise." All he really wanted to talk about was Florence or, failing that, to find somewhere private to think about her. Already America seemed distant, on account of having no Florence in it.

"Do you know," said Rowena, "when you first came home, I had the impression you might decide to go away again."

"Why do you say that?"

She shrugged. "I imagine traveling must be a great adventure. At least, I should find it so."

"I can't say I didn't enjoy the freedom, but I find I'm glad to be home after all." He could feel heat travel up his cheeks.

"Good." Rowena made brusque sweeps at her skirts. "Well, the Butterworths are gone at last!"

"Yes."

"I thought Florence was a very fine girl."

Philip hesitated at the doorway, tempted for a moment to pursue the conversation in this new direction, then thought better of it.

It was going to rain again. The cool evening smelled moist.

"Puss?" Mrs. Trimble called into the twilight. "Puss?"

The cat had got out somehow when she hadn't been looking. Another train was due. It would frighten him.

She pulled her shawl closer against the air, and her fingers found the smooth hollows of the leaf pin. The man who'd sold it to her outside the asylum gates where her husband was shut away had said it was silver, but it wasn't silver. They let some of them sell things they made, the ones who were no danger to themselves or others. It gave them a bit of income. The man had been chained to an iron ring. He said he wandered in his wits, which was why they didn't let him wander very far. The day she bought the pin was the first and only time she ever visited Richard. Afterwards there were always good reasons not to. Then one April morning he had hanged himself.

Asylum meant refuge, and there was none of it within those stout howling walls. "Puss?" Tears stood in her eyes. They were not for the cat, nor for Richard, but for her own deliverance.

Six years ago last June and that wretched fool Georgiana More had not seen her children from that day onwards. You might take a penniless scribbler as a lover, but you mustn't take a tradesman or an artisan, or whatever a painter was. Society closed its doors on her until the day of her death, which had come soon enough. After the divorce, More sued Delgado for the money his wife had lent him, with no success. The whole family was bad with money one way or another.

These past years Mrs. Trimble had come to see her dismissal as a form of retribution. Richard had died alone, by his own hand, and she had gone on working. She had visited once, put him out of her mind, and gone on working, working, working. When the working stopped, and she had stopped, there had been time to think about that.

She called the cat.

A train roared past and she realized how seriously she had been entertaining the idea of throwing herself under one. Beyond the blotted ink of the apple branches, the ground cut away to the track. Along the line, the cinders were dying to ash and taking their light with them.

A soft shape whirred against her skirts. "Where have you been?" she said, bending down, the cat's tail a knobbly rope through her fingers. Then she went indoors, pinching the bridge of her nose, wondering how she was going to turn an outbuilding into a school.

6

The Janus Cup: 1889

In the house a deep familiarity settles over the rooms. Stretch out a hand and you touch a brown-and-white pottery cow you have known since your childhood half a century before and your grandchildren now play with. Walk down the hallways and memories come to greet you, the same inconsequential thoughts every day, nothing momentous.

There are improvements, of course, and upkeep, necessary renewals and repairs. But on the whole things remain as they are, year to year.

Above stairs, it's an ordered life, all the more pleasant for being predictable. Below works an army to keep it that way, lighting fires, blacking grates, winding clocks, cooking meals, washing laundry, sweeping floors, and dusting every nook and cranny. Thirty labor in the gardens alone. It's so long since the house has known hardship, it has forgotten what it is.

The tree was almost twelve feet tall. Its sharp pine scent filled the staircase hall; sometimes you could catch a hint of it along a corridor when you were least expecting to.

"It's a good one this year, isn't it?" said Florence Henderson, turning to her husband. "Well proportioned. They aren't always. Sometimes they're a trifle lopsided or have bare patches." She reached out to grasp one of the lower branches, ran its needles through her hand, and made the baubles jingle.

"A fine specimen," said Philip, nodding. "Very handsome."

"Do you remember the first? It must have been twenty years ago. Everyone thought we were mad."

"We were mad," said Philip. "We nearly burned the place down. That candle . . ."

They both stared up at the Christmas tree, each gravely considering fire buckets, and whether there were enough of them, and then went through to the library, where they had fallen into the habit of spending the latter part of the morning. Today there were the arrangements for the holidays to discuss.

"I thought we might put Rowena up in her old room," said Florence, sitting to one side of the hearth, where crackling logs sent showers of sparks gusting up the chimney. Rowena was due to arrive from London the next day. "She won't mind, will she?"

"Of course not. Why should she?" Philip propped his stick against his desk.

"It's simply that I meant to replace the wallpaper when we were redecorating that side last year and somehow never got round to it. She will find it rather shabby."

"She hates a fuss." Philip eased himself into the chair facing hers.

"A cushion for your back?"

He accepted the cushion.

Florence consulted a list she had made, ticking off items with a gold mechanical pencil Philip had bought her in Paris. "Then Adelaide and William can have the east suite, which leaves the red bedroom for James and Matilda. It's going to be rather a squeeze in the nursery with the little ones, but it can't be helped. Just as well Constance and Flora have decided to spend the holidays in town or we should have been truly overrun."

Philip smiled at the woman he had loved for forty-five years. She had kept him waiting a long time before accepting his proposal of marriage, a day he still counted as the happiest of his life. Four children they'd had—Constance, Flora, Adelaide, and James, in that order, James the youngest by far. Eleven grandchildren now and one on the way.

"I think it's a pity Constance and Flora aren't coming."

"I knew you'd say that." Florence squinted at the page in front of her, holding it at arm's length. "Time for them to make their own family traditions. It's what we did."

"That's true."

"I've given instructions to Mrs. Burgoyne regarding Matilda's condition. Christmas fare can be indigestible at the best of times." Mrs. Burgoyne was their cook, and Matilda's condition was one she shared with many young married women.

"Fatherhood," said Philip, "I hope it settles James down. When I was his age . . ."

"You were a very intense young man. It rather alarmed me."

"You got over it."

"And I'm very glad that I did. I think Matilda will make James an excellent wife."

Philip was not entirely sure about that. Or rather, he was not sure that James would make an excellent husband.

A maid came into the room to replenish the log basket. Coal they had for most of the rooms, but a wood fire was company as much as it was heat.

"Mary," said Florence, "I find I need my spectacles."

"Yes, ma'am. I'll fetch them for you directly."

"And Mary?"

"Yes, ma'am?"

"You haven't done your skirt up properly."

"I'm sorry, ma'am. I'll see to it." The girl bobbed her head and left the room.

"Oh, I love Christmas," said Florence, stretching her hands to the flames.

By the following week all the family had arrived and the house was busy again: more bedrooms to make up, fires to light, and children to tend to, along with the seasonal preparations. It was a great deal of work. However, the Hendersons were always generous with their Christmas boxes, which was something to look forward to when the fuss was over.

On the Thursday Dulcie was rushed from pillar to post, answering one ringing bell after another, fetching and clearing this and that. One of the children upset a basin in the nursery and there was a puddle to mop and a rug to dry. By late evening she was tired to the death and should have been in bed like the other housemaids. Instead she was trudging through the woods to the old estate cottage where her great-uncle lived.

A light wavering at the upper window answered her lantern. Bare branches crackled and creaked; stars were fierce pinpricks in the night sky. In the cold, dead heart of the year all the creatures were asleep in their burrows or stiff under hedgerows. She lifted the latch, let herself in, and stamped feeling back into her feet.

"Who's there?"

"It's me, Dulcie."

The cottage had a stale smell of mice and old men. She went up the stairs and pushed open the bedroom door.

The old woman sitting in the chair was a crazy bundle of shawls and coverlets. Mrs. Jakes blinked in the glare of the lantern, knitting needles ticking over of their own accord. "You got away, then."

"I did." Dulcie Godwin rubbed her hands. "My goodness, it's freezing in here. There's frost on the flags downstairs."

"Mr. Hastings was never a one for home comforts."

Her great-uncle Hastings, the former steward of Ashenden, lay in the high iron bed. Age was sucking the life out of him, breath by breath. His dark eyes were sunk under the nutshells of their lids and his nose was a prow. Only the large bony hands were restless, plucking at nothing and each other.

"Won't be long now. He'll be gone before daybreak. Pass in his sleep, I expect."

No one laid out a corpse as beautifully as Mrs. Jakes. In any case, you couldn't shake her off the end of a life if you tried. She liked to keep her ear pressed to the keyhole of death's door.

Dulcie put out her lantern and sat at the bottom of the bed. It was either that or the floor. Something stirred with a yelp, which shot her upright again.

"No need to take on, it's only the dog." A whiskery snout poked out from under the bedclothes, growled, and disappeared again. "Bless him. He'll be nice and warm in there."

The dog was called Fly and he was mostly terrier, a snapper at heels. She had never known her great-uncle to be without a dog, and Fly would be the one who survived him. Ninety-six was a long life whether you measured it in dogs or years.

"They do say the good die young," said Mrs. Jakes. "Mr. Hastings always had that much vinegar in him, it's no surprise he's lasted all this while. Mind you, Nan Turner, she was eighty-two when she went and she never had a bad word to say about no one." The knitting needles clicked away. "Cold enough to snow tonight."

It didn't smell as if it were going to snow. Snow had a smell, like iron. You could taste it at the back of your tongue.

"Gravedigger's going to have a hard burying. Still, it would be nice to have a white Christmas." The candle spat and hissed on the ledge. "Family arrive safe?"

"Yes, they're all there now, Mrs. Jakes. Those that are coming."

"You have your hands full, I expect."

"We do."

"The happy times that house has seen," said Mrs. Jakes, with a heavy sigh that suggested the house had seen the very opposite. She ran her crooked fingers down the shapeless length of her knitting. "How's that fellow of yours, Dulcie?"

"Well enough. Jack's out with the singers, the waits, tonight."

"I thought we'd have seen the pair of you in the church by now."

"You know how it is."

"You don't want to be wasting your good years, Dulcie. Take it from me, there's precious few of them. You're not getting any younger."

Dulcie was not yet twenty. At home she'd shared a bed with her sisters until the oldest got married at sixteen, by which time her youngest brother had shifted out of their parents' room to fill the gap. In most families round about it was the same. The infants went in drawers or were tucked up with their parents, and the older ones were three or four or five a bed. What one caught, you all caught, itching and sweating and coughing through childhood, sleeping with an elbow in your back, or a knee, never knowing whose dream you were dreaming. At the maids' quarters up at the house it was no better: there was temper, crying fits, and sulks. Marriage, of itself, was no answer. Her sister had three children by now and she was still cramped under the roof of her in-laws.

"We mean to set up on a good footing in our own place." She wondered at the even tone of her voice and what a lie it told.

"Then let's hope it's true what they say and your old uncle's got money put by. Lord knows he never spent any." Mrs. Jakes wheezed a laugh. "You've been that good to him these last months, why shouldn't you have expectations? I'd be the same in your shoes."

Dulcie pinched her leg through the thick wool layers of her skirts to stop words tumbling out. A blush scalded her face. How could your body make so much heat on a cold night? Where did it come from? She was glad it was dark.

When she was a little girl and her mother had taken her to visit the cottage deep in the woods, her great-uncle had frightened her. He had a shock of white hair and a sour, downturned mouth meant for complaining, and there was always a dog that sniffed her in private places and decided it didn't like her. "I know what you're about," her uncle would say to her mother as she sat in the chimney corner darning his clothes or knelt to rake out his hearth. "I'm no fool. You might save yourself the trouble. I'm not about to remember you in my will. Climb up here, little missy, and I'll show you my pocket watch." Then Dulcie would have to climb on the old man's lap and be shown the watch and be told how it was a token of long years of service and was very precious on that account. "Got your nose!" he would say at the end, snapping the watch shut in her face and laughing when she cried. Her mother said he wasn't used to children.

Soon after she and Jack had begun to walk out, her mother had suggested she call by the cottage whenever she could find the time. "You never know," said her mother, with a tilt of her head that stood in for whatever she couldn't bring herself to say. So Dulcie went along on her half days. The new dog, Fly, didn't like her any better than the old, dead dogs had done, but her uncle let her tidy and clean and straighten, mumbling and shifting in his creaking ladder-back chair, his wet eyes following her as she lined the pantry shelves with new paper or cleared up the mouse droppings, her Jack cooling his heels outside, impatient for her to come back and rebuff his kisses. You can't be frightened of a harmless old man, she told herself. Then afterwards she would come out into the sunshine or the rain or whatever weather it was and she would feel like she'd left a shadow or a weight behind.

Jack didn't have much time for Mr. Hastings, living out his last days rent-free, when others too old or too sick to labor for a wage finished up in the workhouse, their families broken, scattered, and ruined. His father had been fined in the magistrates' court many years back for trespass and for helping himself to a couple of branches that weren't strictly speaking dead wood, being attached to trees at the time, and that was all down to her uncle, who knew every hedge and hollow of the land, every oak, spruce, field maple, lime, chestnut, yew, and hawthorn like the back of his hand. Some had names. Old Bob was the yew in Easter Field, and Simon's Seat was the two-hundred-year-old ash down by the gatehouses. Her uncle had been a scourge of boys, scrumpers, poachers, tenants behind in their rent, trespassers, never happier than when he caught someone out.

Work was hard to come by these days. There was next to none on the land. Jack went for a job on the railway and didn't get it. He was big and strong, fit for anything, and stubborn with it. When he got an idea in his head, there was no dislodging it. Some of those ideas had been put there by Arthur Young, who gave talks once a month on Sunday evenings in the upper room at the Ploughshare. Arthur Young was a man of the world. He came from Reading and had been to London, where he'd seen Hyde Park with all the railings down and the police clubbing heads in Trafalgar Square.

"They need a groundsman up at the house," Dulcie had said, back in the summer, when she was walking with Jack by the river. "Someone to help with the coppicing. You could do it. I'll put a word in, if you like."

"You'll do no such thing, Dulcie. I wasn't born to cut down trees some rich man planted on the commons that was stolen from us in the first place." The land belonged to the people, which was them, and didn't belong to Mr. Henderson no matter how many walls and fences and hedges he put round it. "Property is theft."

Property was theft. That was hard to get your head round when you were saving for your own place. Property invited theft, she could understand. The butler, Mr. Williams, was always at pains to point out that the house contained many valuables and they must be careful about answering the door to strangers. Up at the house, everything that could be locked was locked—doors, boxes, drawers, glass-fronted cupboards, cabinets, bookcases—and Mr. Williams jangled with keys to them all. There was a safe somewhere, but none of them had ever seen it, that's how safe it was. "Lock a box and you tell a thief there's something inside worth having," her great-uncle said. He kept his watch in an old Huntley & Palmers biscuit tin printed with scenes from the Queen's Golden Jubilee.

"It's just a job. Can't do any harm, can it?" She slipped her arm through his and laid her head on his shoulder. "I'm not saying it has to be forever."

"I'm not doing it, Dulcie, and that's that. I won't slave for a filthy usurer like Henderson. Not while working men slice their feet to ribbons tramping from parish to parish in search of a crust."

Usurer. That was an Arthur Young word. "Then who will you work for?"

"Anyone who will give me honest employment."

"What's wrong with coppicing?"

Since Arthur Young had started giving his talks at the Ploughshare, what Jack understood by honest employment had narrowed
somewhat. Any minute now he would get on to the millions of poor
in London.

"There are millions of poor in London," he said. "Millions and
millions living in filth. Does Henderson care about them? Does he
give them a moment's thought when he's sitting in his bank counting his money?"

"We need a roof over our heads. Nothing else has come up for
months."

"I'm not doing it. I will not work for that man."

She withdrew her arm and moved away. "I don't think you want
to be married."

"Think what you like."

That had been the start of their first proper quarrel and it was a
bitter one. Afterwards they had made it up more thoroughly than
Dulcie had intended, although at which point what she had intended had given way to what she hadn't intended was never clear
to her. She hadn't let it happen again, which you might say was a
clear case of shutting the door after the horse had bolted.

The other day when she was lugging a coal scuttle up the cork-
screwed back stairs, her arm wrenched out of its socket, a sour taste
rising in her throat, she wondered what, after all, had been the point
of her schooling. Once she thought learning might lead to something, and her teacher had encouraged her in that thought, giving
her books and finding quiet places where she could read them. That
was before her father's accident and she had had to go into service.
What she had discovered then was that no one paid you for knowing verses from the Bible, the kings and queens of England, or poetry by heart unless it was to teach them to somebody else. She had
enough learning to know that she didn't have enough learning to
teach, and might never have it. When her duties took her into the
library, the shelves of leather-bound books made her resentful.

Jack didn't go for the job at the Park and it went to Billy Wells. Wee Willy they used to call him and he wasn't much bigger now. Billy had cut down the tree that stood in the hall and filled the house with its sappy pine scent. It had been one of the spruces that grew along the railway line.

Her uncle's hands were busy again. Up and down, up and down, putting things on a shelf or climbing a ladder.

"Look at him," said Mrs. Jakes. "Perhaps he's trying to tell us something."

Dulcie reached across, laid the fluttering hands on the bedclothes and felt their sinew and bone, the slow beat of blood under the tissue of skin.

"You wouldn't credit it now," said Mrs. Jakes, tugging the yarn, "but Mr. Hastings asked me to marry him once. I was sixteen and he must have been forty if he was a day. There weren't a female for miles around he didn't ask, the plain ones and all. Never had no takers. No one so much as walked out with him so far as I know. We must follow our hearts, my love, however hard the road, that's what I say."

There was no money, Dulcie was sure of it. Nothing in the cottage said money. Bare floorboards, plaster threaded with horsehair crumbling away from the laths, greasy work shirts hanging from the peg rail, worn through at the elbows. It was a sorry place.

She slipped off the bed and lit the lantern with the candle.

"Where're you going?"

"I won't be a minute."

Downstairs she heard mice scrabble into the corners. The lantern's sway shouted up shadows on the pocked walls. Out back on the scullery shelf she found the Huntley & Palmers biscuit tin, rust creeping along its edges. The watch was inside, where it always was. It had stopped ticking years ago and the gilt plating was almost worn off. A cheap piece, her mother had said. "They think we don't know quality."

Dulcie fumbled in her skirts, drew out what she had wrapped in a scrap of washrag, and pushed it down into the biscuit tin. It was a close fit. Then she closed the lid, her heart hammering, feeling giddy and sick.

The waits stomped their feet in the inn yard and breathed on their hands.

"Mills, Steadman, Brookes. And here comes Wells, with the drum. Who's missing?" said the vicar, raising his lantern to their faces. He was a slight man with a light voice, well wrapped in a worsted muffler.

"Jack Pierce," said Dick Steadman, the pigman.

"He'd be late for his own funeral," said Billy Wells, joining them.

"That's a good one," said George Mills, smith, son of smith, and grandson of smith. All weathers his face was burned red and his hands were calloused and scarred, the black worked so far into them it wouldn't come out. "He'd be late for his own funeral. I never heard that one before."

"Horse kick you in the head lately, George? Or are these the wits you were born with?" Billy was a joker. You needed to be if you were short.

"We'll start without him," said the vicar. "What shall it be, boys?"

"'Good King Wenceslas.'"

"'While Shepherds Watched.'"

"'Angels from the Realms of Glory,' I think, boys," said the vicar. "That's a good beginning. We'll sing the others later."

They were used to the vicar asking for their opinion and not taking it.

"Are we ready?" said the vicar, blowing a note on his wind instrument. It was a shawm, a long wooden pipe that ended in a large flared bell.

They sang the first verse of the carol, fine and clear, to the door of the Feathers, and the rest of the verses inside, the reedy blast of the shawm and the drumbeat crowding the snug nicely.

"A small one for a small one," Billy said to the landlord.

The landlord poured the ale. "For a small one you make some noise with that drum. My ears is ringing."

"Billy's always had plenty to say for himself. One way or another." Jack Pierce had come in towards the middle of the last verse and brought the cold with him.

"Here you go, Jack," said the landlord. "Get that down you. You'll need it on a night like tonight."

The vicar said they would do the public houses first, then the cottages strung out along the upper road, and finish at the big house. "Mr. Henderson has given us leave to sing up at the Park, which is most accommodating of him. I hear they've a beautiful tree."

"Don't I know it," said Billy. "I cut it down."

"Don't we know it," said Jack Pierce.

They went along to the East Arms, past the shuttered village shop and the tiny post office next door. The vicar was talking about the waits and how in the olden days every town of consequence had its players, paid for out of the public purse, a band of musicians who performed on civic occasions and wore their own livery. This history lesson they had every year, along with the pedigree of the shawm, a venerable instrument and a fine example of wood turning, which he had been fortunate to come across in an antiquarian shop in Oxford before he took orders. "Some say that singers at Christmastide should not properly be called waits, and perhaps they are right. However, I can see no harm in perpetuating the memory of such an ancient, worthy institution in our modern usage." He had written a letter to *Punch,* explaining the difference between rowdy street musicians disturbing the peace in the small hours with menaces and gentle parishioners singing carols and collecting alms for the poor, but it hadn't been printed, through a clerical oversight. "Wassailing, on the other hand," said the vicar, "that is an entirely different matter and quite pagan in origin."

"Cold night," said George Mills. "It wants to snow."

"It doesn't smell like snow," said Jack Pierce.

The nails in their boots rang out like rifle shots. "Ground's hard as iron."

"You'd be the judge of that." The old people thought that on nights like these the spirits came out of their graves and warmed their white, picked bones by the fires. "You seen any ghosts about the forge, George?"

"I seen my father once. Plain as day. 'What you doing here?' I says to him. 'You're dead. Get back in your box.'"

"What did he say?"

"Nothing. Ghosts don't say nothing. They're just firmaments of your imagination." George rubbed his cheek. "Well, he might have said, 'Keep the fire going,' or something like that. But I can't say I really harked at him."

The East Arms was lively. They sang "Silent Night."

"Ah," said the vicar afterwards, "perhaps not the best choice. George, if you don't know the words, would you not la-la-la quite so loudly? It puts the rest of us off our stroke, as it were. Onward!"

Where the East Arms was bright and cheery, the Ploughshare was sour, dour, and all but empty. The pubs faced each other across the road like a pair of brothers who had never got on and had stopped speaking to each other.

"What do you say, vicar? 'God Rest You Merry, Gentlemen'?" said Billy.

The two drinkers at separate benches raised their heads. The landlord put down his clay pipe and frowned.

Afterwards Billy took round the hat. "A penny and two farthings. What you'd expect from the paste-pot brigade."

"Mind how you go, Jack," said the landlord, with a nod, as they went outside.

"At least we know he's got a tongue in his head," said Billy.

Six weeks ago the police had paid a visit to the Ploughshare and threatened the landlord with the loss of his license if he continued to allow his upstairs room to be used for the purposes of rabble-rousing. Jack Pierce had been one of those they'd hustled outside and roughed up a little. He'd had the printed bills down the back of his trousers at the time and would have been roughed up a little more if they had found them.

WORKERS!
UNITE TO ABOLISH PARLIAMENT!
FREEDOM FOR IRELAND!
NEITHER GOD NOR MASTER!
LAND FOR ALL!
March for Solidarity, Peace, and International Brotherhood
In Memory of Our Fallen Comrade Alfred Linnell
Sunday 24 November, 2 p.m. Assemble Forbury Gardens, Reading

A few hours after the police let him go off with his bruises, he pasted bills around the village. Nothing remained of them in the morning. The next night he pasted more up. Perseverance was what you needed, said Arthur Young. They knock you down and you get up again.

They'd knocked Alfred Linnell down at a march in London two years ago and a few days later he died from his injuries. The march had taken place a week after Bloody Sunday, when three people had been killed protesting against the government's brutalities in Ireland.

Linnell's blood, Arthur Young said, his eyes closed, swaying on his feet, was spilled for all of them. The three who had died on Bloody Sunday. The injured hundreds, women and children among them, who had been beaten by police fists and truncheons, crushed by the infantry, and trampled by the cavalry. The oppressed of all nations.

The waits went up the road in a long straggling line, the vicar, Wells, Mills, Pierce, Steadman, and Brookes, stopping at doorways, singing, and collecting alms. There was a smell of drying mortar as they passed the new school. The old school, round the side of the vicarage, had been one room, baking in summer and freezing in winter. Jack Pierce remembered Dulcie, a long plait to her waist, always shining with the answer whatever the question was. Their teacher, Miss Owen, could not keep order and they made it their business to torment her, as children will do when they smell weakness. "Don't look so pleased with yourself," his mother had said, when he told her. "You're supposed to be learning, not fooling. Mrs.

Trimble, God rest her soul, would never have stood for it." Now Dulcie's hair was pinned under a starched cap, while she crept up the back stairs at the big house.

"What do you want to stop there for?" he had said to her. "They pay you next to nothing. They make you wear a uniform as if you're in the army, and if they happen to see you taking away their chamber pots, you're supposed to pretend they don't have to relieve themselves like common people."

"I don't empty chamber pots. There're water closets at the house. Mr. Henderson put them in years ago."

"They changed your name."

At the big house Dulcie was Mary.

"That doesn't mean I forget who I am."

When Dulcie was angry, the burnished frizzes of her hair sparked and her eyes, which were no one color and many, darkened. It excited him and he imagined his fingers on the hidden white places of her body.

At the far end of the upper road was Prospect Place, where the Stainers lived. They were new to the village and widely talked about. Two years ago they had leased a pair of abandoned farm laborers' cottages from the estate, knocked them through, put in drainage, laid quarry tiles over the beaten earth, and filled the place with country furnishings they had bought in London. They had no children but many weekend visitors. At one Sunday meeting at the Ploughshare Frank Stainer had been moved to speak against the use of violence in the struggle for social justice. His wife, Agatha, had subsequently talked about the rights of women, although no women were present apart from herself, which she said proved her point. They hadn't attended since.

As soon as the waits began to sing, the door opened. "Ah, 'Masters in This Hall,'" said Mrs. Stainer. "One of our favorites. Do come in, all of you, and have a cup of punch." It was flavored with sloes gathered from Ashenden hedgerows, she said.

The punch was strong and there was a dense fruitcake to go with it. Mr. Stainer admired the shawm and was told the story of the shawm. Then he said to the vicar that he had heard the village had Roman origins.

"Indeed, yes," said the vicar.

"We have always found this part of the country to be quite uncanny," said Mrs. Stainer. "The old lore, the pagan ways. One senses it particularly by the river."

"Mmm," said the vicar, and announced they must go.

The waits emerged into the cold and walked up the dark road to the Park. Passing between the gatehouses, they came out onto a graveled drive, which crunched under their boots and bore them up a shallow incline towards the house. Bare branches scraped against each other and evergreen needles shushed and whispered. From the stable block nestled down in a hollow came the sweet odor of warm horse and the knock of hooves against stalls. Jack Pierce had meant to excuse himself and turn back before they came this far. Now he was inside the domain, there seemed to be little choice but to go onwards. The gates clanged behind them. Then the trees thinned out and suddenly there were stars.

Dick Steadman whistled as the house came into view. Great hanging lanterns framed in brass flooded the frontage with light and turned stone into gold. The house was a vast treasure chest set on a hill, an unreal thing.

"My word," said the vicar.

They went along in silence, straightening collars and cuffs, tugging at caps, wishing they had newer trousers, better boots, cleaner hands and fingernails, worrying about their manners.

Billy said, "You'd think we was going to a funeral," and got a laugh.

The butler, Mr. Williams, let them in and indicated where they should wipe their feet. A maid came out of a room midway down the long corridor and disappeared into an interior gloom. There was a faint smell of nutmeg and cooked apples. The waits wiped their feet and stood to one side by a marble pedestal, caps off.

"We're quite ready," said the vicar, fingering the shawm. "Let us know when we should begin."

The butler was balding, and amused. He had an air of the city about him, a slick veneer, and was said to have an eye for the girls. It was hard to imagine him leading the household in prayers.

"No, not here. Follow me. We have been waiting for you."

"Of course," said the vicar, clearing his throat with a little "ahem."

Now they were abashed. Now they felt like fools.

They followed the butler up a twisting flight of stairs, turned a corner, and came into a soaring space with another staircase in it. A dark fir tree glowed with colored glass and blazed with candles. Above its star the hall rose up and up. It shrank them down to ants, to specks. This wasn't a hall, as they understood a hall, or a room, as they understood a room, or a stair, as they understood a stair. It served no purpose except to be a lavish emptiness within the house. Under their feet was matting laid over carpet, on the walls were pictures, and set against the walls were carved chairs, cabinets, and side tables bearing cargoes of ornaments and bowls of fir cones. The whole household was there.

The vicar was the first to recover himself and went over to speak to the family grouped around the tree, the tall, stooping elderly man with side-whiskers, leaning on a stick, who was Mr. Henderson, the smiling elderly woman who was Mrs. Henderson, and the stout elderly woman who was Miss Henderson, the founder of both the original village school and some sort of mission in London. Flanking them was one of the married Henderson daughters and her husband, along with a grinning fellow and a pale young lady, who would be the son and his wife. A number of children ran about, liberated from bedtime.

Jack Pierce was looking for Dulcie but could not spot her among the other maidservants ranged on the stairs, neat, pert, obedient, and grateful in their black uniforms, white caps, collars, and cuffs. That was a disappointment and also a relief. He didn't want her to see him singing to a family he wouldn't work for, or deal with the nagging afterwards.

Billy leaned over and murmured in his ear, "She's not here. Mr. Williams gave her leave to sit with her uncle. He's on his last legs."

The old man had been dying for months, taking his time about it. When the bugger was dead and gone, he would dance on his grave. His eyes drifted to the tree, the pictures and ornaments. How much money was there in this one room? Thousands.

Billy edged closer. "At least that's her story."

"What do you mean?"

"She's not well. The girls say she's sick in the mornings, off her food. She fainted in the pantry last week. Mr. Williams was asking the other day whether she walked out with anyone. Your name might have come up."

A hint of alarm trickled down his back. "She's said nothing to me about it."

"Most likely she's waiting for you to make an honest woman of her. Or perhaps that's against your religion."

"What are you saying?"

"Put two and two together. Looks like there's a nipper on the way."

The vicar beckoned them. "'Angels from the Realm of Glory,'" he said, putting his lips to the shawm.

Jack Pierce opened his mouth and not a sound came out of it.

As hard as she tried, Dulcie could no longer maintain the fiction that the worst hadn't happened. Every morning she retched and all day tiredness hung like a heavy velvet curtain between her and the world. Her breasts were sore and swollen. She hadn't bled for months. It would be all right, she told herself, the child would slip away, like the two her mother had lost. A mess on the sheets and it would all be over. It wouldn't be all right, she told herself, remembering the three that tugged at her sister's skirts. She had told no one, first because that would make it true and second because of the consequences.

"Well, he's still with us," said Mrs. Jakes, as she came back upstairs. "You were a good while. Find what you were looking for?"

The old crone. "Call of nature."

Which was true, after a fashion. She couldn't do up her waist-band anymore. What was inside her was stubborn, as stubborn as Jack Pierce. He was not going to find employment, honest or otherwise, and marry her. She had been a fool to think it. He would sooner marry Arthur Young.

When her sister had fallen with her second, she had tried to get rid of it. A woman in the next village could bring it off, so they said. Failing that, you wanted to jump out of a hayloft or drink gin. Dulcie's sister had drunk the bitter tea the woman in the next village made from the rue she grew in her garden, she'd thrown herself down the stairs, and she'd made herself sick on cider. They called the baby Bertha, after her mother, and the next one was Fred.

Go away! Dulcie told the baby growing inside her. Die!

You love them once they're here, her sister had said, as careworn as a woman of forty. You wouldn't be without them.

Dulcie twisted her hands in her lap. It was only a matter of time before Mr. Williams turned her out. The other girls were already talking, whispering to each other under the bedclothes and on the back stairs. She couldn't lay another burden at her mother's doorstep.

Her father, Fred Godwin, hadn't left his bed since he had slid off their roof in a hailstorm when he had been trying to mend a hole in the thatch. They'd given him a makeshift bench to slope across his lap, an old pallet sawn in half, and when he was propped up, he could work for a while. The last time she was home, he'd been plaiting willow wands. Down on the river, they cut the withies from the willows that grew on the eyots, the midstream islands, tied them into bundles, and planted them thick end down by the water's edge to shoot. Once they had grown tall enough to harvest, the old women and children would cut the rods and strip them of their bark, whipping them through pieces of iron bent into the shape of a Jew's harp. She'd done it herself, on occasion. "People will always need baskets and chair seats, Dulcie," her father had said, reaching for another white wand. "I like to keep useful."

Before the accident her father had been a carter. The basket was poorly woven, good for nothing. "You have to humor him a little," said her mother. The cheer she tried to give their surroundings—the threadbare rag rugs, the cracked jug on the windowsill filled with holly berries—was pitiful and shaming. A sour-sweet musty odor, the smell of poverty and sickness, clung about the place. "Thank you." She pocketed the coins Dulcie handed over. "You're a good girl. That'll help. Bless you."

"What's that awful noise?" The rasping made her think of woodcutting, the saw going back and forth, catching on the bark.

"Dab his mouth with the flannel," said Mrs. Jakes. "I'd get up but my knees ain't what they were."

Dulcie moistened her great-uncle's lips. They pursed and sucked on the wetted cloth. She'd seen a newborn peck and root for a nipple like that. People were childish in death.

The wrinkled eyelids fluttered open. "What time is it?" said her uncle.

She gave a violent start and dropped the flannel. "Late."

"Who put the grass on the ceiling?"

"No one, Uncle." She stole a glance at Mrs. Jakes, who shook her head.

"I'll have him, whoever it is," said her uncle.

Then the wrinkled eyelids fluttered shut and the rasping began again. She sank back on the bed and pressed her hand to her heart, which was racing. A little later and her uncle's breathing was a dry, papery whisper.

Mrs. Jakes put her knitting to one side and yawned. "Long night. Let's hope them waits pass by and liven things up a bit. You want to step out with your Jack awhile, it's all the same to me. They do say a wedding comes after a burying."

"I told you, Mrs. Jakes, there's no wedding planned."

Most girls in her predicament would rush their fellows to the altar on the strength of it. Dulcie was damned if she'd do the same. She wouldn't spend the rest of her life yoked to her own gratitude or someone else's resentment and disappointment. She'd rather shift for herself.

That morning she had been dusting in the staircase hall when the doorbell rang. Mr. Williams was called away and left one of the cabinets open. What came next was the work of a moment and she didn't realize what she had been thinking to do until she had done it.

The cup was about five inches high and had a look of age and foreignness that suggested value. It was a curious thing. One side was modeled into the face of a youth with a straight nose, smooth brow, and curly hair; turn it over and you saw a wrinkled, balding, and bearded old man. Gold, all the same, not too big, not too small. In a flash it went into her pocket, where it knocked against her leg. Then she rearranged the contents of the cabinet, an inch to one side, an inch to the other, until there wasn't a gap.

Dulcie had never stolen anything before. Her dishonesty was the cowardly kind. There had been occasions when she had done something wrong, kept her mouth shut about it, and a brother or sister had taken the blame. Such deceptions had always lain heavy on her. This act was so reckless she could almost convince herself that someone else had done it, or that the cup had been hers all along.

She was unnecessarily dusting the mahogany sideboard in the dining room when she heard Mr. Williams come back into the staircase hall.

"Mary?"

"Yes, sir."

She stood in the doorway, her knees trembling against each other. He locked the cabinet and put the keys away.

"Leave the dusting for now. I'd like you to lay drugget over the hall carpet. We've the waits coming in tonight and I don't want dirty boots all over it. You'll find the rolls in the stores downstairs. Ask one of the footmen to help you if they're too heavy." He paused. "We don't want you fainting again."

Was she imagining the threat? "Yes, sir." She could feel the weight of the cup in her pocket.

"Off you go."

It was now or never. "I beg your pardon, sir. May I ask a favor?"

"What is it, Mary?"

"I wonder if I might sit with my great-uncle tonight. He's dying, sir, and I have been told that he will not see the morning."

"Your great-uncle was steward here."

"That's right, sir. He was. For many years."

Mr. Williams consulted some interior authority on domestic management, which he did by closing his eyes for a time. "Very well. We'll take your next half day in lieu."

She dipped her head.

"I shall expect you back first thing, in time to lay the fires."

"Thank you, sir. That's very kind of you."

The waits had sung all the carols they knew and at the end everyone in the staircase hall had joined in. Then they'd been given cups of spiced wine and it was "We Wish You a Merry Christmas" all round.

"I think that went off very well," said the vicar, whose cheeks were pink. "Yes, I should say that went off very well. I shouldn't be surprised if we weren't invited back next year."

They came out into the night and stumbled down the hill, as noisy as children released from school. The vicar's lantern bobbed ahead. It was icier going down than coming up.

Dick Steadman slid, landed on his backside, and got up cursing. "Shut your mouth, Billy. It ain't funny."

"Well, I'm one over the eight and all," said George.

Jack said he would see them tomorrow.

"Where you going?"

"He's off to see his lady love," said Billy. "Give her a kiss from me, won't you? Or whatever it is you give her."

Jack plunged down the path, a roar in his ears. A fox caught in a gin will bite off its own leg to get free. He'd seen that. Snares and nets: they came in all forms and some of them had plaits down their backs. It was the oldest trick in the book and Dulcie was the last person he thought would have played it. He couldn't be a father, or a husband. He wasn't yet himself. Somehow he had to make that clear to her.

His mother approved of Dulcie. "You need someone to keep you on the straight and narrow. The Godwins are decent people, for all their troubles."

It wasn't decent to lay a trap for a man and wait for him to walk into it. She wasn't what you'd call a beauty but he'd never seen a girl he liked better and didn't expect to, and she was cleverer than him by a long chalk. The trouble was her horizons were narrow and his were as wide as the world. Marriage was an outdated institution, Arthur Young said. "Keep your head out of the noose is my advice. I wish someone had told me that when I was your age."

The cottage was hard by the eastern boundary of the estate, near the river. There was a light at the upper window, and as he came closer, he could hear the dog howling.

"Animals know a thing or two," said Mrs. Jakes, rising from her chair, her knees restored by some miracle to full working order. "I shouldn't waste your tears. He's gone and nothing's going to bring him back."

Dulcie dried her eyes on her sleeve. She wasn't crying for her uncle. It was more the case that his death had allowed her to cry for herself.

"Open the window, my love. Then you can push along to the house if you like. One of us might as well get a decent night's rest."

Dulcie opened the window and Mrs. Jakes stood by the bed, flapping her hands like a clothesline in a strong wind. "You have to let the spirit out. I don't want spirit tricks here, and I've seen spirit tricks in my time, I can tell you."

The candle guttered. Dulcie leaned on the sill and stared into the black night.

"Set a kettle to boil before you go, if you don't mind," said Mrs.

Jakes. "A nice wash in warm water is the least we can do for the departed, I always say. Not that he'll know one way or another. Lord preserve us, what are we to do with this dog?"

Fly, who had left off howling to lick her uncle's face, jumped off the bed and went to hide underneath it. At that moment someone began to sing down below.

What cometh here from west to east awending?
And who are these, the marchers stern and slow?
We bear the message that the rich are sending
Aback to those who bade them wake and know.
Not one, not one, nor thousands must they slay,
But one and all if they would dusk the day.

"That's not a carol," said Mrs. Jakes, weighting her uncle's eyelids with pennies she produced from her pockets and which had weighted other eyelids in their time.

"No, it's not," said Dulcie. More tears fell and she rubbed them off with the back of her hand. Her throat was thick, as if someone had stitched it shut.

"I know the tune, but I can't rightly think what it is. Who's singing?"

"No idea," she lied. The singer was Jack and the song was by William Morris. She'd heard it so often she could have sung it herself.

They will not learn; they have no ears to hearken.
They turn their faces from the eyes of fate;
Their gay-lit halls shut out the skies that darken.
But, lo! this dead man knocking at the gate.
Not one, not one, nor thousands must they slay,
But one and all if they would dusk the day.

Here lies the sign that we shall break our prison;
Amidst the storm he won a prisoner's rest;
But in the cloudy dawn the sun arisen

Brings us our day of work to win the best.
Not one, not one, nor thousands must they slay,
But one and all if they would dusk the day.

Downstairs Dulcie lit the fire, set the kettle to boil, and went outside. A few paces off she could hear twigs and bracken crackle under footfalls that paced back and forth.

"What are you doing out here, Jack?" she said into the dark.

The footfalls came in her direction. "Paying you a little visit."

"I thought you were with the waits."

"I was. How's that old uncle of yours?"

"Dead." There was a pause. "And don't say you're sorry." As he came closer, she could smell his breath and the sweat and smoke on his clothing. "You've been drinking."

"Butter wouldn't melt in your mouth, would it, Dulcie?" His laugh was bitter and harsh.

She pushed him away. "Go home and sleep it off."

"What's the matter? Didn't you like the song I sang to you?"

"Not especially."

"That's a pity. I like it better than any carol. You know why, Dulcie?"

"No idea."

"There's more truth in it."

She was tired, tired of everything. "Go home, Jack. It's late."

He leaned towards her. "I'm not going anywhere until I get a few answers. Come along, Dulcie, you know all the answers. You always have. You at the front of the class and me at the back."

"What do you mean?"

"Billy told me what they're saying."

"And what's that?"

"For God's sake! What sort of fool do you take me for? Was I to be the last to know?"

She could feel the bulk of him in front of her, the rage and despair that were seeping through his skin. A pulse beat in her throat.

"I may not be quick like you, Dulcie, but even I can spot a trap when it's lying there right in front of my feet ready to step into. Is it true? Or are you trying to shame me into marrying you?"

"Wouldn't dream of it." She picked up her skirts and swept past him. "Not in a thousand years."

"Where are you going?"

"Back to the house. While I've still got a position. Which, to be honest, won't be for much longer." The lantern shone her way ahead, a narrow path of light.

He caught up with her and they walked through the woods in a seething silence, side by side and utterly apart. The lantern light glanced off tree roots. A fox barked, a strange unearthly sound, inhuman and barely animal.

"What will you do?" he said, and it seemed to her that his voice was the coldest thing in the cold, dark world.

For a long time she didn't answer. She smelled the pines in the woods and the soot from the railway and knew she would never be happy again. The years stretched ahead, all of them hard and painful.

"I stole a cup from the house today. Mr. Williams was called to the door and left a cabinet open. It's old and gold. I reckon it'll fetch enough for me to live on for a while. I'm certain it's valuable."

He tugged at her arm and swung her round. "You did what?"

"You heard me. I stole a gold cup from the house."

"Have you taken leave of your senses?"

"Property is theft. Isn't that what you always say?"

"Oh, God." He was breathing hard, as if he had been running. "That's—that's just a way of looking at things. Christ. They catch you, you'll go to jail." There was fear in his voice and something else that she didn't recognize.

"Then I'll have to be careful."

"Where's the cup now, Dulcie? Where did you put it?"

"Somewhere safe."

"Where is it?"

"You don't need to know."

"Where is it?"

"In a biscuit tin back at the cottage. Now let me go, if you don't mind."

"No."

"Please." She stumbled. "Lord, I'm so tired. I could sleep for a year."

He blocked her way. "Listen to me. You shouldn't have stolen the cup. You must put it back straightaway."

"Let me go."

"No!"

She beat a fist against his chest. "What am I supposed to do? Go home and tell my mother she's got another two mouths to feed and less to do it on? Walk the streets? Drown myself? Believe me, I've considered all of them. You didn't come out here to sing a song, you came to tell me you can't be a husband, you can't be a father, because there is a road you haven't gone down yet and you mean to see where that will take you. And I'm saying that I won't stop you from going down any road you please." She was crying now. "I'll have to make the best of it, won't I, because I don't have a choice in the matter. I don't have a choice in the matter! Not like you."

"Dulcie!" He took her face in his hands. "Listen. No, listen. Stop crying. Go back to the cottage and get the cup."

"Can't do that."

"Go get the cup and take it back to the house."

"Can't do that. They search our boxes."

"Then give it to me, I'll take it out of the Park, and we'll think how to put it back later. You don't want to leave it in the cottage. They'll find it, and when they do, they'll know who took it."

"What do you care?"

She was crying harder now, great wrenching gusts of sobs that bent her in two, and he was reaching down to her and saying, "Oh, Dulcie, Dulcie, please stop crying, please, please. I promise I'll never leave you, I promise I'll look after you, we'll work it out somehow, we will."

By the time they reached the cottage, she was calmer. The dog began to bark. He agreed that it would be best if she fetched the cup herself, and then he settled to wait outside, as he had so often waited for her while she tended to her uncle.

Now the old man was dead and it was no cause for celebration. Some people said that Mr. Hastings had savings, and on the way back, he'd asked her about that. She said no, there wasn't any money, she was certain.

His mind couldn't grapple with what had happened. It was hard to believe any of it. A couple of hours ago he'd been singing and drinking, and here he was almost a husband and a father and the handler of stolen property. A couple of hours between one kind of life and another, between one kind of future and another: he looked back over that short time and it was as if he were an old man remembering the days of his youth and mourning them.

The dog stopped barking. He was beginning to worry that she had slipped out the back somewhere or, worse, that she had been caught, when she appeared, took his arm, and led him quickly up the path.

"What took you so long?"

"Mrs. Jakes wanted to know why I came back. I had to make something up."

When they were in the woods, she showed him the cup, holding the lantern so he could see it properly.

"That's it, is it?"

"It's gold."

"I can see that."

He held it in his hands, turning it round, feeling the modeling of the faces on the front and the back, tracing the curves and indentations with his fingers. For a clever girl, she could be very stupid. No question about it, the cup was valuable, but it had stolen written all over it. It wasn't a half dozen silver teaspoons that could be anyone's, no questions asked; it wasn't even a plain gold cup. He doubted if any fence or pawnbroker for miles around would touch it with a bargepole. The only way she'd make any money out of it was if George melted it down into a featureless little lump in his forge and she flogged it for its weight.

"How on earth did you think you were going to get rid of this?"

"I was going to ask Arthur Young," said Dulcie. "I expect someone like him knows how it's done."

Arthur Young?

He started to laugh and then he couldn't stop. It was as if someone had turned a key and everything that had been pent up inside him was falling over itself in the rush to come out.

"What's so funny?"

"Nothing." He caught his breath and rubbed his eyes.

Arthur Young had never broken a law in his life. He'd never so much as scrumped an apple or hopped on a tram without paying the fare. The youngest Young was ailing and needed the doctor, so that week Jack had borrowed half a crown from the landlord of the Ploughshare and paid his back subscriptions in a comradely way. That was all the money he didn't have in the world.

"Perhaps I should return the cup myself," said Dulcie. "No one's missed it yet."

He shook his head. "They will, and when they do, they're bound to suspect someone from the house. Give it to me and I'll think of something." What he was thinking was that first thing in the morning he would pack up the cup in brown paper and post the damn thing.

"You want to watch out for the gatekeeper."

"I'm not going out the gate."

There were ways in and out of the Park, and what he had in mind was a lowish stretch of wall that dropped you down in a lane by the river. He put the cup in his pocket and kissed her. Kissing was different when you were kissing the mother of your child, so much sweeter and somehow so much sadder.

All the Pierces could find their way in the dark. The stretch of wall was where he thought it would be, and it was a good deal lower than it had been when he was nine and had first tackled it. The footholds were in the familiar places, and he was up and over the top.

On the other side they were waiting for him.

"Stop weeping," said Mr. Williams the next morning. "Have you packed your box?"

Dulcie nodded. Her eyes were almost swollen shut and her heart was a twisted lump in her chest.

"Where's your uniform?"

"Upstairs." The white apron and cap, the cuffs and collar, the black bodice and skirt were lying on her narrow bed like the skin of another life. She twisted her handkerchief in her fingers.

"What on earth were you thinking? The Janus Cup is the most valuable treasure in the entire house. It's *Roman*." He seemed to be suggesting that she should have taken something different, something less rare and conspicuous, but that could not be so. "The family have been very shaken by the news, although naturally relieved at the outcome."

"What did you tell them?" she said in a dull voice. She, unlike Jack, had always liked the family and hated the thought that they would think badly of her.

"I told them I discovered the theft after the waits left last night, which is true. I told them that Pierce had the cup in his possession when he was caught, which is true. What I didn't tell them was that he had an accomplice."

Fresh tears fell. "Jack wasn't my accomplice. He didn't know I'd stolen it. He said it was wrong. He was going to put it back."

"Maybe he would have and maybe he wouldn't."

"I don't understand." Her lips were dry and cracked with salt. "How did you know he'd have it?"

"I didn't," said Mr. Williams. "The person I was expecting to catch was you."

She caught her breath and raised her eyes. "You left the cabinet open. I don't suppose you told them that."

"Don't think about going to them with such a story. Or to the police," said Mr. Williams. "It won't make any difference to Pierce. And no good will be served by both of you going to prison. Or the three of you, I should say."

"What do you mean?"

"You are fortunate that the Hendersons are charitable people. Miss Henderson, Miss Rowena, was particularly concerned to hear about your condition and wishes to help, which is frankly more than you deserve."

"You are protecting your position," said Dulcie, as the truth of it dawned on her.

He folded his hands. "You should also know that Pierce has confessed to the crime, which may lighten his sentence."

Jack Pierce was sentenced to eighteen months' hard labor and imprisoned in Reading Gaol, where he had been held on remand since he was arrested. Twelve months, or even six, would have been the expected sentence for a first offense where the property had been recovered, particularly when the accused had pleaded guilty, but the judge was of the opinion that the high value and rarity of the cup, together with the high standing of its owners (with whom he had had the pleasure to dine, although he did not mention this in his judgment), amply justified a longer term.

The week before the trial, Dulcie went to see Jack. She had written him many tearstained letters, begging him to take back his confession, and had had no replies. The vicar drove her to the jail in his little trap, but she would have walked the frozen miles had no other form of conveyance been available.

The visiting room was partitioned into three small separate compartments by iron bars. Jack sat on the far side, Dulcie by the door, and in the middle was a jailer to ensure that nothing, other than words, passed between them.

They were allowed twenty minutes. Hard as it was to speak in the presence of the guard, Dulcie said what she had come to say: that Jack should tell the truth, that he should take back his confession, that he should not sacrifice himself for her. If she had imagined or feared that the jailer, overhearing their conversation, would have her arrested and detained in his place, she was mistaken. Instead, the guard, a huge solid man, sat mute and impassive on the prison bench, his fleshy hands hanging down like sides of ham.

Jack was still wearing the clothes in which he had been arrested. He looked gray and beaten, and she was distressed by how much he already seemed to be part of this awful place, with its thick walls and clanging gates, its heavy, oppressive air and stenches.

He said very little, other than to refuse what she asked. "Have you told anyone what happened?" He glanced at the jailer.

"Just my mother. Williams knows, of course. He worked it out, as I wrote you."

"Then tell no one else."

At the end of the twenty minutes, she got up to go, tears welling in her eyes. "I'll come next week before the trial. The vicar said he would bring me again."

"Don't," said Jack, looking at her directly for the first time. "It makes it harder."

When she next saw him, he was three months into his sentence. Before a trial you could visit a prisoner every day; after a conviction it was every three months. She was showing now, her skirt belled out in front of her. The change in him, however, was shocking.

Partly it was the rough prison uniform, bright yellow down one side and purple-brown down the other. There was some sort of awful hat, too, which he was allowed to take off in the visiting room, but which had a long flat peak that hung over his face. (The vicar had explained to her that the prisoners were not allowed to communicate with one another and the hats were designed to discourage this.) The worst was his dull, dead eyes, and his fingers, the nails torn and bleeding.

"Oh!" she cried out before she could stop herself. "Whatever have you done to your hands?"

Jack looked at his hands as if they didn't belong to him. "Picking oakum," he said.

"What's oakum?"

He considered the question for a time. "They give us old tarred rope and we've to shred it."

"But that's harsh," she said.

Another pause. "Better than stone breaking."

He asked how she was, and when she told him that she had been getting by on a little sewing work sent down from the Park, that her mother had been kind, and many in the village, too, and that every-one wished him well (she omitted to say that Billy Wells had asked her to marry him), she could see that his concentration was waning. They fell into a silence.

"Time's up, C forty-two." The jailer, a different jailer, pointed at the clock.

"I'm sorry," Jack said to Dulcie. "My mind wanders these days. I'm not used to speech."

"It won't be long," she said. "It won't be long until the baby is born. Then I can find proper work, and when you're released . . ."

He put up a hand to stop her words. Then he smiled. It was a lovely smile, full of the old Jack, and she folded it away in her heart for safekeeping.

The baby was born in early May. For months, she had resented the child growing inside her and heaped on its unborn head all the causes of her misfortune: her stealing the cup, Jack's arrest and im-prisonment, the loss of her position. Yet the instant the child was laid in her arms and began to suckle, she fell in love. She called the boy Peter.

Her confinement meant that she had missed the next occasion on which Jack would have been permitted a visit. She wrote to him and told him that he had a fine son and whispered in the baby's ear that soon he would meet his father, his brave, stubborn father.

A week before the date of the visit, she was changing the baby's napkin, marveling at his little fat legs kicking in the air and the wisps of hair that curled on his head, when her mother brought a letter for her.

It was from Jack and it was written in pencil on rough prison paper. It read:

Dear Dulcie
Theyve told me youve asked to visit nxt Weds and Ive said that
I wont see you. Its fore the best. Well Im halfway thro my Term
and when I come out Ive been thinking to go away and make a
start Somplace else. Billy Writ me a letter and the long and short

is he wants to marry you. I shld say its a good Offer and with my
blessing take it shld you wish. Youve been true Dulcie none better
and you deserve the best.

Yr loving frend Jack Pierce.

She didn't hear from him or see him again, although she learned from his mother that after his release he sailed for Canada. And, one day, listening to the voices of her children, watching blossom blow down a dirty Reading street in between the tramlines, she did find herself happy again.

7

The Boating Party: 1909

Every farm for miles around now belongs to the estate. Land makes money, as it always does, and the greater the number of acres, the larger the income. New cottages, almshouses, and a pumping station have been paid for out of its earnings. But there are other uses for revenue and that is to fund tastes acquired in more exotic locations, in casinos, for example, and the grand hotels that face the sea on sunny esplanades, or to maintain discreet furnished apartments in the better districts of European capitals.

Jimmy Henderson was so rarely at Ashenden these days that he had forgotten how agreeable it could be, in its own staid and old-fashioned way. He preferred life to be more vivid, on the whole, and since his parents' deaths he had spent most of his time on the Continent, for Jimmy was of the opinion that there was no need to endure gray skies and rain when sunshine was reliably on offer. Weather, of course, was not the sole attraction of foreign climes. If other temptations—horse racing, cards, certain liaisons and entanglements—had led to his divorce three years ago, he could not say he particularly regretted succumbing to them, merely the money they had cost. Divorce was shockingly expensive.

That day of reckoning, which was continuing to drain his pockets long after the lawyers had finished their business—schooling for the child, a London town house for his erstwhile wife, Matilda, didn't come cheap—was the principal reason for his visit to the estate and the weekend party he had assembled here. Jimmy had plans. These centered on one of his guests, Mrs. Carrington, even if she was not as yet fully aware of them. He was conscious of time ticking past; a recent communication from the Banque de Paris had rather focused his mind.

Saturday morning, Jimmy had risen early and was nursing a thick head with the aid of sweet black coffee. It had been a cool, wet summer and he was glad of the fire that was burning in the drawing room, where breakfast was laid out on a sideboard. The previous evening had gone well, he thought. Much laughter, much gaiety around the piano, significant glances by the score, and the warmest good-night kiss at the end of it all. In fact, everything had gone so swimmingly, he had been rather disappointed to hear no patter of feet making their way to his bedroom door in the middle of the night. Still, all boded well for today's diversion, a little boating trip he had organized. Nothing like a river trip for dalliance: there was a spot he knew, shaded by willows, that would be just the ticket.

Half an hour later, most of his guests had come downstairs and were helping themselves to kedgeree, sausages, eggs, and kippers. They were rather an odd party, he had to admit. To encourage Mrs. Carrington to accept his invitation for the weekend, he had cordially extended it to her own houseguests, Maus and Helga von Stamm, nieces of her late husband, who were spending the summer with her. He had thrown in the lure of Bradshaw, the American essayist and playwright, who was a particular favorite of hers and no rival to him, or any other warm-blooded male. At her suggestion, he had also invited Paul Lyell, her godson, and his Oxford friend, Max Koenig, neither of whom he had met.

The Germans girls, Maus and Helga, had gone to bed early the previous night before he had formed much of an impression of them. In the light of day Helga, with her crown of dun-colored plaits, revealed herself to be a rather stolid fräulein. As for Maus, who gave the impression that she might run up your trouser leg and nip you, he could well see where the nickname originated. They were apparently over here to perfect their English, although there was nothing wrong with it except that it was too perfect, as the English of foreigners tended to be.

"Good morning," said Bradshaw, coming into the room impeccably dressed in a blazer and flannels.

Americans, in Jimmy's experience, failed to understand that what you wore in the country ought to look as if it had been worn in the country on at least one previous occasion. He himself was wearing a favorite old cream linen suit, with frayed cuffs, baggy knees, and strained buttons.

"Sleep well, I trust?" said Jimmy.

"Wonderfully, thank you."

Bradshaw approached the sideboard, where Paul Lyell was already returning for a second helping. They began to resume a conversation they had been having the previous evening about *Parsifal*.

Not a sporting type, Paul Lyell, thought Jimmy, who held sporting types and the schools that produced them in the highest regard. From what he had gathered the previous evening in conversation with Mrs. Carrington, the boy had upset his father, who was a wealthy industrialist, by insisting on a medical career and was now midway through his clinical training at the Radcliffe Infirmary. "I think that is rather noble of him," Mrs. Carrington had said. "It takes courage to turn your back on what is mapped out for you and make your own way in life." Paul Lyell didn't strike Jimmy as courageous. Privately, he could no more imagine the boy in an operating theater than on a battlefield.

The dark horse of the gathering was Max Koenig, a small, neat man in his early twenties, with sharp black eyes, a prominent nose, and a closely trimmed beard. Quite a typical specimen of his race. Koenig described himself as a "mathematician," which struck Jimmy as neither a profession nor a hobby but rather a boast.

All in all he was relieved when Mrs. Carrington, the last one down, made her eventual appearance. What she was wearing had a jaunty, nautical look, and as she paused a moment in the doorway, something mocking in her expression acknowledged the theatricality of her choice.

Letitia Carrington had been a great beauty in her day and was still handsome at forty. As Letty Lee, she had been making a name in the halls when Gerald Carrington, an armaments manufacturer many years older than she was, had persuaded her to marry him, having seen her act dozens of times and presenting a bouquet at the stage door on each occasion, some of which were said to have had diamond bracelets and emerald earrings concealed among their foliage and blooms. Gold digging on her part, most people had assumed, but Jimmy, who had seen the couple together at Biarritz on a number of occasions, thought they had seemed genuinely fond of each other. Not a trace of Letty Lee now remained, not in accent, vocabulary, or bearing, and he thought that admirable. She and her husband had had no children and she was now very rich.

"How dashing you look, Letitia," said Jimmy, rising to his feet. It was no more than the truth, but he would have said it anyway.

"You are too kind," Mrs. Carrington said. "In view of our excursion today, I thought I'd dress accordingly."

Bradshaw looked up from his newspaper and smiled. In his experience, few actresses could resist the opportunity to play to an audience, whether they were still on the stage or not. He wondered whether anyone now remembered the costume Mrs. Carrington had worn back in the days when she was performing, the skimpy white robes, the goose-feather wings that sprang from angular shoulder blades that were like wings in themselves. (Bradshaw had arrived in England long after those celebrated appearances but had turned up a picture postcard of "Miss Letty Lee, the Cockney Seraph" on a barrow in Farringdon Market on a wet March morning soon after he had met her. Although the postcard was over ten years old, he had been mildly shocked at its casual indecency.)

"What is the excursion?" said Koenig.

"We are going on the river," said Mrs. Carrington, who was heartily looking forward to it. She had been somewhat disappointed the previous night when no footsteps made their way to her door. Jimmy was highly amusing and she missed male company.

"I thought we'd motor down to Caversham late morning and make our way back at our leisure," Jimmy said to her.

Mrs. Carrington buttered a slice of toast. "That sounds like a charming day out."

"Yes," said Koenig, gazing round at the table. "A river trip would be most pleasant."

The Germans girls agreed, with great enthusiasm.

"Oh, I am sorry," said Jimmy. "But I have made arrangements at the boatyard only for myself and Mrs. Carrington. Quite a small boat, you see. I thought the rest of you might enjoy exploring the grounds while we're gone. Plenty to do."

"But surely we could hire another boat?" said Koenig.

"There may not be another boat," said Jimmy.

"Ha," said Koenig. "That is funny. There is bound to be another boat at a boatyard."

Across the table, Mrs. Carrington caught Jimmy's eye and smiled ruefully. "Shall I see Cook about the picnic?" she said. "We'll need more food."

This assumption of a wifely duty pleased Jimmy sufficiently to give him hope that the outing might still turn out well.

The boatyard occupied a quiet inlet downstream of the lock at the end of a muddy lane. Flat-bottomed punts, skiffs, outrigger canoes, and pleasure craft in varying states of repair and riverworthiness were tied up to mossy landing stages, bobbing at their moorings in water the color of strong tea. Seas, thought Jimmy, smelled mineral, rivers vegetable. From somewhere came the sound of banging, the hard metallic ring of hammer against nail. As he neared the yard, striding out in advance of the others, a man in oil-stained clothing clutching a tin mug emerged from the long, low shed that crouched on the bank.

"Hello there," said Jimmy. "I've a booking. May I speak with the proprietor?"

The man took his time to approach. "That'll be me, sir." He pointed to a small slipper launch. "And that'll be yours. Just the two of you, if I remember rightly."

"I'm afraid there's been a slight change of plan," said Jimmy, as the others came down the lane. "There seem to be seven of us now. We're going to need another boat."

"That won't be a problem," said the proprietor.

"Are you certain?" said Jimmy, his heart sinking. He'd hoped there would be a problem.

"It hasn't been the best summer for hirings, to be honest." A youth of about eighteen or so came out of the shed. "Peter!" shouted the proprietor, waving. "Is *Mirabelle* ashed out?"

"Done her last week." The boy approached. He was barefoot and had hair like fine coils of spun metal.

"Good lad. Come with me, sir."

The proprietor walked Jimmy round to a launch moored at the far end. Made of varnished teak with a canvas awning raised like a flat lid over the middle seats, it had "Mirabelle" painted on the stern in gold letters outlined in black.

"She'll take twelve, with room to spare." The proprietor was gazing at *Mirabelle* as if he might marry her one day. "Almost brand-new. Two-foot draft, so you'll glide through the shallows. Bellis and Co. compound condensing engine and they don't come finer. Birmingham-made."

"I had rather been thinking of *two* boats," said Jimmy.

"Two boats?" said the proprietor. "But you'll all fit in this one."

"So we will," said Koenig, who had come up to join them. "Won't we, Mrs. Carrington?"

All of them were there now. Mrs. Carrington shrugged and gave Jimmy another rueful smile. Koenig, who was carrying one of the hampers, got into the boat. Paul Lyell, who was carrying the other, followed him. They settled themselves in the stern.

"You'll need a skipper for the day," the proprietor was saying. "These engines have a lot of power to them. We don't go in for drowning parties at this boatyard, sir. Not like some I could mention. Peter?"

"Right you are, Mr. Benn," said Peter, stepping on deck.

Anyone else while we're at it? thought Jimmy. Uncle Tom Cobbleigh and all?

The proprietor turned to Jimmy. "Don't be fooled by his age. There's nothing Peter Wells doesn't know about engines. Or about this river, come to that."

"Upstream or downstream, sir?" said the boy, uncoiling the rope.

"I was planning to picnic at Maple Durham," said Jimmy, thinking regretfully of the willow-shaded bank and the crowd that would now shelter there.

"Upstream, then."

"Never mind," said Mrs. Carrington to Jimmy as they puttered out of the inlet. At least they were sitting next to each other, although that had been touch and go for a while. She patted his sleeve. "We'll have a lovely day and then there's always the evening to look forward to." And the night, she thought, resolving to make better use of it this time.

And the night, thought Jimmy, shifting his leg closer to her skirts and feeling what he was certain was an answering pressure in return. Across the boat, Bradshaw was chatting to the German girls, and Jimmy took the opportunity to launch into a steady stream of flattery, beginning with the daintiness of Mrs. Carrington's feet and proceeding upwards. He had to admit, it all went down very well.

After Caversham Lock they passed a walled enclosure for bathers, beyond which loomed the tall chimneys of big brick factories, hedged by a monotonous pattern of low terraced streets blackened by soot. A couple of boys on the broad towpath halfheartedly threw stones in their direction, which plopped in the water some yards shy of their intended target.

"What is this town?" said Koenig.

"Reading," Jimmy said, raising his voice over the turn of the screw. "I'm afraid the river is rather dismal around here. It improves past the next bridge, I'm happy to say."

"I have heard of Reading Gaol," said Maus. "Oscar Wilde was imprisoned there."

"He was," said Bradshaw.

Mrs. Carrington, whose eyes had just been compared to heavenly stars—"so pellucid!"—favored Jimmy with a lingering glance from them. She hadn't felt so happy, so cherished, since her husband died.

Above Caversham Bridge, a sturdy structure of iron girders and pillars, the water was broad and deep, free of weeds. A trim modern boathouse perched on the Oxfordshire bank, surrounded by an old, well-established garden with rose pergolas and shaded walkways which rose to high ground planted by firs. As they skirted an eyot, the river now running strong and fast, a train sped past close to the bank, then dived down into a deep cutting, out of sight but not out of hearing.

Things were progressing very nicely, thought Jimmy, who allowed himself a little daydream of a future life in which he was married to the grateful Mrs. Carrington (she was over forty, after all, the age when women ought to be grateful for any attention), he had her money to spend, and there was a little popsy tucked away somewhere.

"What is that, Jimmy?" said Mrs. Carrington, pointing at a clumsy-looking vessel moored on the far bank. "Is it a dredger?"

"It's a horse boat. The towpath changes sides round here and they need to ferry them across for the barges."

"Why does the towpath change sides?" said Koenig.

"Because the people who own these stretches of riverbank can't agree over the rights of way. They're always falling out."

"Falling out?" said Koenig. "You mean falling in."

"No," said Jimmy, with one of his sudden laughs. "Falling in is what you would do if someone pushed you overboard." Which was not a bad idea.

A bend in the river took them away from the railway line. Then farther along they came into a tranquil reach overhung by a whispering, shushing green vault of spreading branches. Wood pigeons cooed and small insects flew at their mouths. Beneath the clear water, where ducks paddled, weeds furled and unfurled like streamers as the launch puttered through.

The German girls trailed their hands in the water.

"Ah," said Mrs. Carrington, turning her veiled face into the breeze. "How glorious."

"What a marvelous figurehead you'd make, Letitia," said Jimmy. "You've the profile of the Venus de Milo. I've always thought so."

Mrs. Carrington laughed and struck a pose.

"Yes, yes," he said. "I can see you now at the prow of a ship."

"The *Hesperus,* I daresay."

"Oh, my dear, no. The *Golden Hind,* or Nelson's *Victory* at the very least."

Bradshaw, who was by nature, profession, and inclination an observer, a listener, half closed his eyes. At breakfast he had thought Mrs. Carrington was playing a part; now he was not so sure. He was very fond of her, and since the death of her husband she was lonely, he knew. Overhearing her and Jimmy Henderson batting gallantries to and fro reminded him of the disquiet he had felt the previous evening. While the champagne had flowed, along with their host's flattering, solicitous attentions, he had noticed Mrs. Carrington looking around at the house as if she were measuring for curtains. Ashenden, as neglected as it was, represented a step up from the more modest Queen Anne house in Harcourt St. Mary her husband had left her, and if there was one thing Mrs. Carrington knew how to do, it was to climb ladders. In other circumstances, he might have wished her good luck with it, but he could not shake off the sense that under the bonhomie there was something cold and calculating about their host, something, in fact, a little malignant.

Jimmy was apologizing for the weather. "Of course, if it were a better day, one would have to put up with ghastly shrieking hordes grappling with boathooks. In fact, I don't know what's worse, mindless pleasure seekers or those oarsmen who look down their noses at motor launches."

The water mill at Maple Durham came into view.

"Shall we stop here, sir?" said Peter.

"Anywhere you please," said Jimmy, waving a hand.

The boy cut their speed, steered the launch to the bank away from the tumult of the weir pool, and looped the painter round the trunk of a willow alongside a sign that said "No Mooring." As soon as he did, there was a patter on the canvas awning, and then the heavens opened and it began to rain in earnest, fat drops pocking the brown river, water splashing into water.

A shout and Paul Lyell and Koenig made a dash for cover. The fact that the awning did not extend over all the seats meant that there was a certain amount of confused scrambling and squashing up, like a game of musical chairs, which left Jimmy separated from Mrs. Carrington by Helga, and Koenig sitting at the center of the party next to Maus.

Koenig shook the rain off his hat. "Ha!" he said, after a moment. "That is so English. 'No Mooring.'" He pointed at the riverbank. "And those others. 'Keep Off.' 'Private.' 'No Fishing.' I am surprised we are permitted to look at the trees."

Lyell, who had squeezed alongside Bradshaw, twisted his head round to speak to Mrs. Carrington. "Max has paid out a fortune in fines to the college. He will keep walking on the grass in the quad."

"Why not?" said Koenig. "In Germany, we are free to wander wherever we please. On Sundays, everyone walks. *Im Wald und auf der Heide, da such ich meine Freude.*"

"I find my joy in the woods and on the heath," Helga translated helpfully.

"You'll find that in England," said Jimmy, unhappy to be usurped, "we respect property rights. I shouldn't want anyone tramping about *my* woods without a by-your-leave."

Over lunch, Jimmy found Koenig even more irksome, if that were possible. They had barely made a start on the contents of the hampers—bread rolls, potted shrimp, foie gras, pressed tongue, quail's eggs, strawberry and lemon tartlets, Stilton, oatcakes, ginger beer, and several bottles of excellent hock—when the mathematician began to hold forth about Göttingen, where he had studied for his first degree, and about his tutor there, Professor Hilbert, someone of great importance of whom none of them had ever heard.

Twenty interminable minutes later, Helga whispered in Mrs. Carrington's ear, a deep blush rising from her neck to her cheeks. They murmured together, then rose and stepped across the launch, the boat rocking lightly under their feet.

"If you wouldn't mind handing us out, Jimmy," said Mrs. Carrington, "now that it's stopped raining, we'd like to take a little walk."

Jimmy, thinking of the opportunity this presented for a little tête-à-tête, said he would come with them. Mrs. Carrington gave him a meaningful look, whose meaning escaped him, and said that would not be necessary. "We won't be long." They headed down a path into the bushes.

Later, Jimmy would understand why Mrs. Carrington had shepherded Helga to the bank and into the undergrowth and realize that he could have avoided their embarrassment by instructing the boy to take them on to Pangbourne for the picnic, where they could have moored near inns and other conveniences. Yet it was not the most significant failure of the afternoon. That was to follow, and he was never to comprehend it fully.

When Mrs. Carrington and Helga came back to the launch, Jimmy had hopes that the conversation might take a more frivolous turn. It didn't. He had always understood that mathematics spoke only to those who were reluctant to communicate its mysteries to anyone else. It seemed he was wrong.

"I don't understand how numbers can go on forever," Maus was saying. "It does not make sense. Everything has a beginning and an end."

"Ah, well, to imagine infinity," said Koenig, his eyes fastening on Maus like a pair of black boot buttons, "you must imagine a grand hotel."

"There is a grand hotel in Baden," said Helga. "It is called Brenners and it's on Schillerstrasse. We spent a fortnight there once."

"It was very boring in Baden," said Maus.

"Oh, I do agree," said Jimmy. "Baden is lethally dull."

"Never mind," said Koenig. "Brenners will do for our grand hotel. Napoleon and Queen Victoria have stayed there, which means it must be very grand. So, it is the summer season and this grand hotel in Baden is full. All the rooms are occupied. Yet here comes a visitor to inquire at the reception desk. *Ping.* This visitor, Herr Braun, rings the bell and asks for a room. He has come for the treatments and perhaps a little gambling to while away the time between the treatments." Helga leaned forward, her mouth open. "'So sorry to disappoint, mein Herr,' says the clerk on the desk, 'but the hotel is fully occupied. There are no rooms available until next Tuesday.' 'But I must have a room!' says Herr Braun. 'I have come all the way from Berlin!' The hotel clerk scratches his head."

Koenig paused and scratched his head. Theatrical in the extreme, thought Jimmy.

"'Ach,' says the clerk"—Koenig raised his hands—"'but there is something we might do. We can move Herr and Frau Klein from room one to room two, and Herr and Frau Buchwald from room two to room three, and the Frankel sisters from room three to room four.' And so on. *Und so weiter.* And because this grand hotel in Baden is a hotel with an infinite number of rooms, our visitor, Herr Braun, moves into room one and everyone is happy, although naturally a little inconvenienced with the packing and unpacking. Although not too inconvenienced, because at a grand hotel there are many maids and porters to take care of such things. The paradox, which is Hilbert's paradox, is that the grand hotel is always fully occupied but always has room for one more guest. That is infinity."

"Bravo!" said Mrs. Carrington.

There was an intense look of concentration on Maus's face, then a swift dawning of understanding, like light moving across water.

Koenig nodded. "You see it, don't you?"

"I did. For a moment." Maus flushed, her eyes shining.

"Well, I think it's all utterly fanciful," said Jimmy.

"Of course it is fanciful," said Koenig, "that is the point. To explain such concepts one needs to be fanciful. Hilbert had a student once who quit his class to study poetry. 'Good,' said Hilbert. 'He did not have enough imagination to become a mathematician.'"

It was the laughter that followed that did it, or possibly the four glasses of hock that Jimmy had drunk by that time. In any event, he found himself dominating the conversation at last, which he did by embarking on an uninterruptible Cook's tour of places he had found most noteworthy abroad. Menton, Le Touquet, Lake Como. "Now, Sintra is a most pleasant place. I wintered there last year. Have you ever been to Sintra, Letitia?"

"No, but we went to Lisbon once."

"Yes, Sintra," he said. "I should love to show it to you. An enviable situation and quite a mild climate, considering. And, of course, one doesn't get so many Jews, which is a distinct advantage."

"Jews?" said Paul Lyell.

"Oh, they've quite overrun Biarritz. You know what a nuisance they are." He flapped a hand. "All money with them and endless vulgarity. On the Continent, there's scarcely a bank they don't own. We shall all dance to their tune ere long, mark my words."

And here the boating party fragmented, like shattered glass, thought Bradshaw, whose ear was attuned to such things. Koenig colored, and the German girls shrank into themselves with an emotion that was impossible to read. Mrs. Carrington turned her head and stared into the distance from under the brim of her hat.

"That's a foul point of view," said Paul Lyell. "And a remarkably ill-informed one."

"Don't trouble yourself," said Koenig, muttering to his friend.

"What did I say?" said Jimmy.

"You were most rude," said Paul Lyell in an even, dispassionate tone that conveyed more disgust than rage would have done. You could see how he might have stood up to his father in the matter of the medical training.

"Don't," said Koenig.

Jimmy, sufficiently drunk to be pleased with himself, smiled at Koenig. "Oh, present company excepted, of course."

*   *   *

They were all quiet on the way back. Unspoken conversations charged the heavy air.

Whitchurch, Pangbourne. Under the circumstances, it was as well that the business of the locks served as a lengthy and regular distraction. Gates opened, gates closed. Lockkeepers: stern or cheery. Small dogs running along the towpath, barking. Red flowers in window boxes. Rushing weirs, gliding swans, fierce geese, scuttling coots and moorhens.

At Ashenden they moored at a splintery landing stage.

"Aren't you coming, Letitia?" said Jimmy to Mrs. Carrington, as the others scrambled onto the bank.

She turned and gave him a cold look he would be in no danger of misinterpreting. "I'll be along shortly."

Bradshaw, who was just about to set off down a path bordered by the creamy froth of meadowsweet, noted this exchange with relief.

Water lapped the side of the boat, a soothing, repetitive sound. Mrs. Carrington took off her hat and breathed in the green smell of the river. "Oh, Jimmy was always spoiled," she remembered her husband telling her, "coming so late after those girls. He hasn't a single bone of responsibility in his entire body." Responsibility, she thought, was not all Jimmy Henderson lacked. She shivered.

The boy left off fiddling with the engine and asked if she was cold, whether she would like a rug from one of the lockers? His coppery hair was alive with light, and she noticed how well made he was, how assured and competent. There were smuts on his face, streaks of ash, and she wanted to wet her handkerchief and wipe them off.

"No, thank you, Peter. I'm all right."

Mallards came up to the side of the launch and made a nuisance of themselves. She found a roll in one of the hampers and fed it to them. Something about tearing the bread into crumbs and throwing it in the water, watching the ducks make their absurd fuss, lightened her mood a little.

"How long have you been working at the boatyard?" she said to the boy, who was leaning on the brass rail, staring over the water.

"A few years."

"You must know the river well."

"I should do," he said, with a wry smile. "Never been anywhere else."

A drake, with his bright green head, was darting about, scooping up the bread, while the females were circling and quacking near the bank.

"Look at him," she said. "You'd think he'd give the ladies a chance."

"Not likely," he said.

To delay the moment when she would have to return, she asked him if his father was on the river too.

He shook his head. "I never knew him."

"I am sorry."

He shrugged. "You can't miss what you haven't had. My stepfather works at the biscuit factory and so does my mother. They used to be in service here"—he nodded at the riverbank—"up at the big house."

"Here? At Ashenden?"

He nodded again. "My stepfather was an undergardener and my mother was a maid before she had me. Factory's better, they say."

"My mother was in service. It's a hard life."

He was surprised.

"You're wondering how I got so posh." Moving her vowels from east to west, from poor to rich, hadn't been hard: she'd always been a good mimic, a quick study. Learning the rules, the rites, the codes, however, had been the work of years. "Well, this is what I used to sound like." She cleared her throat, widened her mouth, and pointed to a cob grazing by the riverbank. "Dat bleedin' 'orse ain't worf 'arf a crahn if you arsk me."

He laughed. "How do you do that?"

She was tempted to reply in his soft country burr but thought better of it. "I was on the stage before I married. You get an ear for these things." She gathered up her hat and her bag, along with a wrap that Helga had left behind. "You ever been to the theater?"

He shook his head.

"What do you do on your days off?"

"Tinker about with engines."

"That sounds like a busman's holiday to me."

"Engines are interesting. I'm saving up for a garage."

"Are you?" She considered a moment, opened her handbag, and handed him a banknote. "Good luck with it. And thank you for all your efforts today. Much appreciated."

He gave her a sudden, transforming smile that warmed her heart to see. Then Letitia Carrington, who had once gone by the stage name of Letty Lee, and who had been born Hatty Cohen in Whitechapel, stepped off the boat.

Bradshaw's comedy *The Boating Party* opened at the Adelphi the following spring to good notices and even better takings at the box office. Mrs. Carrington, who had been one of the play's angels, and who was widely believed to be the model for Mrs. Hancock, the leading female role, could not have been more delighted at its success.

8

The Photograph: 1916

In some parts of the country near the south coast you can hear a dull murderous boom come over the Channel, an ominous blood pulse. Not here. Here a dog's bark annoys the ordinary silence the way it has always done and will do again, a wood pigeon hidden in a beech tree utters its lilting, repetitive coo, a freshening wind shivers through the leaves and drops again to a hush. The plow turns over the earth to the jingle and creak of the horses' harnesses and their heavy hooves thudding down the furrow; in a cobbled courtyard the bicycle bell of the delivery boy rings out.

But the house, which is not standing idly by, which is serving honor and saving it, encloses other sounds in a veil of discretion. Voices mutter private nonsense to themselves. Old music-hall songs bang out on an untuned piano. Shouts and cries rupture sleep, and horror is fought in a rustle of bedclothes and a pacing of floorboards.

Pale sun, as fragile as an egg, lay in lozenges of light across the desk, across his knees. Lieutenant Harrison put a cigarette between his lips and struck a match, holding one hand with the other to steady it. The match went out. The second time he managed to light the thing. Not bad. Some days it took five or six goes.

It was an odd little room, some sort of office downstairs in one of the service wings, and looked out over the kitchen courtyard. If he wanted a view, almost any other window in the house would have given him one. But he didn't want a view. He didn't want any sort of prospect. This small, low-ceilinged room suited him and no one had turned him out of it yet. Well, if you knows of a better 'ole, go to it! as the men said.

In front of him on the scratched deal desk, table really: his tobacco tin, his cigarette papers, a box of matches, a Wedgwood ashtray filled with stubs, and a black notebook with mud on the cover. A letter. The morning's paper. A packet wrapped in oilskin. *Robinson Crusoe,* Shelley's *Prometheus Unbound,* and *Little Dorrit*—a small stack of books that he had raided from the library.

"Raid" was the right word, because in the beginning it had taken all his nerve to confront the fierce symmetries of the house. Everything lined up with everything else, placed you like a chess piece on a board. When they had first arrived, and were grouped in the hall with their stinking kit bags, the heavy wooden interior doors had been open, revealing stark views in every direction. Later he would learn how silkily and snugly they closed, but on that day they were flung back. You could see it all. In front of the house the land fell away and rose again to a gentle hill. He couldn't work out where they had put the guns. He could hear them, but he didn't know where they were.

So much exposure. He had wanted to sink to the ground and crawl. Even now he sometimes found himself hugging the walls or zigzagging across the floor. First lesson. Keep moving. Don't give them a clear shot at you.

If he could have chosen a time to be in England, it wouldn't have been late November, the skies gray, the ground soggy. They might as well have been in France. Somehow, when you were out there, all you remembered were long sunny summer days, not the fact that you were close enough to home to share the same weather.

They were a mixed lot. Mostly officers from the Sixth Battalion, Royal Berkshires, as he was, but there were a couple of NCOs, one from Hampshire, one from Essex, and a padre from London. Without their uniforms and in the democracy of bad dreams, it was hard to tell the ranks apart.

They were always tired. Terror woke them at night and sleep ambushed them by day, delivered them onto the fire steps of their imaginations.

A hand on his shoulder. "Sir? Lieutenant Harrison?"

"What!" He jerked awake, panting.

"You were shouting."

"Was I?" He caught his breath. "Sorry."

Mullins, a short, barrel-chested man, said not to worry. He was a sergeant from one of the Hampshire regiments, about thirty-five, and on his first furlough home after nearly a year in the trenches. He wrote to his wife every morning after breakfast, the way some people brushed their teeth.

"Thought I'd better remind you that the photographer from the local paper's coming this afternoon to take a few shots. In case you'd forgotten."

He had forgotten. The photographer coming to take a few shots.

"You might want to spruce yourself up."

"Thanks, Sergeant. When is the photographer coming?"

"Half two."

"Oh." Something else he had forgotten. "I've a visitor this afternoon."

"All the more reason to spruce yourself up." Mullins reached across the desk and picked up the newspaper. "May I? They've been asking for it."

"Help yourself."

Mullins nodded. "Lose the beard, sir. I should. The whiskers. Such as they are."

"That would mean looking in the mirror."

"Has to happen, sir, has to happen one day. You'll feel better for it."

He doubted that. What would make him feel better would be an end to the waiting. You could get used to war. You could almost get to like it.

*   *   *

The house was not another hospital: that was made clear. (They'd seen enough of hospitals.) Instead, they should think of it as a place of rest and recuperation and take advantage of the opportunities and amenities provided. The park was extensive for those who liked to walk and well stocked with game for those who liked to shoot. Otherwise, they might want to fish or take a boat out on the river, play billiards or improve their minds in the library. Menus for the day would be posted up on the notice board in the lower hall each morning. Those on a prescribed dietary regime should make themselves known. They would all agree that Mr. Henderson had been very generous in making his house available to them. Were there any questions? The secretary, or housekeeper, or manageress, whoever she was, a trim female with polished brogues and a lovat tie, peered over her wire-rimmed spectacles.

"What are the local girls like?" said Pettigrew. "As nice as you?"

The secretary ignored the question and the laughter that came after it. "Next?" she said, pointing.

"I wondered if th-th-th-there would be any b-b-b-basket weaving."

Bolton turned his head and winked at Harrison. Harrison winked back.

The secretary consulted her clipboard. "No basket weaving is scheduled. If you would like to make a request, I'll see what I can do."

"Thank you, m-m-m-miss," said Bolton. "I f-f-f-find it helps with the tr-tr-tr-trench foot."

Harrison expelled a laugh as solid as a pellet. He almost expected to see it roll away across the floor.

Late morning and Harrison decided he would go for a walk. The idea had occurred to him after he finished shaving. While he stropped the razor and lathered his chin, he thought he might leave a mustache behind, but in the end, mesmerized by the scrape of the blade plowing clear tracks through the white soap, revealing the blue veins in his neck, he carried on until all of it went and his face, naked, thin, twenty-two years old, peered out of the mirror like a skinned rabbit. Mullins was right. He did feel better, even if he didn't look it. When he buried his head in the towel, for a moment he was back home on a Sunday morning, the smell of cooked bacon coming from downstairs, his mother with her hat on, coins for the collection plate in her gloved hand, ready for church. Coming? she would say, and he would shake his head and say he'd rather go for a walk.

Turning away from the mirror, Harrison stared round at the room where he shared nightmares with Newman, the two camp beds, sheets and blankets all rucked up, half falling on the floor, the faded floral wallpaper, the brown-and-white pottery cow on the mantelpiece filled with cigarette stubs. In the washbasin bristles floated on the scum. He ought to do something with the dirty water, but he couldn't think what. Tip it out the window? Instead, he came out of the room, went along the corridor, and felt his way down the cantilevered stairs into the great void of the hall.

"What did I tell you?" said Mullins when he poked his head round the door of the library. "That's the ticket."

The air was blue. A fug of coal fire, cigarette, and pipe smoke hung like a pall over the room. It could have been a railway station. There was the same sense of transit, of marking time or shuffling through. The padre was writing at a desk in front of one of the large windows. Two of the men were playing cards. Bolton was rocking himself in an armchair and Pettigrew was over by the drinks table. The others were probably in the billiard room.

"Care for one, Harrison?" said Pettigrew, waving the stopper of a decanter.

"No, thanks."

"Are you sure?" asked Pettigrew. "Never too early for a stiffener. Buck you up no end."

"No, thanks."

"Feel better, don't you?" said Mullins.

"Much." He cast his eyes around. "Where's Newman?"

"Having his dressing changed. Sister's here."

"Of course." He nodded. "Have you seen this morning's paper?"

Mullins gave him a cautious smile. "I took it off you, remember? About twenty minutes ago?"

"Oh yes," he said. "I forgot." He rubbed his chin. "Well. I think I might go for a walk."

"Outdoors?"

He nodded.

"Want company?" He was a good man, Mullins, salt of the earth. He shook his head. "I think I can manage."

"Right you are, sir." Mullins said. "Lunch in an hour. Cauliflower soup to start. Mutton to follow. Spotted dick for afters."

"That's something to look forward to."

"Isn't it just, sir?"

Getting out of the house was easy. He went down the side stairs and left by the door that led into the kitchen courtyard. There he peered through the window into the office where he had been sitting earlier, as if he were looking for himself, and saw that he had left his tobacco tin and his cigarette papers behind. He went to fetch them. When he returned to the courtyard, he wondered if he might need his notebook and went and fetched that, too. He was putting it into his pocket when Mullins came out.

"You still here, sir?" said Mullins.

"Looks that way."

"Are you certain you don't want company? I could do with stretching my legs."

That might have been a joke. Mullins, who had a wound in his groin that hadn't healed yet, used a cane.

He shook his head. "Kind of you all the same."

Mullins lit a cigarette. "Force of habit, sir, in case you're wondering. The wife doesn't like me smoking in the house. Can't seem to bring myself to smoke indoors wherever I am."

"Quite right."

"The lads say, 'Sergeant Mullins, smoke in the dugout! The Hun will have your head off.' And I say, 'Blame the wife!'"

The courtyard was cobbled. It had rained earlier and the cobbles were slippery. Across the yard a door stood open. Harrison went over and looked inside. It was some sort of outbuilding, a storeroom, and it was full of coal. He picked up a lump and dropped it again, sniffed his fingers. He'd forgotten how much he liked the smell of coal. Pasted to the back of the door was a poster that said that if every family in Britain saved a lump of coal every day, it would mean eight million more tons for the war effort. He couldn't quite do the sum.

"That's the way out, sir," Mullins said, behind him. "Over there."

"What did you say?"

"The other direction."

"Of course."

He turned round and saw the archway, the land on the other side of it. The big gray sky and the watery sun.

"Lunch in half an hour, sir," said Mullins, throwing away his cigarette. "You wouldn't want to miss the mutton."

"No," he said. "I wouldn't want to do that."

Mullins limped inside and took his kindness with him, which was a relief.

Through the archway he could see the land, dotted with stands of trees. There was no one there. For once the guns were silent. A hush fell on his ears.

Some of them had a great need to be alone, as he did. Most preferred company and distraction: cards, billiards, singsongs round the piano. Yet he knew it was not as simple as that. He knew, for example, that he only tolerated being alone because he was attached to the others, however loose and circumstantial the connection was. Because they were there, he was able to set himself apart. For those who preferred company, he suspected it was the other way round, that distraction was their way of keeping their solitariness to themselves. Similar thoughts had occurred to him in a trench. You were never alone in a trench, and you were always alone.

The open countryside that he could see reminded him of a dog they'd had when he was growing up and the way the dog covered the ground, doubling back, circling, off at tangents, sometimes deaf when called. You might keep to a path, set off towards a destination, but a dog describes the terrain, brings it home to you, as if it is all within your reach or compass. He pictured the dog running across the fields and he saw her blown to bits, the bits blown up and buried time after time. Her feathery tail severed in the mud.

Land was something else now. It was graves. Perhaps it had been graves all along. You might think no one was there, the fields were empty, but they weren't. They were full of flesh.

He stood in the archway for some time, feeling the protection of the house to either side, a protection he did not feel in the booming indoors, and thought his parents would be impressed by the place if they could see it. It was the sort of house they would appreciate, and his father would know about the architecture. Perhaps he ought to take them up on their offers to visit him, which came regularly in letters, along with the local news. They had come to see him in hospital at a time when he was in no position to refuse. All he remembered about the visit was his mother being brave with a handkerchief, the cheap bird brooch he had given her for her birthday when he was sixteen pinned to the collar of her coat, and his father talking about the first eleven at the school where he taught. To get them to leave, he'd started to moan—the pain was real, but the moaning was a performance—and Sister had come with a syringe.

"There you are," said Mullins, back again.

"Lunch?"

"Yes, sir. The gong's gone."

He nodded. "Wouldn't want to miss the mutton."

"That's right, sir. Enjoy your walk?"

"Very much."

Miss Wells got down from the train. Doors slammed behind her, a couple of people went off, and she stood on the platform, dressed in her best gray tweed coat and clutching a small, square mock-leather handbag. The air was cold on her neck. It was one twenty-two by the station clock.

The roof that extended over the platform was trimmed with white-painted wooden slats, pierced and shaped like the edging of a petticoat. A pair of fire buckets hung from the brick wall, and three tubs planted with winter-flowering pansies were placed at exact distances from one another. On the opposite side of the tracks the same scene was repeated. She thought about crossing the footbridge and taking the next train back.

"Can I help you, miss?" said the stationmaster.

When's the next train to Reading? she wanted to say. Instead, she said she was visiting one of the soldiers in the convalescent home and she was not sure how to find it.

"Which one? There's two. One for the officers and one for the Tommies."

What a surprise. Of course there would be two. "Ashenden Park."

He told her where to go. "You can't miss it. Twenty minutes' walk at best."

Near the station a stone bridge crossed the river. Peter would have known this reach, she thought, would have navigated it many times. Peter was her brother, or rather half brother, and the reason she was here.

Up the hill trees creaked in the wind. The bare branches clawing at the sky reminded her how war poked its ugly crooked fingers into lives. No one was left out, not even the children, especially not the children. She saw it all the time. One day a child would be rosy, skipping, noisy; the next it would be a silent white face and another father or brother would be gone. They almost never cried or missed a day. Sometimes a strange viciousness would take hold of them and they would torment other children in the playground simply for the sake of inviting punishment for their actions. To feel bad was to be bad, to inflict pain was a way of suffering it: that seemed to be how it was. It had got to the point where you didn't ask. What she taught with the battered primers and on the smeared blackboard was nothing compared to what they were learning out of school. The ones you worried about were the ones who stayed the same, who froze it all up inside.

There was so much grief in the country, it was impossible to mourn. Loss had lost its status. No one could be comforted, because that was to claim a privilege that was not yours. Before the war, when her mother fell headfirst into the tray of digestives she had been sorting, her dead weight dragging the whole lot crashing to the factory floor, people brought their whispered remembrances to the house in their Sunday coats and hats. Her father shouldered, elbowed his way round the front room after the funeral, nodding, shaking hands, agreeing it was the best way to go—"out like a light." Later, when they all left and while her brother banked up the fire, he talked with a kind of wonder about how their mother had smelled of sugar, about the crushed biscuits in her hair. "They weren't even her favorites." These days, the telegrams came, you lowered the blinds or pulled the curtains, and sat alone with the news. They were making shell cases at the factory now.

When she got to the house, she was told by an unsmiling woman wearing spectacles that the men were still at lunch and shown to a side chair in a massive hall. A muted gray light came down from above, and she sat in it as if she were waiting to be called to an examination room. Inside her clothing was the tiny gold heart on a chain that her brother had brought home on his first leave. It had been meant for Ida Firth, but by then Ida Firth had married someone else and he gave it to her instead. She tugged it up and free, put it to her cheek, and felt the warmth it had stolen from her skin.

"Miss Wells?" said the woman, returning. "Lieutenant Harrison will see you now."

Her first sight of the house, sitting smug on its hill, had brought buried anger to life, flared it up. She had seen the columns on the frontage and thought: politicians, generals, judges. Us lot up here and you lot down there. Now, following the woman's important footsteps down the stairs, along corridors, and through a courtyard, her anger grew. Everywhere she looked was the privilege of exclusion: those chairs, that cabinet, the wallpaper, the echoing stone floor. Old things, old money. Even the shabbiness was grand. It was only later, after she left, that she realized that it was the house where her parents had been in service years before she was born, which struck her as an irony of a kind.

They stopped outside a door. The woman consulted her watch. You could see how time gave her a purpose in life.

"We've a photographer coming in half an hour."

"I shouldn't think it will take long."

"Good. He's through there."

"Miss Wells," said Harrison, standing. There wasn't much room in the little office, but he brought another chair up to the table and turned his own round so they were facing each other. "Please have a seat."

She sat down. So did he. He wanted a cigarette but he didn't trust his hands. He didn't know what fits and starts they might get up to.

Miss Wells put her bag on the table, took off her gloves, and laid them on top. She was like some sort of fierce woodland creature. Small, with pointed features and large hazel eyes. He wished she would take off her hat so he could see her hair. When had girls started cutting their hair? It was very odd. From what little he could see of it, he thought it must be like her brother's, curly and coppery. Otherwise she didn't look much like him at all.

"I'm sorry. I know this must be difficult."

She bit her lip, lowered her eyes, and nodded. The instant she came into the room and saw this damaged, twitching man, hardly more than a boy, anger receded and in its wake came the foul swill of shame that had been lapping round her life for months. Most people got a telegram. That's what you feared, a telegram. They had received a letter in the post from the War Office, which was worse. *Dear Sir. We regret to inform you that your son, Private Peter Wells of the 6th Battalion, Royal Berkshires, was sentenced to death for cowardice and shot at dawn on the 9th of August.* That was what it said. That was all it said. They never even knew there'd been a court-martial. Her father had kept the letter in his trouser pocket for the past three months so that no one could find it and read it. Her hands were clenched, her knuckles white. How much more shame did they want them to feel? She raised her eyes.

"Why did you want to see me, Lieutenant?"

Harrison reached across the desk, picked up the packet wrapped in oilskin, and handed it to her. "First let me give you this. These are his effects."

She put the packet in her lap without taking her eyes off him. Her greeny-brown eyes. The colors of the English countryside, he thought.

He wanted a cigarette badly. *Effects?* Why had he come out with that? It was the sort of word a padre would use. Start again. "Miss Wells, I knew your brother and he was no coward."

She was as good at silence as he was, which was saying something. After some time she asked him how old he was, as if she were asking whether it was raining or not.

"Twenty-three next month." Worse and worse. Now he sounded like Sergeant Mullins, who was "getting on for five foot five." Which was to say, five foot four. He gave in to his craving and began the long, jittery process of rolling a cigarette and lighting it.

"I know Peter wasn't a coward," she said, as his fingers twitched and leapt. She wondered whether she should help him and decided against it. "Which is why I can't understand what happened."

Somehow he found the courage to look her in the eye. "Things are different over there."

None of them wrote what it was like in their letters. You wrote "Thank you very much for the socks" or "Thank you for the scarf, much appreciated" or "We all enjoyed the fruitcake" and "How are you all at home?" To write down the truth of it would be to admit that it was real. That it was as much a part of the world as anything else, which was unimaginable.

"Please be assured, Miss Wells, your brother was a fine soldier and you and your family have nothing to be ashamed about. I wrote to you because I wanted to tell you that in person."

His mouth was dry and it was hard to swallow. It was hard to speak over the shame of his failure. A silence fell.

"Is that why you brought me here? That's it?"

He lit the cigarette, inhaled, felt the smoke catch at the back of his throat. What had he expected? That his *assurances* would be enough?

"Forgive me," he said. Then he began to talk to a patch of crumbling distemper on the wall.

"I first met your brother a few months before the offensive. He was running dispatches from high command to the field and back again, mostly by motorbike. Lines of communication, they're as important as lines of supply. The staff officers need the intelligence from the ground and you need the orders. You might think that's an easy job. It isn't. You never know what you're going to come across. Things change day to day. There are mines and snipers. We have pigeons, you know, carrier pigeons, but a man's more reliable in the long run.

"And your brother was good with engines. Out there, they're always breaking down. Sometimes it's the weather, the mud, the dirt, the dust, the wear and tear. Sometimes they're just substandard. Whatever the problem was, he could always fix it. So he was doing an important job and doing it better than anyone else could have done."

He paused.

"Go on," she said.

He swallowed. "Then we were sent to the front. We'd been training for months behind the lines. We knew the terrain. The plan was that we would shell their trenches, wire, and artillery batteries. Mine their gun posts. Destroy the lot. Then we would walk across and take their positions.

"The bombardment went on for a week. Shell after shell after shell. During the day there was nothing coming from the other side. Nothing at all. You could stand up and walk around as if you were off for a picnic. But at night the enemy were still shelling us, so we knew the barrage hadn't been as successful as they said. The morn-

ing of the attack, the mines were to be detonated a couple of minutes before the whistles went, and we were told not to cheer when
we came up the trench ladders. Those were the general orders. In
the south sector ours were slightly different. We were to advance a
little ahead of the appointed hour, to get as far forward as possible,
and that turned out to be the right decision in the end, despite what
happened."

Another pause. "You don't want to be hearing this."

"I do," she said. "Go on."

"Our position was opposite a machine-gun nest, which had
been mined," he said. "When we came over the top, the Germans
started firing from it. The engineer in charge of detonating the mine
saw that we were already out there, in the way of the blast. But if he
didn't go ahead and explode the charge, we would be mown down
anyway. The problem was, when the thing blew up, it went in all
directions. The charge hadn't been laid deep enough. Those first few
minutes after the blast, your brother saved two men that I know of.
One of them was me."

The patches of peeling distemper seemed to make a map of
somewhere. He smoked his cigarette and was back in the weather
of that summer morning, the red mist of blood and burning debris,
the heavy earth rain, the obscene hail of body parts thudding onto
the chalky ground. His knees began to knock and jump in his trouser legs. The weather of that morning.

When he came back to himself, he noticed that her silence had a
different quality, which helped. He rubbed his chin, which was still
bare and clean-shaven, and went on. "We took the crater where the
machine-gun nest had been and the trench lines around it. By the
end of the day we had taken all our objectives. We were luckier than
some. In the south sector our orders were to vary our formation if
we had to. If things didn't go according to plan. Farther north, they
were told to keep to theirs, whatever happened. And they were carrying more kit."

He was leaving out a lot. "The cavalry never arrived like they
were supposed to. Not at the end of the first day and not afterwards.

It became clear there wasn't going to be any breakthrough. That we would be fighting over each field, each yard. Then three weeks later, the third week of July, we were sent to relieve the South African First Infantry Brigade. They'd suffered heavy casualties taking a wood. Delville Wood. Only it wasn't a wood by then."

Heavy casualties was one way of putting it. Just a fifth of the brigade left alive was another. He only realized that he'd stopped talking when she prompted him again.

"Lieutenant?"

He stared at the flaking distemper. "To be honest, I don't remember much about it. My memory's not so good these days." He was lying. Shattered stumps, waterlogged craters, corpses piled four deep: he remembered all of it, and whenever he forgot it for a time, his dreams were happy to remind him. "We advanced in daylight, which was a mistake. There was heavy artillery and machine-gun fire. They called it a tactical victory." He twisted round and stubbed out his cigarette in the Wedgwood ashtray. "Which is their way of saying it didn't change anything."

There were footsteps outside. A peremptory knock. "Lieutenant Harrison?"

He frowned at the door. "What is it?"

"The photographer has arrived. The men are assembling in the library."

"I'll be along shortly."

"As soon as possible, please, Lieutenant," said the officious voice. "The photographer says that the light's going and there isn't much time."

The photographer can stuff his light, he thought. And you can stuff your bloody photograph. He turned to the girl.

"Delville Wood," she said.

"Yes." He fumbled with his tobacco tin and cigarette papers.

"Let me." She took the tin and papers, rolled two cigarettes, and handed him one. "May I?" she said, holding up the other.

"Of course."

She lit the cigarette. "What's the matter? Haven't you seen a girl smoke before?"

He smiled and moved the ashtray within her reach.

"Delville Wood. Was that where it happened?" she said.

"Where what happened?"

"Where my brother was arrested."

"No, that was somewhere else."

Delville Wood. Shattered stumps, waterlogged craters, corpses piled four deep. "We advanced. There was heavy artillery and machine-gun fire coming from the hill. I don't remember much about it." (The remnants of the brigade marching out of the wood to the pipes of the Black Watch.) "The last time I saw your brother, he was dragging one of the wounded to cover, except there wasn't much cover. Later, afterwards, we discovered he was missing. I thought he must have been shot."

"Missing, presumed dead," she said.

"When they eventually found him, he was alive and a long way from the front."

She leaned forward. "What are you saying? Are you saying that he deserted? That he ran off?"

"He was confused. He didn't know where he was. He'd been wandering about for ages and wasn't making much sense. What happened to your brother could have happened to any of us. Now they say two days is enough. After that you're supposed to be relieved. We'd been at the front for weeks. Fighting or under attack a lot of that time."

"But being confused doesn't make you a coward!"

"No, it doesn't."

"Then why did they arrest him?"

"Because he was alive and he was a long way from where he was supposed to be. Because he wasn't wounded. That's enough for them. That's the way it is."

He picked up the letter from the desk and handed it to her. "You don't have to read this now. It's from the chaplain who was at the court-martial. When he heard they were shipping me back, he asked me to give it to you. I've been in hospital for a while, otherwise you would have had it sooner. I'm sorry about that."

She opened the envelope, took out the letter, and began to read. It was two pages long. When she got to the end of the first page, she gasped. She read the letter twice, then looked at him. Her hazel eyes were like the English countryside in the rain. Greeny-brown. Wet.

"He refused a blindfold."

He nodded. "He was the finest soldier I've ever known. The bravest. The best."

The door banged open and Mullins barged in. "They want you upstairs now, sir. For the photograph."

"Anyone ever teach you to knock, Sergeant?"

"Sorry, sir."

Miss Wells stubbed out her cigarette and put the letter into her handbag. "It's time I was going in any case." She got up and turned to Harrison. "Peter was my half brother, you know. But he was never half of anything to me. Thank you, Lieutenant."

"It was the least I could do."

"It has meant a great deal."

He could see anger, resolve in her eyes. She wasn't wearing it like a shield, she was carrying it like a spear.

"I'm going to see to it that his name is cleared," she said.

He didn't want to discourage her, so he nodded. "Good luck."

"Good luck to you too."

She put on her gloves, gathered up her things, and together they went across the courtyard, up the stairs, and through the echoing house, with all its symmetries and sight lines. On the portico, the land falling away in front of them and rising to a gentle hill, he shook her hand, and then he went off to the library to have his photograph taken.

9

The Treasure Hunt: 1929

It's a simple equation: spend more than you earn, no matter how little or how much that is, and there's trouble sooner or later. That time has come. With the land gone, sold to pay off debts run up in the pleasure spots of Europe, the house has fallen under the hammer.

Trapped in the looking glasses here and there are pale reflections that rise out of their depths and fade away again. So much has been left behind and little of it is of any consequence or value. Broken shooting sticks, burnt saucepans, cracked china, discarded clothes in abandoned wardrobes, clothes that no one will ever wear again. A nursery so long shut up that no one remembers it is there. Touch the curtains and they threaten to drop from their rings into huddled heaps on the floor, the threads disintegrated, eaten away by sunlight and dust.

"What a Dazzler!" read the gossip column headline.

Tantalizing news has reached our ears that the winner of the eagerly anticipated treasure hunt at Ashenden Park will find themselves in possession of a diamond bracelet. We call that *very* generous. Property dealer George Ferrars, who recently acquired the house at auction, refuses to say how much the

Cartier sparkler is worth but has confirmed that society's favorite good-time girl Dido is among those invited to the glittering *soirée*.

George Ferrars, sitting in his silk dressing gown in his Bayswater flat, set the paper aside and stared out at the busy London street. It was late April and trees were budding in the gardens and squares. Ever since the article had appeared a week ago, he had received a flurry of acceptances by each post. None from Dido, but that was to be expected; they had made their arrangement on the telephone. As he understood it, normally there was no telling whether Dido would show up and make your party a success or go elsewhere and consign it to oblivion. In this case, however, he thought he had probably weighted the scales sufficiently in his favor.

Depending on whom you talked to, Dido was a dustman's daughter, the errant wife of the headmaster of a famous public school, the lover of a Russian sculptress, or the current mistress of the Prince of Wales. The one thing that was known for certain was that she was in the papers every week, mostly the gossip columns and court circular, sometimes the news, and occasionally the law reports. The press followed her everywhere, which was why he had invited her. If all went according to plan, in a few days' time he would have the publicity he needed for the house and the bold idea he had conceived for its disposal.

Property was no business for a gentleman, someone said to him recently, the sort of someone whose property he often sold. Hard times for that class now, he thought, not taking it personally. What income tax started, the war had finished off. You didn't have to be titled to feel the pinch. Even the bankers and City gents, with their make-believe estates an hour's train ride from London, were having to retrench and upset the wife.

Ashenden Park was the largest property Ferrars had ever bought, and the most distinctive by far. A beautiful house, even in its present abandoned state, a national treasure that the nation could no longer afford. He was under no illusion that these days you could sell a place this size to a private buyer in England. A speculator with deeper pockets than his would simply tear it down and turn a profit by cramming lots of little jerry-built houses on the land where it used to stand. Ferrars's intention, he liked to think, was much more honorable.

The American market was where the future lay. Anyone could see that. America was full of new money and new money loved old things. A million dollars was a reasonable sum, he thought, to dismantle a historic house, ship it across the ocean, and reerect it on behalf of whichever patriot wanted to put his name on a museum, college building, or public library, or who wanted a private residence with a past.

Such a sale and the house would be preserved, as it deserved to be, though admittedly not in its original setting. Such a sale and he would have the capital he needed to develop the estate into a pleasant Home Counties suburb. In his mind's eye he saw decent houses with airy rooms and fair-sized gardens grouped about well-tended greens where children bicycled and mothers sat overseeing them, where fathers arrived home on the five-fifteen from Paddington. George Ferrars was a romantic who believed he was a visionary.

On the evening of the party, anticipation crackled through the house like electricity. Every minute held the expectation of something happening, some momentous balloon of pleasure lying in wait, just out of reach. Dido would be coming, and meanwhile here was an abandoned house, an enchanted attic for the imagination to rummage about in.

Outside Ferrars paced up and down the portico, lighting cigarette after cigarette. For the occasion, he'd had the great brass lanterns lit and the frontage was bathed in gold. Behind him, through the closed glazed doors, he could hear the noise of the party grow, rising from a murmur to a loud, insistent droning hum punctuated by the odd vibrating shriek that rattled the glazing. From time to time another motorcar would arrive and more people would trip up the stairs, laughing. It was approaching ten o'clock.

No Dido.

One of the staff he'd hired for the party came out and said people had been asking when the treasure hunt was going to start.

"Tell them soon," said Ferrars. "Very soon."

Below the pressmen skulked, smoking, shuffling their feet on the gravel. As if sensing his unease, one of them called up, "She's going to show, isn't she, squire? Or are we wasting our bleeding time here?"

"Oh," he said, with an assumed lightness, "Dido is Dido. A law unto herself."

"Are we to take that as a no, squire?"

He ignored the question. "Have you everything you need? Would you like more sandwiches?"

"More drink would not go amiss," said the pressman.

"A pint of your best bubbly for me," said another.

Just then a long black car drew up, its headlamps raking the drive. Ferrars leaned on the balustrade, squinting into the night. A chauffeur got out and opened the rear doors. There was an explosion of light.

"Dido!"

"Dido!"

"Over here, Dido!"

Whoosh, pop, pop went the flashbulbs.

Dido got out of the car, one hand shielding her eyes, a rope of white beads the size of quail's eggs hanging down to her hipbones.

"Gentlemen," she said to the press, "we meet again."

Ferrars, who had never seen Dido in the flesh, was surprised that she was even more beautiful than her pictures in the papers would have led you to believe. The light, breathy sound of her voice, however, he remembered.

Whoosh, pop, pop went the flashbulbs.

"Dido!"

"Dido! Over here!"

"Are you going to find the bracelet, Dido?" said one of the pressmen.

"Who knows, Sammy?" she said.

Out of the other car door emerged a man who came swiftly round and took Dido's arm, shepherding her up the stairs. "They love you, baby," the man was saying as they came out onto the portico.

"They do, don't they?" she said.

Ferrars came forward, rinsed in relief. "Dido, so glad you could make it. Welcome to Ashenden Park."

"Who are you?"

"George Ferrars. We spoke on the telephone."

She touched the tips of his fingers, her mouth half open, her eyes half closed. "Oh yes, Mr. Ferrars. Pleased to meet you."

Her companion, a tall, thickset man in a camel-hair coat, introduced himself as Connor. First name or last name, Ferrars was never to know.

"Come through," he said, opening the doors onto the party's blare. "Let me fix you a drink and then I'd better start the ball rolling."

In the library Ferrars poured out the malt. "Here you are. Good for whatever ails you."

Connor in his camel-hair coat was staring around at the empty bookcases, and the camp bed, folding table and chairs Ferrars had brought up from London, signs of his temporary occupancy.

"How much did you pay for this place?"

Who is this person? thought Ferrars, registering a slight air of menace that emanated from him. "A good part of the land was sold a couple of years ago. The house has been empty a long time. So less than you might think."

Connor said he hadn't been surprised to see the estate up for auction. He'd heard Henderson had debts. "What are you going to do with the house? Live in it?" He had an unpleasant laugh.

"No," said Ferrars. "I have other plans."

"Sweetie," said Dido in her baby voice, "I could do with a little lift."

"Of course, my angel."

From an inside pocket Connor took out a hand mirror and paper packet. Tipped white powder from the packet onto the mirror and chopped it up with a razor blade.

Dido inhaled through a fine silver tube. "Mmm," she said. "Limehouse's finest."

"You are so good to me, Connor, darling," said Dido. Then she turned her glittering eyes on Ferrars. "Show me the bracelet."

For a moment, as Ferrars opened the jewelry box and flashed the diamonds, Connor wondered whether the point of all this was to get Dido into bed, but he didn't detect any of the usual overtures, and he had a very good nose for them.

"I get to keep the bracelet," said Dido, who could not take her eyes off it.

"I know that, my angel." But what does Mr. Ferrars get? thought Connor.

Dido's entrance to the party had caused a sensation: first a beat of silence, then an upsurge of sound as she was ushered into the library at end of the hall.

"Did you see that?" said Sylvia Lanchester. "She's wearing Fortuny. That takes nerve. It must be ten years old, that gown. I knew I should have borrowed Mother's."

"Don't be ridiculous," said Vivian. "You would never have carried it off."

The Lanchester sisters had driven down with Hugo Lyell in his father's Daimler Double Six, along with Frances Dunne, Hugo's cousin. The saloon car had been a hothouse of crushed flowers: Vivian's lily-of-the-valley scent, Sylvia's gardenia, and Frances's lavender eau de cologne.

Hugo, who was nineteen and about to go to Oxford, was the younger son of a wealthy industrialist; his elder brother, Paul, had been killed in the war. Ever since he had gained his place at university and left school, he had found himself at lots of parties—circus parties, swimming parties, fancy-dress parties—although he didn't particularly consider himself to be the partying sort. He helped himself to a glass of champagne.

"Don't get too tight," said Vivian. "You're driving us back, remember?" Her frock shimmered with tiny glass beads and ended at her knees in a series of overlapping triangles, like teeth.

"Don't you get too tight either," said Hugo. "Or you can get a lift from someone else. My father will murder me if you're sick on the seats."

"Chin-chin," said Sylvia. Her eyes were ringed with kohl, each forearm an armature of bangles from wrist to elbow. "You'll miss all this gaiety next year. Up in your ivory tower. Hunched over your dusty old law books."

"History," said Hugo. "I'm reading history."

His cousin Frances was standing silent beside him and he registered her discomfort with a pang of conscience. His mother, who had refused to let his younger sister, Winifred, come to the party, much to Winifred's outrage, had told him to be kind to his cousin and to look after her. Frances had nice brown eyes but wasn't wearing any makeup and didn't have the right figure for her dress, which was to say she had a figure whose curves disturbed its straight lines. No girls had bosoms now; what precisely they did with them Hugo was not entirely sure, but he understood it involved elasticated undergarments of the kind Frances evidently did not possess.

At that moment Ferrars came out of the library, stood on a chair, and waved them all to a hush.

"Pray silence for mine host," said Vivian.

Ferrars's speech had a natural and unrehearsed quality, as if he were conversing with friends over a supper table. First he told them when the band would be playing, and what there was to eat and drink and where to find it. Then he moved on to the treasure hunt. On a side table they would find cards printed with clues. The object of the game was to solve the clues and then find an object corresponding to the answer from somewhere in the house or the immediate vicinity. The winner or winners would be the first to find all six items.

"You will no doubt have read about the prize." There was a cheer as he produced the red leather Cartier box from his suit pocket and a gasp when he opened it. "Good luck, everyone."

The effect of diamonds on jaded appetites was nothing short of miraculous. As Ferrars got down from his chair, there was an immediate rush for the side table.

"I like this Ferrars person," said Sylvia. "He's my sort of chap."

"Which chap isn't?" said Vivian. "Coming, Hugo?" She waved a card.

"Yes," Sylvia said, "we're going to need your brain."

It was clear that Frances was not included in their invitation, and for a moment Hugo was torn. "No," he said. "You two go ahead." He glanced at his cousin and her eyes said thank you.

"*This king has his pride.* Four letters. Well, that's obvious, isn't it?" said Frances.

They had gone through into another hall with a staircase in it, an echoing, hollowed-out space, and Hugo could hear a band tuning up in a room that led off it. "Where do you suggest we find a lion?"

"A cat might do for a lion," said Frances.

"I don't really think that's precise enough," said Hugo. "Finding a picture of a lion will probably be our best bet."

"Picture?" On the walls were no pictures, just pale rectangles where pictures had once been. "Oh, I know where to look," said Frances, her eyes lighting up.

"Where?"

"I'll show you."

He followed her up the curving stone stairs with its wrought-iron balustrade, and people begin to spill into the hall down below, the girls like moths in their light dresses, flitting and phosphorescent. More girls than men, and a couple of the men with empty sleeves pinned to their sides or across their chests, one with an eye patch. He thought about those who hadn't come back, about his brother, and Vivian and Sylvia's brothers. Frances's brother had been too young, like him, but her father hadn't been. At first they had put him in a convalescent home; then they moved him to a private asylum.

At the top of the stairs was a gallery leading to a corridor dimly lit by shaded electric bulbs. Frances went along it, trying handles, opening doors, peering inside. They had all been bedrooms or dressing rooms, judging by what was left behind: a couple of washstands, a broken brass bedstead, a pair of brocade curtains drooping on their rail, a small armless chair with fringed upholstery. A large over-mantel mirror, of the ornate Victorian kind he remembered from his grandmother's house, reflected the last of the light in its cloudy foxed depths. A film seemed to lie over everything, not merely of dust and neglect, but of past expirations and hopes.

In the last year of the war, by which time his brother Paul had been dead for eighteen months, killed when his hospital tent was shelled, his father's driver, Jim Sugden, was called up. Occasionally they had postcards from him in an upright school hand, generally in response to parcels his mother sent, and once the war was over, he returned to ask if the position was still open. That would have been just after Christmas, early in the new year, because he could remember the sleet lashing the windows and how Jim, who had taught him to drive in Hyde Park before he had left for the front, had sat warming himself by the cook's fire, drinking tea, the wet steaming off his army greatcoat. From where Hugo was sitting, watchful on the top step, neither in the kitchen nor out of it, Jim looked more or less his same square self, which puzzled him as much as it comforted him. This was at a time when the fortitude of his parents had been an impenetrable thing. He seemed to remember Jim tousling his hair on his way out, or that might have been an earlier occasion. The position was still open but Jim never came back to fill it and they learned a little later that he had died from the Spanish flu. Afterwards Hugo himself had come down with a mysterious illness that kept him away from school for a term, which the doctors could not get to the bottom of, and which passed in due course.

"Ah, here we are," said Frances, opening another door. "The nursery."

He stood for a moment, feeling the weight of the past. The room was empty and desolate. Part of the ceiling had fallen down, exposing the bare laths, and a litter of distemper lay on the floor. "How can you tell?"

"Bars at the windows. We had them in ours, didn't you?"

Sure enough, when he looked more closely he could see, as well as the bars, the curling remnants of a faded wallpaper that put rhymes into his head. "We're not going to find anything here. There isn't anything here."

"O ye of little faith." Frances was tugging at a cupboard built into an alcove beside the chimneybreast. It opened with a creak of protest and she began foraging inside. Before long she was surrounded by a disorderly heap of spinning tops, lead soldiers, and aged dolls with painted porcelain faces. "Ha," she said, sitting back on her heels. "This looks promising." She drew out a battered wooden box with a pitched lid set on a thick tapered base and spilled the contents on the floor. "The animals went in two by two." She held up the lion and the lioness, both with broken tails, the coloring half worn off.

He laughed.

"Good, aren't I? I thought perhaps a picture book, but a Noah's Ark is somehow much more satisfactory." She handed him the lions, stood up, and wiped the dust off her dress.

"Both of them?"

"In case anyone else has the same idea."

Lanterns had been lit. The hall was a crush. As they came down the stairs, Hugo saw a group of people screaming at each other. One of them was Edward Furneval, whom he'd hated at school.

"It's got to be a lion," said Furneval.

"It could be Henry the Eighth," said a girl with a feather in her hair.

"It's a lion," said Furneval.

Frances said, "I thought that clue was too easy."

Hugo thought that if anyone was going to win, it shouldn't be Edward Furneval.

"See here, what we really should do is solve the clues first. Otherwise we'll waste time running about from pillar to post."

"Good idea," said Frances, consulting the card. "*Eros arranged to give you a flower.* Four letters."

"Rose."

"Yes, that's what I thought. This one's harder. "*Drink is initially the easy answer.* Three letters."

"Tea."

"Why?"

"First letters of 'the easy answer.'"

"*Record points on page.* Nine letters."

He considered for a moment. "Points are usually points of the compass."

"North, east, south, west?"

"Or north, east, west, south. Ah, newspaper."

"My goodness." Frances pushed her spectacles up her nose. "*To find it take a little money.* Five letters. I can't see this at all."

"Let me look at it," said Hugo. "Lemon. It's hidden in 'little money.'"

"Last one," she said. "*This is time to pour.* Is it four, as in teatime? No, it can't be. It's five letters."

"You're thinking too literally," said Hugo. "T for 'time' and rain for 'pour.' Train."

Connor had worked it out. The game was publicity. Ferrars was not after Dido, nor was he some counter jumper looking to rub shoulders with a better class of person. He was trying to flog the house. It was obvious from the way he was showing them round, pointing out all its fine features.

"The doors are Spanish mahogany," said Ferrars.

And I'm a Dutchman, thought Connor.

Leading them from room to room, Ferrars was a little worried. His original idea was that Dido should pretend to search for the treasure-hunt items, with more than a little assistance from him, as he knew where he had hidden those he intended her to "find."

Yet, somewhat ironically, he had not entirely reckoned with the way fame worked. They had only to enter a room and it would immediately fill up with people craning their necks to see her. Every move they made was under the scrutiny of dozens of pairs of eyes. Meanwhile, there was the unsettling presence of Connor.

"Well, I have to say I admire your optimism," Connor was saying as they stood in the dining room.

"What do you mean?" said Ferrars.

"It won't be easy to shift a pile like this, whatever you paid for it."

"What exactly do you do?" asked Ferrars.

"This and that."

"I'm desperately thirsty, Connor," said Dido in her baby voice. "Perishing."

"What do you want, my angel?"

Dido gave it some thought. "A sidecar," she said.

"The bar's downstairs," said Ferrars.

"There," said Dido. "Isn't that clever of me! Didn't you say lemon was on your little list, Mr. Ferrars?"

"Yes," said Ferrars.

"A sidecar's got lemon in it."

Downstairs, the party had reached the stage where it was taking matters into its own hands, and a number of paper lanterns had been removed from where they had been strung across the walls. People were swinging them, carrying them like glowing orbs or suns, holding them up to each other's faces. You could see the appeal of it, how the hunger for pleasure led you to make mischief. And it was beautiful, so beautiful. The pale moth-like dresses, the flickering orange light, and the guilt of their unearned youth.

"Now, what next?" said Frances, fishing a slice of lemon out of her lemonade and putting it in her bag.

"Newspaper, perhaps," said Hugo. "That can't be hard to find."

"Darling?" Sylvia stood in front of them, the kohl outlining her eyes smudged a little. She slipped her arm into Hugo's and her bracelets jangled. "I wondered if you could give us a teensy-weensy bit of help with these clues. They're awfully hard."

Hugo was distracted by the sight of Furneval and his friends dragging a stone urn across the floor, a snarling lion carved on the front.

"Just a little help," said Sylvia.

"Which clue are you having trouble with?" said Hugo.

"All of them."

He bent and whispered in her ear and she gave him a kiss and tottered off.

Frances glared at him. He shrugged.

"She's tight. Two minutes from now she won't remember what I told her."

"Does she always get so drunk?"

"Quite often."

"About the newspaper," said Frances, somewhat mollified. "I've been thinking. Our cook always lined her drawers with it. It's hygienic, something to do with the ink. No, don't snigger, not those kinds of drawers."

In the kitchen, which they eventually located in one of the side wings, they found half an inch of stale tea and a rose-patterned eggcup, along with a number of implements and utensils that the passage of time had silently severed from their functions. No newspaper, however.

"What do you suppose this is for?" said Hugo.

"It's a jar opener," said Frances. There was the sound of voices outside. "We'd better make ourselves scarce."

They hid in a little low-ceilinged room nearby, peering out of the window, a small deal table between them, scratches and inkblots in the grain.

"It doesn't have to be tea," said the girl with the feather in her hair, her voice carrying across the courtyard. "There are lots of other drinks that have three letters. Gin has three letters. So does rum."

"So does ale," said Furneval.

"Good job you emptied the caddy," said Frances.

"I'm learning," said Hugo.

A few minutes later Furneval and his friends reappeared. "What did I tell you?" said the girl with the feather in her hair. "It can't be tea because there isn't any."

Hugo said, "There's a name for that form of reasoning, but I can't remember what it is."

Frances, who was busy opening the drawers in the table, elbowed him in the ribs.

Words asked you to read them, whether you wanted to or not. They leapt into life, into sense, as soon as you looked at them. "No," he said, staring at the newspaper. "We can't use this."

"Why not?"

"It's a casualty list. It's not on, can't you see that?"

"It's lining a drawer."

"Even so, it's bad form."

"Don't lecture me." Frances spoke to his back. "We're all casualties, one way or another. Do you know, we don't go to see Daddy anymore. There's no point. They say he hardly speaks and it's too upsetting for Mummy. She's met someone else now. I don't like him very much, to be honest, but he says he'll pay for me to go to secretarial college. A girl like me can't rely on marriage these days. Far too much competition."

He turned. "I'm sorry."

She flushed and handed him the brittle, yellowing sheet. "Put it in your pocket. I've folded it the other way round. Now where do we find a train?"

"In a railway station."

"Not a bad idea."

"You could do worse than sell these doors," Connor said, running his fleshy hands up and down the panels.

They were back in the library, Ferrars having given up his original plan in favor of simply handing Dido the treasure-hunt items to wave in front of the photographers. With difficulty, these he had retrieved from their various hiding places. His concern now was that as time went by, there was the increased chance that someone would genuinely win. He knew enough about the way things worked to understand that no newspaper was going to run a picture of Tom, Dick, or Mabel on their front page, bracelet or no bracelet.

"A little more marching powder?" Connor said to Dido.

"Oh yes, please."

The girl had the constitution of an ox, thought Ferrars.

"Care for some?" Connor said to Ferrars.

"No." Ferrars looked at his watch. "I think we should get this over with. The press won't wait much longer. You can tell them how you found the lemon in your cocktail," he said to Dido.

"Doors, chimneypieces, even the plasterwork at a pinch," said Connor, chopping up the white powder. "All worth a bob or two, if you know where to flog them."

Ferrars had had a bellyful of Connor. The tawdriness of the man: it was contaminating. Who did he think he was? More to the point, how dare he imply that he was the sort of philistine who would strip the house bare for the sake of cash in hand? (Not that cash in hand wouldn't be welcome right now.)

As Dido sniffed up the line, Ferrars fetched a brochure from the card table and almost threw it at Connor. "If you must know, this is what I'm planning." He folded his arms. Some people had no vision at all.

Connor read the brochure and handed it back. Then he burst out laughing.

The car's headlamps whitened the rushing hedgerows on the steep ascending bends. The air was sweet with new growth, new green. When Hugo and Frances arrived back at the house, great brass-framed lanterns lighting up the frontage, another car drove up behind them and half a dozen people, including Furneval, spilled out, dragging an inn sign behind them.

"The Rose and Crown," said Frances, clutching the poster of a locomotive she had removed from the station platform. "Clever. Never mind. We find Ferrars and we've as good as won." She was triumphant. "We'd better split up. It will be quicker to find him that way."

But Ferrars was nowhere. No one had seen him. Those Hugo asked were either treasure hunters and wouldn't tell him, or were drunk, or were drunk treasure hunters. He searched from room to room, pushing and elbowing his way through the crowd, and what had seemed so beautiful earlier was now fractured and nightmarish: scarlet lipstick smeared on the rim of a glass, lanterns trampled on the stone floor, the smell of sweat and hair oil and the shrill braying of utter rot and nonsense. Four girls were doing calisthenics, shrieking, on the upstairs landing. In a bedroom off the corridor, he surprised a couple, the girl with her dress hiked up, the man crouching, pumping between her white thighs. He could only have been standing there a matter of seconds, but it felt like an hour. Then he backed out and shut the door on the disgust he felt at his own arousal.

"Frances," he said, colliding with her on the staircase coming up from the lower hall. His heart was thudding. "Have you found him?"

All the while people were tramping up and down the staircase in a restless, purposeless parade. He leaned against the wall, his sides heaving. Someone trod on his foot. Someone else trod on his foot.

"I have," said Frances. Her face was closed, shut in on itself.

"Well, where is he?" Someone trod on his foot. "Stop stepping on me!" he said. "These people are mad!"

"He's on the portico. Having his photograph taken."

"Why didn't—"

"No point. He's already presented the bracelet to Dido."

"Dido?"

"Apparently she's *won*," said Frances, with a look of disgust. "By the way, Vivian's been trying to find you. Sylvia's passed out."

It seemed to take forever to get Sylvia through the hall, out onto the portico, and down the stairs. Hugo had his arms wrapped under her humid armpits and across her chest; the others had hold of her feet.

With every step her bracelets rang and her dead weight threatened to send them all tumbling. He felt the strain in his shoulders
and thighs; a little below, Frances's face was white and taut.

"Is she breathing?" said Vivian.

"For God's sake," he said. "Set her down a moment."

Vivian said, "I can't tell whether she's breathing or not." Her
voice went up an octave. *"Is she breathing?"*

"Shut up, Vivian," said Frances.

He recovered himself, tightened his grip, and somehow they
struggled to the bottom. Outside they laid her on the gravel while
he opened the car; then they eased her onto the backseat. "You best
get in the front," he said to Vivian. "Frances, make sure she stays on
her side. If she starts choking, tell me and I'll pull over."

He stood a moment to catch his breath.

"You know, it was bad enough that they fixed it," said Frances.
"What really gets my goat is that she didn't even pretend to take part."

On the way back, Sylvia was sick all over the seats and into the
footwell.

10

Love in Bloom: 1938

A t night, when the rain beats on the roof and clouds chased by the wind scud across the sky, fear grips like a vise. The storm lifts slates and shatters them down below, where they'll be swept up and worried about in the morning, mows down the flowers that wave like brave flags. Worse is coming. The certainty waits round the corner.

Neglect's one thing, and almost expected; mutilation's another. In the dining room the walls are flayed. The doorways are open wounds. Drafts whistle down chimneys, where fireplaces have been torn away from their hearths, and rattle the loose sash frames. Unhappiness and dread spread through the empty rooms like an infection.

An afternoon in late October and Ferrars was watching a group of hikers from an upstairs window of the north pavilion. Half a dozen or so of them, all in plus fours, climbing up the hill towards the stand of trees on the horizon. Their intrusion wasn't so unusual. From time to time people wandered through the park or drove past the house, curious or simply lost; sometimes they even knocked on the door. Ferrars had sold off the entrance gates a few years ago and there was nothing to stop them.

"Love in Bloom" warbled on the gramophone next door in the

sitting room. If Ferrars had once been indifferent to Noël Coward, he thoroughly detested the man now. These days his wife kept playing the bloody song over and over and over again, until he thought he would go out of his mind. Perhaps that was her intention.

"Amanda," she had introduced herself to him when they met at the Chelsea Arts Club, shrieking over the roar. "As in *Private Lives.*" Little did he know that seven years later Noël Coward would be torturing him by the hour, that he would be married, let alone to Amanda, and that their marriage would be every bit as fractious as those depicted in the play, only a good deal less amusing.

She wasn't his type: that was his first impression. Too brittle, one of those voices that cut glass, long cigarette holder, penciled eyebrows. Half an hour in her company and it was obvious that she reveled in the attention of men, women, an aspidistra given half the chance. He thought she was tiresome.

He was unable to locate the man he had come to the club to meet, someone who had expressed an interest in buying the plasterwork decorations at the Park, and he allowed her to drag him out to the garden to hunt for the famous tortoises. The light was leaving the sky, but they found one—"Isn't it simply divine?"—motionless like a dull green boulder on a mossy paving slab.

"I hear you're in property," Amanda said, exhaling extravagantly. All her gestures were extravagant, as if she were semaphoring her intentions to the back row of the stalls.

"I dabble a little."

"A little bird tells me you have a great big house in the country. Clever you."

Since the Crash, Ferrars had lost confidence. Partly it was the timing—to buy a bloody big house just before Wall Street collapsed was bad timing, if anything was, and of course he was suffering financially and had given up the London flat as a consequence. Mostly it was some sort of unease that he couldn't identify but which made him wonder if he was losing his touch or had wandered so far off the road map of his life, he would never find his way back again.

Yet despite the unfavorable impression Amanda first made on

him, over the course of the evening he found that he was enjoying being with her. She made him laugh, she made him feel better; she made him feel like he used to feel, which, among other things, was younger. He began to see that she might be *fun*. For a while.

He never intended the affair to last once it started and gave it a few months before he tired of it or she did. Instead, day after day, week after week, he found he grew to depend upon her view of him, the possibilities she seemed to see in him. It made his previous successes, such as they were, less remote, the future more alive and promising. One thing led to another. And one of those things, in due course, was his daughter, Pudge. Amanda was four months pregnant when they married. Pudge was nearly seven now, and if anyone was the love of his life, she was.

So here they were, the three of them, at the Park, where they had set up a home of sorts in the north pavilion. A roof over their heads; others were not so lucky. These days he rarely went over to the main block, except to check no one had broken in. As a tangible reminder of the failure of his grand scheme, it depressed him; stripped of its doors, doorcases, a couple of fireplaces, and eventually the plaster-work decorations in the dining room (which had ended up, via a dealer in architectural antiques, in a hotel in New York), it made him feel guilty and small. It made him feel, in fact, as if he had turned into Connor.

He had already begun the process of making the pavilion habitable before he met Amanda. Cleared all the old rubbish out of the Victorian kitchen, moved some of his furniture down from London, knocked a couple of small rooms together upstairs at the back to make a sitting room with views towards the river, turned a small room downstairs into an office. It was more or less sound, tolerably warm if you kept the paraffin heaters going, and spacious enough for the pair of them after they married, for the three of them once Pudge came along. Yet Amanda complained ceaselessly—about the poor facilities (the freezing bathroom and lavatory in particular), the isolation, the lack of staff. Although a succession of slow-witted, obstreperous girls from the village cleaned the place after a fashion, and they'd managed to hang on to Len Stubbs, the head gardener, and a couple of other boys to help out in the grounds, it had been a while since they'd had a cook. Amanda could make a cocktail, but she couldn't boil an egg, so he'd taken on most of the cooking. It was either that or eat out of a tin.

In other circumstances, he supposed he and his wife would have gone their separate ways by now. But for him, divorce, separation, living apart were unthinkable so long as there was Pudge. He didn't trust Amanda to look after Pudge properly on her own—she was far too selfish—and if they had parted on bad terms (and on what other terms would they part?), he wouldn't have put it past her to refuse to let him see his own daughter. His great dread was that she would run off anyway and one morning he would wake to find them both gone.

It began to rain and the hikers Ferrars had been watching out of the window were nowhere to be seen. Next door, "Love in Bloom" started up on the gramophone again. He went down to the kitchen to fix himself a drink.

Pudge was sitting at the deal table, swinging her legs. She was making something with snippets of yarn, hard to tell what, watched by the cat, a large tabby, who was batting at the loose threads.

"Shoo the cat off the table, Pudge," said Ferrars. He disliked cats, but he tolerated this one because there were so many mice.

"He likes sitting on the table." His daughter was an eager little thing, with the self-containment of an only child. She was wearing a blue corduroy tunic, and her light-brown hair was cut in a bob just under her ears and in a fringe straight across her forehead. It pleased him that she resembled neither himself nor Amanda, only herself. She had round cheeks and thickly lashed eyes. "It's his proper place."

"No, it isn't, darling. He's a cat."

"Cats can go where they like. *Everywhere* are their proper places."

Ferrars put the cat on the floor and the cat leapt back on the table again in one fluid movement. Washed a paw.

Pudge said, "Can we go to the glasshouse, Daddy?"

"It's raining, darling." He fetched a clean glass from the draining board and uncorked the whisky bottle.

"I'll put on my mac."

"Maybe later, when the rain stops."

"But it might get dark. Please, Daddy, I haven't been for ages and ages and ages."

Not since the day before yesterday, in fact. Only one of the glasshouses was still in use; for some reason he couldn't fathom, it was Pudge's favorite place. She could play there happily for hours. Ferrars took a sip of the whisky and let it roll round his mouth, which didn't improve the taste. Then he set the glass back on the draining board. He couldn't afford the good stuff these days.

"All right, then. Just for a short while."

Pudge wanted to go to the glasshouse because she wanted to see the people. She couldn't tell anyone about the people because the people were secret. Very small and very secret. She had been making some food for them. They must be hungry because she hadn't been to the glasshouse for ages and ages and ages.

Her father fetched her mac and she put it on. It was navy blue and had a belt that you buttoned up. It wasn't her favorite coat. It was just a coat. Her best coat was fawn and had a dark-brown velvet collar.

Len was in the glasshouse. Len had hair growing out of his ears, and his fingernails were very dirty. Rain tapped on the glass roof like it wanted to come in.

Pudge walked down the slatted floor between the rows of seed trays to the place where the ferns grew. Her father was talking to Len. Len was washing out plant pots.

The glasshouse had a special smell, which she liked. The smell was stronger the closer you got to the beds at the back. Under ferns in the corner the little people were waiting for her. She crouched down and gave them their dinner. They didn't have very good table manners. They talked with their mouths full. They put their elbows on the table.

Her father was still talking to Len. Len was still washing out plant pots. She was talking to the people very quietly in her head.

"Pudge, darling. Didn't you hear me calling you?" said Ferrars. "It's time for tea."

His daughter peered up at him and shook her head. She had squeezed herself in among the ferns, where she had arranged her tiny snippets of yarn in the dirt.

"What are you doing down there?" he said.

"Playing," she said.

"Well, you'd better pick up those bits and bobs," said her father. "You don't want to leave them for Len. He likes to keep the glasshouse tidy."

The people had finished eating. Pudge picked up the bits and bobs and put them in the pocket of her mac. Her fingernails were dirty, just like Len's.

Six weeks later, a fortnight before Christmas, carols on the wireless and frost in the park. One of the paraffin heaters had packed up. It was a little after eight in the evening and winter gloom had settled in the sitting room.

"Who was on the telephone?" said Amanda.

"You mean this afternoon?"

"Obviously." These days the telephone rarely rang.

"A chap who saw the advert in the *Times*. Seems he's interested in the garden urns. Coming out to have a look at them tomorrow."

He had placed the notice in the classifieds: *For sale. Antique garden furniture, statuary, ornaments, urns. Price negotiable.*

"Tomorrow's Saturday."

"Some people have to work."

"They do," said Amanda pointedly. "Well, I suppose you might make half a crown if you're lucky."

Ferrars winced and nursed his glass of whisky. "Hark! the Herald Angels" sang.

"Pudge said the funniest thing this morning. I meant to tell you earlier. She said there are people living in the glasshouse. Tiny people."

Amanda was perched on the settee, one leg tucked under her, sewing in the lamplight. A cigarette burned in the ashtray. She was working on a little white shirt. More little white shirts and a couple of navy sweaters banded in emerald green were nestled in an open parcel beside her.

"Tiny people in the glasshouse. I see."

He had only mentioned it as an uncontroversial topic of conversation. There were few enough of them.

"It explains why she's always so keen to go over there all the time."

He took a sip of his drink.

"She has far too much imagination for her own good."

"I wasn't aware one could have too much imagination," said Ferrars.

His wife didn't answer.

"What are you doing?"

"What does it look like?" Amanda bit the thread with her teeth. "Sewing in name tapes."

"Name tapes. For school?"

"Of course for school. Why ever else would one need name tapes?"

Pudge, his daughter, his beloved daughter, was asleep in her bedroom next door.

"That isn't the uniform for St. Mary's."

St. Mary's was the infants' school in the village, which Pudge had been attending for a term.

"How observant you are, George."

It had reached the point where Ferrars and his wife were sleeping apart. There were no spare bedrooms in the north pavilion, so Ferrars was bunking on a camp bed in the office downstairs, the same camp bed where he had slept when he was plotting the sale of the house, when he still had a flat in London to go back to.

"Are you going to tell me what this is all about? Or am I supposed to guess?"

Amanda pulled another little white shirt out of the paper wrapping, smoothed it over her lap, and turned back the collar. Threaded a needle.

"She's starting at Silcott House next term."

"Silcott House? What's that?"

Amanda raised her eyes wearily. "It's a boarding school in Windsor."

"*What?*" Ferrars got up, crossed the room, and turned down the wireless. "But we agreed no boarding school, at least not until she's older. She's only six."

"She's nearly seven. And she's learning nothing at St. Mary's, which is hardly surprising, since it's chock-full of children with nits."

As a boy, he had had nits on numerous occasions. He didn't recall them interfering with his education.

"She likes it there. She has friends."

"If she had proper friends, there would be no need for imaginary ones."

Ferrars tried not to raise his voice. It rose all the same. "Pudge is *not* going to boarding school. It's out of the question. She's far too young."

"Her name," said Amanda, "is Dinah, not Pudge. And it's all arranged. My mother has very kindly agreed to pay the fees, so you needn't concern yourself on that account."

That, at least, did not surprise him. Amanda's mother, in some shape or form, lurked at the bottom of nine-tenths of their disagreements. Which was odd, considering how she had featured so largely in his wife's decision to give wedded life a go.

"Correct me if I'm wrong, but your mother has never shown the slightest interest in contributing to our household expenses."

"She simply wants the best for her only grandchild."

Ferrars shook his head. "Well, she's gone too far this time. I'll ring her tomorrow and tell her so. And I'll ring the school, whatever it's called, and tell them there's been a mistake."

"You'll do no such thing," said Amanda, "if you care about your daughter."

"What's that supposed to mean?"

"The coming months are going to be difficult. She will need to be somewhere safe and settled."

"I'm sorry, I hadn't realized that you and your mother were on speaking terms with Herr Hitler. We don't know when this bloody war will start. We don't even know if there'll be a war."

"I'm not talking about war," said Amanda. She put down her sewing. "I had been planning to wait until after Christmas to tell you, but as you're being so frightfully unreasonable, you might as well know now that I'm leaving you."

You could dread something happening, expect it, wait for it, and still feel the shock when the chasm opens up under your feet. His mouth was dry.

"You're leaving me."

"Don't beg me to stay, please. That really would be the limit."

"And what do you propose to do? Once you've left."

"I intend to get a divorce."

"I see," said Ferrars. "Then I'll fight you for custody."

"You won't get it."

"Have you seen a lawyer?"

Amanda brought her penciled eyebrows together in a little frown. "Of course. You haven't a leg to stand on."

He was not taken in by the evenness of her tone or by her un-natural composure, in itself a form of exaggeration. This was still a scene played out to the back rows of the stalls.

"What do you mean by that?"

She picked up her sewing again and made a couple of swift, stabbing stitches.

"I said, what do you mean by that?"

She raised her eyes and played her card. "Edie Baxter."

"Who?"

His heart was hammering and he could feel some sort of foolish expression occupy his face.

"You heard me. Not a name, I admit, previously familiar to me from our small circle of acquaintance."

That was the moment Ferrars knew it was over. Edie Baxter had been a stupid lapse—a moment of temptation or weakness, call it what you like—and the devil of a job to get disentangled from.

"How did you find out?"

"You're a poor liar, George, which I count as one of your better qualities."

"It meant nothing."

"Not to *Edie,* it seems," said Amanda, handling the name in the tongs of quotation marks. "If you must know, she rang me after you finished with her. Went into a great deal of rather unpleasant detail. I don't know what you promised, but the stupid bitch was jolly disappointed not to get it. Hell hath no fury, et cetera. She's happy to make a statement if necessary. Spill the beans, as the Yanks say. But of course one would hope to keep matters civilized for Dinah's sake."

Ferrars threw his whisky glass across the room. Then he hurled the ashtray after it. For good measure, he knocked over the lamp. The bulb shattered.

"For God's sake, George, act your age."

"Is Mummy paying for this too?"

"Be quiet. You'll wake the child," said Amanda.

He went over to the window, parted the curtains, and tilted his forehead against the cold glass, panting.

Behind him, he was aware of her tidying up, rustling the packaging in which the school clothes had arrived, coming and going between bedroom and sitting room, heels tapping on the floor.

It was a beautiful day for a drive to the country, clear and crisp. For the Lyells, newly married, every outing no matter how ordinary was weighted with significance. The war, with its threat of separation or worse, loomed over their future. In defiance of it, they were nest building.

"I thought we might take the roadster since it's fine," said Hugo.

"Yes, why not?" said his wife, Reggie.

"You won't be too cold?"

"A little fresh air never hurt anybody. And after last night it would be good to clear one's head."

"That's what I was thinking."

Hugo watched his wife wrap her dark-brown hair in a head scarf. Perhaps there would come a time when he no longer noticed the grace she gave to an ordinary gesture, but he couldn't imagine it.

The previous evening had been frightful. Old friends of his family, who lived in Belgrave Square, had invited them to dinner. As soon as the drinks were poured, and tongues loosened, Hugo regretted accepting the invitation. It wasn't so much the friends as the friends of the friends.

"Anything rather than war" was not an uncommon sentiment after Munich. You heard it and read it often enough these days. What had been aired around the lamplit room, however, had strayed into open admiration of the German regime. It disgusted him. So did the remark someone had made that if you hadn't fought in the last one, you couldn't possibly know what you were talking about. He thought of Max Koenig, a professor of mathematics, who had arrived from Göttingen the previous month on the boat train with his wife and two daughters, all that remained of twenty-five years of research and domestic life crammed into four small suitcases. Max and Hugo's elder brother, Paul, who was killed in the war, had been great friends at university. Honoring that bond, Hugo's father had helped the Koenigs get out, found them a tiny flat in West Hampstead, and was paying the rent until the professor could find work. "They froze his bank accounts and confiscated his wife's pearls and engagement ring," his father had said, adding that when he'd shown them the flat, with its shared bathroom down the hall, the wife, Maus, had cried like a child.

In the hall of their tall, narrow house in London, Hugo patted his pockets.

"The keys are in the dish."

"So they are."

"What's the name of this place we're going to?" said Reggie, as he held the door open for her.

"Ashenden Park."

The first time Hugo saw Reggie, she was on horseback. A college friend had asked him to Leicestershire for the weekend, and they'd gone along to a point-to-point for the want of anything better to do between lunch and dinner. Hugo didn't ride himself, or at least not well enough for the daunting fences and hedges, and was standing with the other mud-flecked spectators at the halfway mark when a horse and rider flew past and cleared an enormous ditch as if it were a crack in the pavement. His immediate companion, an elderly woman in tweeds with rheumy eyes, noted his astonishment and passed him a hip flask. It was a chill, overcast day, threatening rain.

"Who was that?"

"Oh, that was Reggie."

He shook his head. The name meant nothing.

"Regina Fitzalan. Daughter of Patrick Fitzalan, the trainer."

"I don't know the racing world very well."

"Patrick hasn't had a winner for a while. Through no fault of his, I might add. He's a superb horseman." The Fitzalans had a yard near Kilkenny, the woman went on to explain. "Poor as church mice, of course."

Later he would understand just how short money had been and how much that had contributed to the independence and resourcefulness of Reggie's character. At the time, as incredible as it was to him now, he had thought nothing more about her until that evening, when he was standing with his college friend in the drawing room before dinner.

"Reggie!" said his friend, waving. "Over here."

Hugo hadn't recognized her out of her riding clothes. She came across the room and his heart swerved in his chest.

They were introduced, they talked, and when he complimented her on her riding, she said that he should see her father in action. "No," she replied in answer to his next question, "he didn't really school any of us. His approach is pretty much to tell you not to fall off. And then to tell you to get back on when you do." There was a quality to her voice he found irresistible, not so much an accent but a different sort of music.

His previous affairs had been acquisitions. He would see some-one he wanted, get her, more often than not, and then stop want-ing her after a while. This had nothing to do with the inequality of possession. This was like finding a part of yourself that you hadn't known was missing and having it restored to you.

An hour after the Lyells left London, they were driving along the narrow lanes that twisted through the Chilterns, up and down one green hill after another. While the white roadster was a plaything and a thoroughly impractical color, Hugo had to admit it cut a dash. As they came through the village, children ran after them, waving and calling. They passed a church, a couple of pubs, and a war me-morial, and he began to laugh.

"What is it?"

"I was remembering that dreadful woman last night who thought your dress was by Worth. The look she gave you when you said you'd made it yourself."

"She was shocked, wasn't she? You know, she came up to me after-wards and asked whether you gave me a decent allowance, and that if you didn't, it was a scandal considering how well-to-do you are."

"I hope you sent her away with a flea in her ear."

"Well, I told her I liked making things and that she had a good eye because Worth have used the same cloth themselves."

Hugo smiled to himself. One of the things he cherished most about Reggie was her generosity of spirit.

"I think this should be the turning," he said.

The trees thinned out, revealing a house set in open parkland.

"How beautiful," said Reggie, as they came up the drive.

The late-morning sun brought out the honey color of the stone-work, and the great house seemed to glow. Something about it tugged at her, stirred her imagination in a way she could not put into words.

"Most of the house is shut up, apparently," said Hugo. "We're to go through that courtyard over there and ring the bell."

As they stood waiting on the doorstep of the pavilion, they could hear music coming from above.

"What is that insinuating tune?" said Hugo.

"'Love in Bloom,'" said Reggie, and they laughed.

Ferrars had stored the garden furniture, statuary, and stone urns in one of the outbuildings beyond the kitchen garden. As he switched on the light, a bare bulb festooned in cobwebs, he realized that he ought to have tidied up a bit: the place was a jumble. But after Amanda's announcement the previous night, and the amount of whisky he had put away afterwards, he was in no mood.

It did not help that the couple—the Lyells—were a handsome pair. To rub salt further into the wound, they were obviously smit-ten with each other. The woman was young, graceful, and beautiful. The man was a little older and, judging by appearances, well-heeled, and he envied him on all accounts: wife, wealth, and tailoring. Care-less of their expensive clothing, they were crouching down examin-ing a pair of urns with snarling lions carved on the front, discussing whether or not they were too big.

"We live in London," said Reggie, smiling up at him. "Our gar-den is tiny."

Hugo stood up. "Do you deliver?"

"I could arrange transport," said Ferrars. By which he meant that he could borrow a van and drive the urns to London himself.

"And how much are you asking for them?"

"Six guineas." Ferrars had been intending to sell them for four, but he was feeling savage. "They're eighteenth-century. Original to the house."

"We'll take them." Hugo got out his notecase, then hesitated a moment. "If you don't you mind my asking, how long have you been here?"

"A good while," said Ferrars. "Why?"

"There's something awfully familiar about this place. I seem to remember some sort of party."

The treasure hunt, thought Ferrars, with a further sink of spirits. What a hiding to nothing that had been.

"I don't know how one could ever forget a house like this, darling," said Reggie. She wouldn't forget it, she knew.

"Well, it must have been nine, ten years ago."

Ferrars shook his head. "Before my time." He ushered them from the outbuilding and snapped off the light.

11

Hut C: 1946

Blackout. For six years every factory, home, and institution in the country has done its bit for the war effort and the house is no exception. While you might think it's risen to the occasion, it's had no choice in the matter. Its requisitioned rooms, to which only ghosts of glamour still cling, fill up with filing cabinets and uniformed personnel; its staircases echo to the pounding tread of regulation boots. Tape crisscrosses the windows, tanks tear up the turf, and planes drone monotonously overhead. Troops training for invasion invade the park.

Now nights are no longer broken by the crump of falling bombs or the wail of sirens. But the war isn't over for everyone.

In his dreams Walter Beckmann sometimes saw the house from above. He did not know what trick of the imagination allowed it to appear to him from this perspective—he had never flown in a plane—and yet the positioning of the house on the hill, the distribution of its chimneys on the roof, the crisp shadow it cast over the park were accurate so far as he could tell. Such soaring, billowing visions often came towards morning, which is why he remembered them. Unremembered were deeper, darker, more fragmented ones.

When the war ended, they had expected to be shipped home in a few months. Instead repatriation was slow, and out of eighty beds in the hut only twenty-three were empty. There was a rumor that the new German government would pay a mark a day in compensation for those who remained in the camps after the turn of the year. He wondered whether it would mean that Vogel, who had given the *Heil Hitler!* salute when he'd been summoned for his interview before the panel, and sentenced to a further six months as a result, would be rewarded for his loyalty to National Socialism at the same time he was punished for it.

Eighty men a hut, two tables, four benches, one stove in the middle of the room. Ten huts in the camp. Previously troops had been stationed here preparing for the landings, and he thought it a particular British efficiency—no one could have called it over-confidence the way the war was going by then—that as soon as the huts emptied of soldiers, the bunks were free to accommodate the prisoners they took. As the months wore on and the camp filled up, they played skat, told stories, took English lessons. English lessons were popular. Kaplinski played his mouth organ in the evenings when they came back from digging ditches, dredging, hedging, bone weary and stunned by air and labor.

The first thing Walter did when he woke up this morning was pull out the drawstring bag from underneath his bunk and spill the wooden blocks across the iron-gray blanket. Twenty-six of them, sanded smooth, each one carved with a letter of the alphabet, and on the other side a picture. A for Apple. B for Boat. C for Cat. It had taken him weeks to make them and tested his vocabulary as much as his woodworking skills.

Frisch, the *Lagerführer,* threw open the door to Hut C and the corrugated iron shuddered on its timber frame. The cold air brought in a sharp smell of autumn bonfires. Most of the men were already up and yawning, heading out to the latrines.

"Beckmann," said Frisch, approaching.

He pulled up his uniform trousers, P for Prisoner painted on the side of them. "Sir."

Frisch handed him his day pass and inspected the blocks by peering down at the blanket, his hands clasped behind his back.

"Good work. Christmas gift?"

"Birthday present."

"Not long now," said Frisch, who had a round face that looked as if it had been carelessly formed out of putty and might be re-formed any minute and not necessarily in a better fashion. "You're on the next list. Expect an interview soon. Your conduct has been good. No tarts, no fights, no Nazi talk. And you've seen the films. You know what they want to hear."

Walter nodded. He'd seen the films. They screened them in the chapel once a month. Reeducation was what the British called it, those jerky, grainy images of emaciated corpses and walking dead in their wire-fenced circles of hell. The first time, Kaplinski had barely made it outside before he'd thrown up, which left you wondering what he'd seen on the eastern front and wouldn't talk about. Vogel had said, and carried on saying, that it was propaganda designed to humiliate them and that the newsreels were faked.

Walter watched the films with compulsion and dread, silent in the flickering light, storing the images with the other heavy truths the war had taught him. The biggest truth, and perhaps the worst, was how easy truth was to ignore, how fragile it was when delusion combined with self-interest. An entire country, a people, could will their eyes and minds away from it while their acts demonstrated a terrible knowingness and purpose to the contrary. A few years before the war, his father acquired a Jewish business in the small town where they lived, the premises and stock, the old upright cast-iron cash registers and a small motorized delivery van, "for almost nothing" he had announced over the evening meal, as if the transaction had been a triumph of his own commercial acumen. Later he remembered accompanying his father to make an inventory and finding in the darkened flat upstairs a heavy coat with a fur collar hanging in a wardrobe smelling of camphor. What had arisen in him was a feeling of shame so intense he had quickly closed the wardrobe door to trap it inside. Now when he watched the films, the wardrobe door swung open and shame came tumbling out. He wondered if you could ever get used to it, as you could get used to a cough in the mornings.

Frisch said, "If you need packing materials, come by the camp office. I'll see what I can do."

"Thank you, sir, but that will not be necessary."

Frisch laid a hand on his shoulder. "Home soon. We shall all be home soon."

After breakfast Walter went to the chapel where the interdenominational pastor talked about plowed fields and scattered seeds. You got a good mark on your record if you attended chapel, although that was not why he had come. He was there because there was nothing else to do until ten o'clock, which was the time when his day pass came into effect.

During the service a memory came back to him. It had been a summer's day soon after the bombing of Hamburg and he'd come home on a forty-eight-hour leave. When he'd arrived, hot and tired, at the railway station, it was crowded with bewildered refugees laden with cheap luggage and reeking of smoke, many with singed hair, raw faces, and dull, empty eyes. He recalled one couple—they could not have been much older than he was—and the woman was murmuring to a child wrapped in a dirty shawl. The child was burnt black and quite dead.

Coils of barbed wire surrounded the camp, enclosing machine-gun posts and gun batteries trained on the rows of huts. He presented his pass to the guard at the gate.

"Open your bag," said the guard, stamping the pass.

Walter opened his bag and the guard examined the wooden blocks with absent curiosity, nodded, and waved him through.

Release was a birth. Soon the camp lay behind and the world fell away in every direction. To his right was a stand of trees, clumped together for company, beyond which the land dipped down and rose again to the hill where the house was situated. To his left were fields rutted by tank treads and littered with rusting oil drums. Farther in that direction was the American airfield, overgrown with nettles and other choking weeds that encroached upon the abandoned runway.

The path that bisected the fields was mud striped with chalk, knobbly flints cast upward giving a grip underfoot. The colors were what he described to himself as English: a sharp yellow and a dull blue that answered it, the rest dirty green, gray, and brown. Above, the sky was streaked and indefinite.

He had been captured somewhere near Caen and brought across the Channel with other prisoners on a barge laden with wounded Allied troops, the sea foaming red near the beach and many men screaming and dying before they reached the port. He didn't remember much about the crossing; he thought he must have slept or blanked it out. Afterwards a train—with upholstered seats, to his astonishment—took them to a football ground serving as a holding station, where they were deloused and interrogated. To get to the football ground from the train, they were marched in columns down the main street of the town. He had been expecting to be spat at or beaten, at least abusive words, but they had passed through silent stares, the women with their hair wrapped up in head scarves, smoking, the gray men lost in their thoughts, the sharp-eyed children brandishing polished bits of shrapnel.

Name, rank, company, papers. The purpose of the interrogation was to determine how zealous a Nazi you were. Regardless of their answers, all members of the Waffen-SS were given black cloth badges to sew on their uniforms and sent to wild parts of Scotland and similar remote places. Gray badges were given to party members whose loyalties were more ambiguous. They were also assigned to camps away from the cities. After a series of questions barked at him in a clipped voice by a man with a mustache behind a desk, translated by a Pole (although his *Hochschule* English meant he understood the greater part of it), Walter had been given a white one, which graded him as an ordinary enemy. Then he was sent to Ashenden Park. There were many men to process and it was not an infallible system. Vogel was proof of that.

He slipped on the path and almost fell. All captives eventually learned that if they were going to survive their imprisonment, they had to live in the monotonous present. Now, as he steadied himself, holding the drawstring bag up and away from the mud, it was the future he was protecting, something precious, tender, precarious, and unexpected.

Alison watched her father out of the kitchen window. He was digging and wore no coat or jacket, braces over his shirt hitching up his work trousers. In the far corner of the garden a small fire sent wisps of smoke into the air like a regular in a public house drawing on his pipe. By her feet the child played.

"I do wish there was more in the shops," said her mother, for whom cooking was clattering. "One wonders when it will ever improve!" She did battle with an oven tray. "How tired we all are of cakes made of carrots. I know I am." The oven door slammed and the child, Thomas, reached up his arms, uncertain. Were all war children so uncertain? wondered Alison, bending down to pick him up. "You do spoil him," said her mother, resting her hands on the sink. "Sugar, in proper quantities. Is that too much to ask, after all we've been through?"

"Go have a rest," said Alison, the child tugging her hair and her earlobes. "I'll watch the cake."

Her mother said, "Oh, Lord, now the cat's being sick."

"I'll clear it up. Go have a rest."

"You'll let the cake burn."

"I shan't, I promise."

Her mother went off in her apron, and Alison heard her go along the passageway and up the far stairs, and all the slight adjustments and tidying she made as she went along. She set down the child, who immediately reached up his arms to be picked up again, and wiped the cat sick off the quarry tiles with a floor cloth.

Long ago Prospect Place had been two separate cottages and the rooms were little, low-ceilinged, and duplicated one another, which meant that it was difficult to assign to each a settled purpose. That hadn't mattered so much when they had evacuees billeted on them and everything was chaos, but now the ambiguity that she remembered from her childhood had returned. There had always been too many rooms for the three of them, yet somehow not enough space. Her parents' bedroom, with its old Morris willow-pattern paper, was on the upper story at the front. She and the child slept over the kitchen, which isolated their noise. It used to be the spare room, and she could recall wet afternoons when she and her school friends had tugged the feather mattress off the bed, placed it at the bottom of the stairs, and taken it in turns to hurl themselves onto it.

Her father came in the back door and the cat shot out of it.

"What's up, Sunny Jim?" he said to the child fretting on the floor, turned on the tap, and scrubbed his hands with a nailbrush that had seen better days. "Where's your mother?"

"Gone for a rest."

Hanging on a peg beside the mackintoshes was the tin hat her father had worn when he was fire watching on the roof of the insurance company in Reading where he was employed. There had been nights early on in the Blitz when she and her mother had huddled under overturned armchairs, waiting for the all clear, a sick taste in their mouths; then the raids eased off and the second wave of evacuees had come. The biggest explosion they'd heard in the following months was when a land mine close to the big house was detonated, which had set off a fresh round of bed-wetting among the youngsters. That was about the time an incendiary bomb dropped by a straggler off-course had set a field on fire at Grange Farm and the smoke from the burning stubble had hung over the village for days.

Alison looked at the clock, a skip and a flutter in her chest. Almost eleven. In the chipped white enamel colander on the draining board, blackberries leached purple juice. Her father dried his hands on a souvenir of a rainy summer holiday in Bournemouth.

"Remind me," he said, "what time is this extravaganza?" He was a slight, dark man, with a bald patch on the crown of his head.

"Dad," she said, with a smile. "You know. Teatime."

"Birthday boy," he said, bending down to touch his roughened knuckles to the child's reddened teething cheeks. It would not have occurred to him to pick him up, any more than it would have occurred to him to change the sheets or lay the table.

"I'm just going to put him down for his nap and pop out for a bit."

"Right you are." He winked at her. "Don't let the cake burn, will you, or I wouldn't want to answer for the consequences."

Love was hard to hide in a village. Sometimes Alison wished she lived in a bombed-out part of London or was back in the cramped flat in Reading where she and Geoffrey had spent the early months of their marriage, anywhere indifferent and anonymous. Here you couldn't post a letter without Mrs. Peat, the postmistress, saying, "Run out of stamps already, Alison?" or Mrs. Harris, a curtain twitcher who lived across from the postbox on the corner of the green, wondering in the butcher's queue whether you'd taken up a correspondence course and, if so, how you managed to find the time to study with a little one to look after. Even your thoughts weren't safe. "Penny for them," the milkman said. "Lucky chap, whoever he is."

Half eleven, the cake was cooling on a wire rack on the kitchen table and the child was asleep in his cot, his dimpled fist pressing the satin bias binding of his blanket close to his cheek. She let herself out of the house and headed off down the lane towards the river.

These were great moments of freedom when Alison felt wholly alive. Her prewar self would not have recognized this person wearing an old navy-blue jersey and a pair of trousers, her face bare and her hair anyhow. Perhaps if Geoffrey had survived and come home, he would have met this person and they might have arrived at a different understanding of one another. "When there's a flap on and we've all got the wind up," he had said on his last leave from the airfield, "I remind myself what a looker I married. What a lucky bugger I am." Then he'd pulled her towards him and kissed her, and all she remembered afterwards was the revulsion she'd felt at his urgent wet mouth. That involuntary shrinking had come back to shame her in the long blank months after he was killed, when she was carrying his child and guilt and grief were one and the same thing.

Alison thought that if she ever had a daughter, she would tell her to beware of first impressions, particularly the ones you created yourself. After she'd met Geoffrey at a dance at the social club, dressed up to the nines, she'd let herself in for hours of applying lipstick, curling her hair, and straightening the seams of her stockings, knowing all the while that she was constructing a person who didn't exist and whom she didn't much like the look of in the mirror. If war had taught her endurance, how to put one foot in front of the other, it had also taught her the fine art of being herself.

Where the lane met the river was a low stretch of wall that was easy to climb. On the other side of it, in the grounds of the park, her heart began to quicken.

The cottage in the woods had been abandoned as long as she could remember, in childhood a place they dared each other to go into, a witch's lair or haunted house. These days the walls were scribbled with obscenities and part of the roof had fallen in. She saw Walter before he saw her, framed by a rear window, and the quiet way he had of looking inwards, of self-examination, moved her as much as it had done the first time they had set eyes on each other, the afternoon her father had taken pity on a prisoner laboring in the heat and suggested that she go and give him a glass of water.

"He's a German. He can die of thirst for all I care," she had said.

"He's a human being," said her father, handing her the glass.

"Walter?" she said, and his face turned into the light. Everything she loved about him and knew about him was written on it in that unguarded moment.

It hadn't been love at first sight. First sight established Walter as the human being her father believed him to be and awoke nothing more than fellow feeling in her. Deeper feelings came later, watch-

ing Walter work without complaining the way some of the prisoners did, overhearing the halting conversations he had with her
father, seeing his face light up when an eleven-month-old Thomas
took his first steps down the back garden.

One summer's day after VE Day she invited him to afternoon tea.

"Steady on," said her mother. "We don't want the village talking."

"He's just a lad away from home," said her father. "Can't do any
harm now."

By then Alison knew she was in love. What she didn't know yet
was whether she was in love with a person or forbidden fruit. In the
village "love thine enemy" did not extend to Germans.

It was true that Walter didn't look especially German. He was
dark-haired, not blond. His eyes were brown, not blue, and the
shape of his head would remind no one of a bullet. But he had P
for Prisoner painted on the sides of his trousers, and his English,
although good, had the accent they had all learned to hate.

They'd had their tea out in the garden since it was such a lovely
afternoon. Reaching for the milk jug, his hand brushed hers, and
she felt such a sudden heat in that gesture, as if it had left a mark
on her skin, that she looked directly at him, her mouth fallen open,
color rising in her cheeks.

Later that week, she received a letter from him and it was after
that they began to meet, often at the ruined cottage. The first time
they kissed, a door opened inside her and stayed open.

"I say, you do scrub up well," her father said to her mother, giving
her a little pat on the backside.

"Don't be ridiculous, Malcolm." She touched her hair and tied
her apron around her waist. "I didn't realize it had got so late.
Where's Alison?"

"Here I am," Alison said, coming down the stairs into the
kitchen, the child drowsy in her arms.

"The cake's soggy in the middle. You must have taken it out of
the oven too soon."

"Oh dear, did I?"

"Well, look at it."

"Never mind, I'm sure no one will notice."

Her mother eyed her up and down. "Aren't you going to change?"

"What for?"

Her parents exchanged a glance.

"Your mother's gone to a lot of trouble," said her father.

Her mother said, "I know it's only the Drummonds and Walter, but you could make an effort."

She shrugged. "I'd rather be comfortable."

"Suit yourself."

"Do you want a hand with the table?"

"You might iron the napkins, I suppose."

She put the child down, opened a drawer, and took out the napkins.

"Not those!" said her mother. "The little green ones with the scalloped edges."

Thomas lifted his arms, fretting.

"Ignore him," said her mother. "He's got to learn you're not at his beck and call."

"He's teething." She picked him up. "It hurts."

Her mother said, "He's winding you round his little finger is what he's doing."

"I'll be out back if anyone wants me," said her father.

Three-quarters of an hour later, the little green napkins with the scalloped edges had been ironed, folded into triangles, and laid beside each place setting. Plates of paste sandwiches, their crusts cut off, sat on the cross-stitched cloth, and the milk jug was covered with lace weighted with beads. In the center of the dining table, beside a green glass vase filled with the last of the Michaelmas daisies, was the cake, its sunken middle disguised by a spray of artificial lily of the valley that her mother had saved from a bottle of scent her father had given her before the war.

"Look upon my works, ye Mighty," said Alison, "and despair."

The doorbell rang. It was the Drummonds. Alison could hear

them saying to her parents that they were sorry they were early, but after all they hadn't far to come. When she brought the child into the sitting room, they were all standing equidistant from one another as if the occasion warranted some greater formality.

"And here's the birthday boy!" said Mrs. Drummond. Thomas turned his face away. "Don't be shy, Tommy. It's only Auntie Mavis and Uncle Bob from next door."

The child clutched Alison's leg and she picked him up.

"She does spoil him," said her mother.

"I gather the German lad's coming," said Mr. Drummond. "Quite a fixture round here these days."

"Sherry?" said her father, as if there were an alternative.

The bottle lived in the cupboard underneath the wireless, which seemed to have shrunk a little since the war had ended and become something to dust between gay bursts of the Light Programme.

"Wouldn't say no," said Mr. Drummond.

"We've brought a little contribution," said Mrs. Drummond. She rummaged in her handbag and produced a tin. "Now what do you think of this?"

"What is it?" said her father, sherry bottle in hand. He wasn't wearing his spectacles.

"Peaches," said Alison.

Mrs. Drummond said, "All the way from Australia. We had a parcel from Deirdre this week. Still no idea when she'll be de-mobbed, but of course her work is very hush-hush."

Her father handed round the sherry glasses.

"Cheers. Bottoms up," said Mr. Drummond.

"They talk about the Yanks and whatnot, with their hams and nylons," said Mrs. Drummond. "And good luck to you if you've got the connections. Who am I to say you shouldn't have a nice bit of ham on your table? Who am I to deny a young lady the chance to show off her legs?" She glanced at Alison's trousers. "But to be honest, and put it down to my sweet tooth if you will, I'd much rather have peaches in syrup. I always think," she said, "that they taste of *pure sunshine*."

"Thank you, Mavis," said her mother, accepting the tin. "That's frightfully generous of you."

"Deirdre sent us half a dozen," said Mr. Drummond. "You can imagine the postage."

There was a little silence.

"Do excuse me," said her mother. "I'll be back in a moment."

"Well, that's trumped the cake," said her father out of the corner of his mouth.

"Never fear," said Alison, out of the corner of hers. "There are cards up the maternal sleeve."

"Tell me you don't mean the boiled sweets. They've been sitting in that jar in the larder since nineteen thirty-nine."

"I was thinking more along the lines of table decorations."

"The rose-patterned tea service?"

Alison nodded. "She's brought out the artillery."

"Pass the little lad over to me, Alison, dear," said Mrs. Drummond, moving within earshot of their murmured exchange. "I'm sorry we were so early. You obviously didn't have the chance to get yourself ready."

The doorbell rang. "I'll go," said Alison.

Walter was standing on the doorstep, holding the drawstring bag, whose contents he had refused to divulge to her earlier. She had seen photographs of him before the war, family pictures that he kept in his tunic pocket; since then his face had sharpened and developed hollows and lines, but the dark hair and eyebrows were the same and so was the quizzical look, which she had previously ascribed to difficulties understanding English, or the English. Laughter came from the sitting room.

"I am late?"

"No," she said. "You're just on time."

"Happy birthday, Thomas," he said to the child.

"Wattah," said Thomas, wriggling out of her arms and making a run at him.

He lifted the child high up into the air and set him back on his feet. "My goodness. What a big boy you are."

"Wattah," said Thomas, with his first smile of the day.

"Come through," said Alison. "We're having sherry. The Drummonds are already here." When she turned to lead him indoors, she saw her mother standing at the end of the passage, silhouetted against the light.

"Then those chaps from the RMC hoisted her up on top of the bus shelter and she sat there singing 'Run, Rabbit, Run,'" said Mrs. Drummond. "Do you remember? She was tight as a tick."

"How could anyone forget?" said her father.

"VE Night," said Mr. Drummond. "Best night of my life, I don't mind telling you."

"Have you heard from Geoffrey's people?" said Mrs. Drummond.

"Still in Scotland," said her mother. "They sent a lovely card and some of Geoffrey's things that the little lad might appreciate when he's older."

"They want to draw a line under it," said Alison.

"Oh, nonsense," said her mother.

"I've seen them three times since the wedding, and the second was the memorial service. At the christening they hardly even looked at their grandson, much less held him. Too painful, they said."

"Help yourselves to more sandwiches," said her father, passing the plate.

"And when will they be sending you back, Walter?" said Mrs. Drummond, speaking in capital letters. "Any idea?"

Her mother got up from her seat. "Time to give this little chap his presents, I think. I'll light the candles."

Thomas, sitting in his high chair, was transfixed by the two candles and indifferent to the mimed huffing and puffing that followed. In the end, Alison blew them out and everyone clapped. Then she placed her present on the table in front of the child and helped him to unwrap it. He was transfixed now by the paper.

"Oh, look what it is, Thomas!" said her mother. "It's a funny little rabbit, isn't it?"

"I'm very taken with your rabbit, Alison," said Mr. Drummond.

"I sewed the ears on backwards," she said.

Thomas put one of the ears in his mouth.

"It's the thought that counts." Mrs. Drummond reached across the table to hand her two half crowns. "This is from us. Buy him something he needs, dear."

"That's very kind of you."

Her mother gave her a small packet wrapped in tissue paper that contained a sky-blue cardigan.

"Oh, that's lovely," said Alison, identifying the source of the wool as one of her mother's sweaters. "And the red buttons are so jolly. Wherever did you get them?"

"That would be telling."

Then her father left the dining room and returned wheeling a little wooden wagon that had been comprehensively repaired and newly painted British racing green.

"Dad, you kept that quiet."

"What's a shed for?" he said.

She lifted the child out of his chair and he began pushing the wagon round the room into table legs and skirting boards.

"I say, young lad, steady on," said Mr. Drummond.

"Now, Thomas," said Walter. "My turn. These are for you." He opened the drawstring bag, took out the blocks, and loaded them into the wagon.

"Good Lord," said her father as the blocks kept coming. "How many are there?"

"Twenty-six," said Walter. "It is an alphabet."

Mrs. Drummond craned her neck. "What are they?"

"Building blocks," said Alison, a catch in her throat.

"Wattah," said the child, picking up a block and testing it against his gums.

"Let me show you, Thomas." Walter crouched on the floor. "You can stack them like this and we can make your name. Look, here is M for Mouse and here is O for Owl and here is a T for Spinning Top."

He stacked the blocks and the child knocked them over with a crow of delight.

"Excuse me," said Alison. Out in the passage, she gave way to tears.

The dining room door opened and her mother came out and handed her a handkerchief.

"Alison," she said.

"I know what you're going to say."

"He's a good man. It's a pity he was on the wrong side."

"That wasn't his fault."

"He mightn't see it like that, the way things have turned out. Others mightn't see it like that either. Here or in his own country."

"I don't give two pins what other people think."

"You'll break your father's heart."

"Why does no one care about mine?" She blew her nose.

Her mother rubbed her arm. "Come in the kitchen and help me work out how to make four peach halves go round six and a half people. Half a dozen tins. Isn't that the limit? They could have at least brought us two, don't you think?"

"Mother."

"We'll talk about it later."

When they came back into the dining room with the dish of peaches cut into slices, Mrs. Drummond was smoking and the three men were discussing woodworking.

"We are allowed to carve. It passes the time. Many of us carve," Walter was saying. "These blocks are made of oak, your English oak. A tree came down and we could take some branches and so on." He turned a block over in his hands. "It is a wonderful wood, but difficult to work. It takes a long time. I would like to color the letters and the pictures, but there is no paint. Only black paint. Not so cheerful for a toy, I think."

Her father rubbed his forehead. "I take my hat off to you."

"Mmm," said Mr. Drummond, and set down his teacup.

"It's nothing, truly. My father was in the furniture business. So I know a little about wood."

Mrs. Drummond said, "You'll be going back to join the family firm, then, will you, Walter?"

"No," he said, shaking his head. "There is no business now. The factory was bombed, my parents' house also."

The child bashed the wagon against the skirting boards and all the blocks tumbled out. For a second his face trembled; then he bent down and began to put the blocks back into the wagon one by one.

Walter watched him and smiled. "He is so solemn. Solemn. Is that the right word?"

"He's a bit of a fusser, if that's what you mean," said her father. "They do go through these stages, of course."

"He's teething," said Alison. "But you're right"—she nodded at Walter—"there is something solemn about him. I've always thought so."

"Peaches," said her mother, pointing, "blackberries, and cake."

"Yes, please," said Mr. Drummond. "I'll have the lot."

"Let's go mad," said Mrs. Drummond. "A little of each for me, too."

"Blackberries, please," said Alison.

"Do try the peaches, Alison, dear," said Mrs. Drummond. "Plenty to go round. They taste of *pure sunshine,* I always say."

"I'm sorry," said Alison, winking at her father, "but I'm awfully allergic to them."

"Really?" said Mrs. Drummond. "I knew an elderly lady once who was allergic to strawberries. She couldn't eat a single one without coming out in the most dreadful itchy hives all up her arms. But I've never heard of tinned peaches causing such a reaction."

"Runs in the family, I'm afraid," said her father. "Peaches have much the same effect on me. I'll have the blackberries and a slice of that delicious-looking cake."

"I will have the blackberries also," said Walter, glancing around the table, the quizzical look back on his face. "And some cake, Mrs. Milner, please."

"Well, it just goes to show," said Mrs. Drummond. "No matter how well you think you know people, there's always something new to discover."

Around the table was the scrape of dessert spoons. Around the room the wagon crashed and the blocks tumbled.

"You haven't said when you are going back, Walter," said Mrs. Drummond.

"No." Walter paused a moment. "To answer your question, I am not going back."

"Oh?" said Mr. Drummond.

"I didn't know that was an option," said Mrs. Drummond.

Alison bent her head to her plate to avoid the look on her mother's face, a look that was trying very hard not to be a look.

"Naturally there are difficulties."

Mr. Drummond cleared his throat. "I imagine there blooming well are."

"It helps if you have employment."

Her father said, "And do you have work?"

"Yes," said Walter. "Freeman's have asked me to stay on."

"Have they?" said her father.

"Freeman's the builders?" said Mr. Drummond.

"Walter was one of the prisoners they hired when the war ended," said her father.

"I find construction satisfying," said Walter. "To make something for the future is a good thing, I think."

"Surely there's a great need for construction in your own country, Walter?" said Mrs. Drummond, tapping ash into a souvenir of Weston-super-Mare.

"Perhaps he'd rather build here," said Alison.

Her parents glanced at her, then at each other.

"Alison," said her father. "Shall we clear away?"

Her mother handed him the teapot. "I think we could all do with another cup."

* * *

Her father put the plates in the sink, which was always the extent of his efforts at washing up. Beyond the window, the garden darkened and you could no longer see the river.

"Those blocks must have taken him weeks to make."

Alison set the kettle to boil. "He's fond of Thomas."

"I'm not blind," said her father. "Even I can recognize a labor of love when I see one."

She was tempted to ask him what he meant, but it was obvious what he meant and to pretend otherwise would be rude and dismissive as well as pointless.

"You're a grown woman. I can't tell you what to do. But the two of you need to know what you'd be letting yourself in for," he said. "It wouldn't be easy."

She shredded the skin on the side of her thumbnail. "I don't care what other people think."

"Even so, you'd have to live with the consequences." Her father lit a cigarette and stared out of the window.

"If this is about Geoffrey," she said. But she knew it was not about Geoffrey.

Her father said, "Remember the fuss in the village when people found out the POWs were getting the same rations as our lads in the forces? That they were getting more to eat than we were?"

She nodded. The "fuss" had gone on for weeks and a couple of the prisoners detailed to help bring in the harvest at Grange Farm were badly beaten up.

"Then you've got to think what it's going to be like when they start coming home and find Germans in their old jobs being paid union rates. People will put up with it for now, because everyone can see there's work to be done and not enough men to do it. But that's not always going to be the case."

"I know," she said.

He drew on his cigarette and opened the window to let the smoke out. "Did you know he'd decided to stay?"

"He's been talking about it for a while."

"And the job?"

"He told me this morning."

Her father smiled to himself. "So that's where you popped out to."

The kettle boiled and she spooned tea out of the caddy and into the rose-patterned teapot.

"Tell me," said her father, still staring out of the window, "what would you have done if he'd decided to go back?"

"Gone with him."

He nodded. "That's what your mother's been afraid of."

She knew, without him saying, that he'd been afraid of it too. "Dad?"

He turned, his eyes resting upon her. "I should never have made you take him that glass of water." Then he patted her hand. "You do what you think's best. So long as you're both happy."

She brushed off the tears that threatened to fall. "Thank you."

"Tea's brewed, I expect." He put out his cigarette. "You realize, I suppose," he said with a smile, "that neither of us is going to be able to eat a peach in this village ever again. I don't know how your mother kept a straight face."

"Practice," she said.

12

The Waiting Room: 1951

There are many ways of killing a house. You can set fire to it, you can flood it, you can tear it down to get your hands on the land where it stands. Or you can pulverize it with bombs, which is how two million homes have been lost in the Blitz. These are quick methods.

Slower methods work just as well in the long term and require absolutely no effort. Nothing: that's all you have to do. Let nature take its course. It will. Nature is strong enough to topple stone, given time.

All around the country, the great houses are dying. Four or five a week and their deaths are slow and lingering.

Reggie Lyell turned over the pages of *Country Life* while rain streamed down the windows. A nurse wearing a white uniform, white stockings, and white shoes came into the waiting room on hushed feet, straightened the magazines on the circular rosewood table, and said, "Mr. Collins sends his apologies, but he is running a little late."

"Not to worry."

The war had left 91 Harley Street more or less unscathed. Unlike the bombsite a few streets away where buddleia, purple loosestrife, and rosebay willow herb grew, its Georgian frontage and fanlight with delicate glazing bars were unmarked save for some pocks and gouges in the brickwork, which might have been shrapnel damage. Earlier, when she had pressed the bell set in the polished brass nameplate, smelling coal dust and cooking odors that rose from the basement to the damp pavement, she remembered the faint astringency of surgical spirit that would greet her inside. By now she was more than familiar with the back copies of *Punch*, the hunting prints, and the oatmeal-colored wallpaper of these consulting rooms, where women in hats suspended in their own predicaments avoided each other's eyes. Today the waiting room, although empty, retained a presence of their quiet desperation.

Her sister had recommended the doctor. Royalty went to him to be treated for the consequences of their indiscretions, she had said, but she shouldn't let that put her off. "He's the best gynecologist in London."

Murmurs and footfalls came from the corridor, and it was only by craning her neck to stare out of the window, through the obscuring gauze of its drapery, that she spotted the departing umbrella of the previous appointment. One paid to be so anonymous. She reread an article deploring the numbers of great country houses that were being lost to the nation every week without taking a word of it in.

The door of the waiting room opened and the nurse said Mr. Collins would see her now. Reggie replaced the magazine on the table and tried to disguise the fact that her gloved hands were trembling.

This morning the best gynecologist in London was dressed in a chalk-stripe suit, a scarlet silk handkerchief blooming in his breast pocket, his silver hair swept back from his forehead and curling a little over his stiff white collar. When the nurse with the hushed feet showed her into the wainscoted room, he rose from behind his kneehole desk, which would not have been out of place in a solicitor's office, and shook her hand.

"Do have a seat, Mrs. Lyell," he said, pulling out a chair for her. She noticed, as she always did, how clean his nails were.

Reggie was not easily embarrassed or a prude, and she was comfortable enough in her own skin and with the functions of her body not to find physical examinations by well-qualified strangers especially revolting. Even so, she was pleased that today there would be no need to "slip off her underthings" and lie on the examination table with her feet in stirrups while the consultant penetrated her with his cold speculum or pressed her abdomen with his manicured hands. If there was anything unpleasant about the procedure, it was her nagging suspicion that he enjoyed it more than professionally speaking he ought to have done, and she wondered if this was true of other gynecologists or only those at the top of their profession. This did not mean that what would follow would be anything less than an ordeal and, as she sat in the chair, she steeled herself against it.

"You will be anxious to know the results of the tests," said Mr. Collins, seating himself on the other side of his desk and drawing a buff folder in front of him. He put on a pair of half-moon spectacles, opened the folder, and ran his finger down the first page. Then he pulled the spectacles down his nose, peered over the top of them, and smiled. "Good news, Mrs. Lyell. I am pleased to say that there appears to be nothing wrong with you whatsoever. All is in working order, so far as we can tell."

The words fell on her ears and she didn't know how to respond.

He turned over the notes. "We have already established that your husband is capable of fathering children . . ."

She nodded quickly to stop him from saying any more. The worst part of the whole exercise had been divulging that particular piece of information, so personal to them both and which, although it concerned an event that had predated her meeting Hugo and their marriage, was something that had grown more painful to her over the years, not less. Hugo had been at university, the girl had miscarried; now this temporary calamity was part of her own medical history.

"Which means," said Mr. Collins, taking off his spectacles and laying them on the desk, "that it is simply a question of time. You are not in the first flush of youth, that's true, but even so you are only thirty-six and I have known women over forty to conceive and bring their babies to term. War takes its toll—rationing, separations, anxiety, and so on—and I have no doubt that you will be writing to me very soon to announce a happy event."

Out in the cold, rainy street, Reggie, awash with a mixture of emotions, one of which was relief, thought about canceling her lunch. She found a phone box and put a call through to Hugo, who was in a board meeting and unavailable. Then she hailed a cab and asked to be taken to Paddington. The Reading train was departing from platform 11 and she caught it with only a few minutes to spare, wondering if she was doing the right thing.

Bunny Anstis was waiting at the station in his little car and, as soon as Reggie got in, he turned the key in the ignition and began complaining about Kenneth, in a way that was more acerbic and less diverting than usual. Kenneth wouldn't be joining them for lunch, he had got much too grand for his friends, was sitting on some Festival committee and never home, and any moment now their cottage would be full of tubular furniture and hideous Scandinavian earthenware and they would have to entertain socialists at the weekend.

"The Swan do you, darling?"

"Perfectly, thank you."

"Goring," said Bunny, as they drove through the village. "It always makes me think of bulls."

Bunny was a thin, wiry man with a beaky nose and a lock of hair that persisted in falling over his forehead no matter what he did to tame it. He was working in publishing when Reggie first met him; since then he'd tried his hand at selling antiques and at interior decoration, and from time to time he talked about opening a restaurant. "I'm a natural-born dabbler, darling," was how he explained it. "Can't be helped."

They had a table by the waterside, with a view of the weir and the lock.

"Lovely weather for ducks," said Bunny. "Or swans. Raining in London, was it?"

"Yes," she said, "quite heavily."

"Good," said Bunny. "Kenneth forgot his umbrella. With luck, he'll catch pneumonia."

Reggie watched rain drip, drip, drip into the river while Bunny ordered the drinks, a gin and tonic for himself and a sherry for her, which gave her an excuse to ignore the unspoken conversation he was having with the waiter and the looks they flicked between them.

Halfway down the gin, Bunny remembered his manners and said how well she was looking. "Austerity agrees with you."

"Thank you," she said, gazing round the room at the pink table-cloths and the dessert trolley, which thanks to rationing had few desserts on it.

"Oh, darling, what an idiot I am. You've hardly said a word. Something's on your mind, I can tell."

She nodded.

"Out with it."

The waiter came with large menus clad in maroon leatherette and Bunny waved him away.

Bunny was an old friend of them both, and she had never understood the English inclination to speak in code to those closest to them, or to grow privet hedges in front of their lives, so she explained that she'd been seeing a doctor in London, undergoing tests to find out why she couldn't get pregnant, and this morning she had found out that there was nothing wrong with her at all.

"Of course there isn't, darling Reggie," he said. "You are absolutely splendid in every way. Surely this is good news."

"Oh yes. Yes, it is," she said. "I have been so worried."

Bunny looked at her over the rim of his glass.

She plucked at her napkin. "And yet it doesn't change things, I suppose. All this waiting is torture."

Human difficulties often presented Bunny with the opportunity to draw analogies with something or other that his pugs, Noël and

Gertrude, had done or were doing, and he had even been known to bring their thought processes into it. On this occasion, he simply rested his chin in his hand. "Considering how you and Hugo feel about each other and how long you've been married, it can't be for want of trying, can it?"

"No." She laughed.

"Well, it strikes me that you need a diversion and another drink, not necessarily in that order." He beckoned to the waiter, who came flourishing the menus. "I *don't* recommend the veal Marengo, by the way. It isn't veal and it certainly isn't Marengo."

Every time Reggie got into Bunny's car, dog leads and blankets in the back, she remembered, too late, what a terrible driver he was, both slow and dangerous, with an alarming habit of turning to talk face-to-face to his passenger while the road was left to its own devices. After lunch, seeing that the rain had stopped, it was his idea to take a spin in the country and her idea to point him in the direction of Ashenden Park, which she guessed was nearby and confirmed by looking at a map she found in the glove box, along with a crumpled paper bag of dog biscuits that shed crumbs all over her tweed coat.

"We visited the house one day before the war," she said, shrinking as hedgerow screeched its green fingers along the side of the car, "and I've often wondered about it. Since we're so close, it seems a pity not to see it after all these years."

What she also had in mind was to stop, get out of the car, and prolong her life a little.

"You are a one for punishment," said Bunny. "And here I am trying to cheer you up. We're losing four, five of these places a week, so I was reading just the other day in *Country Life*. So depressing. The big houses will survive, of course, one way or another. I can't see Blenheim or Chatsworth going to the wall. It's all the charming middling ones that will be lost. Expect to be disappointed. It's bound to be a ruin."

A horse-drawn cart laden with milk churns was up ahead, and

Bunny, oblivious to the discrepancy between its speed and theirs, began to inveigh against the country's infatuation with modernity, which led him back to Kenneth and the Festival.

"I've nothing against contemporary design," she said, shielding her eyes. "Some of it is very refreshing."

"You wouldn't say the same about contemporary designers," said Bunny, swerving just in time to avoid the milk cart. "The ones I have met are exceptionally tedious, I can tell you. Of course, Kenneth would not agree. Have I mentioned he's got his eye on a Picasso, of all things? Why not a little Vuillard or even a Derain, seeing as I'm going to have to look at it too?"

"Funnily enough, this morning at the doctor's I read that same *Country Life* article you did," she said, in an attempt to change the subject and letting out a breath she had not been aware she was holding as they left the milk cart behind.

"Darling Reggie. One can always rely on you for a non sequitur."

"Over there." She directed his attention back to the road. "According to the map, that should be the turning."

They drove through an open gateway. "Ministry of Works" said a board nailed to a stake. No one was about.

"I think Hugo and I must have driven in the back way that day. I don't remember these lodges or"—she craned her neck—"those stables."

She did remember the war looming over them and their fear of separation. That had never happened. Hugo had served in army intelligence during the war and they had traveled round the country together, setting up home in temporary billets wherever he was posted, barely spending a night apart. Things never turn out as you expect.

The car, confused about which gear it was in, bumped over a pothole, stalled, and came to a stop.

"What did I tell you?" said Bunny, yanking up the hand brake.

The house was both smaller and larger than she remembered, the grounds completely overgrown, choked with nettles and brambles, littered with old boots, and rutted with tank treads filled with water, almost up to the weed-infested drive. She looked up and saw that not a single window was whole.

"Is this enough for you?" said Bunny. "Or shall we make ourselves really miserable and go inside?"

During the war, when they had time together in the evenings, she and Hugo had started to read books and articles about the Georgian period, at first in a "Look thy last on all things lovely" sort of a way, when the bombing was destroying so much that was lovely, and then with a growing interest and appreciation of eighteenth-century architecture and design, and its descent via Vitruvius and Palladio from the classical orders of ancient times. The Vitruvian notion of "commodity, firmness, and delight," applied to buildings as much as to silver teaspoons, had been something sustaining to cling on to in dark and uncertain days. It was then that they had discovered that the architect of Ashenden was a Yorkshireman called James Woods, who had otherwise built little in the south, and that the house was considered one of the finest late-Palladian buildings in the country.

She had anticipated the dereliction she now saw around her. What was unexpected was how resilient and solid the house appeared despite the signs of decay and creeping undergrowth, its symmetries and architectural intent still intact nearly two centuries after it had been built.

"Yes, I would like to if they'll let us. We weren't able to before. You don't have to come, if you don't want to."

"Wouldn't miss it for the world," said Bunny.

They tried the door at the lower level, found it unlocked, and wandered inside. Two workmen in overalls down at the far end of a dim vestibule ignored them, which they took as permission of sorts, and as they ventured farther into the house, they could feel the penetrating cold and damp that seeped from the walls; it was, if anything, colder and damper than outdoors, and it was a raw day.

"What's that funny smell?" she said.

"Dry rot," said Bunny.

For the next hour or so, they toured the house, pointing out damage to each other as if they were a pair of government inspectors. The cloying smell of dry rot, which she thought she might never get out of her nose, was stronger on the principal floor, and the scuffed walls, painted those familiar utility wartime colors of cream and hospital green, were crudely scrawled with names and cartoons of the "Kilroy woz 'ere" variety. In a room she would later identify as the original library, there was a large puddle of water on the floor, which corresponded to a missing portion of ceiling above, where the plasterwork had fallen down to reveal fire-blackened joists. They came across a few paraffin stoves, one in working order, but only two chimneypieces remained, and whole sections of moldings were missing, along with most of the doors and doorcases in what would have been the main reception rooms. Everywhere was the litter of military occupation: abandoned filing cabinets with dented drawers, heaps of old sacking, crates and boxes full of rusty nails, screws, and unidentifiable lengths of webbing.

"What might have been," said Bunny.

They were standing in the center of the house, gazing up at a stone staircase cantilevered from the wall, gaps in its wrought-iron balustrade, light pouring down from clerestory windows too high to be mended in any fashion. It was the one part of the house where damage was less evident, and the walls were decorated with delicate plasterwork wreaths, whose mere existence, in such a ravaged setting, seemed to fly in the face of everything they had seen so far.

Her eyes traced the fine leaf shapes and lingered on a pair of griffins. "How on earth did these survive?"

A voice behind them said, "This room was boarded up until a year ago. That's how."

They turned and saw a man in his late forties or early fifties with a pouchy face, wearing a light trench coat over a dark suit. "How do you do? Charles Marling." He put out his hand and they shook it in turn, introducing themselves.

"Are you from the Ministry of Works, Mr. Marling?" said Reggie. "I do hope you don't mind, we've been looking around. When we arrived earlier, there didn't seem to be anyone to ask whether or not that would be allowed."

"No, I'm not from the ministry," he said, with a wry smile. "Rather the opposite. I'm here on behalf of my client, who owns this place. And so far as I'm concerned, you can look round all you like. But do take care, won't you, particularly if you go upstairs. Some of the floors are not sound."

Marling went on to explain that the house was due to be derequisitioned shortly and he was there to ensure that certain repairs had been carried out satisfactorily.

Bunny gave a snort.

"I know what you're thinking," said Marling. "Grim, isn't it? I last came six months ago and I thought at the time it couldn't get worse. But it has."

"I imagine your client will be dismayed at the lack of progress," said Reggie, watching a spider scurry into a crevice.

"No, he'll be glad to hear that at last they've done what they said they were going to do. You can tell from where we're standing." He raised his eyes upwards and they followed his gaze. "One of their so-called workmen flogged off the lead from the roof over this staircase. Naturally the whole thing soon rotted and fell down. Mind you, I see they've put it back the cheap way. That ceiling used to be vaulted."

Marling brought out a pen and a small notebook from his coat pocket and wrote a few lines.

"We noticed the fire damage in the room off the entrance hall," said Reggie. "Someone must have caught it just in time."

"That happened in forty-six, when the military were still in residence," said Marling, putting the notebook away. "I don't know where the puddle keeps coming from. I dread to think. No compensation for that sort of thing, of course."

"So much is missing," said Bunny.

"I must confess that's not entirely due to the war." Marling gave another wry smile and did not elaborate.

To explain their intrusion, which she felt she had not adequately accounted for, Reggie said that she had been curious about the house ever since she had first seen it, and had wanted to know how it had survived.

"When was that?"

"The year before the war."

"In which case, you might have come across my client. Mr. Ferrars lived here in one of the side wings until thirty-nine."

"Yes," she said. "I remember him. He sold us a pair of urns."

"A pair of urns?" said Bunny.

"The ones in our garden."

"Oh, *those,*" said Bunny.

"We never saw inside the house," said Reggie. "It appeared to be shut up, although it was not in such a bad state as this."

"Yes, it's taken a lot of punishment since those days."

Bunny asked what the house had been requisitioned for.

"All sorts," said Marling. "Tank practice in the park, as I expect you must have noticed. Yanks, too, training for D-Day. By the end of the war there was quite a big POW camp in the grounds—over towards the woods, there are still a few Nissen huts remaining—and the house was used as a mess for the officers in charge of them. Then the military clerks moved in and now the Ministry of Works, bless its soul, is billeting some of its staff here, while they work on the construction of Harwell. But not for much longer, I'm glad to say."

"Harwell?" said Bunny.

"Some sort of nuclear establishment, I gather," said Marling, checking his watch. "Though possibly I shouldn't be telling you that."

"I'm afraid we're holding you up with all our questions," said Reggie.

"Not at all. But unfortunately I do have another appointment." He reached inside his trench coat and fished around in the pocket of his suit jacket. "Here's my card. Do drop me a line if you want to know anything more, and I'll try to answer to the best of my knowledge."

"Thank you," said Reggie, putting the card into her handbag.

"If you don't mind my asking, what plans does your client have for the house?"

"Plans?" Marling laughed. "He's been trying to sell it for twenty years. If no one wanted it then, they're hardly going to want it now." He pointed to an open doorway at the side of the staircase. "Have you been through there?"

"Not yet," she said.

"Pity I've got a train to catch." He belted his trench coat. "I'd have been interested to know what you thought of it. It's an unusual space, what's left of it."

"We were saving it up for last," said Bunny. "The end of the enfilade, you know."

"The end of an era, if you ask me," said Marling. He shook his head. "It's a shame really. So many of these places going to rack and ruin. You'd never think we'd won the war."

"You wouldn't want to be in his shoes, would you?" said Bunny, as they watched Marling leave. "Or in the shoes of Mr. Ferrars, come to that. Managing decline, it's a frightful business, but I suppose we must all get used to it."

"Must we?" said Reggie.

They went through the doorway into the room Marling had indicated.

"Oh, look," said Bunny, twirling about, ballroom dancing to unheard music. "It's octagonal, darling."

Reggie took a couple of steps across the floor and stopped, greatly moved. The walls were bare and scrawled with the usual graffiti, but overhead was an ornate ceiling composed of recessed painted panels and surrounded by an elaborate frieze. The three windows, set into adjacent sides of the octagon, didn't have an unbroken pane among them, but the central one was arched and flanked by two pairs of slender columns. She could sense the house poised on a precarious equilibrium, willing itself to survive. She could feel it waiting for a verdict or a judgment to be passed on it.

Bunny, who had stopped twirling and reassumed his forensic role as damage inspector, was now crouching down under the central window. He beckoned her over. "Come and see this," he said.

"What is it?"

"Just come and see."

"Not more scribbles," she said.

"Not exactly."

She crossed the room and bent down next to him.

"This portion of wall must have been paneled at one time," he said. "You can tell where the wood's rotted away."

"I can smell it too," she said. "What am I looking at?"

"Initials," he said, pointing them out. "M. G."

"Oh yes, so there are." The letters, incised in the plaster, were crisply made and finished with a flourish of serifs as fine as pen strokes.

"They weren't put there recently."

"No," she said. "I can see that they weren't." She rubbed her fingers across them.

"The paneling must have protected them," said Bunny, and she could hear the thrill of discovery in his voice. "I wouldn't be at all surprised if they didn't date back to when the house was built. A maker's mark of some kind. Kenneth would know."

They walked back down the central axis of the house, from the octagonal room to the staircase hall, and from the entrance hall out to the portico. The elevated vantage point of the terrace allowed them to see more of the scarring the war had left behind, rolls of barbed wire and the remains of huts, scrub taking the place of what had still been grassland the last time she saw it. Part of the balustrade was succumbing to ivy. She stood there, trying to work out the contours of the landscape, the bones that lay beneath, and didn't want to leave.

Bunny, who had been quiet and reflective since he'd shown her the initials under the window, laid a hand on her sleeve of her coat. "I'm glad we came."

"So am I."

The atmosphere of the house had made such an impression on her that she realized she had not given a single thought to what the doctor had said for the entire time they had been inside.

Bunny began picking at the ivy, easing its tendrils away from the stonework. "Hugo told me that you two are looking for a place in the country."

"We are."

"In the Home Counties."

"Yes. Preferably near London."

"A manor house or rectory is what he said."

"Something of the kind."

"Sensible," said Bunny, "considering the rationing of building materials and all the red tape these days. Anything more ambitious would be quite an undertaking."

"An uphill struggle, I should think."

"An expensive uphill struggle," said Bunny, glancing at her. "To rescue somewhere like this, for example, one would need a great deal of money and a great deal of time, as well as patience, knowledge, and sensitivity, if one were to do it properly."

She tore her eyes away from the landscape and smiled. "Wouldn't this be a marvelous place for horses?"

"For *horses*?" said Bunny, raising his eyebrows. "Oh, undoubtedly."

Afterwards, things seemed to happen rather quickly. Many times in the weeks and months that followed, Reggie found herself apologizing to the house, explaining in her head, as the clearing and stripping and probing went on, that it must get worse before it could get better. There was something almost surgical about the restoration, at least in those early days. One wondered, always, whether the patient would survive.

The dry rot was extensive. Its treatment was brutal, a hacking away and a dosing with foul chemicals. Materials were in short supply and permissions took ages. Reggie had never been happier.

On her birthday, 12 September, they had a little party, sitting in deck chairs in the staircase hall, with candles in saucers. Bunny and Kenneth, Hugo's sister, Winifred, and her husband, Jeremy Minton, were there.

"Cheers," said Hugo. "To Reggie and the house."

"To Reggie and the house."

Glasses were raised.

"I must show you something," said Bunny to Kenneth. "You will be interested in this." He took up a candle and led him through to the octagon room.

"Top up?" said Winifred. She had been a nurse in the war, which was where she'd met her husband, who was a doctor.

Reggie shook her head. "To be honest, I've a headache. Probably all these chemicals we've been spraying everywhere. They are really rather oppressive."

"Well, it is quite a white elephant you've taken on, I must say."

"Do you mind? I think I'll go outside for a moment."

Out on the loggia, Reggie drank the air and rejoiced. The deep drag of tiredness like a tidal undertow, the odd metallic taste in her mouth, the strange and unsettling revulsions that toothpaste and bacon aroused in her: even though she had never experienced such symptoms before, she knew what they were and gave thanks. To the house, primarily, for she had no doubt this child had been its gift. Three periods she'd missed now.

13

The Interview: 1966

L avender clings to laundered sheets folded on the cedar shelves of the linen closet. Vases of velvety roses sit on tables polished with beeswax. On summer evenings, the sweet perfume of night-scented stocks drifts through open windows, blended with the astringency of cut grass, the sharp acid twist of lemon in a gin and tonic. From the kitchen come warm savory aromas of bread, coffee, and roast chicken, which mingle with a faint hint of wood smoke and damp dog.

Contentment, order, and well-being: the house smells of it. Breathes it in. Inhales and exhales.

"Who rang?" said Reggie, sipping her coffee. "I heard the telephone."

"Did you?" Hugo came into the room with his copy of *The Times*. "It wasn't anything important."

"Bit early for a call."

"Just someone from the office."

"What did they want?"

He squeezed her shoulder and avoided her eyes. "The usual nonsense."

She buttered her toast, reached across the breakfast table for the marmalade, and knew that he was lying. If you'd been married as long as she had been married and your husband was habitually truthful, you gained an instinct for such things. He was a poor liar: good ones could be specific on the spot, but he could only retreat behind vagueness whenever a fabrication was called for. The intelligence work he'd done in the war had not required him to lie, simply to keep the official secrets to himself, and keeping a secret and lying were not always one and the same thing.

"Coffee?"

"Please."

While she poured him a cup, he unfolded the paper to the crossword, took out his fountain pen, and began inking in the squares, as he had done every morning of their life together. For him, it was a necessary prelude to the day, as much a part of the ritual of rising as brushing his teeth or combing his hair, and she knew better than to disturb him while he put his mind in working order. Instead, she watched him across the table, her heart wrung with love and unease. He was so very much himself, she thought, and becoming more so.

Hugo had always been distinguished-looking rather than handsome and had the type of features you grew into, the type that tended to improve with age, which he wore as well as the knighthood he'd received in the Birthday Honours five years ago. Despite his reassurances, she was conscious that it could never be the same for women, who must always be rubbing cream into their faces and worrying if fashion had left them behind, or whether to color the gray. She wondered what he had been lying about and who had been on the telephone. For a moment, anxiety seized her by the throat and it was hard to swallow.

He finished the crossword, checked his watch, and capped his pen. "Twelve minutes, not bad going. Got a little held up in the southeast corner." He helped himself from the toast rack, the toast stone cold by now, she would have thought. Toasting bread and then airing it in racks so that it cooled again was a strange English custom to which she had never grown accustomed. ("Better cold than soggy," Hugo always explained.)

"What are you doing today?" he said.

"Well, first of all, there's the interview this morning."

Hugo, who had a sweet tooth, chose the strawberry jam over the marmalade.

"Oh yes. I'd completely forgotten about that. When is it?"

"Eleven o'clock."

"Do you think you could make a start without me? Only I've arranged to see Beckmann about the pavilions at half ten. I shouldn't think we'll need more than forty minutes or so, but you know how thorough he is and it could run over."

They had wanted a local firm to carry out the work on the Park and had chosen Freeman's on the grounds of their reputation and because they were, in Hugo's words, "small enough to care and big enough to cope." Beckmann, who had been the foreman at that time, had almost single-handedly been responsible for rooting out all the dry rot, pursuing it through the timbers of the house as if it were his own mortal enemy. He had been the head of the firm ever since Freeman retired six years ago and so much part of the fabric of the house and its restoration that they no longer found it surprising to think that he had once been a prisoner in its grounds, and had to rely on the reaction of people who heard the story for the first time to remember how unusual the association was. They knew they had been very lucky to have Beckmann on their side in the battle against decay.

She laid her napkin beside her plate. "And then this afternoon I thought I'd go to see Bunny."

He gave her a sad smile that she interpreted, correctly, as equal parts sympathy and concern. "I must run over there myself later on in the week."

Out of the windows of the drawing room she could see the sunlight in the summer garden. This room was where they always had breakfast, and they now knew enough about the previous inhabitants of the house and pattern of its occupancy to understand that they were following a long custom. It was among the first rooms they had completed after the dry rot was dealt with, and the pink-and-green ceiling, Greek gods depicted at each end, was the only example of original eighteenth-century paintwork in the house. She had tried to be guided by its faded delicacy when it came to selecting the furnishings, and she thought she could remember every country-house sale and auction where she had bought them, if she put her mind to it.

Tonight, when Hugo's cousin was coming to dinner, they would eat here as well. Three was too few for the dining room. One might argue, thought Reggie, pushing back her chair to get on with the day, that two was too few for the house.

"Reggie?" said Hugo, as she was getting up. "There's something I want to ask you."

He looked perturbed, she thought, and she felt unease pulse in her throat again.

"What is it?"

"I've been thinking about what to buy Charlie for his birthday." Charlie was their nephew, the son of Hugo's sister, Winifred. He was about to turn thirteen.

Reggie considered for a moment. "Well, he's at school most of the time, so it's probably best not to buy him something too valuable that he might mislay. It's not very imaginative, I know, but boys his age like to have a bit of extra pocket money."

"I was thinking about a camera."

"A camera?"

"When they were over at Easter, he was showing me some of the pictures he's been taking. He's got a good eye, but not a very good camera, I'm afraid. I thought about getting him a proper one."

"A proper one?"

"A Nikon F, perhaps. I hear they're very good."

"Are they very expensive?"

"Quite."

"Mmm," said Reggie. "I think you'd better ask Winifred." On that side of the family there was a certain degree of sensitivity on the subject of money, which was not always disguised. It sometimes made for an atmosphere at get-togethers. "We wouldn't want to outshine anything they are thinking of getting him."

*   *   *

A little after eleven Panton came to tell Reggie that the journalist and photographer had arrived and were waiting in the entrance
hall. She and Hugo had agreed to be interviewed for the article,
which was for one of the new Sunday supplements, on the basis that
it would provide them with the opportunity to encourage people in
their position to save other houses in danger, and to demonstrate
what could be done. The commissioning editor had assured them
that there would be nothing personal about the piece and that it
would run in the arts or design section, or possibly as a special
feature on Britain's historic heritage, depending on how the photographs turned out. For that reason, she was somewhat surprised to
find that the journalist was a young woman in her mid to late twenties, wearing a sleeveless cotton gabardine shift with an optical print
and a hem four inches above the knee, and that the photographer
was a similar age with a long Beatles fringe and a number of lenses
slung from his shoulder. Then she told herself to stop thinking like a
middle-aged woman and showed them both into her sitting room,
explaining that her husband would be joining them shortly.

"Would you care for coffee or tea?" she said, after they had identified themselves as Lucy Costello and Paul Parker.

"No, thanks," said Lucy Costello, taking a spiral-bound notebook and a sharpened pencil out of her bag. Her hair, which was
blue-black, skimmed her cheekbones at angles that made you think
of the scissors that had cut it.

Paul Parker said that if no one minded, he'd wander about and
take a few snaps while they were talking, and left the room. Panton,
sending Reggie a signal that indicated *he* very much minded, followed him.

"Is he your butler?" said Lucy.

"Technically," said Reggie, wondering how to convey the extent
to which they depended on Panton. "We've been very fortunate
with our staff and I can say they have all been as much a part of the
revival of the house as we have." By way of illustration she told the

story of how she, Panton, and their cook, Mrs. Marsham, had spent days disentangling an old chandelier she'd bought at auction, washing each beaded rope and crystal drop in Fairy Liquid before hanging it in the staircase hall. "Only Panton could have worked out what went where. It was quite a puzzle. The next time we cleaned it, we put the bits in numbered boxes."

Shorthand flew across the pages of the notebook. "And how many other staff do you employ?"

"There are ground staff, of course, with a park of this size. I suppose half a dozen work for us, off and on."

Lucy looked up through eyelashes clotted with mascara. "Just how big is the park?"

"About four hundred acres."

"Gosh," said Lucy. "And how many children do you have?"

This was always a dreadful question. Over the years Reggie had found no good way of answering that didn't betray her daughter by denying her existence or lay guilt on the unassuming and unaware who'd asked it. The truth was that they had no children but had had a child. She couldn't remember if this was recorded in *Who's Who*, but she could hardly go and consult it now.

Their daughter had been born on a stormy March morning and lived two days. The birth had been easy. Nothing easy about the death. They had named her Grace because in the short while she was with them, grace was what she had brought. It hadn't occurred to either of them to photograph her while she was fighting for her life, and after she died it seemed the worst thing to do. Reggie could no longer remember what she looked like, although she lived every day with the hole her daughter had torn out of her center.

"We have many children who visit," she said, opting for indirection. "Nephews and nieces on both sides."

The shorthand flew again and the wings of Lucy's hair swung down.

Several more questions followed, whether they had dogs, what the dogs' names were, how long was the drive from the gates to the front door?

"And horses?" said Lucy Costello. "I noticed horses in a field as we arrived."

"Yes, we also have horses," said Reggie.

Six months after Grace died, a period about which she remembered very little, Hugo had woken her one morning, opening the curtains with all the delicacy of a nurse removing a bandage, and announced they were going to a sale. Another house sale, she thought, pulling on the clothing she'd worn the day before and chafing her hands.

Not a house sale, as it turned out, but a horse sale. They stood in the arena, with its sweet smell of wood bark, and he pointed out some fine, expensive horses with good bloodlines, elegant, nervy creatures, the sort she used to ride, and she had responded dully and had wanted to go home and get back under the covers. Then towards the end of the proceedings a dealer had led out a cob. People were leaving by now and, among those that remained, there was widespread indifference.

It was not surprising. Piebald, sturdy, the mare was no oil painting. She had big feet, which she planted round the ring, one after the other, as if she'd been there before and didn't expect anything to come of it. When the dealer led the horse past, the mare looked at Reggie with dark, kindly eyes, as if to say, "No matter how rough the going, I will get you home." She found herself gripping the rail so hard that splinters worked their way under her skin.

"That one?" Hugo was incredulous. "Bit of a dobbin, isn't she?"

Horses can heal you and that mare had saved her.

"Domino?" said Lucy.

"Black and white, you see."

"Oh, I get it," Lucy said.

Reggie had little experience of being interviewed and had imagined the whole process very differently. A series of questions, certainly, but with some sort of discernible order to them.

"It would be much easier for you to get an idea of what the house was like when we bought it and what we did to it if I took you on a tour."

"That would be lovely," said Lucy, lifting her head and giving Reggie an enormous smile.

"For example," said Reggie, "the room where we're sitting now was the first room we were able to occupy. We camped here for months."

Lucy looked around as if expecting to see a tent pitched somewhere among the French and English antiques.

"My wife is too modest to say that almost everything about this house is the result of her efforts and resourcefulness," said Hugo, coming into the room.

"This is Lucy Costello," said Reggie.

"Pleased to meet you, Miss Costello," said Hugo, and proceeded to conduct the interview the way he wanted it to go, beginning at the beginning, clearly setting out the problems they had faced and the remedies they had come up with, going into detail where detail was required and avoiding it where it wasn't. The tour was put on hold.

"Carrying out historical research is a bit like being a detective," Hugo said. "Early on, we knew we needed to know more about the work of James Woods in order to interpret what he had built here at Ashenden, so we traveled to Yorkshire and saw various houses he designed, including Faraday Hall, which sadly no longer exists. What we discovered was that Woods, like many at the time, adhered closely to a particular pattern in his architecture. You might say he repeated himself. When Faraday Hall was sold and broken up, we were able to acquire a number of doors and chimneypieces for Ashenden. They fitted like a glove."

Reggie could see that he had captured the young woman's complete attention and that he was not unaware of the fact. It amused her, but it also made her uneasy, thinking about the phone call earlier and the hemline six inches above the knee, rather more than four inches above the knee sitting down. In due course the chandelier story came up again, but he wasn't to know she'd told it earlier. Lucy wrote it down for a second time.

"Twelve, fifteen years ago," Hugo was saying, "it was possible to acquire many objects and furnishings of the right period quite reasonably, which was a great help. The most important thing, however, was to strike a balance. We couldn't have put everything back the way it was and it would have been wrong to try. Of course, one needs to be guided by what remains, and an important part of that is atmosphere. But one also wants these places to live again, and my wife has a genius for making that happen."

For some time Lucy had asked no questions, except to check a spelling of an unfamiliar word or name. The enormous smiles, however, were much in evidence, all directed at Hugo, along with encouraging murmurs of appreciation. At last, having taken charge of the interview almost the entire way through, he brought it to an end by asking her if there was anything else she'd like to know before they showed her round.

"Yes," said Lucy. "How much did it all cost?"

It was a fine evening and they had drinks outside before dinner. The gardens that sloped down to the river were only now beginning to come together, landscape taking longer than buildings to be restored, needing to go at its own pace. In the early years they had cleared the undergrowth around the house and reseeded the lawns; then they had begun to think about uncovering the underlying structure of the terraces and how to plant them. Reggie's particular project, the rose garden, where earlier she had cut the flowers she had taken to Bunny, was at its best in June, and she caught a teasing whiff of it in the evening air, along with the night-scented stocks she had decided to grow where their heady perfume could waft into open windows on summer nights.

"Balm for the soul, this view, after London," said Frances, staring into the distance, her eyes unfocused behind her spectacles. Hugo's cousin had been briefly married to an anthropologist called Benton Fenwell; it had been one of those wartime marriages that hadn't lasted, and she had reverted to using her maiden name, which was Dunne. She worked for the BBC, where she was regarded as formidable. "I must say, I've had an extremely trying day, but the aggravation seems to melt away sitting here."

"We've all had a trying day," said Hugo. "Reggie went to visit Bunny this afternoon."

"How is he?" said Frances.

Reggie shook her head. "Not good. Hugo was planning to visit later this week, but I've told him he must go tomorrow. I don't think it can be much longer."

"I'm sorry to hear that," said Frances. "Do you know, I don't think I've seen him since your wedding."

That wasn't surprising. Before the BBC, Frances had worked for the British Council, which took her abroad for long periods, and she'd spent much of the war in Cairo, where she'd met the anthropologist.

It was dusk, the time of night when the bats came out, and Reggie trained her eyes to see if she could spot one flit past. Whenever she did, it always felt like a gift or an unexpected blessing. The dogs snoozed at her feet. No bats came.

Hugo said, "And this morning, a journalist came to interview us, which was an interesting experience and possibly one we shan't repeat."

"Oh yes?" said Frances. "Did he grill you? The papers these days seem determined to prove that there's a skeleton in every cupboard. Happy couple in beautiful house: must be something wrong somewhere. Canker in the rose, trouble in Eden. You know the sort of thing."

Reggie flinched at the thought of trouble in Eden, remembering the telephone call that morning.

"Are you cold, darling?" said Hugo.

"Thank you, no. Not at all." She turned to Frances, whom she admired but also found intimidating. "It wasn't a grilling. Far from it. Until Hugo took matters into his own hands, the questions didn't seem to be getting at anything, really. And it wasn't a he, it was a she."

"Girl in an alarming dress," said Hugo. "Rather like a walking Bridget Riley."

"Short?" said Frances.

"Very short."

"They all wear them like that, surely you must have noticed. There's one at work who comes into the canteen, skirt up to her ears, and the men practically drop their trays at the sight of her. They can't believe their luck. I suspect you protest too much."

"Other men might drop their trays," said Hugo. "Personally I feel as if I'm being invited to a party I have no wish to attend."

Reggie thought that comment was for her benefit. "She asked us how much we had spent."

"What did you tell her?" said Frances.

"Somewhere between almost nothing and quite a lot."

"Did you show her the clever bargains you found, such as those Regency bed hangings you bought for ten pounds, and all those curtains you made yourself?"

"She wasn't very interested in curtains," said Reggie. But she was interested in my husband, she thought.

Over dinner, Hugo talked about the pavilions and their plans to convert them. "It's too late now to show you the courtyards, but last year we laid them with the bricks we were able to salvage from the broken-down glasshouses. That's worked out quite well, I think."

"I can't believe how much time and patience it takes," said Frances, "more than I've got, to be sure. You've been at this for years."

After coffee, Reggie rose from the table, excused herself, and said she must go to bed. The dogs lifted their heads, querying this next move.

"You go up, darling," he said. "We shan't be long."

Reggie kissed Frances, and the dogs followed her out of the room.

"She looks tired," said Frances. "Beautiful, as always, but tired. As if a light has been dimmed. It isn't like her. She always has so much energy and spark."

They had gone through to the library and were having a nightcap, sitting opposite one another on either side of the unlit fire. Frances had kicked off her shoes and tucked her feet under her; she had never lost these girlish gestures and it touched him. A number of catalogs were spread across the desk, open and heavily annotated. A sale was coming up and there were one or two pictures he had his eye on.

Hugo said, "She's more upset about Bunny than she lets on. They have always been fond of each other, and if it weren't for him, I don't suppose we would be here."

"I think it's something else," said Frances.

"Her sister rang from Dublin this morning. She's pregnant again."

"Oh no. How many is it now?"

"It will be six."

"Good Lord. Have you told her?"

"Not yet."

Frances said, "Then tell her. You know how good Reggie is at picking up signals. She will know you have something on your mind and will be worrying what it is."

He swirled the brandy in his glass.

"And how are you about it all?" she asked.

"What do you mean?"

"In such situations, people often say what a tragedy it is for the wife, forgetting that the husband is childless too."

"Of course it saddens me that I can't have children with the only woman with whom I've ever wanted to have children," said Hugo. "And I'm afraid that I'm old-fashioned enough to think that it's a pity no son or daughter of ours will inherit one day."

"The house doesn't have to stay in the family," said Frances. "Have you thought about the National Trust?"

Hugo frowned. "I'm aware that's an option, clearly."

"Not keen on the idea of these beautiful rooms open to the public?" said Frances.

"I hope I'm not so hidebound as that. Nor as snobbish." He struggled to put his feelings into words. "It's simply that when one has lived here, one gets a sense of what the house wants, if that doesn't sound too fanciful. Which is to be lived in as a *home*. Not gawped at from behind a crimson rope."

"Then what are you considering? I take it that you *have* considered?"

"Reggie and I have discussed leaving it to Charlie."

"Just Charlie?" said Frances.

"Primogeniture. Closest male relative on the male side. Straightforward that way."

"Now that *is* old-fashioned." Frances wagged a finger at him. "Charlie has a sister. Why not leave it to both of them?"

"Friction, in a word. Can't guarantee they'd want the same thing."

"You can't guarantee anything in life," said Frances. "These houses take a lot of looking after, as you should know. If you're so keen to keep it in the family and ensure that it's lived in, you would double the chance of that happening."

"Perhaps," said Hugo, sighing. "At any rate, all this is an embarrassment of riches, however you look at it. That was one of the unsettling things about the interview this morning. You suddenly see this place through someone else's eyes. It's been such an obsession for so long."

"For you both," said Frances.

He nodded. "For us both."

They stared into the unlit fire.

"Women our age start to become invisible," said Frances after a while, "to ourselves as well as to other people. It's the time of life. I should know, having gone through it. From Reggie's point of view, a door is closing for good, and I think what is worrying her is that she is realizing that it will never close for you. I shouldn't be at all surprised if Miss Miniskirt hadn't rattled her. And all the other legions of Miss Miniskirts out there."

"Reggie's too sensible for that."

"No one's too sensible for that. You can't override such feelings with intellect or common sense."

"If you'd met the girl this morning, you'd realize how silly and empty-headed she was. I had to spell 'escritoire.'"

"Silly, perhaps, but young, available, and fertile."

"You are very blunt."

"So they say." Frances lifted her spectacles and rubbed her eyes. "What Reggie needs right now is to feel wanted."

"She is wanted and she knows it. She's always known it."

"Perhaps she needs reminding of the fact. All couples fall into habits. Those that remain couples for long enough, that is. Tell her about her sister and show her how much you care about her. And whatever you do, don't propose a holiday or a cruise. Or buy her anything. That would be fatal."

"I'll tell her in the morning."

"Tell her tonight, if she's still awake."

"And spoil her sleep?"

"She may sleep all the better for hearing it. It's not her sister that she's worried about."

"Perhaps you're right."

"Of course I'm right," said Frances. She laughed. "I so often am."

"Are you awake?" he said, coming into their bedroom.

"I think so," she said.

One of the lamps was burning, and the great bed with its hangings seemed to him to be like a ship resting at anchor, darkness looming over the tester and beyond towards the windows. A moth flitted against the lampshade, doomed to crash again and again in its thirst for light. He thought about what Frances had said, debating with himself—and with her in his mind—whether he should tell his wife about her sister now or leave it to the morning. His mother's belief that procrastination was a great evil, which she had instilled into him when he was very young, had served him well in business over the years, and he decided, acknowledging this higher authority, as mothers remained even when one was fully middle-aged, that he must be guided by the same principle on this occasion.

He undressed and got under the light summer covers, shifting the dogs with his feet.

"Reggie." He reached an arm around her. "There's something I must tell you."

"What is it?"

He could feel her nerve endings coming to life all the way down her body.

"I'm afraid your sister's pregnant again."

"Was that the call this morning?"

"It was," he said.

She turned over in bed to face him.

"I'm sorry. I should have told you straightaway. It's been on my mind all day."

They lay in silence for a while, then she let out a long sigh. "Well, I have to say that's a relief. I knew you were keeping something from me and I was beginning to imagine—oh, never mind what I was imagining."

He stroked her face. She had always had such smooth skin. "I would never do anything to hurt you, you must know that. Never have and never shall."

An embarrassment of riches, he thought, and nothing more prized than their life together. Twin compass points was what they were: he remembered his Donne, although he would never have quoted poetry, not even after a good dinner.

She moved closer towards him. A little air came in through the windows. Everything was still, except the moth pattering against the shade.

"My poor sister. It won't be easy at forty-five."

She reached over to switch off the bedside light, and the next time he asked if she was awake, he didn't get an answer.

By the time the article was published six weeks later, Reggie had forgotten all about it. In the interim there was Bunny's funeral, with all its attendant sadness and regret, followed by Charlie's birthday, which was celebrated at the Swan in Goring.

Reggie was conscious that she was subdued throughout most

of the birthday party, looking out over the rushing weir, awash in memory of the time she had lunched here with Bunny, all those years ago when they had visited the house together. The restaurant had been redecorated since then, veal Marengo was off the menu, and the dessert trolley was laden with a monstrous trifle. The table-cloths were still pink, however.

After they finished eating, a waiter brought a cake lit with can-dles and embarrassed Charlie, who tried to dive under the table. Then there were presents. Hugo slipped Charlie an envelope, and he tore it open long enough to register the amount and mutter his thanks.

"Blimey! You lucky thing!" said his younger sister, Ros, peering over his shoulder.

Afterwards, Winifred produced a square package wrapped in blue-and-silver paper. "And this is from us."

"What is it?" said Charlie, shaking it. He was a vivid boy, with a slight air of devilment about him.

"Don't shake it," said Winifred, whose hair had been rigidly set for the occasion.

As Charlie unwrapped the package, a look of sheer wonderment and joy spread across his face. No gift giver could ever have hoped for a better reaction. For a time, he was too stunned to say a word.

"Are you going to let us know what it is?" said Hugo, smiling.

Charlie held up the box. "It's a Nikon F," he said, his eyes wide.

Jeremy, his father, cleared his throat. "Well, if one is going to pursue a hobby, one might as well take it seriously."

"Thanks, Dad. Thanks, Mum. I can't believe it!" Charlie was al-ready opening the box, lifting the camera out of its packaging, turn-ing it over in his hands.

"Good suggestion," murmured Winifred, on her way to the la-dies'. Reggie glanced at Hugo and read nothing in his expression.

In the car on the way home Hugo said, "At least he got his camera."

The article, when it finally appeared the following Sunday in a paper they did not normally buy, was called "The Way We Live Now." It was as bad as Reggie had feared. She was described as a "svelte brunette in her early fifties," Hugo as a "titled industrialist said to be worth millions"; the article alluded to their childlessness as if this had been a matter of choice—"the two of them rattling around in a huge Georgian mansion on their own"—and got the names of the dogs wrong. Barely half a paragraph was devoted to their restoration of the house, rather more to the numbers of staff they had "waiting on them hand and foot." Retold, the story about Panton and Mrs. Marsham helping Reggie to reassemble the chandelier became a tale of exploitation. The second half of the feature contrasted the "Lyells' lavish stately home set in thousands of acres of rolling Berkshire countryside" with the three-bedroom council flat with "condensation running down the walls" occupied by the Travers family of Poplar, an unemployed docker, his wife, and five children.

Much to Reggie's surprise, Hugo found it funny. "I'm absolutely certain," he said, throwing the supplement to one side, "that the heading must have been the sub's idea. I'll eat my hat if that girl's read a word of Trollope."

Reggie felt no such equanimity. After breakfast, she fetched her secateurs and went out into the garden, where she deadheaded roses for the remainder of the morning with rather more savagery than strictly speaking was necessary.

14

The Fête: 1976

You can reach a turning point without realizing that's what it is; most people don't. Afterwards, with hindsight, you make it out, but at the time it seems like more of the same—another year gone past, the habits that creep up on you which were innovations in their time but have become traditions through repetition. It's hard to spot the moment when you get old—the date won't be on the calendar. Harder still to tell when you've done enough, when there is nothing more left to do except bow out with grace.

This year no one speculated what the weather would be like. Everyone knew the weather would be the same as yesterday and the day before, and the week before and the weeks before that. No need to worry about it raining or to gaze up at the skies, which were as blank and blue as a Mediterranean destination; no need to check for incoming weather systems and depressions over the Atlantic that might spoil things. All summer, days of endless sun had parched the ground, turned what was green brown and dusty, yielded up the ridgebacks of ancient barrows and Saxon settlements. A holiday mood prevailed, which made people bare parts of their bodies that had never been bared in public before. "Mustn't complain," they said, fanning themselves, shoulders and arms burned lobster red. The Ploughshare put picnic tables in its garden, and the landlord was surprised when after a few weeks the saloon bar became noisy again with the chuntering of the fruit machines and the ringing fall of coins. As the heat wave went on, only the children, swooping on their bikes across melting tarmac, were in seventh heaven.

The Upper and Lower Ashenden combined village fête was always held in the first week of August in the grounds of the Park. Proceeds of the event went to Lady Lyell's charity. In the old stable block, cakes, fruit, flowers, and vegetables would be presented for judging, a marquee would serve as a tea tent, and scattered around the paddock would be the usual stalls: trestle tables laid out with knitted items and gingham-topped jars of jams, hook a duck, the coconut shy, guess the weight, and the tombola with its ticketed prizes. For three years, the same bottle of port hadn't been claimed and now had dusty shoulders and disturbed sediments.

Izzie Beckmann was eighteen. In her bedroom she tried on various outfits in front of the mirror, ideology rather than coolness and comfort uppermost in her mind. When she was satisfied with what the mirror told her, she went downstairs.

"My God, Izzie," said her mother, coming along the passageway. "What on earth are you wearing? You'll roast. Put on a skirt or some shorts. And what's that on your fingernails?"

"Nail polish, Mother."

"Mother" was new; it gave Izzie the distance she wanted from "Mum" and she enjoyed using it.

"Green?"

Izzie spread out her fingers in front of her and nodded. "Green."

Alison Beckmann winced, not at the nails, but at hearing herself turn into her own mother. Who was she to comment on her daughter's cropped puckish hair, green polish, and combat trousers, with their pockets and pouches down the legs? She wondered whether coming back to the village had hastened the process or whether it was inevitable wherever you were.

Both her parents were gone now. After her mother's death last October, they could have sold the house and got a reasonable price for it, but Walter, who was nearing retirement, wanted a change and a garden of a decent size, and so they had sold their Reading terrace instead, and now, almost thirty years since she had last lived here, she was back in her childhood home. Tom was up in London, and Izzie, who had protested about the move, although not more forcefully than she protested about all the other things she protested about, had had only a term of long bus journeys to and from school before her examinations were over. University loomed in the autumn and then she too would be off.

The doors were open front to back, letting in a through breeze. Even in these unprecedented temperatures the house remained cool, as if it retained the climate of other times.

Her mother, whose fractious spirit hung about the place, had been a vigorous, scouring cleaner. When carpets were beaten, dust had circled in the air, too afraid to land. Dust had never been afraid of Alison and on this hot summer day lay mocking her on every ledge and along the tops of skirting boards. Cobwebs too. Walter had plans and had shown her drawings that demonstrated how the house might be modernized with the knocking down of walls and the opening up of hallways and reroutings of passages, by which she had understood that his retirement from the building trade was going to mean more of the same. When she imagined the house transformed, French windows leading from a large remodeled kitchen on to the garden and the river view, she thought how well he had anticipated the fact that they were both going to need something to look forward to once Izzie had left. All their married life there had never been just the two of them, and to become a couple for the first time would also be something new.

"I want to put flowers on Grandma's grave," said Izzie, confirming in the hall mirror what the mirror upstairs had told her. "Can I take these?" She pointed to the vase on the hall table and, not waiting for an answer, hoicked out the brassy marigolds.

"I took some a couple of days ago. They should still be fresh."

"What are you saying? Are you saying I shouldn't go?" Izzie's memories of the grandfather who had doted on her were sketchy and based largely on photographic evidence; her grandmother, however, was her own personal property. "It's a special day." There was scorn in this statement, an implied negligence, although Izzie had been the first to complain about the errands, sickbed visits, and all the other time-consuming attentions an elderly mother required. "You know how much she always enjoyed the fête." The stems dripped all over the floor.

Alison counted to ten in her head: she didn't want an argument. Walter handled Izzie better; their temperaments weren't so much alike. So far as appearance was concerned, her daughter had the pick of both their features, as if she had been presented with a checklist in the womb and ticked them off: I'll have Dad's mouth, ears, and height—oh, and Mum's nose, eyes, and legs while you're at it. And please make me blond, just to confuse them. Sometimes Alison thought that Izzie wasn't conscious of her beauty. At other times she was convinced that the determined ugliness of her clothing was her way of calling attention to it. That was to say nothing of the contrast between Izzie's sharp mind and the fecklessness of Stuart Moss, who was the current boyfriend (and whose combat trousers they were).

Pray God, thought Alison, that Izzie will get the grades, go to university, and leave Stuart behind. She could not imagine that there would be Stuarts at university. Universities would not let in Stuarts.

"You won't forget to call next door and pick up Mrs. Drummond's cake, will you? The entries have to be in by a quarter to eleven."

"No, Mother," said Izzie. "I won't forget."

"Don't. She's hoping to win again this year."

"Of course she'll win," said Izzie. "They fix it. She'd win even if she didn't enter. Where's Dad?"

"Up at the Park. He's helping them set up. I'll see you later, shall I?" she said to the slamming door. Then she went to open it and let the air back in.

Izzie, heading to the churchyard with the marigolds, peered at her reflection in the butcher's window and straightened the khaki bandanna she had tied round her head. She definitely looked like a militant. When she got to university—unlike her mother, she'd no doubt she'd get the grades and believed her teachers when they told her so—she'd decided to join one of the far-left organizations, perhaps the Socialist Workers Party, or the Workers Revolutionary Party or the International Marxist Group. A socialist worker of some kind sold papers outside the record shop where she had a Saturday job, and she'd bought one once, intrigued by the headline "Scum." The paper was full of savage rage, calls to action, and exclamation marks, which appealed to her very much. For the past six months she'd been vegetarian, which had made her mother, who didn't believe that meat was murder, worry about the number of eggs she ate and what it was doing to her bowels and cholesterol levels. Unlike her vegetarianism, which couldn't be disguised, she was keeping her political conversion to herself for now. Once she was at Sussex, she had visions of her parents turning on the television one evening after supper and seeing her with a placard at the head of a demonstration, or raising a clenched fist and spitting in the face of a policeman. Although her father was a naturalized British citizen, his German birth allowed her to entertain ideas of being distantly related to Karl Marx or perhaps one of the members of the Baader-Meinhof Group.

She lifted the latch of the lych-gate. The ancient graves near the church had slanted tombstones covered in gray-green lichen, the lettering old-fashioned and blurred. Her grandmother shared a plot with her grandfather at the far end, where the newer graves were. Ever since she had been a little girl, Izzie had had a favorite, a small stone inscribed "Grace Lyell, born 12 March 1952, died 14 March 1952." This child gone before spoke to the child she was then, before she had known who Grace was, before everything she learned about the Lyells had kissed her life with glamour. As she passed the grave, which was always well tended, she laid a marigold on the ground and told Grace that it was for her. Over the years, she had left similar offerings: handfuls of daisies picked from the long churchyard grass; once, a small plastic cowboy for reasons she could no longer remember.

There wasn't a breath of air. Sweat ran down her forehead and into the khaki bandanna. Her grandparents' memorial tablet was

mottled brown granite with a high shine and deep black letters. The
ground was cracked, bone dry. "Hello, Grandma," said Izzie, crossing herself with the solemnity of those who aren't religious. "These
are from your garden." When she remembered her grandmother, she
was always in her garden, staking things, deadheading roses, teaching her names of plants. Lady's mantle was one of them, with its
tiny lime-green stars and crinkled leaf-fans whose furry hairs turned
raindrops into crystal beads. She bent down and picked up the grave
vase, catching, as she did so, a hint of her reflection in the polished
stone. Then she tossed her mother's flowers onto a neighboring plot
and went to fill the vase at the tap. Only a trickle of water emerged.

Izzie believed the dead liked to hear news. Back in the churchyard, as she sat inserting the marigolds into the holes in the aluminium liner of the grave vase, she talked about the bring-and-buy stall
at the fête she'd be running—"for the first time ever, isn't that good
of me?"—what the weather had done to her skin and hair—"I'm so
tanned you wouldn't believe it and my hair is almost pure white"—
and how irritating, incompetent, and ridiculous her mother was
and all the ways she had been irritating, incompetent, and ridiculous lately. "Well, good-bye, Grandma," she said, crossing herself
again. "I'll be back soon to tell you how it went." She got up, thought
about leaving her mother's flowers where she had discarded them,
then gathered them up and gave them to Grace on the way out.

In the stable block the judges were having a discussion. Down the
length of a trestle table the entries for the flower, fruit, and vegetable prizes were spaced at intervals, like shopping at a supermarket
checkout. Although the village gardeners had done their best, the
weather had taken its toll. This year the potatoes and onions were
puny, the peas were pellets, and the floral entries were down by a
third. The exception was a display towards the door: two enormous
marrows presented in the class C "size and weight" category.

"He says he's been siphoning his bathwater," said Mr. Southcliffe.

"My eye," said Mrs. Cottingham. "Mrs. Simmons sees him every night out there with his hosepipe. Watering freely. Those are her precise words. *Watering freely.*"

Petra Curtis, who had been examining a scabrous carrot with a nose, which was entered in the class F "amusing vegetables" category, said that the rules made no mention of watering methods.

"We simply cannot let him get away with it," said Mrs. Cottingham, putting much vehemence into "simply," as she did into all of her adverbs. "Watering in secret during a hosepipe ban sets such a bad example."

"You can't do anything in secret if you live next door to Mrs. Simmons," said Petra. "It seems perfectly straightforward to me. These marrows are obviously the best in class. We've no choice but to give them first prize. Although I do agree that a quiet word with Ted might not go amiss."

"He's a decent sort, all in all," said Mr. Southcliffe, glancing from woman to woman and giving the change in his pockets a sharp, decisive jingle. "You have to remember he's not been well."

Mrs. Cottingham folded her arms. "Well, I for one shall be bringing this up with the committee at the earliest opportunity."

The door opened and Izzie Beckmann came in. "Am I too late?"

Mrs. Cottingham checked her watch. "Five past eleven, I make it. The rules clearly state—"

"Is that Mrs. Drummond's cake?" said Petra. "I did wonder where it had got to."

"I was visiting my grandmother's grave and lost track of time," said Izzie, who knew how to look innocent and angelic when she wanted to.

"Put it over there, dear," said Petra, pointing to the end of a trestle table on the opposite side of the stables, where the jams, chutneys, and cakes were displayed. "You'll see her entry card."

Izzie smiled, set down the cake, and left.

"Lovely girl," said Mr. Southcliffe, shaking his head. "Lovely girl. She'll break a few hearts in her time, I expect."

"All the girls look like boys these days," said Mrs. Cottingham. "And vice versa."

"My dear late wife was wearing trousers when I met her," said Mr. Southcliffe. "Practical garments in wartime. Fetching on the right person."

Izzie had met Stuart one Saturday when he'd come into the record shop with a few of his friends. They'd crammed into one of the booths at the back, sharing the headphones to listen to the latest Judas Priest album, and then left without buying it. Afterwards the booth reeked of patchouli and cigarettes.

At the record shop Izzie sold Herb Alpert and James Last and songs of humpback whales. Fourteen-year-old boys would come in to snigger over the naked women on the cover of *Electric Lady-land* or to ask for a James Brown record so they could say "sex" out loud. "That song I hear on the radio all the time" was another request they often had. Depending on how bored or busy she was, she would either suggest whatever was number one that week or ask the person to sing the tune, which was always good for a laugh. Iris, the manageress, had psoriasis and a crush on Al Pacino.

The week after he'd listened to Judas Priest in the booth with his friends, Stuart had come into the shop on his own and spent an hour flicking through the empty record sleeves in the alien and despised territory of folk, which happened to be the rack closest to the counter where Izzie was serving. The next week he'd done the same. "Here's love's young dream back again," said Gregory, raising an eyebrow and nursing his cup of instant coffee. Gregory was in charge of the classical music section upstairs and a devotee of Sibelius, Steeleye Span, and Hollywood musicals.

The following Saturday Stuart asked her out and they went to a pub after she finished work. The trees were budding, Elton John was on the jukebox, and they kissed right there in the public bar after she finished her rum and black. In the upper fourth there had been a girl who believed you could get pregnant from kissing, she remembered halfway through the snog, which wasn't to say she wasn't paying attention to the thrilling twang of her nerve endings or the heat deep in her loins. She'd had boyfriends before and was familiar with the way that sweaty hands inched along the backs of cinema seats or landed on you as if they had unexpectedly dropped off the ends of arms up in the circle. Stuart, however, knew what he was about— "experienced" she told herself as his tongue went in her mouth—and had long sideboards, which made him seem older. He shared a maroon Ford Anglia with his brother. She fancied him like mad.

That spring, they spent a lot of time in pubs or in the car, parked in side streets or down country lanes, steaming up the windows. Afterwards she would come home flushed and confused, her body saying one thing and her head another. One night, a month or so before they moved to the village, her father had given her an awkward speech in the kitchen of their old house, where he was sitting waiting up for her, pretending to work on his accounts.

"You have your whole life in front of you," he'd said, his accent pronounced, as it always was at times of stress or emotion. "I'm sure that this Stuart is a nice boy, but there is no need to be serious about one person at your age. What is that on your neck, Izzie?"

"Nothing, Dad." She tugged her hair across the love bite; this was before the haircut.

"Have a glass of water before you go to bed." He ran the tap and poured it for her.

"Have you Done It yet?" they giggled at school. (Doing It was always capitalized in the sixth-form common room.) No, was the answer she kept to herself, while trying to imply otherwise. Lust tugged at her when she was with him, particularly in the car, and walking hand in hand or going to meet his friends in some pub or other gave her a warm sense of importance and necessity, as if she were a prize that had been won. Trevor, who had a beard and wore blue eyeliner, used to pretend her school scarf was a telephone, putting one end to his ear and talking into the other. Other friends paid tribute: "Like the new haircut," said Mick. "Suits her, don't you think?" said Stuart, running his hand over her shorn head. "Shows her lovely little ears." Yet at other times something like boredom would ambush her, she would stop fancying him, and he would become as insignificant as someone she would pass in the street. Even his name would become unattractive. He went away to London after Easter to hang about with different friends (he had already left school) and wrote her poems that were like bad pop lyrics. She hid them from herself at the bottom of her underwear drawer, where she wouldn't be tempted to read them and remind herself how awful they were and how childishly they were spelled and punctuated. Aside from the poetry, however, she found that she did miss him, which was all very confusing.

During the exam season, she wasn't allowed to go out much and she became a young girl again, fed by her mother, tested by her father, crossing off the revision chart in her bedroom with a black Magic Marker. Now the exams were over, lust and boredom were back warring with each other, and her mother was frenzied with disapproval, convinced that Stuart was going to ruin her future; that his general lack of ambition was going to rub off on her; that she would get pregnant and end up living on the dole. Izzie knew that there was no place for Stuart in her future. The question was whether it would be better to sleep with him and lose her virginity before she went to university, or wait until she got there and had met someone else who wouldn't bore her quite as much. As it wasn't an exam question, and virginity was not like impacted wisdom teeth, which she was due to have extracted later in the month, she didn't know the answer to it.

When Izzie told her grandmother that she was running the bring-and-buy stall, it wasn't strictly true. What was true was that she had agreed to help out behind the stall later in the afternoon for an hour or so. During the weeks before the fête, her mother had been the one to collect the donations from the houses in the village and the postwar council estate that adjoined it, quietly dispose of what was pure rubbish—the much-worn pair of plimsolls, for example, or the carrier bag filled with stained tea towels—and ticket the rest with white stickers on which she wrote the prices.

"Is twenty pee too much, do you think?" she had asked Walter one evening earlier in the week, holding up a pewter platter with "God Bless Our Daily Bread" stamped on it in Gothic letters.

"I'd pay twenty pee never to see it again. But I wouldn't mind this." He picked up an old wooden plane.

"Yours for fifty pee," she said.

"Oh, come on, Allie. The blade is rusty."

"You'll sort that out in no time. Besides, it's all in a good cause."

He ran his fingers over the plane. A certain distance descended on him from time to time, and over the years she had learned, the hard way, not to say, "What is it?" or "Anything the matter?" or, worse, "Out with it."

She got on with her stickers. The clock ticked.

Alison may not have wanted to turn into her mother, but she missed her all the same. The incapacities of her old age, the worsening arthritis and the series of strokes, had been a trial to them both, duty chafing at her love, the indignity of physical decline chafing at her mother, each of them locked into it together. If her father's sudden death of a heart attack thirteen years ago had been a brutal severance, her mother's had been what people call "a release," which didn't make it any easier to bear. When the envelope arrived in two weeks' time and Izzie got the grades she was expected to get (fingers crossed), she knew she would not be able to resist the impulse to reach for the phone, the same phone that would have delivered the news to her parents, and then turn away from it saddened that there was no one on the other end of the line.

Walter, having examined the plane from more angles than you would have thought possible, pulled out a chair, sat down at the kitchen table, and sighed.

"The Lyells have decided to move out of the house and into the south pavilion."

Alison put down her stickers and looked at him. "Have they?" And then, "I suppose it's sensible at their age."

"There will be an announcement at the fête, I think. Better not say anything about it for now."

"Of course. Are you sad?"

"No, not sad. A little—what is the word?—wistful. Yes, I am wistful."

She reached across the table to squeeze his hand. "Look at it this way. You made sure the house survived. They couldn't have rescued it without you."

He nodded.

Change, she thought, none of us like it. "I'll make some tea."

"Don't," he said, catching her around the waist as she got up. "Better we should have a toast, I think."

"Good idea." She kissed the top of his head, then pulled herself free and went over to open a cupboard. "Schnapps or Dubonnet? We don't seem to have anything else."

"Schnapps."

They held up their tiny shot glasses and clinked them.

"To retirement," said Alison.

"To retirement," said Walter, keeping quiet about the fact that the Lyells had asked him to finish the conversion of the south pavilion for them and he had agreed.

All day Izzie had been humming with the righteousness of the useful. After she had delivered the cake, she'd found her father in the paddock and helped him with the marquee, hammering in the pegs and standing on the aluminium stepladder to throw the linings across the jointed metal framework. Because of the heat, they decided to leave the side walls rolled up. The canvas smelled musty, as if its folds had trapped the air of an old camping holiday. Lunch was sandwiches sent down from the Park.

"Aren't you meant to be helping your mother with the stall?" said her father.

Izzie picked cress out of her egg sandwich. "That's later. What else can I do?"

Her father thought a moment. "You could take the van and fetch the tea urn from the house."

"Really?"

"Why not?"

"I haven't passed my test yet."

"You've had lots of lessons. And it's a private road." He handed her the keys. "Don't hit a tree. Or anything else."

The van was boiling inside. Izzie rolled down the windows, reversed over the grass into the drive, her driving instructor's mantra—"mirror, signal, maneuver"—going through her head. Lots of lessons, in her case, had not meant much improvement behind the wheel, although that was not the story she told. "You chuffing idiot!" was what Mr. Stubbs said at some point most weeks. It took a couple of minutes at most to reach the house, but she was hugely pleased with the accomplishment. She parked near the courtyard and went through the archway, just as Lady Lyell came out of the house with Mrs. Marsham, who was leaning heavily on her stick, her ankles swollen over the tops of her black lace-up shoes.

"Hello there, Izzie." Lady Lyell was wearing a pale-pink linen dress and was as cool and composed as if she were air-conditioned.

Later Izzie would learn that socialism was not incompatible with snobbery, inverted or otherwise. For the moment, she would have sooner seen her mother as a class enemy than Lady Lyell, whom she had known and admired all her life, her connection with the Park via her father's firm being something that she had always hugged to herself as something special.

"Oh, hi," she said. "I've come for the tea urn."

"Do you need someone to help you with it?" said Lady Lyell. "Mind the step, Mrs. M."

"No, I'm fine. Dad lent me the van."

"Are you sure?"

"Yeah, I'm fine."

The urn, scrubbed and shiny, was where her father had said it would be, and she made a great show of lifting it up as if it weighed nothing at all, which it didn't.

Mrs. Marsham, feeling ahead with her stick, was fussing about the time.

"Ages to go," said Lady Lyell.

"Not a good idea to rush things." Although Mrs. Marsham had been retired for a number of years, she always came back on the day of the fête to reign over the tea tent. "In *my* experience."

"Izzie, since you've got the van," said Lady Lyell, "would you mind giving Mrs. M a lift?"

"OK," said Izzie, from behind the tea urn. She didn't want to admit that she hadn't passed her test yet or turn down another opportunity to demonstrate how useful she was.

It was funny how much difference a passenger could make. The only person Izzie had ever driven before was Mr. Stubbs, who didn't count. For a time she couldn't find first gear, and the three-point turn that should have sent her in the other direction down the drive became a seven-point turn with a hill start in the middle of it. Sweat poured into the khaki bandanna. Then they were off, the tea urn rattling away in the back. Down, down, her mind returning to the virginity, the Doing It question, and just when she was thinking about changing up to second—"Fuck!" said Izzie, stamping too late on the brakes. Metal scratched metal, an awful scritching sound, like fingernails scraping across a blackboard. They were thrown forward, then back. The tea urn crashed onto its side with a loud clang.

"Umph," said Mrs. Marsham.

"Oh, God, are you hurt?"

Mrs. Marsham patted her chest, getting her breath back. "No, dear. A little shaken, that's all."

Izzie rested her head on the steering wheel, panting, dry-mouthed, a sick feeling in her stomach. She heard the clunk of a car door and the other driver bent his head through the open window.

"You all right?"

She raised her head and glared at him. "What do you think?"

"Mrs. M?" he said. "Didn't see you there at first. You OK?"

"You want to be more careful, Charlie. You'll kill yourself in that thing one of these days. I've told you so a hundred times." Mrs. Marsham shifted her legs. "Good job I was wearing my seat belt. They should make it a law with people like you about."

Izzie got out of the van. A long ragged scratch ran down the side to the rear-passenger door. It was worse than she thought. "Shit."

The other driver was in his early twenties, with longish dark hair and bright blue eyes. "Look, I'm awfully sorry, but you were right in the middle of the road."

"So were you! Going like a hundred miles an hour!"

"Yes, but in my case I was actually looking where I was going."

"What do you mean? Are you saying I wasn't paying attention?"

He checked the damage to his own car, a yellow Triumph Spitfire: the front bumper was a bit dented. "Let's just let the insurance sort it out, shall we?" He reached into his jeans pocket. "Have you got a pen and paper?"

"No," said Izzie.

"I do," said Mrs. Marsham, opening her handbag and producing a biro and a small notepad with a William Morris pattern on the cover.

The driver, Charlie, wrote quickly, tore out a page, and handed it to Izzie. "Your turn."

She took the notebook and didn't know what to put.

"You are insured, aren't you?"

Izzie straightened her khaki bandanna.

"Aren't you?"

"Sort of."

"What do you mean?"

"This is my dad's van."

"Are you insured to drive it?"

"He said it would be OK."

"How old are you?"

"None of your business!"

"Christ," he said. "Have you passed your test?"

Izzie cursed the blush that spread up her neck to her cheeks.

"Look," he said, "give me your number and I'll speak to your dad." His eyes really were a startling blue. Dark hair, blue eyes—she and Ruth, her best friend, had decided that was their ideal combination in a man. "I'm sure we can come to some arrangement."

This concession, and the wealth and privilege that she wrongly assumed lay behind it, made her furious. Here, at last, was the class enemy. "I should bloody well think so!"

"Your dad's details?"

Mrs. Marsham leaned across and spoke out of the window. "She's Walter Beckmann's daughter," she said. "Look him up in the telephone directory, Charlie. I do need to get on. Time's ticking past."

"Well, take your life in your own hands, Mrs. M," said Charlie, tapping the van's bonnet. "Good luck."

"Who was that?" said Izzie, trying to stop her hands shaking long enough to turn the key in the ignition.

"Charlie Minton. One of Sir Hugo's nephews," said Mrs. Marsham. "The clever one. Though you wouldn't think it sometimes."

Izzie parked in the shade. The sensible thing would have been to tell her father what had happened straightaway. Instead, she took the urn out of the back and went along to the marquee with Mrs. Marsham, where she helped her set up. By the time the fête opened, she was still there, wondering what on earth she was going to say about the van.

Stuart had begged Mick to come along. The plan was that they would show up at the fête, he would tell Izzie he was chucking her, and then they would go back to Reading and sit in the pub until closing time. Only the pub part of the plan appealed to Mick.

"Can't you do it over the phone? Or just split, man, and let her work it out for herself."

Stuart shook his head. "I can't do that."

"You've done it before."

"Yeah, but this is different."

Since Easter Stuart Moss had been seeing someone called Jan Vickers, who lived in a squat in Shepherd's Bush. Jan was really creative and made these really clever little leather chokers and anklets and things. While Izzie had been revising, he had been up in London most weekends; after she finished school, he went to stay with Jan for odd days and nights in the week. The sex was fantastic.

Proper sex, on a bed. A mattress on the floor really, but same thing. Even if Jan didn't have such a great body as Izzie, the big plus was she let him do things to it. In return she did things to his that were surprisingly inventive. The maroon Ford Anglia had a lot more mileage on it these days. Now Jan was hassling him to move in, and he was all packed, ready to leave. "A rolling stone gathers no Moss," was how he had been putting it.

"Anyway, I'm busy," said Mick. "I promised Tiny Tits I'd take her to see *The Omen*."

"Please," said Stuart. "It's going to be really heavy. She's going to freak out."

"You don't have to tell her about Jan."

"Do me a favor," said Stuart. "Do you think I'm crazy? I'm going to say I need a bit of space."

"You never did get your leg over, did you?" Mick stubbed out his fag. "Don't understand why you didn't chuck her weeks ago."

"She was doing her exams."

"Stuart, mate, the exams have been over for ages."

"Please."

"OK. But you owe me."

Mick decided that if he was going to provide moral support, he needed some chemical support. Stuart picked him up from his house around three and they drove out of Reading along the country lanes.

"Wow, so many trees."

A vague greenness swam past the car windows.

"You sod."

"I'm here, aren't I?" said Mick, tripping on the greenness.

"You bloody sod. You're stoned."

The vague greenness became a vague brownness as they came past parched fields.

"True," said Mick. "Very, very high."

They paid their ten-pence entrance fee and wandered around the trestle tables congested with old people picking things up and putting them down.

"This is cool, this is all very cool," said Mick. "Can you, like, eat this jam?"

"You have to buy it first." Stuart took the jar out of his hands. "See Izzie anywhere? She said she'd be on one of the stalls."

Thwock, thwock, thwock came from the coconut shy, and the shrill cries of children tore the air. A queue was forming by the tea tent, and the St. John Ambulance people were on the alert for heat exhaustion. They wandered about a little more.

"Stuart."

"Oh, hi, Mrs. Beckmann." Izzie's mother was standing behind a table covered with crap, frowning at him.

"I don't suppose you know where Izzie is, do you?"

"No, we just got here."

"Well, if you see her, tell her I need her to come and look after the stall. I've got to fetch Mrs. Drummond for the prize giving."

"OK," said Stuart, as if he was supposed to know who Mrs. Drummond was and why she was giving out prizes.

"Unless," said Izzie's mother, still frowning, "you wouldn't mind tending the stall for me. Everything's priced. All you have to do is take the money and give change."

"Um," said Stuart.

"I won't be long."

"OK."

She gathered up her handbag. "Is your friend all right?"

Mick was sitting cross-legged on the brown ground, staring at it.

"He's not dead keen on the heat."

"For a minute there I thought he was counting what's left of the grass."

"I am," said Mick, looking up and giving her a stoned smile.

"He's interested in nature," said Stuart.

"I see," said Izzie's mother.

The sun beat down. Christ, he had never seen so many old people in his life. Or so many children. There didn't seem to be anyone in between, except him and Mick.

"How much is this?" said an old person with a horrible sagging neck, holding up some sort of metal tray with "God Bless Our Daily Bread" on it.

"What's it say?" said Stuart.

"I can't read the label, I'm afraid. The writing's too small," said the old person in an old person's voice.

Typical. Old people always said the writing was too small or the hill was too steep. They never said their eyes were bad or they were on their sodding last legs. Stuart took the plate.

"It's twenty pee."

"What's that in old money?"

"Four bob."

"Oh dear, no. That's far too much."

"Go on, treat yourself," said Stuart.

"No, no, I mustn't. You have to watch the pennies at my age."

"Well, have it for nothing, then."

"For nothing?"

"Yeah, go ahead. It's on me."

"Well, thank you very much, young man," said the old person. "God bless."

Christ, thought Stuart.

A middle-aged man with poofy hair, short legs, beer belly straining against a striped shirt, came up and stood sifting through the Mantovanis and Perry Comos and Andrews Sisters. From time to time he shot Stuart filthy looks that said, "They should bring back National Service," and "In my day . . ." A kid bought an Airfix kit. Another kid bought a green plastic frog. The middle-aged man with the beer belly said, "I'll take this, thank you very much," and placed coins on the table.

Auf Wiedersehen in Garmisch-Partenkirchen. Lederhosen on the cover.

"Sorry. That's not enough," said Stuart.

"It says twenty-five pee."

"Yeah, it's been marked up wrong. You see, this is kind of a rare album. It's actually one pound fifty."

"One pound fifty?"

Stuart explained that he was the manager of a record shop, giving the name of the record shop where Izzie worked. "Trust me, mate, one pound fifty is a bargain. You could flog it for three times as much up in London tomorrow. Rare pressing."

"You're having me on."

"I was thinking of buying it myself," said Stuart. "As an investment."

"Were you?" said the middle-aged man.

"Yeah," said Stuart, putting the album to one side.

"One pound fifty, did you say?" The middle-aged man got out his wallet.

For the next half hour or so, Stuart decided on his own pricing policy. Everything on the stall was crap. *Sligo and Its Surrounds,* an ashtray with "Souvenir of Weston-super-Mare" written on it, a shower cap in its original packaging. The trick was to work out how much someone could afford to pay, how much they wanted the piece of crap, and multiply that by how much they annoyed him. Most people who came to the stall annoyed him, one way or another, so the cash was building up nicely when he caught sight of Izzie over by the stable block. "Mick," he said. "Mind the stall for me, will you?" But Mick had disappeared.

When it was time for the prize giving, Izzie still hadn't worked out what to tell her father. She saw him coming into the tea tent and escaped out the back, where she immediately ran into her mother and Mrs. Drummond.

"Where on earth have you been?" said Alison.

"Helping Mrs. Marsham."

"You were supposed to be helping *me.*"

"Does it matter?" said Izzie. "I'm still *helping,* aren't I? I've been down here all day. I put up most of the tent on my own." And had an accident. She squashed the thought like a fly.

"She had her hip op yet?" said Mrs. Drummond.

"Who?"

"Mrs. Marsham."

"I doubt it," said Izzie. "She has a stick."

"If she's sick, she shouldn't be serving teas," said Mrs. Drum-mond, who was deaf. "It's not hygienic."

Alison said, "I'm going to take Mrs. Drummond in for the prizes. Why don't you go and relieve Stuart? When I couldn't find you, I left him minding the stall."

"Stuart?" said Izzie. "What's he doing here?"

"I expect you asked him, didn't you?"

Izzie had told Stuart not to come, but she wasn't about to admit that to her mother.

"He's got some sort of friend in tow," said Alison.

"Why are you frowning, Mother?"

"I'm not frowning."

"I'll go after the prizes," said Izzie, who didn't want to see her father, Stuart, or Stuart's friend, whichever friend that was. "Grandma always said the best bit was the expressions on the faces of the ladies who came in third."

"So many ladybirds this year," said Mrs. Drummond, nodding. "The garden's full of them. Never known anything like it."

First prize for cake (class H) had never been awarded to an empty plate before.

"You did remember to fetch it, didn't you?"

"Yes, Mother," said Izzie. "You can ask the old dears if you don't believe me."

Petra Curtis, handing the certificate to a bewildered Mrs. Drum-mond—"Goodness me, for the ninth year running. What a cham-pion!"—said that she had no idea what had happened to the cake but all the judges could testify how delicious it was. "We only ate a slice, mind you, so don't go blaming us!" There was a little laughter. She consulted her notes. "Moving on, and bearing in mind there is no class I. Class J. Chutney. Third prize to—"

At that moment Mick rolled out from underneath one of the

trestle tables, blinked, and sat up, sawdust in his hair and wispy beard, sawdust all down his maroon cords. Then he staggered to his feet, bent over the table, and gouged out a handful of second prize.

"Ace cakes," he said, stuffing the handful into his mouth and gouging out another. "Specially that one." He pointed to the empty plate. "That one was really, really amaaaaazing."

The reaction was immediate and, as it was an English reaction, almost invisible to the untrained eye. People looked and looked away, muttered shock and disapproval, and wondered why no one was doing anything about it and how anyone could wear corduroy in this weather.

"Shame!" said someone at the back, and all the heads swiveled round to see who it had been.

"That's Stuart's friend, isn't it?" said Alison.

Mick stumbled across the floor, throwing his legs in front of him and trusting that the rest of his body would follow. "Hey, Izzie," he said, grabbing her by the arm. "Stuart wants to see ya. He's got something important to tell ya."

Across the stable block Izzie saw Charlie Minton standing alongside Sir Hugo and Lady Lyell, trying and failing not to laugh. The tidewaters of embarrassment rose up her body, up her neck, and closed over her head. She was drowning in a sea of shame.

Her father came through the door, a quizzical expression on his face.

"Izzie? Where are you going?" said Alison.

Stuart was trying to persuade a mother of a snotty-nosed kid that a wicker wastepaper basket was worth a pound of anyone's money— "hand-crafted," he said, and "locally made"—when Izzie came tearing across the paddock with "Fuck you" written all over her face.

"A pound. Seems a bit steep," said the mother.

"Fuck you!" said Izzie. "I never want to see you again. Do you understand? Ever!"

"Crumbs," said the mother, putting her hands over her kid's ears.

"Go!"

Stuart put up his hands. "Hey."

"Go. Now! Just bugger off."

The mother led her child away.

"If you want the wastepaper basket, have it!" said Izzie, throwing it after them.

"Izzie," said Stuart.

"Bugger off," said Izzie, coming behind the table and pushing him away. "And take that fucking old hippie with you! You bastard!"

"Izzie." Stuart had never been the chuckee before and didn't know whether to smirk or push back. On balance, a smirk seemed best.

"Go!"

"OK, OK. Keep your cool."

"Go!"

Stuart went.

Izzie placed her hands on the table and bent over. A dull rumor of pain started in her lower back. Probably whiplash or something. The sun beat down on her head. She stood there for some time, all the embarrassments of the day washing over her in wave after mortifying wave.

"That was impressive."

She lifted her head and was confronted by the startling blue eyes of the class enemy. "What was?"

"I think you would be a lot cooler if you took that headband thing off," said the class enemy, who had a camera around his neck and a drink in one hand. "Here, this is for you. Thought you could do with it." It was a glass of Pimm's. "Courtesy of Uncle Hugo and Aunt Reggie."

Pimm's. Strawberries, cucumber, and mint. The drink looked cool and delicious, but she was certainly not going to give him the satisfaction of taking it.

He put the glass on the table and retrieved the wastepaper basket from where it had rolled away on the ground.

"How much do you want for this?"

"A pound," said Izzie, her cheeks blazing. "What was impressive?"

"Too expensive," said Charlie, putting it back on the table. "You should really take that headband thing off. Let me. There you are. Much cooler, isn't it?"

Izzie rubbed her forehead. "He wasn't my boyfriend, if that's what you're thinking." She picked up the glass and took a sip. "Just somebody I sort of know."

"Oh, I wasn't thinking anything," said Charlie. "Now, are you going to give me your phone number so I can ring your dad and tell him the accident was all my fault?"

"A hot-water bottle," said Walter. "In this weather?"

"You know how she gets," said Alison. "The first day of her period. It's soothing."

"She scratched the van."

"Walter," said Alison, halfway out the door. "You did let her drive it."

"She said she was getting on so well with the lessons."

Alison smiled and shook her head. Upstairs, she knocked on the door of her daughter's bedroom, the bedroom that used to be hers. There was a muffled reply.

"Slip this under the sheet," she said.

The room smelled of antifungal foot powder and deodorant.

"Are you crazy?" said Izzie, her face rumpled and sweaty. "In this heat?"

"It'll help the pain in your back."

"No, I don't want it, Mother." She burrowed her head in the pillow.

"Aspirin?"

"Had some."

"Well, I'll just set this down on the bookcase in case you change your mind." Alison sat on the edge of the bed. "We made fourteen quid on the stall. Can you believe it? The strange thing is I don't know quite how. I only took three pounds or so, if that, and there was quite a bit of stuff left at the end."

No reply.

Her hand hovered over her daughter. Without finding any obvious place to rest it, she sighed and got up.

"All right, then. See you in the morning. Hope you feel better."

"Mum?" From the pillow.

"Yes?"

"Is Dad mad at me about the van?"

"No. He's a little sad about the house. Wistful is how he puts it."

"Why?"

"Oh, I forgot. You missed the speech, didn't you? It was after you ran off. The Lyells are moving out of the house into one of the pavilions."

Izzie shot up in bed, creases all over her cheeks. "Oh no!"

"Much easier for them to manage a smaller place at their age."

"That's terrible! That's so sad!"

"I think it's sensible of them, actually."

"I can't believe you don't care!"

"Get some sleep. We'll talk about it in the morning."

"How am I supposed to sleep now?"

"It's been a long day. I think you'll manage."

When her mother had left the room, Izzie fetched the hot-water bottle and laid it against her back. Then she reached under her pillow where she had put the piece of paper with Charlie Minton's address and phone number written on it. Just to check that it was still there. He had really nice handwriting, much nicer than Stuart's. She wondered how the photograph he had taken of her was going to turn out.

15

The Winter Season: 2010

If these are ghosts, they are friendly ones, who slip past in the thin cold air and leave no disturbance or sadness behind. It's the gentlest form of haunting, really, a smile fading from a face, or a forgotten tune playing in the next room. Ghosts are only to be expected when the house contains so much time.

So much of your own life too, over half a century. The house is your skin, your memory, your thoughts. It's family; all that you've loved.

Reggie awoke to find a glare on the ceiling, a bright reflected uplight that told her that it had snowed again. What did Luke, Charlie's boy, call it? *A snow dump.* There had been another snow dump. Thick drifts plumped the outlines of trees and fences and hedges, hid the world under a goose-feather counterpane. She was standing at the window staring out over the whitened park, the monochrome landscape like an old silvered photograph, perhaps a Brassaï, when her carer, Elaine, came in with the breakfast tray. This morning Elaine was wearing purple leggings and a bulky sweater patterned with gray and white lozenges.

"Oh, I see we're up, Lady Lyell."

She had never been able to persuade Elaine to call her Reggie, one of the small failures of recent years, any more than she had become used to "we," the old-age pronoun. Live past eighty (she was past ninety) and you became a "we."

Elaine set down the tray. "No post, of course. Everything's at a complete standstill. They've been saying for days on the telly this was coming, so why haven't they gritted the roads? Scandal, if you ask me. What do we pay our council tax for is what I want to know. Before I forget, Mrs. St. George rang earlier."

"Did she? I didn't hear the phone."

Elaine poured the tea. "Breakfast first. Then we'll see about ringing her back, shall we?"

"She'll want to tell me the date of the charity auction, I expect." Reggie thought she might need assistance with some aspects of daily life—bathing these days was a chore—but returning calls to old friends like Mrs. St. George was not yet one of them. Waving away Elaine, who was trying to pull out the chair for her, she sat herself down at the table in front of the window, spread her napkin over her lap, and reached for the honey. Hugo used to have a sweet tooth; nowadays she did. She'd read somewhere that one's sense of taste altered with age. Otherwise, she had all her own teeth, all her faculties (reading glasses didn't count), and no arthritis beyond a thickening of the knuckles that meant she couldn't wear her rings anymore. There had been one or two odd little turns, dizzy spells, nothing serious to speak of. Low blood pressure, the doctor said. Her sister, who was eighty-eight, was the same. She supposed it was in the genes. Every evening they spoke on the phone, a little something to look forward to.

"If Mrs. St. George rings again, tell her I'll call her back this afternoon."

"Oh?" said Elaine. "Do we have plans this morning?"

"Yes." The idea, which had occurred to her as soon as she had opened her eyes, as if she had dreamed it, had got a grip on her. It was all she could think about. "I'm going over to the house."

"Lady Lyell." Elaine shook her head as if she'd expressed a desire to take up white-water rafting. "It's freezing out there."

"I'll wrap up well, I do assure you."

"Better stay in the warm. I should. Go another day."

Reggie had anticipated the resistance, and the only way to deal with it was to ignore it. "Would you mind letting Tony know that I'm coming? Say in an hour or so."

Elaine sniffed and said, "We'll go together, then."

"It would be lovely if you would see me across the courtyard, but I shall be fine after that. I'll ask Tony to bring me back when I'm ready. You needn't worry."

"And what if we have another little fall?"

"I won't."

"We can't be sure about that."

"If I do," said Reggie, "I shall press the button."

She held up the panic alarm they insisted she wear round her neck, the electronic tag for an old offender. How Hugo would have hated it. Luke, her grandnephew, was teaching her to google. The first time she had made a search, she had entered her husband's name, but his obituary wasn't online. Hers, she thought, would be.

Elaine consulted her watch and sighed to register her disapproval. "Shall we listen to the news?" The radio, which had been talking quietly to itself in the corner, blared into life. A soldier had been killed in Helmand Province.

Reggie drank her tea and ate a slice of toast. The first carer the agency had sent, Debbie, had left after a few weeks to train as a probation officer. Elaine, the second, had been with her for two and a half years. Her magenta hair had gray roots. Magenta, Reggie remembered someone telling her (it might have been Bunny), was a shade that was unknown before the middle of the nineteenth century, the product of the harsh aniline dyes developed by the new chemical industries, and named after a Crimean battle. The old colors, the preindustrial colors, made from animal, vegetable, and mineral sources, were much subtler and faded in sympathy with one another, the same someone had told her (on the other hand, it might have been Kenneth). What a lot you learned in your life. What a lot you forgot, no matter how hard you tried to hang on to it. When she had realized that she had forgotten Hugo's smell, and could find it nowhere on the few clothes of his she had kept, she knew she had lost him for all time.

They had been living in the south pavilion for over twenty years when he died. During that time they traveled a good deal, around the Mediterranean and in the Middle and Far East. It had been a late education. Hugo was good with maps and itineraries and they saw temples, pyramids, and ancient ruins. Of all their journeys, she thought her favorite had been an early trip to Greece in the late 1970s, when a caïque had taken them from a ferry to an island in the Cyclades and they had stayed in a bare whitewashed cell at an old monastery. She remembered breakfasting on sheep's milk yogurt, bread fresh from a conical stone oven built on the hillside, honey flavored with thyme, the sun hot on her shoulders, a donkey braying. Swimming off rocks in a sea as blue as heaven, as blue as the domes of the island churches.

"Are we finished?" said Elaine. "Lady Lyell?"

Reggie came back to herself. "Yes, thank you."

She screwed the top back on the honey and wiped her mouth, leaving a trace of lipstick behind. Before Elaine had the chance to help her, she pushed back her chair and got up from her seat, perhaps not as steadily as she would have liked, seeing as she was trying to prove a point. She must get over to the house this morning. The urge was not a hunger or thirst; it was more a necessity, like breathing.

Elaine reached for the tray. "Buttons," she said.

"I'm sorry, I didn't catch that."

"*Buttons*. We've done our cardigan up wrong."

So she had. She fumbled with her knotted fingers. "Thank you for telling me."

"Don't mention it," said Elaine. "It's what I'm here for."

Less than an hour later Reggie, dressed in her warmest coat, a knitted hat and gloves, and a pair of thick-soled brogues she'd had for forty-three years, was standing by the door to the courtyard, like a pensioner at a bus stop or a dog asking to go out. At her heels a long line of dogs stretched behind, all of them gone now, of course. She had been given the last one by her sister twelve years ago—it was a few months after Hugo died—and the vet had had to put her down last spring. No more dogs now. Not fair on the dogs.

"Ah, there you are," she said.

Elaine was wearing a quilted jacket and a pair of red-and-white polka-dot Wellington boots over her purple leggings.

"Are we sure this can't wait? It's going to warm up next week, that's what they're saying."

Reggie opened the door and breathed in the sharp, cold air. The snow was so bright, even brighter than from the window in her bedroom. It made her feel light-headed. Across the courtyard a path had been cleared and salted.

"Somebody's been busy."

"Yes, well," said Elaine, getting a firm grip on her elbow and handing her the stick the hospital outpatients department had supplied after the last fall. "We can't be slipping and sliding everywhere, can we? Mind how you go. It's that treacherous."

They inched across the courtyard.

"I spoke to Tony and he's expecting you," said Elaine, her wellies crunching on the salted path.

"Thank you."

They reached the other side.

"Much appreciated," said Reggie.

Elaine released her grip on Reggie's elbow and opened the door to the house. "I think we'd better go in together."

"No need," said Reggie.

"I think it would be best."

"You're very kind, my dear. But I should like to be on my own."

She could see Elaine judging how far to take it. "Well, if that's what we want." Her words made a cloud in the frosty air.

"Do you mind? I won't be long."

"Right, then."

"Please don't worry."

Before she'd left her bedroom, Reggie had taken off the panic alarm, the pendant monitor, and hidden it in a drawer. In its place she'd put on the pearls Hugo had given her for their first wedding anniversary. It had taken her a long time to do up the clasp. Always tricky, that clasp. She could feel the pearls under her coat warming themselves on her throat. Real pearls needed the oil from your skin to retain their luster; one ought to wear them every day.

"I'll see you later."

"What do we fancy for lunch?" said Eileen, rubbing her hand under her nose.

"Is there soup?"

"Leek and potato."

"That would be lovely."

Elaine screwed up her face. She had a son who lived with his dad and a daughter at "uni."

"Back by twelve, OK?"

She was saying something about Tony and the stairs when Reggie went into the house.

Look thy last on all things lovely. The house was warm enough for her to take off her hat and gloves, not warm enough for her to shed her coat. They had to maintain a certain temperature for the sake of the pictures, although humidity was more critical than temperature, Hugo always said.

She spent some time in the lower hall, looking at the framed black-and-white photographs on the walls. When she and Hugo had first taken on the restoration of the Park, they had been so preoccupied by capturing what remained of its evanescent eighteenth-century atmosphere that they had paid little attention to the two centuries' worth of history that had followed. Afterwards Hugo had remedied that. Here were local girls and village women stripping willows down on the riverbank. Here was a shooting party with their dogs and beaters and their feathered heap of pheasants. Here were First World War officers in civvies posed in the library. Here was her father at their yard in his old tweed hat. She wondered what that photograph was doing there. Or whether it was a photograph.

Quarter of the way up the stairs to the first floor she thought that perhaps she should sit down for a moment to catch her breath and decided against it on the grounds that she didn't know how she would get up again. Silly, really. All morning, consumed by the desire to get back to the house, she had completely forgotten about the stairs. Just imagined herself floating about somehow.

Look thy last on all things lovely. Between pushing down with the stick and pulling up with the handrail, she took it a step at a time. So many steps. Stick and handrail. Stop. Stick and handrail. Stop. Unbutton coat. Hugo had bought their first television so that they could watch the coronation, during which news had come of Hillary's conquest of Everest. Hillary and Tenzing on the roof of the world. Stick and handrail. Stop. Stick and handrail. Last step. Her heart fluttered in her chest and she laid her hand over it to contain its wild beating.

The house was a place of ghosts. She wandered from room to room on the principal floor, and the white dust sheets draped over the huddled furniture made it look as if the snow had found its way indoors. Sad that no one sat on the furniture anymore. She thought that she could remember every auction and country-house sale where she had bought each piece, if she put her mind to it.

When she peered round the door of the drawing room, she remembered the ceiling being cleaned for the first time, a task that had taken four people three days with paintbrushes. It hadn't been cleaned since.

Hugo said, "Do you know, I think I'll try the marmalade today, just for a change."

"Why don't you?" she said. "Thick cut. It's very good."

"More patience than I've got," said Frances, although what that had to do with marmalade she didn't know.

"Reggie?"

She was standing bathed in the thin white light pouring down from the clerestory, feeling transparent to the point of X-rayed, when the caretaker, Tony Knoll, came across the staircase hall. Despite the weather he was dressed for action in Lycra cycling shorts.

"Elaine said you'd be over. Sorry I'm late. I've been checking the pipes."

As ever, she wished Hugo were still alive to share the joke. When someone died, you missed their physical presence first, the warmth in the bed, all the tones and shadings of their speech, the footsteps or sighs or rustlings in the next room, even the irritations and annoyances. You missed these things as if your skin had been peeled off in long, bleeding strips. When all that became less painful, you still missed their mind, the consciousness that partnered yours, that gave you bifocal vision. Tony Knoll was conscientious and reliable, no question about that, but something about him had always struck her as hilarious. Hugo would have known what it was and they would have laughed about it.

"So," Tony said, rubbing his hands together, "what brings you over here today of all days?"

Today of all days. All days were the same.

"Have you been here long?" he said.

Had they been here long? "Quite a time. We moved here in fifty-two." She gazed upwards and sketched her fingers in the air. "They've put that ceiling back the cheap way. It used to be vaulted."

"I see." Tony removed a dust sheet from a carved mahogany hall chair (Vyckers Court house sale, 1956, she remembered) and gestured at it. "Take a pew, Reggie. I'll fetch you a cup of tea."

"Oh no," she said. "Not now. I must go upstairs."

Tony rang Elaine on her mobile and got her voice mail. "You'd best come over here right away," he said after the beep. What was the woman playing at? Agency staff, he thought. "Ring me back as soon as you pick this up."

Reggie was across the hall and making her way up the cantilevered staircase by the time he caught up with her. "Goodness me,

Luke," she said, "whatever is the hurry? At my age you learn to take things as they come."

"Let's wait a moment, shall we?" he said, peering over the wrought-iron balustrade. What a long way to fall. As he grasped her arm, she sagged a little. "Shall we sit down here on the step for a time?"

She looked at him with her dark-blue eyes. Her coat was open and there was a stain on the front of her cardigan, an old-lady food stain of some kind or another. "No, I don't think so. Help me to the top, will you? I'd like that, please."

The hall yawned below as they climbed to the next floor under the white light of the clerestory. Something fell out from underneath her coat, and he turned to see a pearl necklace cascade down the stairs. Pick that up later, he thought. He didn't dare let go of her and she didn't appear to have noticed it had gone.

At her insistence, they went along the corridor. Outside what had been the master bedroom she paused, gray about the mouth, leaning on her stick. She fumbled with the handle.

"Do you want to go in?"

She nodded and he pushed the door open for her. "Here we are. Your old bedroom, Reggie, wasn't it?"

"Yes. Yes, it was."

The curtains were drawn against the glare of the winter's day. He went over to switch on a bedside light.

"Want to lie down for a bit?"

"That might be an idea." Her voice was a whisper.

His phone went as he was helping her onto the bed.

"You have a little rest. I won't be long. I'll be back in two ticks, I promise."

The great bed, with its Regency hangings, was a ship lying at anchor. She had left a lamp burning by the bedside, and a moth, drunk on light, pattered against the shade.

"Are you asleep?" said Hugo, coming into the room.

"I think so," she said.

16

All You Want (Tonight): 2010

Who knows what comes next, what lies around the corner? The house can't tell you, nor is the future in its power to determine. But it knows what it wants. What it wants is a beating heart.

It probably wasn't the first time someone had been sick on Skype, but it was a new experience for Charlie. Saturday afternoon and he was sitting in Tony's office in the north pavilion talking into his computer, telling his wife about the discussion he'd had with his sister the evening before, when Rachel went greenish white, lurched to the right of the screen, and disappeared from view. He heard a retching, splattering sound, a groan, and an "Oh, *Christ!*"

"Are you OK?" he said. "Honey, are you OK?"

More retching, and then he could hear her run to the bathroom.

"Think I've got a bug," she said, when she eventually reappeared on his screen, some minutes later, looking if anything greener than before. "Don't feel so good. Understatement." She put her hand to her mouth. "Sorry. That was gross. Oh, God, the wastepaper basket's fucked."

"Don't worry about the wastepaper basket. Do you have a temperature?"

She shook her head. "A little headache."

"Tell Marisa you're not coming in to the shop today."

"I'll see how I am."

He understood her reluctance. Saturday was the shop's busiest day. "Take it easy, OK? Promise me?"

"Promise."

"You better go and lie down for a bit. I'll Skype you later, round about eight your time?"

Rachel pushed the hair back from her face. "No, let's talk tomorrow. I've been really bushed all week. Think I'll go to bed early tonight."

Earlier than eight? Charlie thought. Rachel wasn't much of night owl, but she could usually manage to stay awake until eleven. "You sure you're going to be all right?"

"I'll be fine. Probably just something that's going round."

"OK, then, if you're sure. Love you."

"Love you too."

They touched hands to screens and she was gone.

He closed his laptop, left the office, and headed back to the south pavilion. Probably a bug, he thought, nothing to worry about. Some kind of twenty-four-hour virus. Even so, he should have been there, holding her head, ministering with a cool cloth. It seemed like a failure that he hadn't been.

A short while later, having left his computer, picked up his wallet and, out of force of habit, his camera, he set off down to the village to buy something for supper. This morning Ros had left by the time he woke up. A note on the kitchen table reminded him that Helen, his ex-wife, was dropping off their son, Luke, around five. "See you later," said the note. "Your turn to cook tonight. xx." He wondered briefly where Ros had gone—was the surgery open on Saturdays?—but he wasn't his sister's keeper. There was also the possibility that she had removed herself in protest at the way last night's discussions had turned out. He thought he had been getting somewhere, persuading her that the house should be sold. Perhaps he was fooling himself and they were back to where they started. The idea was depressing and it preoccupied him for most of the twenty minutes it took to walk to Lower Ashenden.

The village had changed a great deal over the years, much more than the house, which was trapped in a time warp by comparison. He remembered it as a sleepy place with a couple of pubs, a post office, a shop that sold everything, except anything you wanted, and an old-fashioned butcher's, which was always empty and displayed mostly bacon in its window. Now, despite the fact that the village had grown considerably in size, the post office had closed and buses to Reading ran only twice a day. The shop that sold everything had become a mini branch of Tesco's, one of the pubs had been converted into a rather swanky house, and the other, the Ploughshare, was a decent, if pricey, gastropub where local farmers were name-checked on the menu. The butcher's had been turned into an organic farm shop-cum-delicatessen, also pricey, which was where he was hoping to buy sausages that tasted of something. In view of Luke's appetite, he thought he might cook sausages and mash tonight, with an onion gravy, although on reflection, after last night's fish pie, he was really going to have to get back to running.

Outside the organic farm shop were wicker baskets containing remarkably dirty vegetables. When he pushed open the door, an irritating bell tinkled. Were bells a sign of authenticity? He supposed so. Ten minutes later, after dithering over the chill cabinet, he came out into the village high street £8.29 poorer, with eight free-range pork-and-sage sausages and a packet of organic beef stock cubes, which came highly recommended by the young woman, clad in a Breton T-shirt and striped apron (the stripes going in opposite directions), who served him. He had forgotten to bring a bag, was too embarrassed to ask for one in an organic farm shop-cum-delicatessen, so one pound of the £8.29 had gone on an unbleached cotton carrier on which was printed, in green cursive lettering contained within an outline drawing of an apple, "Pretty's Organic Produce. Think Global, Act Local." He felt like an idiot with the bag slung over his shoulder and tried to turn it so the slogan wouldn't be visible, but the lettering was printed on both sides. Then, like a traitor to the environment, he headed to Tesco's for cheap, clean, shapely potatoes.

It was when he was queuing at the supermarket checkout with his plastic bag of Maris Pipers and a couple of onions, worrying about Rachel again, worrying about the house, the two worries effortlessly exchanging themselves in his head, that he felt a tap on his shoulder. He turned to see a tall, attractive middle-aged woman, dressed in one of those quilted sleeveless vests, jeans tucked into Wellingtons, smiling at him with an expectant look on her face that told him he was supposed to know who she was.

She acknowledged his bewilderment with a brisk shake of her head and held out a hand. "Charlie? Charlie Minton, isn't it?"

"Yes." He took her hand, although it necessitated a bit of juggling with the potatoes to do so. Who was she? Friend of Ros's? Friend of Reggie's?

"Izzie Beckmann," she said.

"My *God*," he said. "*Izzie*. How are you?"

He hoped she wouldn't think that his inability to place her meant that she had changed out of all recognition, because she hadn't. Now that she had identified herself, he could see the resemblance to her former self. They'd gone out for—what, six months? An intense little period, yet, unlike many of his relationships, one that had ended fairly well. (She'd met someone else just as he was beginning to think about moving on, a form of dovetailing that hadn't happened to him since.) Thirty-odd years down the line, she had worn well. The idea occurred to him that he must have worn well too, otherwise she would never have recognized him.

He was disabused of that notion when they came out of the supermarket and stood in the street talking.

"I'm sorry," said Izzie. "I've got the advantage here, I think. I was at Reggie's funeral and someone pointed you out to me."

He had taken a backseat at the funeral. Ros organized it, and the vicar, who knew Reggie well, gave the address.

"I admired your aunt so much. Always did." Izzie's hair wasn't short anymore, but she ran her fingers through it with an impatient gesture that tugged at his memory. "She was a remarkable woman."

"Thanks," said Charlie. "She was."

"Well, it's been quite a while, hasn't it?" said Izzie. "You're still taking photographs, I see." She nodded at the camera he had slung over his shoulder, along with the Pretty's cotton carrier.

A photograph he had taken of Izzie during their short time together, a delicious black-and-white nude (his Man Ray period), wormed itself to the front of his mind. What had he done with it? he wondered.

"It's what I do for a living," he said. "I sort of stumbled into it after university. Photojournalism mainly. Though these days I mostly teach."

"Oh," said Izzie, "where? In London?"

It piqued his vanity somewhat that she didn't know his work.

"No, New York. I haven't lived in this country for years. And you?"

"I'm in property."

"You're a developer?"

"An estate agent. In a niche sort of a way." She adjusted her handbag on her shoulder and blushed. "You're amused, I can tell."

"A little surprised. You were a Trot or something, weren't you? I seem to recall that owning a clapped-out Triumph Spitfire was enough to make me a class enemy."

"It wasn't so much the car, it was the family connections."

"You can't help who you're related to." As he was beginning to appreciate.

"True."

They were walking slowly down the village high street, past an antique dealer's and a shop selling upmarket furnishing fabrics and reproduction garden urns.

"At any rate, I still vote Labour, for my sins. Although I might vote Lib Dem this time. Anything to keep the Tories out."

He laughed. "What brings you to the village? You visiting your parents?" He remembered that her father's building firm had been responsible for restoring the Park. Ros had turned up some papers relating to the works among Hugo's files.

She shook her head. "They're both dead now. They left their house to me and my brother, and I bought him out after my divorce came through. I've been living here for about two years. It's convenient for my business. Most of our properties are in the Home Counties, and driving across London was getting to be such a drag."

"So what exactly is your niche?" said Charlie.

"Big old houses, in a nutshell," said Izzie. "The sort that other estate agents don't have a clue how to market."

"And you do?"

"Yes, I would say so, judging by results."

"What's the secret?" said Charlie.

"We avoid the usual pompous language for a start," Izzie said. "*Facilities* and *accommodation* and *decorative order*. Maybe that works if you're selling a semi, but people who are going to be spending millions on a house want a story. What they buy is a story."

"A story?"

"Not in the sense of fiction. It's more a question of conveying a sense of history and place. So that people can imagine themselves being part of it."

"I see," said Charlie, although he was not entirely sure he had grasped what she was talking about.

"Then, of course," said Izzie, "you've also got to be perfectly straight with them. If there are problems, you've got to say so at the outset."

"That sounds a little risky." Charlie was thinking, among other things, of the decaying stonework at the house, the damp in the octagon room, the roof that needed fixing. The enormous heating bills.

"I happen to think," said Izzie, "that what's risky is pulling the wool over people's eyes. Better to be up-front about what a survey's going to reveal and pack away the wide-angle lens. The clients I deal with don't want to waste their time. Of course they're after value, but they're in the kind of financial bracket where even quite substantial repairs aren't off-putting if they really want a house."

That Charlie could understand.

They came to the end of the high street.

"Sorry to go on. As my kids will tell you, it's a bit of a hobbyhorse of mine." She smiled. "It's been so great to run into you. I would have introduced myself at the funeral, but it didn't really seem appropriate."

Charlie stepped off the pavement to make way for a young woman pushing a red three-wheeled baby buggy the size of a small car.

"You know, it's funny we should meet and have this conversation," he said, after the buggy had gone past conveying its little emperor, "because as it happens my sister and I have inherited the house."

"Have you?" said Izzie, who knew full well that they had.

Then he found himself explaining the situation, how he wanted to sell but Ros didn't, how much money it would take to run the place, let alone fix it up.

"The surveyors think the stonework needs about a million pounds' worth of work doing to it."

"I'm afraid that doesn't surprise me," Izzie said. "My father always said the house would need redoing in another generation."

"Did he?" said Charlie.

"These places aren't always as substantial as they look."

"The winter hasn't helped."

"No, it can't have done."

"I've made an approach to the National Trust," said Charlie, "but it seems they aren't taking on these kinds of properties anymore."

"That's true, they aren't."

"And obviously, in our case, neither of us is in a position to buy the other out. Ros has got all these schemes. The trouble is, I just can't see any of them working."

"It's a worry," said Izzie.

"It is."

She looked up and down the high street.

"Are you staying around much longer or do you have to get back to New York?"

"I guess it depends."

She hunted round in her handbag and handed him a card. "Look, why don't you give me a call or drop me an email before you leave? It would be nice to meet for a drink or lunch or something."

"It would," said Charlie, and meant it. Rachel would like her, he thought, and the same would not have been true of most of his ex-girlfriends.

"And obviously," said Izzie, "if you do manage to persuade your sister to sell, think of us."

"For old times' sake or the sake of business?" he said, putting the card in his pocket.

"Both. My father loved that house. And we'd do a good job of finding the right buyer for you."

Izzie watched Charlie head out of the village in the direction of Ashenden Park. Had that seemed too obvious? she wondered. Had it been a mistake to pretend she knew nothing about his photographic career? On balance, she didn't think so. Stroke of luck, bumping into him like that, and much better than the plan she had been about to implement, which would have entailed a more contrived approach. She didn't doubt for a moment they would decide to sell in the end. The way things were, they would have to.

Izzie believed that you made your own luck, which meant that you did your homework and seized opportunities with both hands when they came your way. She went home to polish her proposal for marketing the house, and blessed Google and village gossip.

The onion gravy was going a bit wrong. A few minutes ago it was exactly the right consistency, but now it was turning into gloop. Unfortunately the sausages were nowhere near finished. Charlie was a good cook and he didn't make a song and dance about it either, but he found himself defeated by his aunt's old cooker, which confusingly combined a sluggish oven with ferocious electric rings. Sausage and mash was a dish that hardly depended on split-second timing; even so, having the constituent parts ready within something approximating the same hour was proving a challenge. It was not helped by the fact that Ros had not yet reappeared from wherever it was she had spent the day.

"Can I have a beer, Dad?" said Luke, coming into the kitchen.

"Sure," said Charlie. "Help yourself."

Luke opened the fridge and pulled out a can. One of the earpieces of his iPhone dangled down, broadcasting a dance track to his groin. Since he left school, he'd been working for an event caterer and had saved enough money to spend the rest of his gap year traveling in South America. Even for Charlie, who had spent a good deal of his life in dangerous places, his son's itinerary was worryingly loose. It invited kidnapping or worse, he'd told his ex-wife, who quite rightly had pointed out to him that so far as taking risks were concerned, he didn't have a leg to stand on.

Any pride Charlie took in his son, which was a great deal, he was conscious that he owed to Helen, who'd brought him up, provided him with a stepfather he got on with, and ensured that Luke's relationship with his biological father had survived long distances, infrequent visits, and all the many other ways in which Charlie had fallen short as a parent.

Luke pulled the ring tab and the can hissed open.

"So, you going to keep the house or what?"

"I'd rather not, to be honest."

Charlie opened the oven door to check the sausages. They were still lying pale on the oven tray, doing nothing in particular.

"Mum didn't think you would want to. She says Ros does, though."

"It seems that way. You getting hungry?" It was past eight o'clock.

"Mmm," said Luke. "Kind of."

"If she's not back soon, we'll start without her. As soon as the sausages are done."

"I wouldn't mind a place like this," said Luke, leaning back against the kitchen counter, drinking his beer. He had strong features, a nose a little too big for his face, a mouth a little too wide. "If I had, like, a squillion pounds. It would be a cool place for a festival."

"The squillion pounds, that's the problem," said Charlie. "The other day when it rained, Tony had eighteen buckets on the go in the staircase hall."

"Fuck," said Luke.

Charlie ran the tap on the dirty pans in the sink. Turned it off again.

"Seriously, if you really want this place, I'll do my best to hang on to it for you." His gut twisted as he said these words.

"No, thanks."

"Are you sure?"

"Yeah," Luke said, grinning. "I'd rather have the cash any day."

A door banged down the hall.

"Ros," said Charlie, checking the sausages again to disguise his relief. "Finally these are getting somewhere."

Ros came into the kitchen, gave Luke a kiss on the cheek, dumped shopping bags on the table.

"Hiya."

Charlie closed the oven door, straightened up. "Just in time," he said. "Supper in three days or thereabouts."

"It's a bloody awful oven," said Ros.

"You look different," said Charlie.

"Had a haircut."

"Suits you."

Ros fished around in one of the bags and pulled out a bottle of champagne. She felt it. "Good, it's still cold. Get some glasses," she said to Luke.

"What's the occasion?" said Charlie. "No, not those, Luke, you don't drink champagne from tumblers."

"Oh, for fuck's sake, Dad," said Luke, replacing the tumblers and setting down three mismatched stem glasses.

Ros peeled away the foil, twisted off the wire, and uncorked the bottle with a deft flick of her wrist. Poured the fizzing wine.

"A toast," she said. "Here's to sanity."

Luke looked at his father, and Charlie looked at Ros.

"To sanity," Charlie said. "Personally, I'm all for it. In moderation."

Ros took a sip and put her glass down on the table. "This is by way of an apology." She shook her new haircut. "You're quite right, Charlie. You've been right all along. We should sell."

Yes! Charlie was astonished and delighted, in that order. He felt like punching the air.

"No need to apologize, though I have to say I'm really pleased you've changed your mind." He chinked his glass against his sister's. "Here's to the future owners of Ashenden Park. Their very good health."

"To their very deep pockets," said Ros.

"Dad," said Luke. "I think the sausages are burning."

All through dinner, Charlie tried to account for his sister's sudden reversal, the closed door that had fallen open, her epiphany. Was it down to his own powers of persuasion the previous night, or the call from her daughter, Maisie, or was it obscurely connected to her haircut? He had known too many women not to be aware that haircuts often signaled *something*.

After supper, Luke sloped off, not to bed but to iPlayer.

"Well," said Charlie.

"Well," said Ros, raising her glass. "Just so you know, I'm going home tomorrow."

"That's good."

"Before I had my hair cut, I met Geoff for lunch and he gave me a bollocking."

"Did he?" Charlie made a mental note to buy Geoff a drink the next time he saw him.

"He's been dead against me trying to hang on to this place all along. I told him what you said last night and he completely agreed with it. I'm sorry, I've been a bit of an idiot."

No, thought Charlie, a drink was not enough. Geoff deserved at least a good bottle of claret.

"It wasn't ever really going to work, you know."

"I think I knew that deep down. I'll ring the bank on Monday and we'll see about instructing an agent."

"Actually," said Charlie, and proceeded to tell her about his encounter with Izzie Beckmann earlier that day. "Funnily enough, she was a socialist when I knew her."

Ros said, "Some of us still are."

"Can't do any harm to ring her. She knows the place like the back of her hand. Her father restored it."

"I'm not entirely convinced she's the right person," said Ros, "but there's no harm in sounding her out."

She got up, with a scrape of chair legs, to clear the plates.

"I spoke to Rachel earlier," said Charlie, over the clatter of dishes.

"She's got a bug of some kind. She was actually sick when we were talking on Skype."

Ros wiped down the counter with a cloth. "Poor thing."

"She hasn't looked great all week, to be honest, sort of washed out. I was going to call her"—he looked at his watch—"around now, but she asked me not to."

"It's been hard on you being away from her, hasn't it?"

"Yes, in a word." He picked up a spoon and fiddled with it.

"You wait until you've been married as long as me and Geoff. A little break can be just what the doctor ordered."

The next morning Charlie went online and booked a plane ticket. Then, despite the fact it was Sunday, he rang Izzie and they arranged a time to discuss the sale.

Izzie was a quick worker, very professional, he had to give her that. She had already pulled together a proposal when they met.

"Of course, we're going to need decent photographs," she said. "There's someone I use a lot, who's good, but it would be fantastic if you took a few yourself. I checked you out on Google. You've done some really great work."

"Sure, I don't mind doing that," said Charlie, his vanity more than mollified. "How about historical stuff? Ros has dug up a lot of old documents."

"Good," said Izzie. "We can use some of those too. When are you leaving?"

"Day after tomorrow."

"Well, we'll keep in touch by email and so on."

"Yes," said Charlie. "And there's always Skype."

Charlie's plane was forty-five minutes late. Rachel was waiting for him in the arrivals hall. At first glance she looked tired, and a little thin, but as he came closer, he noticed a kind of glittery tremulousness about her. He took her in his arms and buried his face in her hair. He was home.

"How are you feeling?" he said, as he wheeled his bag in the direction of the exit.

"Much better now you're back." She gave him a sideways glance.

"Oh, God, me too," he said. "I've been worried about you."

"Sorry. And sorry about the other day. I got a new wastepaper basket."

"Glad to hear it."

Outside, waiting in line for a taxi, she touched her fingers to his cheek and smiled. "Charlie?"

"What?"

"I've got something to show you."

"What is it?"

She didn't say anything. Instead, she opened her purse and handed him a little white plastic wand with a blue line down the center.

"You're pregnant?" A dizzy rush to his head.

She nodded. "What do you think?"

He pulled her to him and kissed her. Something seemed to have happened to his breath, his chest, his heart, which was skipping about like a lunatic.

"I'm sorry that I made you worry. It just didn't feel right not telling you in person. Are you pleased?"

Tears came to his eyes. "I'm absolutely thrilled."

A blustery afternoon in early April and Ma'lita was living in a hotel again. Admittedly it was a three-room suite in a five-star hotel, but it was still a hotel and in five, six years of touring she'd grown to despise them. The way, for all the personal service and individual touches and original decor, they remained heartless anonymous places, places that couldn't care less about you, which welcomed anyone with a platinum credit card. The suite was decorated in cream and chocolate and smelled of expensive toiletries, fresh linen, flowers, and leather. But she had to check the headed notepaper to remind herself that on the other side of the double-glazed windows that dulled the roar of rush-hour traffic, it was Birmingham out there, not London, New York, or Paris. She was due to give the last concert of her current tour the next evening at the NEC and had spent the day doing sound checks.

By this stage of Ma'lita Lewis's stratospheric career as a performer and recording artist she no longer had need of a surname. Like Madonna and Beyoncé, she was Ma'lita on both sides of the Atlantic, in Europe, Japan, Singapore, and Hong Kong, and just about every other market you could mention. They didn't like her in Finland, but Finland was an exception. Also a small country.

Ma'lita. Some people thought the apostrophe was an affectation, a gimmick, or a PR stunt. It wasn't. It was the way her name appeared on her birth certificate. Although there had been times at school when she'd dropped the apostrophe for a while, it was now part of what her manager, Derwent, called the Ma'lita *brand*. You could do cool things with it graphically. For example, the bottle of her signature perfume had been designed so that the top, the bit you unscrewed, formed the head of an apostrophe that curled down in an elegant tail to divide her name on the label.

Ma'lita was twenty-six, which was the exact same number of countries where her second single, "All You Want (Tonight)," reached number one five years ago. Her third album had just gone quadruple platinum.

The tabloids had a lot of fun with the apostrophe in the early days. *Ma'king Whoopee* when she was papped at four a.m. coming out of a nightclub pissed after her first UK number one. *Mar'vellous* when she wowed the Brits. And *Ma'lita to Be a Ma'ma?* when there were rumors that she was pregnant.

In those days the press had also made a big deal about her being mixed race, the daughter of a Mauritian mother and an absent white father (who got in touch when she started making money, with a little help from a journalist she'd personally like to kill). What was that all about? She was British; it said so on the passport she had to get when she started touring. Born in Britain, raised in southeast London on a sink estate, educated in a failing comprehensive, unem-

ployed and destined for the scrap heap at sixteen. British through
and through.

"Boss?" said Jasmine, coming through from the room next door
they used as an office.

Jasmine was her PA, and "boss," said tongue in cheek, was one of
the ways she reminded Ma'lita that she was a person, not a pop diva.
This kept her feet on the ground, which is where she wanted them.

"What's up?" Ma'lita leaned back against the cream leather of
the sofa and rubbed her eyes.

"Just got this email," said Jasmine. She was a south London kid
herself, only with GCSEs and a couple of good A levels. "You might
wanna look."

"Yeah, what is it?"

"Remember the estate agent who got in touch after the piece in
the *Mail*?"

"Which one?"

"The woman."

"Yeah, I think I remember. She was friendly."

"Boss, they're all friendly when they've got something to sell.
Anyway, she's sent some details through of a house she thinks you
might like."

During the *Mail* interview, set up to publicize the tour, an exhausted Ma'lita had talked about wanting to buy a place, stop touring for a while, put down some roots. As soon as it was published,
she'd been flooded with offers from people trying to sell her property: penthouses in Chelsea (which looked like hotels), penthouses
in New York (which looked like hotels), and a penthouse in Dubai
(which was part of a hotel). Derwent had spent a day on the phone
to the record company reassuring them that she was not about to
retire and depart into the wilderness.

"Have a look," said Jasmine, handing her a bunch of pages sta-
pled together.

Ma'lita remembered the woman better now. She hadn't sent her
details of penthouses. She'd got hold of her number somehow and
rung up to ask questions. Where did she want to live? England.

Town or country? Country. Old house or new? Old. How big? Big enough. Big enough for her mother, who wasn't working as a mental health nurse anymore but was still living in southeast London, big enough for her staff, for a recording studio. She'd felt like a little girl writing a letter to Father Christmas. "I always wanted to live near water," Ma'lita remembered saying. The sea? the woman had said. "Any kind of water."

The house was called Ashenden Park. It was three houses, really, one big one and two smaller ones, although the smaller ones weren't small at all. To Ma'lita it looked like a mum holding two children by the hand. A mum who was really proud of her kids. The whole place was a beautiful warm honey color. She read through the pages, studied the photographs. The house was not far from Heathrow. It was on the river. Prickles rose on Ma'lita's arms and the back of her neck, the same prickles her fans said they got from listening to her music. Then she turned to the first page and read it all the way through again.

Half an hour later, Ma'lita pulled out her mobile and dialed the agent's number.

"Can I speak to Izzie Beckmann, please?"

"Speaking."

"Hi," she said. "It's Ma'lita."

Ma'lita watched the trees go by out of the window of the 4x4. So many trees. It was like drinking in green, breathing it in.

"I'll be perfectly straight with you," said Izzie as they drove through the gates. "It needs a lot of work and a lot of money spent on it."

Ma'lita knew how to work and she knew how to make money. By now, she even knew how to make money work for itself to make more money. It turned out that she was almost as good at that as singing.

"Anyone else interested in it?"

"We have had an approach by an international consortium that wants to turn it into a hotel and golf course. They're probably the most serious. But they haven't made an offer yet."

A hotel, no way, thought Ma'lita. No way.

In real life, the house was both smaller and larger than she expected.

"Wow," she said, getting out of the car.

"I can let you in down here," said Izzie, standing in front of a door on the ground level. "But I think you'll get a better impression if you go up these stairs and go in from the loggia."

"The loggia?" said Ma'lita.

"The porch."

"Oh, you mean the balcony."

Izzie nodded. "I'll go and open up. Take your time." She unlocked the door and disappeared inside.

Ma'lita went up the stairs on the left-hand side. It was like climbing up through a tunnel or something, wondering what was going to come next. Then she stepped out into space and gasped. The roof soared over her head, the warm stone glowed in the spring sunlight, and the land fell away in front of her, rising in the distance to a little hill.

She knew this feeling. She had felt the same way the first time she'd stepped on a stage.

This was where she belonged.

This was home.

Acknowledgments

For those who know Basildon Park in Berkshire (and there will be millions who will have seen it in the guise of Netherfield in the 2005 adaptation of *Pride and Prejudice,* starring Keira Knightley and Matthew Macfadyen), it will be clear that Ashenden is based upon it, both in details of its architecture and decoration and in its patterns of occupancy. A few stories in this book are fictionalized accounts of real people and events; most use its history as a framework or springboard for my own purposes. In other words, I have used certain facts about the house when they have suited me and the story I wanted to tell.

Unlike many great country houses, which are handed down from generation to generation of the same family, Basildon Park's mixed fortunes have often mirrored the times through which it has lived. That basic idea was the genesis of Ashenden.

Ashenden is fiction. Basildon Park has belonged to the National Trust since 1978.

I am indebted to various sources. The most important of these are *Basildon Park* by Charles Pugh and Tracey Avery (National Trust, 2002), "A Casket to Enclose Pictorial Gems" by Dr. Caroline Dakers (*Apollo* magazine, 2004), *Basildon, Berkshire: An Illustrated History* by Clive Williams, OBE (Reading, 1994), *Bath Stone Quarries* by Derek Hawkins (Folly Books, 2011), *Pit of Shame: The Real

Ballad of Reading Gaol by Anthony Stokes (Waterside Press, 2007), "Where Thames Smooth Waters Glide" (http://thames.me.uk), "6th Battalion Royal Berkshire Regiment, The Somme, 1 July, 1916" by Andy Teal (www.6throyalberks.co.uk), and Malcolm Sanders's site about POW camps in Britain (www.kg6bg.org).

My agent Anthony Goff, who has been a constant source of advice and support over many years, found the perfect home for the book. Thanks also to Georgia Glover and Marigold Atkey at David Higham Associates for all their assistance.

At Fig Tree, Juliet Annan has made this a very much better book than it might have been, while her enthusiasm has been fantastically encouraging. Thanks also to Sophie Missing; Ellie Smith for shepherding the manuscript through production; Lesley Levene, whose copyediting skills saved me from myself numerous times; Chantal Noel, Penguin Rights director, who has worked so hard to bring the book to new audiences; and Emma Ewbank, who designed the beautiful jacket.

I would also like to thank the great team at Simon & Schuster for their warmth and dedication: Trish Todd, Molly Lindley, Kelly Welsh, and Jessica Abell.

Thanks to Eileen Gunn and the trustees of the Royal Literary Fund who awarded me a grant in October 2010. Although RLF grants are not intended to fund work in progress, I could not have finished the book without such a breathing space.

Hilary Arnold, Emma Dally, Celia Dodd, Jane Forster, Takla Gardey, and Debbie Postgate have given me support and encouragement of all kinds. Special thanks to Jocelyn Stephens, for always being there, for knowing what it's like, and for making me laugh.

To Ann Fischer, Jenny Hall, and Carol and Nick Justin, I also owe thanks and love.

All love and thanks are also due my family, Martin, Katharine, and Tom Lazenby, who have not only read and commented on various versions, but who have also put up with my absent presence and what must have seemed, at times, an inexplicable obsession.

But the greatest debt I owe is to my brother, Glenn Wilhide, my first, second, and third reader, who taught me how to tell a story, along with that very important lesson, which is how to be true to the work. Thank you for everything, Glenn.

ELIZABETH WILHIDE is the author of more than twenty books on interior design, decoration, and architecture and a coauthor and contributor of many more, collaborating with authors such as Terence Conran, Orla Kiely, and Tricia Guild. Born in the United States, she moved to Britain in 1967 and now lives in the East End of London with her architect husband and their two children.

Simon & Schuster Paperbacks
Reading Group Guide

Ashenden

This reading group guide for *Ashenden* includes an introduction, discussion questions, ideas for enhancing your book club, and a Q&A with author Elizabeth Wilhide. The suggested questions are intended to help your reading group find new and interesting angles and topics for your discussion. We hope that these ideas will enrich your conversation and increase your enjoyment of the book.

Introduction

Ashenden is the story of a magnificent English country house, the estate that surrounds it, and the people connected to it over the course of 240 years. From its construction in 1775 to the present day, we are witness to the people associated with the house: the architect and his nieces to the successions of families, both happy and not, who inhabit it—the maids and servants who tend the house and grounds; a speculator who resides in the house nearly alone; soldiers billeted there during World War I; prisoners held there during World War II; the couple who rescues it from doom in the 1950s and their descendants, who inherit it in 2010. Throughout all the upheavals of a multicentury life, a constant cycle of neglect and regeneration, and the toll of history, the house withstands it all, always strong enough to endure change.

Topics & Questions for Discussion

1. *Ashenden* opens in the present day with siblings Charlie and Ros debating what to do with the house they have suddenly inherited and cannot afford. It then jumps back to 1775 and proceeds chronologically. How does your knowledge of the future of *Ashenden* affect your interpretation of the stories of its past?

2. James Woods, the architect of Ashenden, reflects, "To build was a form of human folly that pitted itself against the forces of nature bent on reclaiming their own. To imagine otherwise, to imagine that what you built might last, was akin to madness." In this case Woods was wrong, and Ashenden survived. What was it that allowed it to do so, when so many other houses like it disappeared?

3. One of the central features of the book is the relationship between the owners of Ashenden and their employees. How do these relationships evolve over the course of the book? What are some moments that display the changing perspectives on having a staff?

4. How would you characterize the relationship between the owners of the house and the people of the town that surrounds it? How do the residents of Ashenden and the residents of the town feel about one another? How does this change throughout the book?

5. One of the book's themes is the cost of neglect and its destructive power. Why do you think some of the characters (Georgiana More, for example) take such bad care of the house and grounds, especially considering the time and money they spend on other things?

6. Wealth is another important theme in *Ashenden*. How do the various owners of the house (the Mores, the Hendersons, the Lyells) differ in the amount of their wealth and their use of it?

How does this affect their treatment of the house, the way they raise children, and the way they treat one another?

7. Each chapter revolves primarily around a single character: Charlie Minton, James Woods and his nieces, Georgiana More, Ada Henderson, Dulcie Godwin, Jimmy Henderson, Lieutenant Harrison, George Ferrars, Alison Milner, Reggie Lyell, and Izzie Beckmann. Who did you find the most sympathetic? Who did you regret having to leave? Were there other characters that you wished the book had focused on?

8. Many of the characters who later become a main part of the story are first introduced as minors characters in earlier chapters. In a similar fashion, many minor characters and their descendants disappear and reappear throughout the story. Discuss how many of these references you caught and which you missed. (For example, Paul Lyell is a guest at the boating party in chapter seven, and his younger brother Hugo later returns for the treasure hunt in chapter nine. Hugo and Reggie then buy some urns from Ferrars in chapter ten, and, of course, later purchase Ashenden itself.) How do you feel about this web of connections as a literary device? Do you find it satisfying?

9. The state of Ashenden is described at the beginning of each chapter. How is the condition of the house reflected in the status of its residents?

10. Throughout the book, there are many characters who view Ashenden and its residents as representative of excess, ostentation, and the unfair privilege of the upper classes (for example, Jack Pierce from chapter six and the interviewer from chapter thirteen). Do you find the wealth of Ashenden's owners unfair or unjust, as these characters seem to? Why or why not?

11. One of the ongoing debates the characters have with themselves and each other is whether to preserve the house and its history or somehow update or change it (see the last part of Hugo and Reggie's interview for an example of this). What do you think of the instinct to preserve old houses just as they originally were,

versus truly living in them? If you were in charge of Ashenden, which would you choose, and why?

12. Books like *Ashenden* and television shows like *Downton Abbey* revolve around the institution of the English country house. Is this a phenomenon unique to Britain? If not, is there an equivalent in the United States?

13. Ashenden also serves as a microcosm of the times through which it has endured. What does the house illustrate about the state of the world in each chapter? How does the state of the house at the end of the book reflect the current state of our world?

Enhance Your Book Club

1. Treat yourself to a few episodes of *Downton Abbey* or *Upstairs Downstairs*. How does the world of Ashenden match up with, or differ from, the worlds depicted in these shows? Which do you find to be the most accurate?

2. Choose an old house and research its origins and story. Try the websites of the National Register of Historic Places (nps.gov/nr) and the National Trust (nationaltrust.org.uk) or your state's historical society. Discuss your findings. What surprised you the most about the history of the house you chose?

3. Much of *Ashenden* is inspired by the history of Basildon Park in Berkshire. Read more about it on these sites: basildon-berks.net/local_history/local_history.html; telegraph.co.uk/news/obituaries/1563144/Renee-Lady-Iliffe.html; and wikipedia.org/wiki/Basildon_Park. Discuss how *Ashenden*'s story corresponds to or differs from the story of Basildon Park.

A Conversation with Elizabeth Wilhide

***Ashenden* is your debut novel, but you've written many books on design. How did you enjoy the process of writing fiction? Was this your first stab at fiction writing?**

I've made up stories (and written very bad poetry) ever since I was a child. Having a novel published has been a long-cherished ambition. I've burned lots of midnight oil to that end. Over the years, I've learned the hard way that nonfiction and fiction are not chalk and cheese. In both cases, you have to be clear; get things down in the right order; and write on a word-by-word, sentence-by-sentence level as best as you can. For me, however, fiction is more challenging and more rewarding, particularly when you find yourself in that rare position where the story is streaming through your hands. Mostly, of course, it's a long slog uphill.

The mastery of history in *Ashenden* is remarkably impressive. Did you do extensive research to accurately depict each period? Or are you already a history buff?

Thank you, but I don't claim mastery! Doggedness, perhaps. I did spend an inordinate amount of time agonizing over details like jelly molds. *Ashenden* benefited hugely from years of research I've had to do for my day job as a writer of nonfiction books on architecture, decoration, design, and interiors of many periods. I had that to fall back on. This was supplemented by more specific research, chiefly online, but also in the London Library. Social history has always fascinated me, and I would single out Mark Girouard's *Life in the English Country House* as a particular inspiration. Otherwise, I am just curious about the past. My investigations into the previous occupants of our own Victorian house in Hackney, via the census records, uncovered the fabulous fact that a tenant here during the nineteenth century was a laundress from Whitby, Yorkshire, called Lily Snowball. You couldn't make it up.

What about the story of Basildon Park struck you as interesting enough to try and fictionalize? How did you come across the story of Basildon?

The novel was directly inspired by a visit I made to Basildon Park in the spring of 2008. My husband and I were spending the weekend nearby and our original plan was to visit a garden outside Henley, which turned out to be closed for the day. Basildon was plan B. When we came up the stairs and walked through the door, my immediate reaction was very similar to Maria's in "A Book of Ceilings." The symmetry tugged at me straightaway. It was so powerful. Then when I glanced at my husband (who is an architect and largely averse to visiting stately homes), I saw that, if anything, he was more moved than I was.

We wandered round that day, and the house got a grip on us both. Then, later, when I was reading the guidebook, I realized how closely the fortunes of Basildon Park had mirrored the times it had lived through. That sent shivers up my spine. I was hooked from that moment on.

You also mention that some of your main characters are based on real people. Was it more interesting to you to try and fictionalize their lives, or come up with someone completely from scratch? Who are some of the real people behind the story?

I enjoyed both fictionalizing real people (which gives you a steady hand on your back somewhere between your shoulder blades) and the freedom of inventing new characters. I wouldn't have liked to sacrifice one for the other.

Some of the real stories attached to Basildon were a gift no one could have resisted. Georgiana More in "The Portrait" is based on Henrietta Sykes, who had an affair with Disraeli (Delgado in my version). Her subsequent affair with the portrait painter Maclise ruined her. The story, which may be apocryphal, was that Dickens based Bill Sykes in *Oliver Twist* on her brute of a husband. It is certainly true that Dickens was a friend of Maclise's (who I fictionalized as Maurice). If you visit the Charles Dickens Museum in London you can see a portrait Maclise made of Dickens's children.

On the other hand, in "Hut C," my sole real starting point was the fact that there had been a POW camp at Basildon during and after the war. The rest was pure invention, backed up by research. Similarly, the springboard for "The Photograph," which takes place in 1916, was a photograph of convalescing soldiers in the Basildon guidebook.

Other chapters are equivalent mixes—a bit of real history and a generous dollop of my imagination.

As someone who clearly knows her English country houses, what do you make of the recent American obsession with this kind of story, in particular with *Downton Abbey*? What first interested you in these houses?

As an American I can perfectly understand the obsession. I arrived in Britain at the tender age of thirteen, having previously lived in cities and towns where few buildings dated back beyond the turn of the twentieth century and most were much newer than that. Then all of a sudden here we were living in a tiny Thames-side village where the local pub was built in 1135. The span of history, which was so tangible, was absolutely astonishing to me; it was like a new imaginative dimension. Although we lived in a "modern" mock Tudor house, at the end of the drive was an Elizabethan cottage, where I used to babysit, worrying about ghosts.

I'm just as interested in these humbler survivors of the past as I am in great houses—Prospect Place in the novel, which becomes increasingly gentrified, is a case in point. However, a country house gives you a much bigger canvas, along with the potential for conflict, drama, and intrigue between the classes. Because their pattern of occupancy often changes over time, these houses can almost be seen as microcosms of society at any given point.

I finished the first draft of *Ashenden* just before the first series of *Downton* aired in the UK. I remember wondering whether anyone would be interested in my book and then, seeing how *Downton* caught on, I began to have some hope. *Downton* is great fun, and as long as Maggie Smith has wonderful lines to deliver, I'm sure it will continue to attract big audiences on both sides of the Atlantic.

One of the things the book does so well is balance the story of the characters and the ongoing drama of the world outside Ashenden and outside England. How did you choose the pieces of the house's history to include? Were there years that you wrote but later cut out?
The episodic structure of the novel was there from the beginning, and quite early on I knew key periods in the house's history I wanted to cover. Some of these were inspired by the most dramatic points in Basildon's history, which I was anxious to include in fictional form. I also wanted stories that contrasted upstairs and downstairs, good times and bad, even seasonal variations. Otherwise, I was interested in those cusp moments—just before or just after great events—which informed my decision to set "Hut C" in 1946 rather than during the war years. I was also looking for points in time that resonated with our own. The period covered by the chapter "The Janus Cup," for example, was a time of great economic hardship in Britain. I liked the irony of "The Treasure Hunt" taking place just before the Crash.

Between the first and second drafts of the novel I made quite significant changes. The framing device of the contemporary story set in 2010 was introduced then, as was the chapter "Stonework," which shows the house being built. Another chapter, later on in the book, which proved to be a bit of a dead end was jettisoned, and others were substantially reworked.

The characters in *Ashenden* represent such a wide array of viewpoints. Which of your main characters were you the most sympathetic to? Who do you see as closest to your own perspective, particularly on houses like Ashenden?
I try to be sympathetic to all my characters, even if I don't approve of some of their actions. I didn't write the book with the intention of arguing a point, and I can equally sympathize with Charlie, who wants to get shot of the house and sees it as nothing but a money pit, and Reggie, who pours her heart into it. Or those who saw it as a livelihood, a status symbol, or a mark of oppression. These houses were all those things.

I must admit, however, to a soft spot for those characters who loved the place, whatever their station in life. By the end of the novel, I came to conclusion that the best future for Ashenden would be to let it go. Ma'lita popped up right on cue to give me the ending I wanted.

Would you want to live in a house like Ashenden if you could? Do you have a particular affection for that era of architecture and design?
Even if I had deep pockets and could afford the heating bills, Ashenden is far too big for me. But while we're in the realms of wishful thinking, I wouldn't mind a smaller Georgian house, say a rectory . . . with perhaps a sea view?

What I particularly like about eighteenth-century design is that it manages to combine a kind of robustness with fine, almost delicate detailing. There's a great clarity to it, and this is as true of teaspoons and chairs as it is of buildings. By contrast, Victoriana is much more heavy-handed and more of a stylistic mishmash. I am also a great fan of good modernist design and was lucky enough to inherit some great mid-century Scandinavian furniture from my parents.

At the end of *Ashenden*, the National Trust has stopped accepting houses, and Ashenden is sold to a wealthy pop singer. Does this reflect something about the current state of old houses in England? Do you think architectural landmarks of this kind should be owned privately, or would you prefer to see them open to the public?
Large country houses have always been expensive to run and maintain, even more so in the current economic climate. Nowadays, visitor numbers alone are often not enough to provide adequate income. Basildon Park, for example, which has been owned by the National Trust since the 1970s, has had a profitable sideline as a film location and that revenue has helped to pay for essential restoration works. Meanwhile, the Trust has shifted its priorities in favor of a broader definition of cultural interest, which is no bad thing.

Whether these houses are in public or private hands—and why not pop stars'?—what's important is that they survive for future generations to appreciate. Vast numbers were destroyed after the war, which is such a shame. One stately home, pulled down in the 1950s, wound up as building material under the M1 motorway, which seems like a kind of willful vandalism to me.

Ashenden is full of hidden connections between characters and subtle historical associations across generations. Did you include these expecting your readers to catch them all? How did you keep track of the story lines of all the families?

An episodic novel like *Ashenden* means the reader has to make jumps, leave characters behind that they care about, and get involved in a new story. From the beginning, I understood that for the book to work as the portrait of a house, some elements of continuity had to be woven in. Some of these were broad-brush—an old steward who lives to a great age—and some of these were almost like clues, so that you meet a brown-and-white pottery cow milk jug in several different chapters and time frames. (It fascinates me how objects, like houses, outlive their original functions and owners.)